D0467575

.20

Not With a Bang

Not With a Bang

Bang

CHAPMAN PINCHER

an NAL-World book

PUBLISHED BY THE NEW AMERICAN LIBRARY

© 1965 BY CHAPMAN PINCHER

ALL RIGHTS RESERVED. NO PART OF THIS BOOK MAY BE
REPRODUCED WITHOUT WRITTEN PERMISSION FROM THE
PUBLISHERS.

PUBLISHED BY THE NEW AMERICAN LIBRARY OF WORLD LITERATURE, INC.
501 MADISON AVENUE, NEW YORK, NEW YORK 10022

PUBLISHED SIMULTANEOUSLY IN CANADA BY
THE GENERAL PUBLISHING COMPANY LTD.

PRINTED IN THE UNITED STATES OF AMERICA

This is the way the world ends
Not with a bang but a whimper.

T. S. ELIOT, "The Hollow Men"

chapter 1

At 12:45 P.M. on any weekday the long bar at El Vino's, the wine shop on the south side of Fleet Street, presents an interesting cross section of professional life. As Shirley Howard was leaving the animal house at St. Patrick's Hospital medical school to go there, the usual crowd of people who have their being in those parts had collected for refreshment. There were reporters who were disinclined to waste their lunchtime eating; barristers who grew rich on the reporters' libelous mistakes; executives of the evening papers, seeking relief from the latest drumhead decision on how to secure an enticing headline for the next edition; a High Court judge, sampling the Amontillado; an ex-convict with a crime-story tip-off to sell; and an Opposition MP seeking a lucrative newspaper assignment during his next Middle East tour sponsored by a foreign government.

In the leather seats near the door the dapper political writer for a serious Sunday newspaper was showing the draft of his next article to the lugubrious columnist of the tabloid *Daily News*, who could be fatherly to young journalists when sober, but in whom the milk of human kindness was quickly curdled by a few drinks.

"Ah! The Defender of the Fetus," the columnist exclaimed loudly, peering over his bifocals at a red-haired man who was leaning against the wine racks talking to a girl reporter from the same tabloid. John Holt, Fleet Street's most assiduous science and medical correspondent, bowed in acknowledgment of the remark, which was an impious reference to his insistent demands in the *Daily Dispatch* for pregnancy tests of every drug, even those in household use for centuries. Holt, who had covered the disaster, back in the early sixties, when hundreds of limbless babies had been born to mothers who had taken the drug thalidomide, had become so emotionally involved in it that he had been a leading figure in the campaign to secure lifelong government support for the victims. But this was the limit of his public service, for, hardened by the insatiable demands of his popular daily for copy, he had long since lost any rudiment of social purpose in his work, and he sought for little more in professional life than continuing solvency.

Being methodical, he had worked out that just about every time he pressed a key on his typewriter it brought him in a penny. This was partly because he was highly paid but also because he was parsimonious with the currency of words. There was no point in wasting them in copy for the *Daily Dispatch*, where the subeditors were dedicated to making two stunted words grow where five had thrived before.

His real name was Simpkins, but Holt made a conveniently short pen name, ensuring that it would be set up in bigger type in a byline; and somehow, Simpkins did not accord with his ebullient personality, which was not one of those in which aggressive purpose is tempered with gentleness. He was an infrequent visitor to El Vino's or any other Fleet Street pub, for he always operated as a freebooter, unlike many of his rivals, who secretly cooperated on a mutual exchange system so that they did not scoop each other—an understandable arrangement in a profession where rockets are handed down from above almost daily. This made him unpopular with other journalists, but he preferred their distant respect to their warm comradeship, for he was bored by their habit of reminiscing over too many drinks.

During the eleven years he had been in journalism, since leaving Cambridge at twenty-one, he had become a peddler of facts rather than a weaver of words, but was still resentful that his work was as perishable as that of the pavement artist. As he once put it, with his usual technical exactitude, "If the poet's name is writ in water, the journalist's is writ in ether." The daily paper recording the hardest-won triumph is quickly wrapping the dog meat, and though praise in Fleet Street might be stratospheric as the splash scoop rolls off the presses at midnight, within twelve hours it is submerged by the immediate needs of the staring blank pages of the next day's editions.

Though long aware that the newspaper's prime function was to sell, Holt considered it a more satisfying medium for his talent than any hardware trade, and he had a genuine enthusiasm for some of the specialities of his field. Among them was the research aimed at increasing human life-span, which was of such guaranteed interest to his readers that his editor encouraged him to attend every major international conference on the subject. At one of them, held in Milan, he had met Shirley Howard and her chief, Dr. Robert Harvey, head of the small Rosenfeld Unit for Research in Aging at St. Patrick's Hospital.

With his interest concentrated on the expected entry of Shirley, who was joining him for a drink before they went out to lunch, John wished the girl reporter would go away, but eligible bachelors are rare in Fleet Street, and she kept the small-talk conversation going. To counter the barrage of boring gossip, he relaxed whatever mechanism it is that converts background conversations into a meaningless drone and opened his ears to them.

"I regard expenses that are actually spent as a dead loss," he heard one reporter say.

"How are we going to reconcile these two conflicting statements in court?" a barrister asked a newspaper lawyer, less concerned with the truth than with the most expedient version of it.

"Your argument's as full of holes as a string vest," announced the *Daily News* columnist, who by that time had been given one Scotch too many. "Your writing's so effervescent that it ends up as nothing but froth."

"Children are difficult," remarked a woman fashion editor, who tried to cope with the demands of a daily newspaper and a family.

"I wish they were impossible," murmured the girl reporter with feeling.

As John smiled, the swing doors opened to admit Shirley, hatless, a trifle breathless, and obviously glad to see him. John excused himself and took her by the arm to a table.

"Sorry to drag you away—you looked as though you were doing all right," Shirley said with her bubbly laugh.

"Oh, she's like the paper she works for—all makeup and no content. In fact, just about the reverse of you."

For a zoologist, a profession that tends to recruit the plainer girls, Shirley was outstandingly attractive. She was well set up, in contrast to the prevailing taste for the bony, ill-upholstered frames with flattened chests and bean-pole legs perpetrated on men by the fashion designers. Of medium height and dark to a degree that supported her teasing claim that she had some gypsy in her, she was, perhaps, a trifle too swarthy to be pretty, but she was gay, vibrant, provocative in the way men like, and an Artesian well of affection, which poured out under pressure.

She and John had been casual lovers since the Milan meeting, more than a year previously. It was an arrangement that had suited them both. With John, dispossessed of time by his profession, sex had always been a catch-as-catch-can diversion, unplaced in his winning order of life satisfactions, and though Shirley had a steady relationship as Robert Harvey's mistress, she was wanton. This alley-cat trait was partly born of a reaction to a strict upbringing as an only child in a Christian Science family, but was more the result of recently acquired resentment at the educated woman's second-class role in society.

Though Shirley had contributed some of the key suggestions that made the age research so promising, it was naturally assumed by Robert that she would do most of the routine tasks—the supervision of the animal house, the dissections, and even the bottle-washing when the lab assistant was ill or on vacation. Their research papers were published jointly so that "Harvey and Howard" were inseparable in the minds of other workers when they referred to the literature, but there was never any doubt in St. Patrick's or outside who was the very senior author. Then, at the day's end, while Robert and her other male colleagues at the hospital could go home to relaxation or further study, she faced the stocking wash and domestic chores.

When men lay temporarily neutered in her arms, she had conquered them to some extent. Besides, she greatly preferred their company and conversation and found these rarely forthcoming without the ultimate favor.

Robert had no idea that his mistress joined in what he decried as "the promiscuity Paul Jones." He was vain enough to believe that he was achieving a rare response when she acquiesced to the limit after he made the first pass at her, under rather shameful circumstances in the hospital X-ray room. Shirley had long anticipated the situation and knew she would offer only token resistance. During her first scientific conference abroad, she had learned that the casting couch is not peculiar to show business and that some eminent professors, who are absentminded only in their capacity to forget their wives, are just as likely to abuse their powers of patronage as a Hollywood director, if given the chance. But Robert's amorous interest had been welcome. From the beginning, though she realized that he had more than his share of self-love, she had been drawn to his lean features, accentuated by the high forehead left by receding hair and dignified by temple grayness. She admired his mind with its quick capability for laying siege to a scientific problem, and she enjoyed listening to his resonant voice, for the beholding of masculine beauty was in her ear as much as in her eye.

Never having experienced ecstatic attraction, Shirley saw no reason to doubt the possibility of being genuinely in love with two men at the same time, and she was confident that when she decided to canalize her emotions in the direction of one, she would be mistress enough of them to do so. Besides, Robert went home almost every night to his wife, so why should she be monogamous?

She eyed John up and down as he stood at the bar collecting a couple of drinks, outlined against the huge, black casks of port and sherry, which emphasized the excellent cut of his light gray suit. Though shorter than Robert, less lithely built and somewhat square-jawed, with a fresh complexion in contrast to the gauntness she preferred, he was far from unattractive. Judged in the strait confines of academic attainment, he was less impressive than Robert but had wider interests, was better known, had a more varied circle of acquaintances, was more suitably aged for a girl of twenty-eight—and had no wife.

John enjoyed her liveliness and wit, and she carried the bonus of being a considerable source of medical and scientific news. They also shared an intense appreciation of music, in which Robert had little interest. When John had explained, after they had met in the tiny La Scala museum in Milan, why a noble aria or majestic symphony was a far more effective tranquilizer for him than any pill could possibly be, she knew that their conversation need never be restricted to scientific shop or pillow talk.

"I agree with you. Music has a therapeutic effect on me too," she had said.

"Have you thought why it unwinds you?"

5

"Not really. Escapism, I suppose."

"More than that, surely. I think it's because when you're listening to great music all pettiness disappears."

The mutual attraction had been enhanced the following day when they explored the cathedral. Shirley had looked so enticing with his white handkerchief spread over her long hair as they stepped out of the sunshine into the darkness of the Duomo. He had made her laugh, almost aloud, in the nave, with his whispered story of how, as a little boy at Mass, he had whiled away the sermons by making private wagers on which of the numerous candles would sputter out next, moving the pennies he had brought for the collection from one trouser pocket to the other as the bets were settled.

She had noticed how, though he claimed to have lapsed years before, he was unusually respectful in God's house—behavior very different from that of the callous reporter she had been warned to avoid. So respectful that he could not help showing that he felt it was wrong when she nestled into him as they stood in the spinney of soaring pinnacles that is the cathedral roof.

"Just a conditioned reflex," John had protested. "Surprising how they linger on. I almost had to stop my hand from reaching into the holy water as we came in."

Shirley's smile was warm with affection as John returned with the drinks.

"Well, what news on the rialto?" he asked. "Any crumbs of copy to throw to a hungry sparrow?"

"We're still getting consistent results with the injections of SP47. I think there's no doubt now that we've found a way of lengthening the normal life span in mice and rats, and nobody's ever done that before."

John hurriedly put down his glass and looked around to make sure that no other journalist had overheard Shirley's startling news.

"Look, you mustn't publish anything about it yet," Shirley added, immediately regretting that she had aroused his interest so much. "Robert may be reading a short report about it to the Physiological Society soon. If he does, I'll tip you off, and you could print something then."

"I hope to hell it doesn't leak to any other paper," John said apprehensively.

"I'm sure it won't. I won't tell anybody, and Robert's being very tight on laboratory security. He's terrified that if someone gets hold of the story they'll blow it up into an elixir of life sensation and make him look foolish. We know nothing about any effects on the human body. SP47 may be toxic, and we wouldn't like another thalidomide."

"How soon before you try it on human patients?"

"Oh, years, I should think. I expect it'll be SP147 before then."

"I'm blowed if I'd take it if it was a thousand and forty-seven," said John, who reported on all the latest drug developments but had such antipathy toward taking any of them that he had invented a term—pharmacophobia—to describe it.

"The pharmacophobe—of which I'm the archetype—is the reverse of the hypochondriac," he explained. "The surest way to detect him is by opening his bathroom cabinet. It contains only toilet requisites."

He knew enough about the structure of the body cells to believe that anything which interfered with their finely jeweled movement must be injurious. He was particularly opposed to the ever-growing use of tranquilizers to subdue nervous excitement and of pep-pills to alleviate depression, and had written a much-quoted article in which he wondered how much of literature, art, and music would have been created if these drugs had been available to depressives like Dostoevsky, Tschaikovsky, Michelangelo, and Schopenhauer. Keats wrote and Chopin composed with imagination inflamed by the toxin secreted by the germs of tuberculosis. Van Gogh was driven by mania. How much would they have produced had they been continuously tranquilized? How much artistic endeavor had already been stifled by the medical appeasement of mental torment?

As for SP47, hadn't Harvey convinced him, when the three of them lingered in that restaurant in the Victor Emmanuel Arcade in Milan, that aging was almost certainly nothing more than the steady corrosion of the cells' fine structure? SP47 was intended to delay this change and perhaps reverse it, but such a massive interference in a natural process was more likely to hasten it, John thought.

7

"No. I'm blowed if I'd take it," he repeated. "Incidentally, how is the learned doctor?"

"I haven't seen him today—he's in Oxford—but he was all right yesterday. I shall be seeing him tomorrow afternoon. I'll give him your regards."

"Well, if the cat's at Oxford, the mouse can be back late from lunch," John said hopefully. "Shall we go to your flat or mine?"

"Mine's untidy," said Shirley.

"Mine should be in splendid order, providing Mrs. Mopp's been," John said as they went out into the April sunshine to find a taxi. "Ecstasy in the afternoon," he murmured. "How wonderful!"

chapter 2

"Love is like an organism: unless it can adapt to changing circumstances it becomes extinct." Dr. Robert Harvey mused on the aphorism which he had just constructed. He liked aphorisms. They were so useful in those closed-circuit discussions with his conscience that always followed, and sometimes preceded, a session with his mistress.

He could never concede that he was no longer in love with Margaret. After all, they had been married nineteen years, and love, fortified by comfortable family habit, doesn't end abruptly, he argued. But if the mental environments of two people diverge, then those carrier waves of communication which bind them, first in passion, then in devotion, can be weakened toward extinction. It wasn't his fault or hers that while his personality had expanded, as he moved in the fertilizing influence of the laboratory, common room, and learned society, she, anchored by the domestic chores which enabled him to do so, had become a victim of mental malnutrition.

It was a warm evening for April, as he waited for the lecture to begin at the Royal Society of Medicine in Wimpole Street. Looking around at the score of other doctors who had arrived early for the meeting, he wondered what they would think had they known that only an hour ago he, a married man of forty-seven, had been in bed with Shirley Howard, his young assistant, in her two-room flat in Chelsea. Or were their private lives as much in conflict with their personal and professional ideals as his was?

Robert despised the carnal weakness which cut across his normally disciplined intellect and prevented his being one of those fortunate, all-or-none men who can focus undivided passion and affection on the same woman. It ate into his time; it eroded his peace of mind; it forced him to be a liar, betraying his dedication to the scientific search for truth; and it threatened his stability. Like many scientists, he had an exaggerated admiration of order and could anticipate the disorder if the discovery of his infidelity blighted his roots. As with most busy men, only about a quarter of his wakened time could have been spent in the presence of any wife, yet the thought of having to adapt to a new domestic situation appalled him. A man of his training and temperament could never think his slippered world, created with such effort, to be well lost for lust.

God, what a release to unseat the demon-rider who hacks us so mercilessly across country we'd rather avoid, he thought to himself . . . but then all the other creative drives would disappear. Who ever heard of a eunuch doing anything original? "Infidelity is a side effect of the creative urge," he announced inaudibly, firing off another aphorism. But his conscience could coin them too. "There's no need to apply any McNaghten rules to adulterers; they always know what they are doing and that what they are doing is wrong," it replied.

A stir of interest and a sudden lull in the buzz of chitchat marked the entry of the chairman for the session. "Well, ladies and gentlemen, there are just a few business details to deal with before I have the pleasure of introducing the first speaker . . ."

Robert had been out of practice and in full-time research so long that he often came to see the cases brought to the society's meetings for demonstration by leading specialists, though he had an additional reason for being there that evening. Almost always there

9

was something novel and surprising, for though he read widely, nobody can span even half the octave of modern medical knowledge. He also derived personal as well as technical enlightenment from the meetings, for to an insatiable observer of the human cavalcade like Harvey, who was the antithesis of the ivory-towered scientist, they offered sobering glimpses of the medical tragedies which are mercifully hidden from most of us.

Though, as often happens, he did not recognize it, the introduction of the first speaker was one of his mutation moments, those chance and sometimes trivial events which alter an individual's life irrevocably. Not only was Robert never to forget the case presented by Dr. Thomas Holmes, but he was to be reminded of it by circumstances transcending the most brutal excesses of nightmare.

Like most of the cases discussed at those sessions, this was a clinical rarity—a case of progeria, a peculiar condition in which children age at an incredibly rapid rate. Holmes, of the East End Hospital and, inevitably, of Harley Street, silver-haired and smoothly professional, first described the syndrome, of which only about twenty-five instances have been recorded in the medical literature.

"These patients grow very little in height or weight," he explained. "The complete absence of hair and subcutaneous fat accounts for their senile appearance. They all look remarkably alike, whether male or female, and appear to have an enlarged head, though this is really due to the smallness of the face. The cause seems to be some disfunction of the pituitary gland—probably of the anterior lobe."

The twelve-year-old patient was then wheeled in, wearing a blue checked dressing gown and slippers.

"Poor little bastard," Robert whispered as he leaned forward in his seat. "If that's one of God's little jokes, it's in appalling taste."

All those who had never seen a progeria case before, and that was almost all of them, were touched by the sight of the wizened creature who now stood naked before them, in spite of their detachment to suffering which long familiarity with it is bound to engender. The boy looked like the last and oldest man out of Belsen. He had never weighed more than twenty-five pounds. He walked with difficulty and spoke in a thin, piping voice. Chronologically he looked a hundred.

When he had been examined by the clinicians and been taken out of the room, Holmes concluded his demonstration.

"The patient is unlikely to live more than another four years. If he follows the pattern of the previous recorded cases, he will die suddenly from coronary disease or a cerebral hemorrhage. There is no effective treatment."

Robert was fascinated. In his mind he tried to relate this human wreckage to his own researches, wondering particularly about the latest trend of his results. It was most interesting that Holmes had mentioned the anterior pituitary.

For four years he and Shirley had been injecting mice and white rats with a mixture of pituitary hormones, sex hormones, enzymes, and chelating agents—chemicals with the capacity to lock onto certain toxic products which collect in the body and so render them harmless. The treatments were intended to investigate why natural life-spans are so finite and whether anything could be done to extend them. The ultimate aim was to elucidate the causes of aging in man, but it looked like one of the longest, plodding hauls in the history of science, for aging was clearly an extremely complex process.

Lewis Rosenfeld, the mail-order millionaire who sold everything from shoes to sewing machines, had put money into it, ostensibly as a contribution to posterity but privately in the wild hope that something might be discovered in time to extend his own life. He had striven so hard under the lash of aggrandizement for so long that when he came to his millions, his material enjoyment of them was severely restricted by fallen arches, a peptic ulcer, and chronic bronchitis, but he was still loath to leave them after so brief an indulgence in the power they provided.

The trials had produced no spectacular results, until Shirley chanced to read a report of American experiments in a biochemical journal showing that certain changes in the protein of living cells could be prevented by the application of an extract obtained from bacteria living in soil. Suspecting that these changes might be a major cause of aging, they added the extract to the mixture, which was code-named SP32, because it was the thirty-second of a series developed at St. Patrick's. The combined effect had been startling. Some of the rats, which at two and a half years of age should have been senile, remained glossy-coated and bright-eyed. They had progressively improved the mixture until with SP47, the latest of the series, there was a much higher rate of survival into hale old age, with almost complete inhibition of the pneumonia and other ailments which normally kill off so many caged animals.

Though Robert felt that this absence of disease was highly encouraging, the discipline and disappointments of science had taught him to be ultracautious. On the basis of his previous experience, the next batch of results might show the first to have been as lacking in significance as a cocktail kiss, in which case another five years of patient endeavor would culminate in a few reports, destined to gather dust in the bound volumes of *Nature* or the *Journal of Gerontology*.

Polite applause signaled the end of the meeting, and the audience broke up into gossip groups, each centered around some mogul of medicine. Robert recognized many of them, but few had heard of him. A professor of physiology, whom he had met at a foreign conference, gave him a faint wave, but was too busy talking to the medical director who could open the coffers of the Nuffield Foundation.

Robert wondered how many of them owed their eminence to the luck which had never come his way. He believed he was as competent as most of them, perhaps more so than some like Sir Ewart Gladstone-Hicks, the radiographer, who had sprinted to success and the accolade after being called in to a royal emergency when his betters happened to be away. In boyhood, Robert had resolved to reach the top of whatever profession he might choose, yet here he was, at forty-seven, past his creative prime as a research scientist, with negligible chance of a university chair or fellowship of the Royal Society.

He had always driven himself hard, but in science, as in life generally, there are no prizes for a worthy try. Only the hoist of luck could lift him out of the rut of mediocrity now. Maybe it was not too late. Alexander Fleming had been forty-seven when his mutation moment came in the form of a spore of penicillin mold drifting through his laboratory window. Could SP47 be his magic spore? An odd coincidence that the number matched his age and Fleming's!

As Robert emerged, he saw Holmes getting into a chauffeured Rolls. While other consultants were calling for taxis, he walked through into Oxford Street, which was thick with jostling bodies and the fumes of the rush-hour traffic. He stopped by a cart stacked with trumpet daffodils, bought two dozen for his wife, then stood with them, rather self-consciously, in the line for the Number 13 bus, which went almost past his flat in St. John's Wood. The procession of buses with every other number except 13 would normally have irritated him into muttering, shuffling annoyance, but he happened to be in no hurry to get home. He needed to insert the longest possible interval between an afternoon in Shirley's arms and his return to the warmth of Margaret's welcome. That, in fact, was the main reason why he had gone to the meeting, for which the description "fateful" would have been history's biggest understatement.

chapter 3

The last stripteaser had shed her last garment and was covered in front only by a small card stating "I give Green Shield stamps." As Shirley laughed at this desperate effort to inject some entertainment into a jaded routine, Robert slyly looked at his watch while pretending to adjust his cufflink. It was past midnight. He had told Margaret he would be working late again in the laboratory on a long series of injections and was beginning to feel his usual uneasiness.

The Roaring Forties Revue Bar in Soho was basically out of character for both Shirley and Robert, but the trouble with a clandestine relationship in a small town like inner London is that it becomes increasingly difficult to find places where one is unlikely to be flushed by inquisitive acquaintances. So they used tucked-away restaurants and pubs to relieve the tedium of Shirley's flat, and sometimes one of the less expensive, dim-lit nightclubs like the Roaring Forties where long-limbed girls in fishnet stockings served drinks and food not too appalling in price or quality. They assumed that their professional colleagues would be unlikely to go there and found the atmosphere strangely conducive to the trivial conversation into which they escaped from their work and to their favorite hobby of people-watching. They both considered the behavior of humans to be infinitely more interesting and unpredictable than that of birds, and one did not have to lie for hours in a smelly marsh to observe it.

Robert, who from boyhood had the reputation of having everything worked out, would have computed emotions with a slide rule if he could. His training and analytical temperament conditioned him to reduce even the gesture of a smile to the conjoint movement of muscles. Since the superbly coordinated mechanics of the human machine were a fount of awesome beauty for him, he could never understand why most women resented such analytical interest as being unromantic.

"Does the fact that I happen to understand the strange sexual arrangements of the primrose detract from my enjoyment of its beauty?" he inquired of Shirley. "Because I know what Shakespeare meant when he wrote of 'pale primroses that die unmarried,' am I thereby less sentimental? Does it detract from my human warmth because I know that, when the bird which sent Wordsworth into raptures makes its unmistakable call, it is always a *cock* cuckoo, since the female can't make that noise?"

As a professional dissector herself, Shirley appreciated such expertise, and as an aid to people-watching they had jointly invented, half jestingly, what they called the "HSR"—the Harvey Satisfaction Rating—a quick numerical method for measuring up the attributes of the opposite sex. They awarded points up to a maximum of twenty for body conformation above the belt, twenty for conformation below, another maximum of twenty for intelligence and wit, and up to twenty more for capacity to elicit passion and transmute it to contentment. A further twenty was available for personality, including charm, warmth, kindness, and understanding, making an unattainable total of one hundred. The final score gave a percentage of perfection.

Robert considered it a useful rough guide because it was flexible. The man who cared little for looks but everything for intelligence and wit could load the marks to award forty for ability between the ears and only ten for conformation: or the sex obsessionist could load it his way. His own division seemed about right for the normally integrated man. With a total of seventy-five, Shirley had scored the highest HSR of anyone with whom Robert had been intimate enough to make a full assessment. They both agreed that anyone unattached should settle with any willing partner who scored seventy or over.

In private retrospect he rated Margaret's to have been no better than sixty when he had married her. Now it was down below fifty. The ravages of forty-three years and three children had slashed her score on conformation. Her breasts were pendulous, her legs podgy and marred by the speckling of ruptured veinlets, which are so often the penalty of fruitful pregnancy. Her skin was desiccated, especially on her abdomen, where Robert found the crosshatch crinkling to be as destructive of desire as an ill-timed telephone call. On intellect, her score had never been high, for by congenital endowment she was a poor absorber of facts.

"Pity the poor absorbers, for theirs is the kingdom of mediocrity," Robert had once pontifically told the students to whom he gave occasional lectures. "Ideas grow out of facts. If the facts have fallen through the cracks in memory's floor, there's nothing to germinate."

The particular gimmick of the Roaring Forties was a square hole in the dance floor through which protruded a long, brass fireman's pole. By opening a small safety gate and sliding down the pole, access was achieved to another bar in the basement, though it was possible to reach it by stairs. Each time anyone slid down the pole, a wailing siren warned those below of the imminent arrival of yet another body.

Robert and Shirley watched from the protective gloom of their candle-lit table and commented on the numerous men and few women who made the slide-down. "Men never grow up. They deserve to be clipped," thought Shirley as two potbellied codgers on an expense-account evening embraced the pole amid gales of laughter. Robert's mind was inevitably on the unseen mechanism that operated the siren. To him such a problem was as insistent for attention as a dripping tap in the night.

"I think the slight wobbling of the pole must actuate a switch,"

Shirley suggested, tilting her head in the appealing way she did when she was puzzled.

"Too complicated," said Robert. "Whatever it is it'll be something simple."

He was right. The girl at the reception desk simply pressed a button whenever she saw someone grasp the pole.

"Told you!" said Robert. "The simple answer is nearly always the right one in science."

It is odd how the obvious so often makes its impact at unexpected moments—in trivial conversation, during the lie-back relaxation of a warm bath, or on the sliding edge of sleep. Ideas simmering in the subconscious suddenly boil over in a creative association. His chance remark about the simple solution had recalled Holmes' final sentence of the previous evening—"There is no effective treatment." Since the entire body was affected in progeria, there must be a simple central cause, his reason told him, and this presupposed the possibility of a simple cure. Might the mixture which seemed to be preventing his rats from growing old undo some of the excessive aging which had taken place in this child? Whatever was responsible for progeria, it seemed to be operating in every cell.

Perhaps without the influence of alcohol his critical faculties might never have allowed him to entertain the idea of approaching Holmes, but he discussed it with Shirley as he waited for the bill, or rather argued it out aloud with himself, for having no medical qualifications she could do little more than serve as a sounding board.

"There's nothing ethically wrong in it," he said as he felt for his wallet. "The boy must be considered a terminal case—certain to die soon anyway. I think we could take a chance on long-term toxicity with this patient. I would if he was one of my own kids. He couldn't possibly be in worse shape. If the parents and Holmes agree, there's absolutely nothing to be lost, but we'll have to do some tests to find out if SP47 is compatible with human serum. I'm confident it will be."

Robert was already satisfied that SP47 would not cause cancer. Most of the ingredients occurred naturally in the healthy young body, and the rest had shown no signs of being cancer-forming. Indeed, the animal experiments indicated that it might even suppress some tumor growths. This bonus, if confirmed, would not be inconsistent. Malignancies begin in the individual cell, and some may be due to internal irritation by accumulated toxic products, which the mixture might remove or neutralize. There was also the question of possible mental effects to be considered. If memory consisted of congealed patterns of electric charges, as seemed likely, it was conceivable that the drug might wash them out—an eventuality which would make it unusable, because all learning, including the power of speech, would then be lost. But numerous tests, in which rats were taught to run in mazes or operate puzzle boxes and were later given the drug, had produced no sign of any ill effects on the brain, and Robert was confident there would not be any.

"The boy might die at any time, and my chances of seeing another case in my lifetime are remote, so there's only one quick way out of the difficulty," Robert said as they got up to go. "If Holmes agrees that the effort's worthwhile, I'll try out SP47 on myself in gradually increasing dosage."

There was nothing heroic in this decision. The mixture seemed unlikely to produce any significant side effects, and self-trials are standard practice among medical researchers.

Mademoiselle Gigi, the stripper with the Green Shield stamps inducement, was saying a broad cockney "Good night" to the manager at the desk. Hard and drawn under her thick makeup, so that the contrast with Shirley was like the difference between a pressed flower and a fresh one, she looked as though she was in urgent need of SP47 if she was to go on exposing herself for a living much longer.

"What's her HSR?" asked Shirley.

"Not more than fifty," Robert replied as they opened the doors and stepped into the garlic air of Greek Street.

Riding back in the taxi to St. John's Wood after dropping Shirley in Chelsea, Robert, slightly drowsy with drink, mulled over his idea again with one eye on the meter ticking up the shillings every few hundred yards.

Maybe he was being too precipitate. Even the animal findings were too tentative for any hint of them to get to the ears of that fellow Holt on the *Daily Dispatch*. As for the possibility of using SP47 on the progeria boy, what a tear-jerking story Holt would make of that gobbet of news. He could just see it—"A brilliant

British doctor is fighting to restore lost youth to a twelve-year-old boy who looks a hundred. Using a startling new drug . . ."

"Why the hell are we always 'brilliant' and why are we always 'fighting'? Yes, we must certainly prevent Holt from getting any smell of it," he said to himself as he put his feet up on the seat.

Twelve shillings on the clock already! He really would have to cut out these taxis. And that bill at the Roaring Forties. Nearly five pounds with the tip!

Slumped back in the seat, he sensed the odor of Shirley's perfume clinging to his clothing and lifted the lapels of his jacket to his nose. It was strong where she had rested her head during the drive back to her flat. He pulled down both windows and leaned unsteadily toward one of them, tugging out his lapels to expose them to the maximum draft. God! What a degrading posture for a man of his pretensions and responsibilities. What would the children think if they could see him? The children, who thought him such a wonderful father that, after a memorable morning when he had taken them around the zoo, they had called him "Superdad." Robert recalled the pleasure of watching their faces at the fulfillment of his unlikely prophecies.

"Give that capuchin monkey this onion and watch him rub it all over his fur. Poke this bit of blue paper through the wire of the bower bird's cage and see it swoop down and snatch it. Ever heard guinea pigs warble? Rattle this handful of money at them and listen."

That's what leisure was for; not for jumping into bed with a girl almost young enough to be your daughter! He would have to be his age and give Shirley up: but he had made that decision too many times before to feel any great confidence that he could implement it without some more compelling cause.

His corpulent promises when intoxicated either by alcohol or by guilt had always been deflated by practicalities when he saw Shirley at her bench on the following morning, neat, efficient, and feminine in her white coverall, preparing the injections or adjusting her microscope. He had the continuing excuse that he could not replace her at that stage of the experiments, nor, once his libido had recharged itself, had he ever wanted to do so. But he was beginning to feel a diminution in that direction. He would soon be fifty, and he felt that the welcome weakening of the demon on his back would eventually enable him to uncomplicate his life in the pursuit of peace and stability. Until then, it was a most convenient arrangement. Margaret suspected nothing and seemed contented, and though Shirley clearly hankered after a common roof over both of them, she seemed to have accepted that he was unwilling to desert his wife and home. But in spite of the intimacy of their relationship, his understanding of her nature was as fragmentary as Margaret's knowledge of his. Immunized by self-assurance against the suspicion that either his wife or his mistress could be unfaithful to him, and tranquilized by Shirley's always plausible account when he questioned her casually about how she spent her last free evening, he believed that her sole purpose in seeing John Holt was to promote the interests of Robert Harvey and his research unit by securing publicity when it was needed.

As a doctor, Harvey was instinctively scared of journalists, for though unable to profit by advertisement, he was fearful of the General Medical Council, attributing to it aggressive, inquisitorial powers it rarely wielded. But as Shirley had pointed out, Rosenfeld would never have put up the money for the research had it not been for the original newspaper publicity about the possibility of extending human life-span, and if the experiments continued to go well, they would soon need a lot more. Robert's yearning for recognition also made him perhaps more susceptible than most to the advantages of publicity, provided it was exactly when and how he wanted it, but, anxious to avoid any responsibility if anything went wrong, he held himself aloof from the newspapers and encouraged Shirley to act as his press relations officer.

Robert was aware that one of the most socially destructive factors in human affairs is the failure of most people to disclose themselves, even to those with whom they share their nights, but he had never considered that its consequences could make much impact on his own life.

chapter **4**

Dr. Thomas Holmes, consultant pediatrician to the Royal Household and confident of an early knighthood, studied the letter he had received from Dr. Harvey. His lucrative practice and hospital work left him little time to know much about old-age research. Even the *British Medical Journals* and *Lancets* lay stacked unread in the lower section of the elegant breakfront bookcase which graced his consulting room.

He held strong views about the use of human subjects for experimentation, believing that many of his colleagues, particularly those engaged on brain research, were going much too far, but when a patient was irrevocably doomed, as the progeria child was, there seemed to be no ethical objection to grasping at straws so long as this did not involve mutilation. This fellow Harvey seemed well qualified, and the two months of tests he had carried out on himself did not contraindicate the use of SP47 on human patients. Holmes did not think the suggested treatment would do any good for he knew well enough that aging and the natural causes of death are the cumulative result of an infinitude of minor changes, which build up like encrusting stalactites in the dark caverns of the body, and he could not see how they could be reversed. Still, many medical advances had arisen through fumbling trial and error and many through lucky accident.

"Bring me the papers on Joseph Greenway," he told his secretary over the intercom. It would be necessary to consult the parents.

The Greenways were working class by birth and by circumstance, the father being a garage mechanic just off the Mile End Road, and Joseph was their only child. Holmes had assured them that the disease was so rare that their next child would not be afflicted, but Mary Greenway had been embittered by producing a son who looked old enough to be her grandfather. She was too frightened that it might be due to "something in the blood" to risk another pregnancy, and the neighbors were no help in allaying this unwarranted fear. In spite of the exaggerated affection engendered for him by his pitiful infirmity, she half-welcomed the prospect of his release from suffering.

Holmes had written to their family doctor suggesting the SP47 treatment if the parents agreed. At first they were repelled by the suspicion that the boy might be used for an experiment, but in the end that was the reason which induced them to consent.

"We think that one day it might help others," Mary told her doctor with sincerity.

So Joseph was taken once more into the East End Hospital where he had already spent so much of his short, unhappy life, and Holmes began a tentative series of injections with SP47 supplied from Harvey's laboratory.

The effect was more than dramatic. It was fantastic. Within a fortnight the birdlike face began to fill out not merely with cosmetic fat but with the underlying bone and muscle. For the first time hair began to appear on the polished scalp. The voice fell to a normal short-trousered register; the body fleshed out; the muscles strengthened. Holmes, usually phlegmatic, was so excited that he telephoned Harvey with the news, and Robert and Shirley went straightway down in her secondhand sportscar to see the patient.

Robert could hardly believe it was the same boy. After examining the physiological checks, which Holmes had instituted before beginning the treatment, they decided to increase the dosage, meanwhile keeping the closest watch on the blood count and other danger indicators.

A month later Joseph was barely distinguishable from a normal child of his age except for his short stature, and there were already indications of a height increase.

Miracle is a forbidden word among doctors, but no other could adequately describe this transformation.

Over a cup of coffee in the hospital staff refectory, Holmes and Harvey were talking over the possible ways in which SP47 had produced these effects so quickly.

"Perhaps it's not so surprising, Holmes. Progeria would seem to be due to the extremely rapid aging of the individual tissues, so maybe it's understandable that the senile changes in them can be equally rapidly reversed. We've hardly any understanding of the biological clocks built into our bodies. You know—what makes some people run down quickly so that, though apparently healthy, they are elderly at fifty-five, while in others the life clocks tick so slowly that they are reasonably young at seventy."

"I'm sure that's a neglected field of research," Holmes replied. "Those odd things we all notice about time must come into it somewhere—you know, how it seems to drag when we're young and fly when we're old."

"Yes, I've often thought that if life was a symphony instead of a discord, the slow movement would come first with the presto at the end. I don't think that it's all just psychological."

"Well, whatever time is, Harvey, we'll need plenty of it to see whether this reversal is permanent and whether treatment will have to be continuous throughout remaining life."

As yet there was no evidence that the boy's life expectation had been increased. In spite of their electrocardiograms and other tests, the doctors had no certain means of discovering whether the internal ravages wrought by the disease had been affected. The coronary arteries, those slender tubules fueling the heart itself, which even in the healthy child begin to show signs of scarification at five and sometimes even at birth, might already have been damaged beyond recovery.

"I'm sure this thought has already occurred to you," Holmes added. "But I was wondering what effect this mixture of yours might have on the normally aging body if taken over a long time. I remember being told about these extraordinary experiments with tissue cultures when I was a student."

"You mean the experiments with chicken cells, which remained eternally young when regularly transferred to a new nutritive medium so that they didn't become poisoned by their own excretory products?"

"That's right. Couldn't this SP47 of yours work by neutralizing those products? If so, it might even *prevent* the natural cell damage of aging."

Robert could have given him some sort of answer. He had continued the toxicity tests on himself for five months, trying out variations in the proportions of the mixture to make it more compatible with the human internal environment, and already there were signs that some reversion of age was taking place in his own body. His hair was more profuse, was regaining its blackness, and seemed to be descending toward its adolescent boundary. The dropsical bags below his eyes were retracting. He felt unusually fit and vigorous and was surprised that nobody, not even Shirley, had remarked on it: but then, most people are unobservant, especially concerning those with whom they are in regular contact. He decided to say nothing about it to Holmes at that stage but to step up the dosage on himself.

"An interesting idea to follow up later," Robert said, parrying Holmes' question. "But, of course, in Greenway's case we may be doing no more than remedying some deficiency not normally present in the healthy body."

"That's more than likely, I suppose. Now what about publication?" Holmes asked with his eye on being the senior author of the clinical report in the *British Medical Journal*, where it would be assured of maximum world publicity.

"Shall we do a joint letter, simply announcing this result, with all the usual reservations about more time being needed to assess the permanence of the improvement? It's no good waiting for another progeria case to turn up. They're as rare as a double bed in a hospital. This is only the second I've seen in a lifetime of pediatrics. Or shall we wait a little longer in case the boy relapses?"

It was a difficult decision. Both men were anxious to secure professional priority—to stake their international claim to recognition by being the first to publish. A brief letter in the *British Medical Journal* would achieve this, but both were sufficiently experienced to know that premature publicity has been the stubbing stone of many a promising reputation in medicine. A letter would also serve to arouse the interest of other research workers, but this too was a double-edged prospect. The sooner that more minds were brought to bear on the leads opened up by their findings, the more quickly they would be exploited for general benefit, but both wanted to consolidate their leadership in the field they had created, before opening it to the big battalions, particularly those of the giant scientific laboratories in America.

This conflict between professional ethics and ambition was conveniently appeased by compromise. The two men decided to continue the treatment for a further month and then to reconsider the question of publication.

"Of course, it's most important that the newspapers don't get hold of any information about this case," Holmes said, thinking of his almost certain election to the General Medical Council. For years he had walked the sharply inclined tightrope toward academic acclaim without fault, while at the same time pocketing a lush retainer as adviser on baby foods to an advertising agency, and he had no wish to be put off balance by too well-informed publicity when so near the handrail of the summit.

"I've already taken the precaution of telling the Greenways that they shouldn't say anything about their son's apparent recovery yet," he continued. "I told them it might be psychologically dangerous for the boy if the press got to hear about it just now. I said they'd badger the hospital night and day to secure photographs and all that private detail they peddle. I've also instructed the hospital staff along the same lines."

Robert nodded assent, but Holmes was nevertheless determined in his own mind to secure the utmost credit from the case when the timing suited him. Like most well-breeched doctors, he pretended to hate publicity but secretly was vain enough to desire it and astute enough to realize the value of carefully managed advertising to professional advancement. Once he had his knighthood and his seat on the General Medical Council, he knew he would automatically join the ranks of those untouchable grandmasters, officially—and often inaccurately—recognized as already being so well known as to be unable to escape newspaper acclaim, and already so loaded with patients as to be unlikely to profit from it.

chapter 5

Mapledurham is a decaying eddy of the Thames left bank not yet overwhelmed by the seeping suburbs of Reading, only six miles away. Robert and Shirley had discovered it one hot afternoon when they decided to duck out of a conference they were attending at Reading University. They were enchanted by the ancient mansion with its high-pitched roof and towering chimneys and by the mill, with its great decrepit wheel, serving only as a nesting site for waterfowl. As they stood among the lichened tombs in the nearby church, where God and the Blount family had been worshiped for centuries, they could watch the color of the patterned brickwork change with the slanting of the sunlight and listen to the quiet quartet of swifts, jackdaws, swirling water, and wind in the aspen leaves. They loved the pastures, fenceless alongside the river, at that point still several hours from its degradation into the bladder of London. They were even more enraptured by the close-by beechwoods, where their mutual affection had since received al fresco consummation many times. To a dynamic self-driver like Robert, any place conducive to relaxation was immensely precious.

They were stretched out under one of the parasol yew-trees which gave them some feeling of special privacy. The early September sun filtered through the weft of straggling branches, burnishing the thick, coppery pile of the beech-leaf carpet. The world's oldest tranquilizer had wrought its well-being on Robert, whose stallion drive had unquestionably strengthened since he had been taking SP47.

"I can't remember when I've felt so fit and satisfied with life," he murmured sleepily, giving unconscious expression to the fact that the normal loss of masculine vitality is so gradual that, without benefit of an artificial boost, the middle-aged man cannot recall the full, effervescent surge of sapling vigor.

Wood pigeons were throating their contented rumbles. In the distance, a cock pheasant threw out his territorial challenge, followed by a flurry of wings. The world outside seemed at peace, but not so the mind of Shirley Howard. Like most unmarried mistresses, she was beginning to chafe for the trappings of legal respectability and, above all, of security, for she was so dependent on what she earned that affection was the only asset with which she could afford to be generous.

"You may be feeling younger, Robert, but I'm getting older, and I need some sense of permanence in my life," she announced suddenly. "Do you think there's any chance you might provide it, or do you expect me to go on sharing you forever?"

Robert had not expected to be faced with such an irritating question. Forced to a quick answer, and being frank with everyone except his wife, he put his hands behind his neck and without opening his eyes replied, "There can be few women in the world who are as satisfying in every way as you are, Shirley. You're a wonderful companion, and you give me something nearer to the total personality experience that ideal sex is supposed to be than anyone I'm ever likely to encounter, but I've a commitment to my wife and three children, and they are my stakes in the future."

"Anyone who thinks he can achieve fulfillment through his children is deluded, Robert."

"For someone who's never had any, that's a perceptive remark."

"Not all that perceptive. I only had to think back to my own relationship with my parents before they died. There's little sense of gratitude after adolescence. I suppose it's against nature that there should be any at a time when bonds should be loosening."

"Yes, that's all part of the grand design," Robert said impulsively, seizing the chance to bring the conversation down to a less emotional level. "If human bonds weren't really flimsy in spite of the sentimental mortar we slap around them, we'd never be able to weather the death of those we love."

"Well, if that's what you think, why can't you give up Margaret?" Shirley retorted, edging alongside him. "You've much more in common with me, and you can't expect to go on having us both."

26

Though determined to continue her career, Shirley was as motivated toward marriage as any woman by the ingrained fear of ultimate loneliness. Further, she was not entirely immune to romantic illusion, and in the hope of achieving its fulfillment, she was not averse to the sacrifice of Robert's family.

"You know it's not really ecstatic love that makes the world go round, Shirley," said Robert. "It's dependability. Civilization can operate only on the basis that most of us will honor our bargains to our families and employers, at least in the material sense. The difference between being a traitor to your family and a traitor to your country is only a matter of numbers. Only a degenerate could desert three children and be happy after it."

"But I'm not asking you to desert them. You'd still look after them. We wouldn't be living far away, and they'd be able to come and see us."

"There's more to it than that, Shirley. To withdraw myself from the home would be tantamount to desertion. I'm afraid we've just got to accept the fact that you and I are in love three children too late."

"Well, now there's an admission," Shirley said, putting her arms around him. "Do you realize that's the first time you've ever said you love me?"

It was not only for fear of committing himself that Robert had always avoided using the word "love" aloud. It was because it was the word reserved for his wife, for the permanent, stable side of his life. To have uttered it seemed a more menacing betrayal than his physical infidelity.

Shirley had met Margaret Harvey many times and often dined at their home. She liked her, but with the woman's primal capacity for protecting lovers at whatever cost to truth, ethics, or morality, she had lost all feeling of guilt about her affair with Robert. Margaret was not suspicious of her husband, attributing the mutually waning interest of their intimacy to the normal erosion of nineteen years of double-bedded wedlock. It was so normal for him to mention his assistant that the increasing intrusion of another woman's name and opinions into his conversation, which would swell the seed of doubt in the mind of most sensitive wives, passed unheeded. For his part, the definition of normality, which he had come to accept through his medical experience, was "the condition in which the separate members of the organism function harmoniously," and in applying the criterion to the two-headed monster of marriage he found that it worked as well as could be expected. Margaret's lack of perception was an advantage to a man who could not stand up to being too closely questioned about where he spent his time.

"You've grown so far away from Margaret," Shirley said, drawing him down toward her. "You know she bores you."

"You mustn't be unkind to Margaret," Robert snapped. "It's not her fault if my personality has changed over the nineteen years we've been married. It's true that she's not particularly loaded with gray matter, but I owe her a lot of devotion."

In fact there was much more to it than that. Robert's aura of self-reliance was fraudulent. Through the intimacies of the years Margaret was incorporated in his own body image, and if he amputated her she would persist in his mind like a painful phantom limb.

The Harveys had met at London University when she had a peaches-and-cream freshness, and married soon after Robert had qualified and completed his postgraduate studies. She had sacrificed her average capabilities as a historian to her husband's career and children with no apparent regrets. Lacking originality, she had obtained her university place, like so many girls, by making verbatim notes of everything her teachers said and cramming it by plodding effort into her memory, where it remained just long enough for her to answer the stereotyped examination questions. She was house-proud, a good mother, and an excellent cook, rising superbly to the occasions when they entertained foreign scientists, who gave Robert hospitality when he attended conferences in their countries. There was a smell of stability about the home which, as he appreciated, played no small part in enabling him to concentrate his mind on his work, for he found it difficult to focus his attention in the laboratory if he was irritated by emotional background noise.

To Margaret, who was temperamentally suited to draw all her emotional sustenance through one taproot, being taken for granted was a sign of her husband's satisfaction rather than a cause for resentment, and she had a further considerate attribute important to a scientist. She did not saturate his leisure with the small talk which robs so many husbands of thinking time and gives lonely bachelors in garrets such an unfair advantage in the field of creative endeavor.

Robert had deliberately tried to keep the laboratory out of the home, but she helped him sometimes—as when she volunteered to act as guinea pig in the human toxicity tests of SP47, after a month's injections on himself produced no observable ill effects. He had no qualms about letting her do so. She was so much a part of his ego that it seemed natural that she should share what he considered to be a pretty mild risk, and it had done her no harm. In fact, when she made her face up, she thought her skin looked far less lined and pore-marked, though that might be wishful illusion. Still, there was no illusion about that unsightly speckling on her thighs, which had embarrassed her so much when she wore a bathing suit. It had become so faint that it was barely discernible. Her breasts also seemed firmer and less in need of support.

Robert stood up, brushed the dried leaves from his gray flannel trousers and sports jacket—the hangover garb of the research man who has never broken his links with undergraduate days.

"Anyway, you know I can't *afford* to get divorced," he said. "It seems to me you need a rich wife who can't sue you for alimony to get divorced these days."

"Well, I suppose I'd better look around for somebody else," Shirley replied with equal bluntness as she rescued her shoes.

"Let's not talk about it until you find somebody," Robert replied, knowing that he would be furiously jealous on the day that she told him she had.

Shirley wondered whether in fact she had already found somebody adequate enough in John Holt. She had never indulged in the fantasy that somewhere there was one ideal man waiting to be met. From her own observations, she realized that women who really want to get married and are mature enough to weather its vicissitudes could make a tolerable match with at least one out of every fifty eligible men they meet. She did not visualize love as an entity, which would suddenly erupt out of the plain of spinsterhood, but as a dry-stone cairn to be built, with effort, of many mutual interests and attachments, and which would need time to settle into solidity. As a woman endowed with more than her share of intellect, she knew that marriage was far too important a step to be left to instinct.

chapter 6

There was no longer any doubt about it. Objective tests showed conclusively that Robert was undergoing a definite change, which could only be described as rejuvenation by any reasonable standards. He had measured the elasticity of his skin, which is one reliable parameter of aging, and in the past month it had increased toward the youthful level by several units. Measurements of muscle strength—of the grip, the biceps, and the back—indicated a regeneration of power. His reaction time was shorter, his ear more sensitive to high-frequency sounds. His intelligence quotient had risen by eight points, indicating a cerebral reversion of ten years on the sharply canted curve showing the average decline in intelligence with age. Similar tests on Margaret after treatment with a variant containing female sex hormones were equally significant.

Robert had also submitted samples of his tissues for biopsy examination by the hospital pathologist. For all these tests the collaboration of colleagues had to be secured, and it was fast becoming impossible to keep their purpose secret. Indeed, the results were becoming so obvious that several people who had not seen him for months did not recognize him when he bumped into them.

Margaret's friends were also beginning to be curious about the phenomenal improvement in her appearance. She was being assailed with so many questions that she had to suspend her mid-morning visits to the local coffee shop.

"Darling, you look as though you've been on the most marvelous holiday. Have you discovered some new skin food? Come on, give!" said one neighbor, as Margaret put her shopping bag down by the side of the coffee table.

"Robert hasn't staked you to a face lift by that wonderful plastic surgeon has he?" asked another.

"I say, Margaret, you're not pregnant are you?" said her most intimate friend, remembering how well she had looked herself in that condition.

Margaret's fair skin was recovering a resilience which almost erased the brow lines and crow's feet. Her hair, which for years she had tinted to conceal its mousiness, was becoming vigorous and truly blonde again. Even the whites of her eyes seemed to have acquired a porcelain quality, enhancing the setting of her sapphire irises.

All this really did seem like a thrust into a new realm of medical possibilities, and the time had come to face the necessity for properly controlled clinical trials. For this Robert needed more money and more research workers in his unit. There was also the urgent problem of publication. The progeria boy was almost normal, increasing rapidly in height, and the prognosis looked excellent. His treatment had been going on for five months, and there was no evidence whatever of any untoward mental effects. The boy was backward, but having begun to learn, he was displaying near-average intelligence, and there was no impairment of memory. Holmes agreed that they could delay no longer. It would soon be Christmas, and they should try to get their letter in the *British Medical Journal* by the New Year. So they decided that Robert should seek an interview with Sir Edward James of the Medical Research Council, under whose aegis the Rosenfeld Unit for Research in Aging operated, to secure permission to publish.

Sir Edward James, who at fifty-five had been the council's permanent secretary for six years, had impressive medical qualifications on paper, but was much more of a politician than a doctor. He needed to be to administer hundreds of research units all clamoring for a bigger share of the shoestring money that the Government allotted him—a sum that, he was fond of reminding his political masters, was almost exactly one-half of one percent of the money they spent on defense. Sitting in his office near Regent's Park, he turned over the short report submitted by Robert, whom he had met when he had accompanied Lewis Rosenfeld around the various research units which the tycoon's money had endowed. The claims, though carefully worded, seemed unbelievable, but they were supported by an enclosure from Holmes, who was noted for his caution, and the sequential photographs of the progeria case spoke for themselves.

"Dr. Harvey, sir," his secretary announced. James, barrel-chested and balding, rose, peered over the top of the rimless glasses which made him look rather American, and said, "I'm sorry, but I must have confused you with somebody else. I was expecting a rather older man." When Robert assured him that he was in fact the rather older man somewhat rejuvenated by SP47, Sir Edward was visibly startled.

"This is certainly something," he said, sitting down and motioning his visitor to a chair slightly lower than his. "Do you think it is likely to have an effect on life-span? Apart from making you look younger, which it undoubtedly does, might it increase your total longevity?"

Robert leaned back and reflected for a few moments. "We have no evidence of that yet on the human subject, of course. But our tests with rats suggest that it will. We now have some young-looking rats at St. Patrick's which are three and a half years old, and we'd have expected most of them to have died of old age or disease about a year ago. All the evidence from other sources supports the contention that aging is not inevitable. It seems to be an unnecessary disease process which, in theory, should be susceptible to being slowed down and possibly reversed to some extent."

Declining the proffered cigarette, Robert continued, "I estimate that ninety percent of all deaths would not occur if people could somehow retain the resistance to infection and injury they enjoy when they are fifteen. It's this progressive loss of resistance which is the underlying cause of death, and if it should prove possible to delay it, absolute life-span should be increased. I'm sure I don't need to point out to you that the maximum life-span of man hasn't changed since biblical times. All that science has done is to enable more and more people to achieve it."

"What addition to active life-span do you anticipate?" Sir Edward asked, making a space on his desk for the morning coffee brought in by his secretary.

"We won't know for a long time, Sir Edward, but from animal studies it seems that the theoretical life-span is about seven times the age during which growth occurs. Human growth ceases at about twenty. So in theory man might be able to live to a hundred and forty, but perhaps a hundred and ten might prove nearer the mark. However, I must stress again that there's no certainty that the effect of SP47 will be maintained at all."

"Have you considered the economic consequences of extending the average life-span even just to ninety?" Sir Edward asked, passing Robert a cup of coffee. "Have you thought of the effects on the social structure of the population, on the balance between young and old? Of its effects on family life? On jobs?"

"Not in detail."

"Then we must do so before we do anything else," said James, snapping the little silver snuffbox in which he carried his saccharin tablets. "Above all we must prevent any publicity of any kind about your researches to date, until I have approached the council for their advice. If the public gets to hear about SP47 at this stage, every aging man and woman will start clamoring for it on the Health Service. That will put the Government in a spot. You can be sure that the chemical manufacturers will exert every pressure to get it released so that they can produce it. What a pharmaceutical field day that would make!"

Robert puckered his brow in disbelief.

"No, Harvey," James continued, wagging a pudgy finger. "As I see it there is possible social chaos in this development unless it's rigidly controlled. The world was entirely unprepared for the sudden advent of nuclear power, and it has only narrowly escaped being destroyed by it. The world is certainly unprepared for this new bombshell, in my opinion."

"Surely, you're exaggerating these dangers," Robert protested. "This is a therapeutic drug, not a destructive explosive!"

But James, whose agile mind was developing the themes which had occurred to him when he had first read Harvey's report, was not to be put off.

"Have you thought about the possible effects of a substantial increase in life-span on world food supplies?" he asked. "There's a big enough problem with hungry bellies with the present rate of population growth."

James peered at his meticulously manicured fingernails as he waited for Robert's reply.

"I believe, Sir Edward, that any world food shortage could easily be solved by the resolute application of science. Anyway, the shame of the unplowed acres of human brain in the world has always cried louder in my ears than the shame of the unfilled bellies."

Robert thought it absurd that while all save the inhuman are appalled at the sight of a body emaciated through alimentary starvation, widespread mental malnutrition is accepted with little comment. He saw that if the minds of most people could be actively visualized, like bodies, the millions of poorly fleshed frames would make the world look like a colossal Buchenwald.

"You have only to look around at the stupidity and inefficiency of people in their business lives to realize that the world is largely populated by dolts who have never been made aware of their real capabilities," he continued.

"I see you don't suffer fools easily, Dr. Harvey. You'll have to learn how to do so if you ever have to run a big staff."

"There might not be so many fools if we could stretch out the effective years. More of us might learn to use our mental machinery to something like its full capacity. We behave like the owner of an expensive car built to move at a hundred miles per hour who never drives it at more than twenty-five."

"I'm afraid most people never will however much time they have."

"Why ever not, Sir Edward? We don't have to wait for the brain to evolve any more. The physical structure's all there—a computer with ten billion parts locked up in every human head! All we need is to learn how to program it—to feed in the information and then ask the right questions."

"If it was that easy, more people would do it now, and I see no sign of any increase in the number of outstanding thinkers."

"There soon would be if we had more peak time. It takes about twenty-five years to train the average human mind to do one job moderately well, and then it has only about the same length of time to operate before it goes into decline. Life may have been long enough when there was little else to do with leisure but sit by the fire or go to bed, but scope for living has expanded so much that active life is now far too short. If only we could stretch out the time between, say, twenty and forty-five so that we have fifty years then, we might solve all the problems you foresee."

"Maybe," James said impatiently. "But that's long-term stuff. In the short term, I must ask you to give me your word that you won't mention your work to a soul until I have consulted the Minister of Science and heard the Government's views."

"But, Sir Edward . . ."

"Naturally, we don't want to interrupt your researches," James hastened to add, forestalling Robert's protest. "What I suggest is this, Dr. Harvey. We'll try to transfer your unit to the Microbiological Research Establishment at Porton. I'm on the advisory board there. There's plenty of room, and the facilities are easily the best in Britain. And most important of all, you'll be free from snoopers. We'll try to give you some more money and staff, and we'll get your family some accommodation in Salisbury. Like some more coffee?"

In spite of this financial carrot Robert was horrified at the thought of leaving St. Patrick's. The prospect of Porton's push-button elegance, with its stainless steel benches, conditioned air, and automatically opening doors, seemed a poor substitute for the friendly reality of the old hospital with its antiseptic smell, its ancient elevator, stuffy lecture rooms, and tiled corridors festooned with thick hot-water pipes. Still more repellent was the idea of working in a secret establishment operated by the Army Department for bacteriological defense. He voiced his objections, but the more James thought about the idea the more he liked it.

"I've been wanting to get a permanent unit into Porton for ages. It might give us a lever for prying out some share of the millions they are spending on defense. I think we might set up a small wing there for clinical trials."

"Surely a hospital like St. Patrick's would be better for those, Sir Edward?"

"We'd never maintain any secrecy there. No, I even think the progeria boy should be transferred to Porton. I'll talk to Dr. Holmes about it," he said, making a note on a pad. "We'll have to do something to keep the parents quiet too. And, you know, it'll be just as well to get you away from your colleagues at St. Patrick's before they get too curious."

"But surely we don't have to work in such secrecy when we're not at war," Robert asked, hating the thought that any medical work, and particularly his own, should be suppressed for political reasons. James was ready, soothingly, for that objection.

35

"It's only a temporary measure, while we consider the problems and how to control them. Until now you yourself have deemed it expedient to keep quiet about the work until you were satisfied that you were ready to publish. All I'm suggesting is that the Government will probably desire the same safeguards. We're having a hell of a job trying to get birth control really going in India, Latin America, and among the poor of our own country, and you come along with what might turn out to be a completely neutralizing advance in death control. The more I think about it, the more it scares me. You really must consider yourself as under the Official Secrets' Acts on this one. They do apply to all Government departments you know, not just to defense establishments."

Robert shrugged resignedly. "You do agree, though, that the ban on publication will be only a temporary measure?"

"Of course," James assured him. "And I hope you appreciate the wisdom of it."

"I suppose so. But it infringes the humanistic principle that all medical knowledge should be shared."

"Well, we kept the method of making penicillin from the Germans as long as we could in the last war," James reminded him. "There are times, you know, when the pragmatic man of expediency is wiser than the blind exponent of principle."

James heaved his frame out of his chair and extended a hand to indicate that the interview was at an end.

Buttoning up his overcoat against the bitter December wind, Robert turned into Park Crescent. "Bloody fool. Pompous, fat idiot," he thought aloud. He hurried into the warm breath of the Regent's Park underground and took the tube to St. John's Wood to warn Margaret of the impending move.

The Harveys' flat, on the first floor of a converted Victorian house, was permeated with the personality of an uncomplicated woman whose life was centered around her glossy, tiled fireplace. The inevitable veneered-oak bedroom suite and the living room sideboard, with its bowl of artificial fruit, smelled of lavender-perfumed polish, lovingly applied. There were French Impressionist prints on the distempered walls. Silver-framed photographs of the children at various ages and souvenirs from holidays abroad encumbered the occasional tables. A hoop of half-finished tapestry with the colored wools Margaret was weaving into it lay on the small stool which it would eventually cover. The latest novel from Boot's library was open on the arm of the chair she had just vacated to prepare the lunch, for which her husband had said he would be home.

"But what about the children's schooling, darling?" she asked anxiously as he retailed the results of his interview. "Simon and Angela are young enough to be all right, but it's going to make things difficult for Paul, who's just coming up to his O-levels."

"We really can't afford to board him," Robert said. "Anyway, you know my views on that. We had the children for us as much as for them, and they'll leave home soon enough without being sent away to a junior monastery. There are some good schools in Salisbury. Besides, it's not certain we're going yet."

Margaret hated the thought of being uprooted, but any woman who marries a doctor knows she may have to put her interests second to her husband's patients or career. She leaned over the back of the armchair in which Robert was relaxed in front of the fire, put her arms around him, and nestled her cheek against his untidy hair, which, as usual, was in need of a trim.

"I'm sure I'll like Salisbury. It's a lovely old place," she said. "Anyway, what does it matter so long as we're together?"

Robert put up his hand and patted her face affectionately. Then, as he sipped the coffee she had made him, he wondered about Shirley. A move to Porton might enforce the break, which he knew he was less and less likely to make himself as the cerebral desire to return to fidelity was overwhelmed by the carnal version, stimulated by SP47.

He would have to offer her the choice of moving with him or finding a new appointment. Would she prefer to stay in London in view of their conversation at Mapledurham? He guessed that she would decide to go with him, and as usual, he was right.

Sir Edward James leaned back at his desk calculating how he would deliver the news of this new development to his political chiefs, who, in his opinion, took far too little interest in him and his department. As he had reached the pinnacle of promotion too early, the government service had little further to offer. One of the big drug houses had already rattled its moneybags at him, and the days when it was considered unethical to accept a post in a field where he might wield influence through his former official position were long since over.

But before he departed he wanted his GBE, and there was even the possibility of a life peerage if he played his cards well with the politicians who exert the power of patronage. This exciting advance in one of his departments was just what he had been waiting for to impress them.

chapter 7

The opening notes of what John Holt called the Cha Sonata awakened him as the kettle of the bedside tea-making machine neared boiling point. The first gray light, filtering through the frosted windows of the cottage, illumined the oak four-poster and Shirley's frilly garter belt which made an outsize ruff for the Jacobean gentleman who, with his three companions carved on the other posts, had looked down on the successive occupants of that splendid bed for more than three hundred years.

As an imaginative journalist, John had been unable to resist a committing nod when the bidding for it stopped at £25 at a local manor house sale near Saffron Walden. It would be hell to get it up the cottage stairs, but what delight to lie in it and contemplate the gossip locked in the wooden heads of those four bearded voyeurs!

The bed had become the subject of much coarse rumor in Fleet Street, where half the girl reporters and several of the better-looking secretaries were alleged to have been initiated into membership of the Four-poster Club. Few of John's colleagues believed his claim that, as a bachelor, he spent almost all his weekends unaccompanied in the Essex cottage which he called the Shooting Box, fifty miles outside of London. Yet, in truth, being solitary by nature and resentful of friendship's avarice for time, he was rarely willing to sacrifice the hours consumed by the small-talk trimmings of flesh indulgence which women will not forgo. For five months of the year he spent every available Saturday shooting, a sport in which, at the farmers' level where he played it, women have no part, except to prepare the sandwiches and cook the results. And he worked through almost every Sunday, alternating short bursts of writing with gardening, carpentry, and other household tasks which helped to generate a sense of permanence he could not derive from life in London. Having always been too energized to secure spectator satisfaction, he was only interested in what he could do himself.

Shirley, who lay beside him, still asleep but stirring slightly as the escaping steam began its counterpoint to the bubbling water, was an exceptional woman, and Christmas morning was the start of an exceptional day, one of the few when John could be reasonably assured of being free from harassment by the office telephone. Robert had retreated into the cosy warmth of his family at the season when custom robs solitude of all its bliss, and Shirley, who, like John, had no living parents, had jumped at the offer of this first visit to the Shooting Box, about which she had heard so much. She had not been disappointed when she had driven down the rutted roadway in the deepening gloom of Christmas Eve. The setting was superb, with a backdrop of plantation spruce, heavily rimmed, and a frozen, rushy pond in front of the garden's low brick wall. Throughout three summers John had spent his weekends repairing the ravages of its previous occupancy by an old spinster, who had lived there with the dry rot and death-watch, as gnarled as the quince tree which had blown down on the night she died.

As the Cha Sonata cascaded into its rousing finale, John reached out a considerate hand into the cold air ready to switch off the buzzer the moment it sounded its raucous alarm, but Shirley was already awake.

"What time is it?" she yawned.

"Seven thirty."

"Good God, why are we being wakened in the middle of the night on Christmas morning?"

It was a fair question, and John could not answer it with his usual excuse of having to collect the newspapers. He was always on edge until he had found out whether his copy had been printed and had worked off his morning hate over the way it had been mangled by the subeditors. But there weren't any papers on Christmas morning, and he was left with the naked admission that he was so appalled by the meagerness of man's ration of time that once he was awake he just had to get up and attack the day, whatever the day.

"That's not very flattering," said Shirley as he handed her a cup of tea.

She looked delicious propped up against the bedhead, for being sparing with her makeup, she had the rare advantage of looking very little different in the morning, whereas the last recruit to the Four-poster Club had proved almost unrecognizable without her warpaint. But John's baser instincts were not readily rousable so early.

"I've a lot to do and I want to leave the bathroom free for you. Mrs. Potter can only come for an hour this morning to cook the breakfast, and she'll be here soon."

"Oh, let's lie in until she comes," Shirley said coaxingly.

But John was already out of bed putting on his dressing gown and switching on the electric heater.

"I want you to come down and see what I've got you for Christmas, but not till breakfast's ready. You'll know when it is because the finest aroma in the world will come floating up through the floorboards. Oh, and will you ruffle the bed in the guest room to make it look slept in? I'm sure Ma Potter knows exactly what goes on, but she'll be offended if we don't go through the motions of pretending it doesn't."

As Shirley luxuriated in the warmth of the canopied bed she reflected on the contradictions in John's character—professionally he was engrossed with the newest in technical advance, while in leisure he surrounded himself with the antique: for his success in securing confidential information he was dependent on people, yet he took no pains to hide his preference for the inanimate.

John had forgotten the names of half the women who had flamed briefly in his life, but he remembered every pool of every river and every stand of every shoot he had enjoyed. When he ruminated on past excitements, his mental pictures were not of

faces but of high pheasants gliding off Arthur's Seat, the paneling
he had bought at a sale, the salmon on Inchmarlo, the tapestry he
picked up in a junk shop, the Wensleydale moors, or the rolling
plowland of North Essex. A pathetic plant thrusting between two
London paving stones was more likely to arouse his sentiment than
the sight of a human misfit.

Yet in the off-guard glimpses he permitted of his kernel nature,
Shirley could discern a stifled yearning for the benison of human
contact. Repeatedly she had noticed that in their shared enjoyment
of drowsiness, of music, or of the countryside, he had a compulsive
need to touch her flesh, as though, against his will, his fingers were
seeking to express sentiments he was too inhibited to voice. "Has
he been hurt in some way I've not yet discovered?" she asked
herself. "Not an easy marriage prospect; but probably more ame-
nable to being changed by a patient woman than Robert."

Shirley understood enough about psychology to know that surface behavior is not always a reliable guide to deep-seated drives
and that nobody's personality is ever fixed. When her father
had warned her that "It's not only *what* you know that matters, but
who you know," while she was studying too hard, at the total
sacrifice of social life, she thought he was referring to what people
of influence could do for her. But she had since learned that what
people could do *to* her was often more important because it made
such a difference to the person she became.

As regards her assessment of John, she was not wide of the mark
when she told herself, as she threw back the bedclothes, "A high
HSR, but he falls down badly on warmth and understanding.
What he needs is the gentling influence that only a wife can provide, and he needs it soon. He's too brusque, too withdrawn, and
in danger of becoming as brutal as the blood sports he worships."

Bacon and eggs and coffee! Shirley slid into her bathrobe and
slippers and clopped down the narrow staircase to be greeted by
Scoop, John's liver and white springer bitch.

The living room was still warm from the hot bricks of the
inglenook, and the resurgent fire of oak and apple logs threw dancing reflections on to the patina of the court cupboard, the Cole-
port plates on the Welsh dresser, and the set of graduated copper
measures arranged along the master beam.

"Where are you going?" John shouted from his tiny study as he heard the front door open.

"Just to get your present out of my car. It was too recognizable in spite of my efforts to camouflage it, so I didn't bring it in last night."

"A shooting stick!" he exclaimed, as she came back shivering. "How wonderful! I haven't got one. Now open yours."

It was a large bottle of *Ma Griffe* scent which he always bought in the duty-free shop at Orly airport to hold in stock for any girl friends.

"How perfect, darling. My favorite," exclaimed Shirley, who had never used it before.

"I like perfume so much I think there must be some Arab in me," John remarked as he rotated the pepper-mill over the breakfast, fussily served by Mrs. Potter. "I think I must have an exaggerated sensitivity for odors because they always evoke such strong memories. The fumes from a percussion cap immediately conjure up glorious days when I was a kid. The smell of nasturtiums brings back hot afternoons collecting caterpillars."

"I've got some funny ones like that, John. The smell of a paint-box!"

"Yes, that's one of mine, too. Stale beer's another. It reminds me of when my father kept a country pub after he came out of the army, and the landlord's son lived like a lord. I had as much riding, beagling, fishing, and shooting as I wanted—and all free. God, I had a wonderful childhood," he added, staring wistfully at the window. "And I knew it was wonderful while I was having it."

"I don't recall mine being particularly wonderful."

"Oh, mine was. Rapture without care! I know Browning coined the phrase for a different purpose, but in my experience it's careless rapture that makes childhood so precious. That exquisite tingling that could be touched off by something as simple as sitting in the cinema on Friday evening and knowing there was no school next day, or finding a rare bird's nest. I've never been able to recapture it since I jumped onto the treadmill of work."

"You think that's because there's always some anxiety in the background?"

"I suspect that's the answer: but my mother used to say it was simply because I'd lost my faith."

42

"Maybe she was right. I believe in God and I'm not as haunted as you are by dissatisfaction. Perhaps to achieve a sense of fulfillment, you've either got to live your life through God or through some other person, and you do neither."

"I wouldn't say I don't get fulfillment. I can get that out of a good scoop, even if it's only temporary. I'm sure you get a kick out of seeing your name on your latest paper."

"I suppose I do."

"Well, so do I. In different ways we both get satisfaction through being first with the news. Incidentally, what's the latest on the old-age front?"

"Oh, we plod on slowly," Shirley answered evasively. "Robert should have an interesting paper out soon, but I can't tell you about it because you'd want to publish it and I should be in trouble. He was quite happy about the piece you did on his paper to the Physiological Society, but the dean of the medical school was very sour about it. He practically accused us of degrading the hospital's name by touting for publicity."

"Sorry about that. Is it more mice again?" John asked as he poured more coffee.

"No, not mice."

"White rats, then?"

"No, not rats either," Shirley laughed.

"You don't mean you've got some human trials going at last?"

"Don't pump me anymore, dear. It really is difficult. I'll tip you off when the paper's coming out," she said, leaning over to brush his cheeks with buttery lips.

"Okay, okay," John said disarmingly.

"Now suppose I interview you for a change, Mr. Holt. Tell me, to what qualities of character do you attribute your success as a journalist?"

"I'm glad you asked me that, Miss Howard. Normally I never speak to the press but, off the record, I'd say that to publish exclusive stories and keep one's contacts requires the combined qualities of a detective, a village sneak, and a diplomat."

"Do you see any significance in the coincidence that the word 'story,' which you journalists use to mean one of your written reports, is also in common usage to mean a lie?"

"No more than in the fact that while doctors regard themselves as superior to vets, to 'vet' a story is creditable while to 'doctor' it is reprehensible."

"Touché," Shirley laughed. "Now, on the record and with no hedging, could you tell us why such an eligible man has remained a bachelor?"

"Ah, that perhaps is another of the essential qualities for success in journalism. The journalist's environment is hostile to monogamy by its nature, and now the burden of taxation is forcing him to work such long hours to retain a decent income that he has less and less time to spend with a wife. Then she gets bored and falls victim to the Three T's."

"And what, pray, are the Three T's?"

Drawing on an article he had once written, which was usually his basis for eloquence in conversation, John replied, "The Three T's are Time, the Telephone, and Transport. In the affluent society the housewife, emancipated by her machines, has Time. With the Telephone she can be quickly contacted, and with her Transport, the family car, she can get to an assignation and rapidly return. With these, the fourth T, Temptation in the form of some man at a loose end, will usually thrive. I reckon it's because of the Three Ts that the Fidelity Ratio—the proportion of unsullied to total marriages—has so steadily declined, especially among journalists."

"But it doesn't stop them getting married. Why has it stopped you?" Shirley persisted.

The truth was that with his habits of working six long days a week and wanting to shoot or fish on the seventh, he diagnosed the inevitable collapse of any union demanding more than his casual attention, and no woman had moved him sufficiently to make him want to disrupt the pattern of his life.

"On the whole, I think I find it harder to resist a good alliterative adjective than to resist a woman," he had bragged to one of his Fleet Street colleagues.

Besides, he argued, whereas it may well pay a young man on a modest salary to tie himself by contract to one devoted wife, he could well afford to employ servants and free-lance for such feminine company as he needed. There was also a slight psychological problem. As a penalty for perhaps a too erotic imagination, John had found that when in the most intimate embrace of any girl he

44

had known for long, he had to think of another whose charms he had not explored.

"Seriously, I suppose it's just that I know I'd be bad at marriage, Shirley, and I can't stand failure," he said. "There's also freedom. Not only the freedom to do what I want but the freedom to do nothing, to have no commitments to anybody, when I feel like it."

"But don't you think that's rather selfish?"

John shrugged. "A lot of people have told me I'm selfish not to want any children, but kids don't make any organ music for me. I contend that my voluntary sterility should be considered as an act of public service when the world's already overcrowded."

"I must say that was a very unsatisfactory interview, Mr. Holt. All your reasons sound more like excuses to me. If I can be absolutely frank, I suspect that the real reason you are still single is because you're astute enough to see that marriage is for adults only and honest enough with yourself to realize that you're emotionally immature."

"For adults only!" John exclaimed, coloring slightly. "Some of the marriages I've seen should have a horror certificate! Now I'm afraid there's an hour's work I must do, if you'll pardon me," he added, rising from the table. "The bedroom will be warm now. Why don't you go up and take your time getting ready and then we'll set off on our rounds. We've three houses to visit for drinks as well as two pubs and we've got to be at the Hobsons' for lunch by one thirty. If I know Phyllis Hobson, it'll be the best Christmas lunch you've ever had. Real Pickwick stuff and you'll be expected to take second helpings. So go easy on the cheese at the Bull's Head and don't forget—pickled onions are barred!"

Ernest Hobson, who farmed nearby at Audley End, had managed to get John into the farmers' shooting syndicate on the edge of a major shoot centered on the magnificent mansion long since delegated to the National Trust. It was expensive, but John managed to fit it into the budget of living each day as though it might be his last while at the same time being modestly provident in case it was not. A Saturday walking the stubble with the springers and retrievers, or waiting at a stand for driven birds with the feel of a walnut stock under the arm, was a wonderful escape from the stress of Fleet Street into an all-male world, where a person sensitive to nature could, at one moment, take delight in the beauty of a sunlit cock pheasant coming over the trees and, at the next, feel even greater satisfaction as it tumbled down neatly shot in the head.

When he toted up the bills at the year's end and found that even this modest syndicate cost him £15 per shooting day, he brushed off the extravagance as an investment in health. It was worth it, he argued, to get some unpolluted oxygen into the blood and the accumulated alcohol of the week's business lunching out of it. He was also able, on occasion, to oblige some high-level contact by inviting him to shoot as a guest.

Hobson, 225 pounds of convivial gregariousness, who could not imagine that anyone could ever be alone without being miserable, had invited John to join his family at Christmas lunch. The tentacle intrusion of government into agriculture, with its price controls and bales of paperwork, had made farmers more interested in politics than most voters, so anyone who kept himself as well informed on Whitehall as John did was welcome to put his legs under almost any farmhouse table. He had been doubly welcome when the Hobsons learned that he had a girl with him. With his name in the newspaper almost daily, and with occasional appearances on television, John was something of a celebrity in such a small village, and there was considerable interest in any possible Mrs. Holt.

"Ernest's terrific," John said to Shirley as they tucked themselves into his car. "It'll be worth the journey just to watch him wedged in the carving chair and sliding the biggest knife you've ever seen around the sharpener."

Early the following morning, as Shirley drove off to London in a curling cloud of exhaust steam, John experienced a sense of emptiness which had never before been generated by a parting guest.

"Take it easy in that car. The cargo's rather precious," he said when she was out of earshot, being no more capable of saying it to her face than he had been of telling his parents, when he skinned his shin on the scuttle while running in from the coal shed at night, that he was terrified of the dark. His delusion that any admission of emotion was a confession of weakness had muted him for the language of affection.

As he turned back into the empty cottage with Scoop at his heels, he consoled himself that Boxing Day was going to be full. The frost was holding, the sky was clear, and the pheasants would fly high in such crisp air.

<h1 style="text-align:center">chapter 8</h1>

Parliament was in recess, and Lord Durrant, the Minister of Science, to whom Sir Edward James was responsible, was touring the United States for a month, beginning with a weekend on the Presidential yacht, a distinction which his Lordship's press officer made sure was well publicized in the newspapers.

"Lord Durrant's weekend with President Walter Brandenberg will be entirely social," the gossip columnist of the *Daily Dispatch* reported. "They first met when the brilliant man who was destined for the White House was a Rhodes Scholar at Oxford twenty-three years ago. Lord Durrant is one of the few Englishmen who knows the forty-five-year-old President well enough to call him 'Brandy' to his face. The President calls him 'Fruity.'"

The President's nickname had been nurtured by his backers during his fight for the Republican nomination. "Brandy is Dandy," "Brandy the Five-star Stimulant"—twisted to "Brandy, the Recipe for Skid Row" by the Democrats—were among the slogans which had festooned the convention halls.

James was glad of the delay, for it gave him more time to think about the implications of Harvey's researches, and the more he thought about them the more far-reaching they seemed. Meanwhile, a fuller report from Robert on a considerably improved form of SP47, for which he retained the old code number outside the laboratory to avoid confusion, had confirmed and extended the previous findings. His biopsy specimens of kidney, liver, and muscle all showed clear-cut rejuvenation changes.

Sir Edward decided to seek the advice of the Health Minister, Hastings Maclaren, whose political judgment he admired, though in general outlook and temperament the two men could hardly have been more different. James was expansive and loved conversation for its sake. Maclaren, a former Oxford don in economics and so Cromwellian that he was known in Westminster as "Old Noll," though not yet forty-five, had a reputation for being unsociable because he had no time for small talk. In one of his rare diversions to raise a lecture-room laugh he had told his students, "Society's direst need is for a semantic filter—some transistor device that could be fitted by law to all human mouths and would let through only those sounds which have real meaning. In most homes the silence would be deafening." One of the few front-bench politicians who really meant it when he read the lesson in church, he was a model of public probity. A fervent exponent of self-help, he practiced his Health Ministry slogan—"Every family its own welfare state"—and seemed incorruptible, unless by his overweening confidence in his fitness to become the Chancellor of the Exchequer.

James was sipping dry sherry when his guest was shown to his table, in a quiet corner of the Alouette restaurant in Jermyn Street. The sound of a Scot ordering a double tomato juice surprised the wine waiter. Nobody could be in doubt about his nationality even without the clues of his name and accent. He had the face so common north of the Tweed, thin, pink, freckled on close inspection, with blue eyes, bushy brows, and thinning hair of a color best described as off-ginger. A lifelong teetotaler, he was averse to alcohol not only on the moral ground that its value as a catalyst to social intercourse is infinitely outweighed by the relationships it undermines: he had the strongest objections to befuddling his mental equipment to the smallest degree. James, on the other hand, had convinced himself that his mind worked more smoothly under alcohol's relaxing influence.

After the ritual small talk, James began to explain the purpose of the lunch, displaying the virtuosity of a practiced table conversationalist by keeping up a running commentary between small forkfuls, so that neither the talk nor the eating lost pace. If the information had come from anybody less authoritative, Maclaren would not have believed it, but James had taken the Harvey dossier along with him, and they studied it over the coffee.

"I think your fears are more than justified," Maclaren declared. "More than half a million people die in Britain every year. Suppose that instead, say four hundred thousand of these were kept in a state of medicated survival by SP47, then every five years the population would increase by an extra two millions. The possibility of counteracting this by a reduction in the birth rate through increased birth control seems remote." Intense about any subject once his mind was focused on it, he went on, "In fact, we must take account of the possibility that reproductive life will be lengthened if aging is delayed in the middle years. Women might be able to go on producing children up to the age of seventy or more. So one might assume a considerable *increase* in the birth rate. In that case the population surge over twenty years could be really explosive."

"I agree, Minister. And, of course, this would happen in every other country, too."

"Just let's stick to this island first, James. I hate to think what would happen to the housing situation. And what about food? Without imports, we can only feed one-third of the population now, and the demand for houses would make further inroads into the agricultural land."

Though he had to be careful how he expressed it on a Tory platform, Maclaren was convinced that state controls would have to be steadily expanded as society increased in complexity. For this reason he had given the maximum backing to the Family Planning Association and other bodies interested in curbing the menace of uncontrolled reproduction. It seemed to him now that there was just as strong a case for controlling longevity.

"This reminds me of the situation the Government faced when you fellows decided that smoking is the prime cause of lung cancer," he said. "The Government had a clear duty to prohibit the sale of cigarettes—as it would have done with any other poison—but it was scared of losing votes, and the tax on cigarettes just paid for the Health Service."

Maclaren leaned back from the smoke of James' cigar which was curling toward him. "As Minister of Health I'm being dishonest now in failing to agitate for some control over the sale of tobacco. Whether one accepts the lung cancer link or not, tobacco is a drug of addiction, and tobacconists should be denounced as dope peddlers along with publicans, brewers, and wine merchants."

"That's a bit harsh, Minister. The habit's so widespread it looks as though the stresses of civilization demand it."

"You could say the same about liquor, James, and my argument still holds. We make it an offense to supply tranquilizers, except on a doctor's prescription, but do nothing about alcohol, the most widespread tranquilizer of all, because that would lose votes, too. My colleagues expect me to go on functioning as a Minister of Disease—providing medical facilities to treat the cases of lung cancer and cirrhosis of the liver which could be prevented by simple political action."

"It's impossible to exert controls like that in a free society," said James, gently swirling the Hine in his brandy balloon. "Look what happened with prohibition in America."

"One should have the courage to try or get out of politics," Maclaren countered. "Who'd have thought we could have got away with the parking meter, which forces people to pay for the use of road space they already own? Yet the public accepted it with hardly a murmur as just another example of how technical progress, which is the end result of scientific research, whittles away the freedom of the individual."

"There's always some penalty for progress. Every drug that saves thousands of lives kills a few people who happen to be allergic to it."

"Yes, but we're now in danger of paying far too much. The laboratory has become the most extortionate clip joint ever foisted on society. The services provided by the scientists who run it are criminally small considering what they levy in money and freedom. You know one day soon the government will have to start putting the brakes on research. Scientists are always bellyaching about the absolute necessity for freedom in research, but why should they be allowed freedom to experiment in any direction they like, when the results encroach so much on ours?"

James was astonished. "But you can't curb curiosity, Minister. It's one of the strongest motives in human behavior!"

"Yes, and it's going to kill us all unless we watch out. When most politicians say that the price of freedom is eternal vigilance, they mean vigilance about the Communists, but I think it's you fellows we need to be vigilant about. Scientists are far too cocksure, these days, that they can predict the results of their experiments in time for society to control them."

Having come in search of official support to counter Harvey's professional principles, James suddenly found himself challenged to defend the vestiges of his own. Shooting his cuffs, as was his habit, and laughing disbelievingly, he said, "Really, Minister . . ."

But Maclaren refused to be interrupted. "Look," he continued, "according to you scientists the brontosaurus became extinct because it grew too big. The chance inherited changes which made it gigantic proved lethal to the whole species. Am I right?"

James nodded.

"Then don't you see that chance discoveries can be just as lethal to man. The brontosaurus was extinguished by changes with which its body couldn't cope. I believe man may be extinguished by changes with which his *mind* can't cope."

James tapped the ash from his cigar and asked, "Can you see any evidence of such changes?"

"I certainly can, James. Why do you think the suicide figures are increasing steadily in every civilized country? It's one of my main worries that whereas suicide was the tenth leading cause of death in this country in 1962, it has now risen to be the fifth. You're a doctor. Tell me why more than half a million people in the world take their lives every year—about ten thousand of them in Britain—and why at least two millions more try to do so."

James stared reflectively at the tapestried wall and replied, "I suppose it's because death becomes friendlier with each accumulated disenchantment, and people now lose their sense of wonder so early that disenchantment has never been so severe."

"No, I look at it this way," said Maclaren. "An individual suicide is due to the fact that one mind becomes unable to cope with a set of circumstances and resolves an intolerable situation by commanding the body to destroy it. These circumstances are usually due to a sudden change. The obvious ones are things like financial ruin, death of a loved one, or disgrace, but those factors have always been in operation. There must be some new and less obvious change that's responsible for the steady increase in suicide. I'm convinced that the basic cause is the pace at which life is changing due to the tempo of scientific research."

"You're thinking of things like space flight, supersonic airliners that get you to New York three hours earlier than when you set off, and suitcase bombs that can wipe out London?"

"Yes. And computers and brainwashing and tranquilizers and pep pills. It's all happening so fast that a mind that's more brittle than average can't cope with it and just packs up."

"I see what you are driving at," James remarked diplomatically, at what he considered to be a free display of fantasy. "In the past the mind had time to adapt itself to changing circumstances. Now it's not getting it."

"Precisely. And don't you see the terrifying implication? I can foresee a sudden situation which might force millions of minds beyond the threshold of what they can tolerate!"

"I suppose the threat of the H-bomb came pretty near it, Minister."

"Mmm, hardly. The danger I foresee is more likely to come from the life sciences—from biology and medicine. This promise of a sudden increase in life span is the sort of thing I have in mind. I can anticipate that many people would be quite unable to cope with a sudden thirty-year increase in life span, which would throw the entire structure of society out of gear."

"I think you are being a little too pessimistic," James said, calling for the bill. "Every technical development carries some risk. Look at the motorcar and the airplane."

"Yes, but don't you see, those examples support my point. The public accepts more than ten thousand hideous deaths on English roads every year because the figure has crept up gradually, and the mind has had time to adapt to the idea of it. But with all this work on life span, and the creation of life itself, the scientists are going to present us with some insupportable change. One day it'll be there. It will be unstoppable and it will do us all in. This SP47 could be the start of it."

James shook his head in strong disagreement. "What science inflicts, science can cure—given time."

"That's just it, James, you may not have time. The Socialists used to be always harping on the inevitability of gradualness. It's the inevitability of suddenness that worries me. You mark my words. If we don't start controlling science, it will soon control us. You fellows are in the power business as much as the politicians. Faraday's birthday was a more decisive event than Napoleon's or even Hitler's. It's a matter for conjecture whether Lord Rutherford's influence will exceed Lenin's."

"Well, as I told you earlier, Minister, we've every intention of keeping SP47 under sufficient control to ensure that the public has plenty of time to get used to it. There's an enormous amount of research needed, and I've told Harvey that the whole thing must be kept absolutely quiet for some months yet. I take it you agree with the idea for moving the unit down to Porton?"

"An excellent precaution! Now, to get to the main point on which you asked my advice. We must obviously tell the Prime Minister about this so that he's in the picture from the beginning. But wait until Durrant returns and do it through him. You know how touchy he is about protocol."

James nodded as he unfolded the bill on the plate.

"Durrant's got the influence to induce the Army Department to give you some room at Porton," Maclaren continued. "If the PM decides to discuss it in Cabinet, which I think he will, we must make sure that you're called in for consultation. We must both do all we can to ensure that this development is properly controlled. We don't want any more thalidomide disasters," he added, pulling a wry face.

Maclaren had inherited the task of administering the fund set up to assist the thalidomide babies. Now they were growing up they needed help more than ever, and he and his wife took a personal interest in their welfare, visiting their special schools and homes.

"An interesting mixture," thought James, as he counted out the tip. "Intellectual brilliance, limitless ambition, and genuine care about the community. Pity he's so humorless."

As they walked past the other tables, dodging their way around the food carts, Maclaren did not even smile as he waved hello to Geoffrey Carslake, the overweight young Chancellor of the Exchequer whose voracity for office was exceeded only by his greed for food.

"There's a candidate for a coronary if ever I saw one," he whispered to James.

chapter 9

The legendary imperturbability of the Prime Minister under the hammering of world events was more than matched by his durability under the hammering of time. His adroit capacity for delegating responsibility had enabled him to have all his stress disorders by proxy. It was the henchmen he chivvied around with insistent memoranda who suffered the ulcers, heart attacks, and nervous collapses, but though his internal constitution was sound, Julian Merton looked all his seventy-three years. His thickset frame was hunched, his legs arthritic. His eyes were weakening and he had just faced up to the ignominy of wearing a hearing aid in the House. But though his scalp was half bald, what the brain below had lost in creative capacity was more than balanced by the cunning of his long experience. A thruster since boyhood, his life wish was strong, and he had no intention of loosening his grip on the reins of leadership. The cloister of retirement held no attraction for him. Indeed, because the elderly have less time to afford, and because he was slower, he was working longer hours than ever.

Merton had been briefed on the subject of the rejuvenation drug by Durrant, who had returned to Whitehall, and he had arranged for a brief discussion about it as the final item on the agenda for the next meeting of the Cabinet—that peculiarly British body designed to protect the Government's policymaking from public scrutiny. He could see that the social implications were immense, and he had immediate personal interest in any reliable nostrum that might spare him longer for public service and private enjoyment, for although he had no desire to hang on in real decrepitude, he was all for dying young as late as possible. He had been intimate with power too long not to bear its scars, one of which was the vanity which made him sincerely believe that a change of leadership would be damaging for the nation.

Sir Edward James was waiting in the small antechamber outside the Cabinet room in No. 10 Downing Street, which had undergone considerable rejuvenation itself at colossal expense in the previous decade. He knew that the loneliness of high decision, which retired American Presidents were so fond of recalling in their memoirs, did not afflict the British Prime Minister, whose decisions had long been a matter for congregation, but was surprised to see so many sitting around the green tapered table. There were twenty-six Cabinet ministers in the black leather armchairs and several outside experts called in for advice. Maclaren, the Health Minister, was facing Merton, who was at the middle of the table, the portrait of Robert Walpole looking over his shoulder. Sir Frank Butcher, the chief scientist at the Defense Ministry, was also there.

Butcher had been called in for advice on a defense item taken earlier in the agenda, and was asked to remain. Though he was well known to be a Socialist, and at one stage had endangered his career by developing a name as an agitator, the Prime Minister had profound respect for his judgment. A pushing little man, round-faced, button-nosed, and balding to the point where he brushed to make every five hairs give the coverage of five thousand, he wore the triple tiara of British science—Cambridge, Fellow of the Royal Society, and the Athenaeum—and had developed an outstanding flair for committeemanship, which made him one of the most influential of the faceless officials operating the Whitehall strings.

Merton began with the barest summary of the situation, which was the first that most present had heard about it. Then, as a firm believer in the necessity of hearing prime-source information as little processed by other memories and mouths as possible, he asked James to begin. "We trust you to be brief and protect us ordinary mortals from the tyranny of technical terms," he added good-humoredly.

Making the most of his first command performance, James told the meeting that the past few weeks had fully justified the original interpretation of the early results. Experiments with improved forms of SP47 showed enhanced rejuvenation effects. It now seemed probable that by carefully controlling the dosage, aging could be held static or put into reverse, though there were signs that the extent of the reversion would prove to be limited.

He explained, "This is probably due to the fact that the process of aging is partly due to the clogging up of the body cells with waste products and partly to the death of cells, especially in the muscles and brain. It is estimated that the adult brain alone normally loses about ten thousand of its cells through death every day. The SP47 seems to work by unclogging the cells and bringing them back into service, but, of course, it can't do anything about those that are missing. In a middleaged person who has not lost too many cells a total rejuvenation effect equal to, say, fifteen years might be possible. In an older person who has lost more the limit of rejuvenation might be less than ten, but this shedding of the years might then be held stationary for an indefinite period by continued application of the drug."

James paused to watch the faces of his distinguished audience as they mentally took ten or fifteen years off their own ages and wondered how they would look and feel. He continued: "Of course, the real long-term importance of the drug would seem to be in its capacity to slow down aging by *preventing* the clogging up and death of the cells. A great deal of disease and debility might be prevented in this way, because the cells might retain their youthful resistance to disease processes, but only time can show us whether this effect is transient or sustained." Then he announced a most significant development.

"Dr. Harvey and his team, who are now installed at Porton, are confident that they will be able to devise a method of giving SP47 in capsule form by mouth. This would make mass medication much simpler. There are others here better qualified to assess the implications of this," he concluded.

The effect of this presentation on the able men around the Cabinet table, each with his own special interests and approach to public office, was fascinating. Lord Ewhurst, the Foreign Secretary, so cadaverous that one could see exactly what he would look like when he ceased to be the fifth earl, and whose pronounced stoop was the deferred penalty for being so tall, was quick to seize on the importance of keeping the information out of the hands of the

Chinese, Indonesians, and Japanese if possible. The population pressure which they were exerting on Australia and New Zealand was already dangerous enough. Cynically, he remarked that the still-secret formula offered a most unusual political weapon for attracting allies, providing it could be restricted to personal use by the world's statesmen.

Hastings Maclaren, always keen to impress, developed the theme of a deluge of people. He had obtained a more accurate forecast of the economic effects of an extension of twenty active years in life-span from the Treasury statisticians, under the guise that it was a long-term academic exercise.

"With *no* increase in absolute life-span, the population of Britain is expected to rise to seventy millions—out of a world population of seven billions—by the year two thousand," he said. "If the life-span is extended by drugs, it could rise up to a hundred and twenty millions, though there are so many possibilities that even this might be exceeded. Of this huge figure more than a third might be old-age pensioners—if that scheme is still going! Whatever the results —and they are by no means all foreseeable—any substantial increase in life-span without the slow social evolution needed to adapt people to radical change will unquestionably bring severe political and economic hazards."

Albert Hodges, the Labor Minister and the only former grammar schoolboy in Merton's Cabinet, pounced on the jobs problem. "If bosses remain active at eighty, they won't want to make room for younger people," he said with Yorkshire bluntness, not at all disconcerted by the fact that Merton was in his eighth decade. He foresaw intense dissatisfaction consequent on the interminable wait for dead men's shoes. "All play and no work'll not only make young Jack a dull boy, it'll make him bloody dangerous," he pronounced.

A devout lay preacher, he viewed the prospect with deep concern as a fundamental interference with God's plan and said so.

"You know what man's epitaph'll be? 'He died of a surfeit of science!' The march of science should be halted until we're able to control it, and that's not yet."

The Chancellor of the Exchequer concentrated on the inescapable widening of the balance-of-payments gap in the event of a massive increase in population, which would involve the importation

57

of more food. "Food imports are already costing more than £1,500,000,000 a year. Without a lot of time to adjust industrial production, to provide the additional exports to pay for any substantial increase, we shall have to abandon the target of doubling living standards, which was to be our main promise at the coming election." He waited to let the significance of this sink in all round, then added, "In fact, we might even have to accept the inevitability of a decline in living standards."

The Minister for Agriculture confirmed that home food production was already at a maximum, in view of the savage assault on farmland being made by the ever-spreading towns and the gluttonous road program. Stung into action, the Transport Minister pointed out that any hope that his road-building would keep pace with the threat of traffic saturation depended on the reasonable assumption that most people would have ceased to drive automobiles by the time they were eighty.

The Housing Minister and Education Minister both grasped the opportunity of disclaiming responsibility for any future failure to provide homes and schools, in the event of a population increase which had been unforeseeable. The Home Secretary, who rarely said anything, relying on the hope that the silence of ignorance would be mistaken for intellectual modesty in pressing his opinions, also intervened. "We should be in the same position about prisons, too," he added lugubriously.

Even Butcher, the zealous champion of untrammeled research, who believed that the locked laboratory keeps more secrets out than it keeps in, was basically in favor of controlling the use of the anti-aging drug. "There are obviously the strongest medical grounds for doing so," he told the meeting. "There are still far too many unknowns about it for my peace of mind. Can we really be sure that it won't prove to be cancer-forming without tests lasting several more years? But I must advise against entertaining much hope of keeping the development secret for long. Attempts to suppress nuclear information have repeatedly shown that success is only temporary. Even if the information doesn't leak, we know that scientists in other countries are studying the problem and must eventually come up with the same answer."

James nodded agreement, but there were several members of the

58

Cabinet who by no means approved of this short speech. In spite of the postwar lessons of espionage, and Russian triumphs clearly achieved without help from the West, they still believed that the Government had the power to suppress official secrets "in the national interest," if only time-honored methods were properly applied. Butcher was slightly suspect as a defeatist on security because he had become so appalled at the sheer numbers of Whitehall documents stamped "Secret" that he ceaselessly campaigned for an all-around review of security classification. To make his point, he had once said, jokingly, that it would pay the Government to sack all the security men and send a copy of every Whitehall document to the Kremlin, with an occasional injection of false information.

"The Russian Intelligence Service would be so overwhelmed in sorting it all out that they would have no time for their real work," he had claimed. This typical Butcherian comment had been quickly retailed on the Whitehall grapevine and was now being remembered in several reactionary minds. Butcher was not unaware of this but thought it imprudent to reveal his suspicion that, because of the value of journalists in promoting the rival interests of ministers, the Cabinet leaked like a badly coopered barrel, and that the subject under discussion was of such intense personal interest to all the men around the table—and to their wives—that he doubted their capacity to keep their mouths shut.

Merton summed up by remarking that opinion was virtually unanimously in favor of control, and since temporary expedients are what most cabinets end in adopting, the brief record of the meeting showed it was agreed that the work should be continued in absolute secrecy until a small committee, to be organized by James and Butcher, could report on it more fully in six months' time.

When the meeting broke up, the Premier asked James to go with him to his private quarters. In the small drawing room with its splendid Adam suite, he thanked him for his foresight and prompt action in transferring the work to Porton. Then, after the butler had poured James a preluncheon sherry and his master the customary glass of milk which was such a joy to the cartoonists, he came to his purpose.

"I would be grateful if I could send my doctor to see you. After a talk with you he might consider that a course of this SP47 might do me a lot of good. That is, if he thinks it's safe enough."

He took a sip of his milk, looking at James with bloodhound eyes. The prospect of going back ten years was irresistible. Though the average age for British prime ministers was over seventy, he yearned for the vitality he had felt at sixty-three, when by superb maneuver within the party he had seized the leadership.

"I've been feeling rather tired lately," he continued. "I sleep only about five hours a night, which I suppose is a symptom of my age. This is absolutely in confidence, of course, and I wouldn't want anyone else to know, but sometimes I feel the strain of trying to cope with fellows as young as President Brandenberg, Premier Turganov, and Marshal Cheng."

James, whose ethical ideals had long ago been engulfed by the quicksands of ambition, could almost hear the swish of the rose-pink and pearl-gray riband of a Knight Grand Cross of the British Empire.

"By all means, Prime Minister. I will be delighted to see your doctor at any time, or if he prefers it I'll go and see him."

Nor was James unduly surprised when a few days later he was invited to dine alone with the Foreign Secretary, who put forward a similar argument but with a little more diplomatic fencing in advance. Though burdened with the disadvantage of a withered arm —or maybe because of it, since female sympathy is stimulated for strange reasons—Ewhurst had enjoyed a peculiar success with beautiful women during his middle years. He warmed to the possibility of recovering his attraction, for since entering the bereavement bracket, with his mourning tie replacing the Old Etonian ever more frequently, he found that the increasing inwardness of life brought no recompense.

As James left the Foreign Secretary's residence in Carlton Gardens, full of good food and wine, he was reminded of the scientific aphorism that many great men do not obey the laws of perspective. The nearer you get to them the *smaller* they become. There was, of course, a precedent for this behavior, he remembered. When the French researcher, Voronoff, had introduced the rejuvenation operation of grafting testicular tissue from apes into elderly men soon

60

after World War I, several French cabinet ministers had found the prospect irresistible.

The requests would not be difficult to fulfill, James thought as he climbed into a taxi. For he had already made arrangements with Harvey to secure supplies of SP47 for himself.

chapter 10

Anthony, the second Baron Fayverdale, who had been left impoverished by the first, had solved the problem of enjoying the best benefits of metropolitan life without subjecting himself to its harrying stresses.

Stretched out on the lime and gold, four-seater divan he had bought to accommodate his long legs, which disclosed the disproportion of his body when in a bathing suit but looked so elegant in sharply cut trousers, he awaited the arrival of his afternoon visitor.

Politically, Fayverdale was a mystery. In his background, speech, and habits he seemed Tory to the bone-marrow and accepted the Conservative whip in the House of Lords, yet he derived his main income from a Soviet diamond-importing concession, was forever visiting Russia on red-carpet tours, and was rarely missing from any important function at the Soviet embassy in Kensington Palace Gardens.

Many suspected that he must be serving some Soviet purpose, possibly as a contact man. His own explanation was simply that he had the rare ability, for an Englishman, to speak and write Russian fluently and to get on with Russians; the Soviet government needed a British entrepreneur for its industrial diamond business, and he had been bright enough to rent out the import concession to diamond merchants, thereby securing a considerable income for no work.

This was also the explanation accepted by MI5. Because of the eminence of many of the people with whom Fayverdale consorted, his dossier, stored with two million others in the bricked-up basement of MI5's London headquarters, had been scrutinized by "DG," the Director General, himself. As Sir Roger Black had peered down his hawk nose at the summary of the thick sheaf of typewritten reports inside the folder, he read:

Anthony Wayland Fayverdale is the only son of the late Lord Fayverdale, a former ambassador to the USSR, who was given a peerage for later service as a colonial governor. He learned to speak Russian as a boy in Moscow. Later educated at Rugby and King's College, London, where he read medicine but withdrew in his second year. Played cricket for Rugby and London University. Worked briefly in an advertising agency, a travel agency, as a male model, journalist, and translator. Has a small inherited income but relies mainly on a Soviet import concession. Was married to the daughter of a wealthy American, but this lasted for only six months. Lives modestly, reasonably temperate, no homosexual tendencies, no criminal convictions. A Conservative peer, he has no political associations with Communism but travels frequently to the Soviet Union on business and is a regular visitor to the Soviet embassy and trade delegation.

Black thumbed into the dossier to see why Fayverdale had given up medicine. The report, culled from a former fellow student, recorded that Fayverdale had been accustomed to buy his evening paper from an old newsdealer in the Strand, known to the students as Trammy, because it was understood that he had been born in a tram. Fayverdale, who had always been somewhat squeamish, quit on the day when the cadaver provided for him in the dissection room proved to be his old friend.

Black smiled and flicked over a few more pages to find out why the marriage had failed so quickly. Sure enough, there was a report based on the evidence of friends, who had no idea that their gossip would end up in the registry of MI5.

It was a simple story of hopeless incompatibility. She had been attracted by his title, he by her future wealth. "She was as devoid of beauty as a gas tank," Fayverdale was quoted as remarking, while she had described him as "owing allegiance only to himself."

Normally, to Black's perceptive intelligence, the chance use of the word "allegiance" would have demanded further inquiry, but in the context of the whole report he dismissed it as a stock remark by a disappointed woman. A peer; the son of a governor; public school; cricket. It all seemed very proper. True, that list of his friends on the last page was loaded with women, but there was nothing depraved about that: as the photographs showed, he was an attractive fellow. A bit weak in the chin, perhaps, and somewhat sad about the eyes when off his guard: but a slight look of helplessness appeals to so many women! Who was that last entry? Coral Carslake. The Chancellor's wife. Well, no point in prying there. It was embarrassing enough when Ministers had to be warned about the people they were meeting. Interfering in the private life of a Minister's wife was right outside his terms of reference. "No requirement for surveillance," he had written on the dated slip attached to the folder, when he placed it in his out tray.

Fayverdale switched on the radio and settled back with a cigarette.

"Mrs. Carslake, sir," announced Kopec, his servant.

"How lovely to see you, darling," said Coral, giving him a hug. "I know I've said it before but I do think that servant is the image of Schubert. Are you sure he isn't a descendant?"

"Schubert was an Austrian, and Kopec is a Pole, or rather was a Pole before he was naturalized. Besides, Schubert didn't have any children. Did you have any luck?"

"Of course. I've got them," she said triumphantly, opening her handbag and taking out a screw-capped phial containing a dozen buttercup-yellow capsules. "Greater love hath no woman. No wonder that they make them yellow: they're more precious than gold," she added, handing them over to Fayverdale. "I say, you want to see what they're doing to Celia Merton. She looks ages younger."

It was that archgossip, the Prime Minister's wife, who had whispered the news of the drug to Coral in the first place, as they had chattered under the hairdrier in the Mayfair salon patronized by a coven of cabinet ministers' wives.

"How did you manage to get them?" Fayverdale asked.

"I just told Geoffrey I must have some more, and he got his private secretary to put the heat on old what's-his-name at the Medical Research Council."

Old what's-his-name—Sir Edward James—had been getting more clandestine demands for SP47 than he had expected. He had turned down the Transport Minister and the Minister of Agriculture and Fisheries, but he felt he could not refuse the Chancellor, who ultimately controlled his purse strings. And the Chancellor, who knew he was grossly neglecting his pretty wife for his work, did not feel he could refuse her.

"Well, what reward do I get?" asked Coral, lowering her blonde head until her forehead rested on his.

"Come on here and I'll show you," said Fayverdale, pulling her onto the settee.

"You're sure Kopec won't come in?" she asked.

It would not have mattered much if he had come in, for though Coral was not aware of it, she had few secrets from Kopec.

Tadeuz Kopec had come to Britain as a young refugee from the Nazis, hoping to work as an electronics engineer, for which he had great aptitude, but he had the misfortune to leave a large number of relatives behind him. So when Polish Communists approached him to work for the Soviet Union, under the threat of ill will to his relatives if he disagreed, he soon found himself with a more interesting electronics job than he had expected.

Fayverdale's Russian benefactors—his Kensington Friends, as he called them—who provided the well-appointed flat, insisted on equipping it with some of the latest advances in Soviet science. These included cunningly concealed microphones, tape recorders, and a lightly silvered mirror attached to the wall which separated Fayverdale's bedroom from Kopec's quarters. By means of an infrared camera, Kopec was able to take sharp photographs of his master's bed while its occupants were illumined by an equally invisible infrared searchlight.

The arrangement suited Fayverdale well, for Kopec was a model servant, never embarrassed him by mentioning the electronic activities, and saved him from the danger of making personal contact with Soviet agents outside the official parties, at which it was normal that he should be present.

64

From the time he became a deb's delight, Fayverdale was a tailor-made target for those Soviet intelligence agents sent out to specialize in cultivating likely contacts who might prove of use in the general campaign to degrade and subvert Russia's political enemies. Being internationalist in outlook, through spending so much of his early life abroad, he was soon in receipt of rubles, though with such a valuable recruit it was all arranged very properly by such methods as the diamond concession. All they had asked for in return from The Doctor, as they code-named him, was information concerning the private lives of people who were, or might later be, of eminence in the national life. Fayverdale never asked why such information might be required in Moscow, and though he was aware that compromising photographs and information had been exploited in the past for blackmail purposes, so far as he knew no use had yet been made of any supplied through him.

"Now don't forget to take a pill tonight," said Coral as she prepared to leave. "It'll help to stop your hair falling out. I must say, though, you don't need the pills as much as Geoffrey does. He's looking awfully tired and old lately, yet in fact he's only forty-one —not much older than you are."

"Oh, we could all do with a little touch of Faust," said Fayverdale. "Geoffrey works too hard and worries too much. He's too ambitious. He should be more like me—relaxed, content to live within his intellectual means, and satisfied with the simpler things of life. Sound hearts are more than coronaries and simple tastes than pulseless blood."

Coral kissed him good-bye and was shown out by Kopec. When the servant returned, Fayverdale handed the bottle of capsules to him without a word. As he lay on the divan he thought how incredibly simple it had been to satisfy the urgent request that followed his report that Coral had told him about a wonderful new youth drug. Within hours the capsules would be in the diplomatic pouch on the way to Moscow for analysis, yet he had committed no crime.

He lit a cigarette. The radio was playing a catchy old tune called "Thank Heaven for Little Girls."

chapter **11**

John Holt was far too astute a journalist to be taken in by Shirley's story that the move to Porton was simply a question of securing bigger laboratory space. He knew how the Army Department had fought to keep the Medical Research Council out of the Porton establishment for years and surmised that there must have been some very high-level backing behind this peculiar invasion. Why had Shirley been so terrified when he suggested he might do a harmless news item announcing that the Rosenfeld Unit for Research in Aging was moving to Porton? His instincts told him that she was hiding something from him, in spite of the growing intimacy of their acquaintance. She had kept him informed about the animal experiments on the understanding that he would not print anything about them until the first technical report was ready, but now she avoided talking about her work at all on her occasional weekend visits to his cottage in Essex or his flat near Regent's Park, or when she did, she made little sense. So he decided to do a little snooping around Porton himself.

As he drove through the chalky Wilshire plains, dotted with prehistoric tumuli, on a late May morning bright with the promise of heat, he pondered on possible explanations, but was still as puzzled when he turned his car into the long private drive leading to the Microbiological Research Establishment, an £8,000,000 redbrick building equipped with every conceivable apparatus for research on the most virulent bacteria and viruses. He decided to seek a direct interview with Harvey, reckoning that his chances of at least a short conversation were greater if he suddenly appeared at the door than if he tried to fix an appointment by telephone. From experience, he knew that even a brief brush-off talk can be wonderfully revealing when the speaker is trying to hide something.

As he was walking toward the entrance with its high glass doors topped by sculptured murals, a tall man with thick black hair and wearing a brown sports jacket, who somehow seemed familiar, came out carrying a briefcase. He spotted John walking over from the parking area about forty yards away and turned back in. John could see him leaning over the reception desk talking to the security guard, so he waited outside until their conversation was finished. When the man had disappeared, he pushed open the door and asked, "Could I see Dr. Harvey please? My name is Holt. He knows me."

"There's no Dr. Harvey here," the security guard replied, firmly thumbing through the telephone extension directory.

"But I know there is. He's in charge of the aging research that has just been moved here."

"Sorry, sir, but you must be mistaken."

John knew the man was wrong because he had frequently rung Shirley up in the laboratory there. He also sensed that the guard was deliberately lying under orders, which greatly intensified his interest and his determination to discover what was being hidden.

He slid back into his car, drove halfway down the tree-lined drive, and lit a cigarette. After deciding to stay overnight in Salisbury to see Shirley and make inquiries around the local pubs, he scribbled a note, put it in an envelope, and parked at the bottom of the drive, seeking someone who might be gullible enough to take the note in if it looked like a letter to his girl friend. As he waited, a large ambulance with eight nurses aboard turned slowly through the white iron gates. John waved it to a halt and called through the open window. "Do any of you girls know Shirley Howard? I have a private message for her."

"Yes, we work in the same department," one of the nurses answered.

"Dr. Harvey's?"

"Yes."

She took John's note and promised to deliver it privately.

As the ambulance pulled away to take the nurses to the door of the laboratory, John decided to wait for its return to question the driver. When it arrived it was full of nurses again—a different lot.

Why the hell are nurses working on shifts at an animal experimental station? John wondered. *Have they started human guinea-*

pig experiments with war germs? In that case they wouldn't be working in Harvey's department. No! The only explanation seemed to be the far more exciting one that Harvey was trying his anti-aging drugs on human subjects and that the tests were being kept secret.

John followed the ambulance to the nurses' home in Salisbury and confirmed that the girls were looking after old patients in Porton, but he did not want to arouse too much suspicion by making further inquiries there.

His note to Shirley had told her he would be waiting for her at the White Hart in Salisbury at seven o'clock, and he sat in the lounge there wondering whether she would come. She came, all right. She was too scared to stay away.

"Let's get out of here, it's too public," Shirley said as soon as they met. They drove off to a tiny inn in one of the nearby villages, and on the way she told him why she was so apprehensive.

"Robert's absolutely furious. He knows I must have told you we'd moved to Porton, though I denied it. There's a hell of an Official Secrets cover on the work we're doing. You'll be in real trouble with the security people if you write about it, and so will I. Please promise me you won't." With skill born of long years of dealing with confidences, John avoided making any firm promise and led her on to more disclosures.

"How did Robert know I was there?" he asked. "Did you tell him I'd sent the note in?"

"Of course not. He saw you. He was coming out of the main door to go up to London by road when you arrived. He warned the security guard not to tell you he was even here."

"But the only fellow I saw was a chap about thirty-five with thick, black hair."

"That *was* Robert."

"God Almighty!" Holt said, staring incredulously. "But Robert was gray and half bald!"

"You want to see what's happening to some of the older patients. It looks as though ten to fifteen years is about the maximum rejuvenation possible, but when it happens to a seventy-year-old within a few weeks, he becomes unrecognizable. Some of our patients have entirely regrown their hair. But the real importance will be with middleaged people like Robert. It looks as though they might be kept at that stage indefinitely."

John's mind raced over the journalistic possibilities of this news. "God, there's a fortune in this," he thought aloud. "Its use as a treatment for baldness alone is worth a mint. And look at the woman's angle!"

"I hope you're not taking this stuff yourself," he said suddenly to Shirley.

"No. I offered to take it when Robert started testing its toxicity on himself, but he wouldn't let me. I was rather annoyed at the time because his wife was taking it and there don't seem to be any side effects."

"Well, you keep off it. I'll bet it has a side-kick somewhere along the line. These drugs need testing for at least five years, and even then there may be some insidious effect nobody's thought about. Remember thalidomide!" he added, waving his finger at her. "And all the others that were withdrawn more quietly."

Shirley considered that John was ultraconscious about medication to the point of being cranky. To her, his "pharmacophobia" seemed as much an expression of morbid preoccupation with health as the pill addiction of the orthodox hypochondriac, but she herself was basically averse to drugs because of the abiding impact of her early upbringing by Christian Science parents, who would never have a doctor or medicines in the house.

"I'll promise not to take SP47 if you promise not to print any of the information you found out at Porton today," said Shirley.

"That's hardly a fair bargain," John replied evasively. "You've no need of rejuvenation anyway, and by the time you have we'll know whether it's safe or not."

Shirley was touched by his genuine concern. Having become accustomed to Robert's somewhat callous attitude, accepting it as his particular imperfection, she had, until that moment, imagined that John was cast in a similar emotional mold, in spite of the sensitivity to human suffering he showed through his work for the thalidomide victims.

John, too, was sufficiently surprised by his tenderness toward her to meditate on the cause of it, as he drove back to the White Hart. There was something different about Shirley for him, and it wasn't only that she had a better mind than any other girl with whom he had been on intimate terms, or that she evoked a unique awareness of femininity. There was a void when she had gone, and a growing intrusion of her into his thoughts.

As he undressed in his hotel bedroom, he was aware that his personal problem was not only to explain to himself why he might possibly be in the process of really caring about a woman for the first time, but why at thirty-three he went on demanding such a degree of freedom that it carried a penalty of loneliness that was increasingly distressing. Of all the ambiguities of his experience, why had freedom-loneliness been so difficult to resolve?

He knew the answer well enough, really: it had fallen out of analysis too many times not to be true: but it was too distasteful for acceptance.

His pretty mother had so resented growing old that she banned the word "mother" when he was ten, in favor of her Christian name; at eighteen she had threatened him with "If ever you make me a grandmother . . ." and she had never stopped reminding him of the unpleasantness of the pregnancy, which she had decreed would be her last. With his father forever advising him that marriage was the brakeshoe of ambition, warning him of the dangers of dependence—"Remember, Napoleon said he always won because he had no allies"—and hinting at the financial sacrifice being made to see him through Cambridge, he had never dared to bring a girl into the home. He remembered how, if he was walking with a girl at night in university vacations, he would pretend to be dazzled and put his hand over his face as car headlights approached, in case he might be recognized by one of his father's customers.

It was this conditioned furtiveness, which had to be justified as well-founded suspicion when it persisted into maturity, that had immunized him against the love requiring a deep sharing of experience. But rather than accept that his parents had been so defective, he saw all his contemporaries who had married as being out of alignment with wisdom—like Pisa seen by the leaning tower.

Shirley was the first woman whose personality had shaken this conviction. On foreign assignments John had eaten alone in the Court of Two Sisters in New Orleans, drunk alone in the Top o' the Mark in San Francisco, lain alone on Waikiki beach, listened alone as the serenade boats went by in Venice, and watched alone, so many times, on the Paris boulevards. Yet never had loneliness assailed him as forcibly as when he had walked down the hotel corridor that night, past the rows of conjugal shoes into the bedroom that was bare of the familiar possessions which deputized for regular companionship.

After arranging an early telephone call, he read himself into a sleep troubled by the dream which had recurred in different forms ever since he was a boy. Always the theme was similar—he was about to fish a famous salmon pool, shoot at Sandringham, or set off on some exciting journey, but he arrived without his rod, his gun, or his air ticket, or could not remember where he had parked his car. That night he dreamed that his brain was overflowing with the material for a journalistic masterpiece but when he opened his typewriter case it was empty.

chapter 12

Next day John sat in judgment on a conflict between his personal and professional consciences on the long drive back to London. He had stumbled on the newspaper scoop of the century, maybe of all time, a story of the most intense personal interest to everyone. Yet though he had found out most of it for himself, he knew that Shirley would be in serious trouble if he wrote it. He was already resolved to ignore the Official Secrets threat, which he knew to be empty. The Government might try to use the blanket security restrictions covering Porton to suppress the story if he sought official permission to print it, but no special Defense Notice on the subject of Harvey's researches had been issued, and he knew that the Government would be powerless to prosecute him. It was only Shirley's personal position that worried him. It would be treacherous to the newspaper to suppress the story but a betrayal of her trust if he did not.

As the soft tar sputtered under his tires he was reminded how in another hot summer he had been forced into a crisis of conscience, involving the only woman with whom he had felt a bond of attachment worthy of the name devotion. Reared in the Roman Catholic faith, he had rebelled against the dogma because he found it did not square with the facts of science, and he could not stomach the ritual because of an exaggerated sense of the ridiculous, which made all ceremony, from the Trooping of the Color to a church wedding, too comic to be taken seriously. He had even had the certificate for his first-class honors degree mailed to him from Cambridge to avoid the pompous presentation ceremony.

His complete break with the Church, ten years after he had been confirmed at the uncritical age of nine, unfortunately coincided with the contraction of a serious illness by his mother, to whom her faith was everything. When, after three years of progressive sickness in which she had stormed heaven with prayer, her symptoms were unrelieved, she began to believe that she was being punished by God for permitting her son to lose his faith. John could see the inevitable request and dreaded it, but when she asked him if he would go to confession and communion because she believed it might cure her, he could not refuse.

On a morning misty with heat haze they had made their way up the narrow passage leading to St. Augustine's Church—the memory was so vivid that he could still recall how their heels beat out the metallic echo peculiar to flagstoned alleys—and John was first into the confessional box.

Through the square of gauze which separated them, he could see the priest intoning quietly in Latin. As he knelt on the hassock, their faces were less than a foot apart, but he was unrecognizable in the complete blackness of his compartment.

"How long is it since your last confession?"

"Three years, Father."

"How old are you?"

"Nineteen."

"Why have you committed the mortal sin of failing to do even your Easter duties?"

"Because I don't believe in them any more, Father."

"Then why have you come to confession?"

"To please my mother, who's very ill."

72

Then followed a brief argument in which the priest tried unsuccessfully to convince John that he should believe because men far more brilliant than he would ever be were believers.

"I cannot give you absolution while you are in this frame of mind. You must go away, and if you feel you can make a genuine act of contrition, you can come back another day."

While his mother was confessing her few minor sins, John had only moments to decide whether to commit the terrible one of taking the communion wafer when not in a state of grace, or to tell her that her son had been refused absolution. In spite of his cynicism, John felt sickened at being dismissed from the confessional box. With the added impact on his fasting stomach of the smell of incense, candles, and the disinfected floor, washed at four o'clock that morning by the nuns, he thought he was going to be ill. Was the deep uneasiness he felt no more than a reflex from the years of inculcation? Or was his disbelief in doubt when subjected to the assault of a positive decision? As the tail of the procession to the altar rail shuffled past his pew, he made his choice and joined it. He would take the sacrament and, if necessary, be damned.

While recalling this painful episode, he knew how he was going to resolve the conflict this time. He would publish and be damned. The news was certain to leak in time, and he could foresee the trouble if it appeared in another paper under the name of one of his rivals with no personal scruples.

"What do I fear more, the sack from the paper or the sack from Shirley?" he asked himself aloud, in the habit of people who spend much time alone. The situation reminded him of the devil-worshipers, who argued that if they worshiped God and it was the devil who proved to be master after death, they would never be forgiven, whereas if they worshiped the devil and God proved master, he might well forgive them. It was conceivable that Shirley might understand and make allowances, but the editor wouldn't.

In order to give the subject the full treatment, John kept quiet about it in the office for a further day, explaining that he was working on a big exclusive which should be available by the weekend. He wanted to write an explanatory feature to go with the news splash before he unloaded the information on his editor. He would write it as deadpan as possible, for the material was surely sensational enough.

A ritual pantomime is played in every newspaper office in Fleet Street round about 11 P.M. each night, when copies of the first editions of all the rival newspapers mysteriously appear, brought there furtively by cloth-capped couriers who somehow secure them in defiance of office regulations that no first edition must ever be removed. The first edition of the *Daily Dispatch* containing John's splash story, under the banner headline "Eternal Youth Drug," caused an explosion in every rival office. The night executives read:

A new rejuvenation drug, which may be the long-sought Elixir of Life, is being given to old people by doctors at a secret government research station.

First results of experiments, which have been in progress for several months, suggest that the drug, code-named SP47, can be used for two purposes:

1. To keep people in a state of suspended youth or middle age so that they do not grow older in appearance.

2. To neutralize the effects of accumulated age so that people look and act younger.

The experiments are being directed by Dr. Robert Harvey, 48-year-old head of the Rosenfeld Unit for Research in Aging at the germ-warfare station on Salisbury Plain.

The Unit, which was formerly located at St. Patrick's Hospital, SW4, was recently moved to Porton so that the work could be continued there in secrecy.

Dr. Harvey has been attempting to rejuvenate animals with a drug mixture for the last five years. His experiments have been so promising that elderly volunteer patients are now being treated in a small ward, specially set up at the Porton establishment.

I understand that some of them have regrown their hair and look ten years younger.

The experiments were started following a case in which a boy suffering from a complaint called progeria (pronounced projeeria), which had made him prematurely old, became normal after injections of SP47 last year.

They will have to be continued for many months, probably

years, before SP47 could be made generally available. The doctors want to be sure that it has no long-term ill effects.

It is not yet certain that the drug will lengthen the total life-span, but I understand that the animal experiments strongly suggest that it will.

The results to date also indicate that it may have to be taken regularly, probably in daily doses, to produce a lasting effect.

There was a photograph of Dr. Harvey taken from the picture-library stock. Inside the paper was a long feature article, developing the possibilities opened up by the experiments for a much longer and healthier life for everyone. John deliberately withheld the news that Robert had been acting as a guinea pig himself, to keep a follow-up story in reserve for the next day, and omitted Shirley's name to avoid drawing the attention of the security authorities to her as a possible source of the leak.

No sooner had the headline been read than telephones began ringing in the bedrooms of every science and medical correspondent and every government public relations officer and official who could be connected with the project, newspaper night editors being no respecters of sleep in such an emergency.

Runners were sent out to the press club and other late-night haunts to ferret out those journalists who think there is no place like home only when all the other places have closed. Cars set off for Porton, and local correspondents in Salisbury were roused and ordered to find Harvey at all costs. Somehow the other papers had to catch up on the *Daily Dispatch* before the printing of the last London editions.

Sir Edward James, who kept his telephone number unlisted to avoid being pestered by journalists and cranks with cancer cures, was the first high official to be awakened. His public relations officer had been deluged with so many calls that he could not avoid seeking advice however testy his boss might be at being disturbed. James was horrified at the news. His immediate reaction was to deny everything, but his shrewdness stopped him. He told his PRO to head the newspapers off by saying that he had heard nothing about any such experiments and that the Secretary of the Medical Research Council could not be contacted. Then James roused the director of the Porton establishment and warned him to alert the security guards. Finally he telephoned Hastings Maclaren.

By 2 A.M. the telephone was ringing in the bedroom of the Prime Minister, who had recently returned from his usual salmon-fishing holiday in Scotland. On his arrival back at No. 10 the newspapers not only remarked how refreshed and well he was looking but announced that he had taken to wearing a toupée. This was, in fact, a subterfuge to cover the growth of black hair which would soon enable the toupée to be discarded.

Merton roused his wife, who was sharing a room with her husband for the first time in twenty-five years. The former Lady Celia Fitzroy had responded to the influence of SP47 even more emphatically than her husband. Indeed, at her husband's suggestion she had, in the past few weeks, been using makeup to disguise her loss of years.

The Prime Minister belted his dressing gown and poured himself a glass of cool milk from a vacuum flask. Being a man used to quick decisions and with unrivaled experience of manipulating the government machinery, he knew what to do. He called up his Cabinet secretary on the green scrambler telephone.

"There's been a bad leak about the old-age experiments at Porton. It's all in the *Daily Dispatch*. Make sure that all the public relations officials involved are told nothing. See that they are given the impression that the whole thing must be a hoax. That will see us through the night and we can discuss what further action to take at the Cabinet meeting in the morning."

The other newspapers secured no information on the story that night. Their editors took comfort from the official statements put out by the news agencies which seemed to indicate that the story might be untrue: that is, all except the editor of the *Daily Dispatch*, who called up Holt for his comments. John had an enviable reputation for accuracy, but this story was incredible. He assured the editor that he could not possibly be wrong. It was 3 A.M.

After the disturbance, John could not sleep for thinking about the inevitable rumpus in Whitehall—and at Porton—next day. Ever since the thalidomide affair there had been no sleeping tablets in his flat.

76

By the time the Cabinet meeting was over, Merton had decided exactly what should be done. Durrant, the Minister of Science, issued the following statement to the news agencies:

The Rosenfeld Unit for Research in Aging has been moved from St. Patrick's Hospital to the Microbiological Research Establishment at Porton. This move, which had been under consideration for several months, is part of a pilot study to see whether it will be possible to hand over a substantial part of the establishment to the Medical Research Council. It is well known that only about ten percent of the work at the Microbiological Research Establishment is directly connected with defense.

The Rosenfeld Unit, directed by Dr. Robert Harvey, is engaged in animal experiments designed to investigate the process of aging. A newspaper report describing this work today is exaggerated and irresponsible in raising false hopes. If and when Dr. Harvey's team produces results of medical interest, they will be published in the medical or scientific journals. It cannot be stressed too heavily that this is a long-term project and that the research is currently at an early stage.

The PROs concerned were instructed to tell reporters, if asked, that as a medical man Dr. Harvey could grant no interviews and that his laboratory could not be visited, because it was in a part of the Porton establishment, where secret defense work was still in progress.

It was a masterly example of "news management." It told no lies but was intended to deceive.

Having organized the political denial, the Prime Minister, who was infuriated by this newspaper intrusion into his time and plans, commanded his Cabinet secretary to institute a full investigation into how the leakage had reached the *Daily Dispatch*. Like so many of his predecessors, he had never been able to grasp why the press was so little under the control of Whitehall, which had so many public relations officers on the payroll. He gave loud lip service to the necessity for a free press on the political platform, and used the newspapers and television with skill in securing publicity when he wanted it, but years of power and custom to obedience had corrupted his judgment. When the press displeased him and particularly when a leakage of official information was involved, he expected it to be brought to heel.

So the Cabinet secretary, who also considered that all government information should be an official secret until released by the machine, ordered the full "leak procedure" to be put into operation. This automatically required the questioning of all officials who might have been concerned by agents of MI5. Sir Roger Black reported by return telephone call that a quick check of the files showed that Holt, the author of the offending article, was friendly with Hastings Maclaren, through their mutual membership on the thalidomide committee, but the Cabinet secretary did not relish the thought of approaching the austere, acidulous Health Minister. So the first man to be interrogated was Dr. Robert Harvey.

chapter 13

Holt was decidedly unpopular in the *Daily Dispatch* office that day. The newspaper telephone exchange was saturated with calls from readers wanting more information and offering themselves as guinea pigs. The editor was deeply concerned about the official statement, which all the rival papers were sure to project next day as a flat denial, as the BBC had already done. The proprietor had expressed his grave displeasure. Questions were to be asked in Parliament, which would inevitably lead to another denial, no doubt with innuendoes about the irresponsibility of the press from the numerous MPs who, in the course of their careers, develop some festering grudge against it. John was on the carpet and indeed in some danger of being sacked, for in Fleet Street, as in public life, reputations built on years of distinguished service can be destroyed by one major blunder.

Though outwardly confident, he was inwardly churned as anxiety cascaded into fear, and in self-defense he told the editor all he knew, including his information that Harvey was taking the drug himself with spectacular results.

"Then get hold of Harvey today," the editor urged. "Take a photographer. Get a picture of him, and if what you say is true, we can print before-and-after pictures on the front page tonight. Take the office helicopter if it'll be any help. We must make this story stand up in the paper tomorrow."

John was scared. He knew that he would have no chance of getting anywhere near Harvey at Porton, and he was loath to race down to Wiltshire when he felt the big news might be happening in Whitehall. He was confident that time would prove him right, but the public's memory is short, and he looked to be the man who on that day—which was all that mattered then—had inflated a few facts into a deceitful sensation. Had John known it, the Government was unwittingly doing his work for him. Displaying their usual disregard of the scientist's loathing of secrecy as the negation of discovery, the politicians made an error which was to prove catastrophic, in sending down an MI5 interrogator to interview Dr. Harvey. When Robert was told that a security man was coming to question him, he could feel his heartbeat quicken and his skin chill, as his blood vessels contracted under the needle of resentment.

By the time the man with the homburg had been shown into his small office, Robert's mood had mounted to complete defiance. His work had progressed rapidly, and he knew that the time was passed when his preliminary results could be withheld without a gross abuse of medical ethics. He was weary of having his yearning for professional recognition stifled by Sir Edward James, and was no longer prepared to carry the responsibility of covering up such an important advance in human knowledge. Even before the *Daily Dispatch* incident, he had decided that he would not remain in imposed silence much longer.

He believed there were some situations in which scientists should be their own decision-makers concerning their discoveries, irrespective of loyalties they might have to government or individuals for financial support. Explaining his stand to Shirley, who was thoroughly frightened by the situation and urged him to reconsider, he

79

had said, "Would it have been right for the patrons of a great composer to have stifled his music just because they had helped him to buy his piano? Well, what we have to offer may turn out to be of greater benefit to society than a thousand concertos."

Robert was confident that his livelihood was assured, for if the Medical Research Council fired him, he could get an appointment at any hospital or drug firm.

"I know nothing about any leak and I'm not going to be subjected to any inquisition," he told the agent curtly. "Furthermore, I'm not going to allow any of my staff to be questioned either. We've more to do with our time here than waste it on such futilities."

His anger was momentarily relieved when, on asking the agent for his security pass into the building so that he could sign it and speed his departure, he found that the man from MI5 had managed to get in without one.

"You might stick to the rules yourself before accusing other people of breaking them," he said testily.

As the grim-faced agent was being ushered out, Shirley came in to warn Robert that John Holt had been on the telephone seeking an interview. "Bloody nerve," she said. "After all the trouble he's caused. I told him to go to hell."

"Get him back on the telephone and tell him I shall be arriving at Waterloo on the 11:33 train from Salisbury. He can give me lunch."

Shirley was astonished, but Robert had made up his mind to unburden himself of the whole story, and Holt was the only journalist he knew well. A crowd of reporters and photographers was hovering around the gate of the establishment as he drove out, but they did not recognize him from the old photograph printed in the *Daily Dispatch*, and he easily fobbed them off when questioned, as they did not suspect that he had been taking SP47 himself.

John was waiting at the ticket barrier and hustled Robert into a chauffeured office car. He had arranged a lunch in the *Daily Dispatch* boardroom in Fleet Street, partly to ensure privacy, partly to get Robert into the office to be photographed, but mainly so that the editor, chairman, and news editor, who were joining them for lunch, could confirm the truth of his story from Harvey's lips. They were not disappointed. Wallowing in the relief of being able to speak freely after so many months of constraint, Robert told them almost everything.

The report, which appeared under John's name in next morning's *Daily Dispatch,* was reprinted in every major paper in the Western world. It revealed the details of the Government's cover-up, was illustrated with front-page photographs of Robert before and after treatment and introduced some glamour by describing Shirley's important contribution. In the column entitled "Viewpoint," the leader-writers fulminated about the ham-fisted attempt to conceal SP47. They concluded:

But for the presistent delving by the *Daily Dispatch,* this towering medical advance would have been suppressed, possibly forever. Should anyone ever doubt the absolute necessity for a free, unfettered press to penetrate bureaucracy and curb the arrogance of politicians, let them recall the events of the past few days.

In the smugness of their triumph they could not divine that the newspaper's brilliant exposure was destined to put every facet of liberty into the utmost peril.

The *Dispatch*'s rivals did what they could to check the information when they saw the first edition at midnight, and to get hold of Harvey who, by that time, was safely lodged at the *Dispatch*'s expense in an out-of-the-way hotel. When they had failed, they simply copied the information, since it was obvious from the mass of circumstantial detail and quotes from Harvey that it must be substantially correct. They, too, vented their anger at being so badly scooped on the Government and howled in their leader columns for the fullest inquiry in Parliament.

Harvey had warned John and the *Daily Dispatch* editor that SP47 was far from ready for general use.

"I hate publicity myself," he had protested. "I'm lending my name to it—and risking my professional reputation—purely to draw maximum attention to this lead. We need international co-

81

operation to find out exactly how the mixture works, what its long-term effects are, and how it can be improved before there's any question of making it generally available."

"We will certainly pass your warning on to our readers," the editor had replied. "I assure you that the last thing we want to do is to raise false hopes."

But such concern meant nothing to Morgan Owen, the fiery leader of the Labour Party, whose motives had been pickling too long in the vat of resentment.

A Welsh miner's son who drifted into trade union politics because a bad chest kept him out of the pit, Owen had fought his way to the top of the Labour Party through his outstanding ability as a spell-binder and his incinerating hatred of the Establishment.

"Outside every Tory is some common humanity trying to get in," he declared. "Good Tories are as rare as mule's milk."

Any injustice aroused his memories of poverty—memories made semifictional by the haze of time, for his early life had not all been the bed of cacti he recalled. He was aware that the canyon of difference between what a politician can safely say in public and what he knows to be true in private might be the reason for Merton's behavior. Yet as he read the extraordinary story disclosed by the *Daily Dispatch* over early breakfast at his house behind Westminster Abbey, he sensed the material for a political scandal, which could be worked up into a great moral issue in the House and might even make a major election theme, far more compelling than the tattered phantom of fair shares for all.

For Owen, it was the differences of political opinion generating the thrust and parry of debates that made life worth living.

"If humanity ever marches in step the monotony will be unbearable," he had observed.

He wiped the trace of egg from his full lips with the napkin tucked into his collar and rang up Holt, with whom he lunched occasionally to keep himself up to date on nuclear defense matters. Even HM Leader of the Opposition is only meagerly informed by the Government on secret issues, which are usually well known to the industrious diggers in Fleet Street.

Experience had taught him that after passage through only one head, the quality of truth is always strained, and since any aggressive challenger in Parliament knows that he should have his facts straight before he distorts them, he wanted them firsthand.

"Do you think you could bring this Dr. Harvey to see me in my room at the House of Commons this morning?" he asked. "I would like to talk to you both about this youth drug affair. Then we could have lunch here at my house in Barton Street."

"I'm sure I can organize it, Morg. I'll ring you back in a few minutes," said John, to whom the meeting not only offered the prospect of another follow-up story but solved the problem of how to keep Harvey occupied, while still hiding him from the rest of the press and from the television newsmen, who were searching for him all over London.

Robert, who had always admired Owen, was delighted with the prospect of meeting him. As John put the telephone down after alerting him at his hotel, he wondered whether Dorothy would be lunching with them. It was largely the money earned by Owen's wife, who wrote highly paid fashion articles under her maiden name of Dorothy Jordan-Bell, which enabled the man who might be the next Prime Minister to live in Barton Street. Holt knew her through her Fleet Street connections, though since marrying Owen she wrote mainly for the glossy magazines. They certainly needed all the big fees she commanded, for not only was she extravagant with clothes and entertaining, but her husband, while puritanically castigating the rich in public, privately embraced the pleasures of affluence with cavalier indulgence.

At that moment, Owen was shouting "Good-bye" to Dorothy up the narrow stairs of the eighteenth-century house, to race across to the House of Commons in time to organize a private notice question for answer that afternoon. Since by Parliamentary tradition the Leader of the Opposition does not put down questions on the Order Paper, Owen had to ask one of his back-bench hatchet-men to do so. The question, in the name of George Watson, MP for Croftbridge, read: "To ask the Prime Minister if he is aware that the security service has been used in an effort to suppress medical knowledge which belongs to all mankind, and if he will make a statement."

Though, as with most sensitive inquiries, the question was more likely to be countered than answered, Owen would get his chance to belabor Merton during the supplementary cut and thrust.

Dorothy, looking well-groomed and beautiful, if slightly faded at forty-two, was stirring dry Martinis in a long glass jug when Robert and John were shown into the Owen's drawing room. Slim, in one of the tailored suits she acquired at cut rates from the fashion designers, she was several inches taller than Owen without benefit of her high-heeled shoes, and her disciplined elegance contrasted sharply with her husband's casual untidiness.

Molded by Cheltenham Ladies' College and polished by metropolitan life, she pandered in her gossip writings to the people Owen most despised and categorized as "born to misrule," yet as a champion of the career woman she had recently made useful headlines for him by publicly vowing that her husband would be the first British Prime Minister to have a working wife. She had even proved an unexpected success in Penrhos, Owen's constituency, through her warmth and ready smile.

"An odd alliance," John thought as she came over to greet them. "But she would certainly make the most elegant Prime Minister's wife of this century or maybe any other."

Dorothy was fascinated to meet Robert because of the unique cosmetic attributes of his treatment, about which she was dying to talk—and write, but she kept her curiosity in bounds. She had realized, without having to be told, that Morgan had high hopes of turning the SP47 affair to political advantage and wanted no sidetracking of his source of information at that moment.

"I have a previous lunch appointment, so I'm afraid I can't stay to hear all the exciting news, Dr. Harvey," she said. "Anyway, I don't suppose Mr. Holt would relish the intrusion of another journalist. He has a reputation for being a lone wolf, you know."

"I don't count you as a competitor, my dear," John laughed.

"Oh, you never know, John, I'm a free-lance. I might sell it all to the *Daily News!*"

"If I know Morg, there won't be much to sell by the time he's finished with it in the House."

"Maybe not. But I'd very much like to write about your work from the woman's point of view, Dr. Harvey," she said, extending her hand to Robert. "Perhaps I could ring you in the morning to fix an interview?"

"Surely. I may have to go down to the laboratory tomorrow, but I am sure we can fix something."

Over lunch Owen avidly absorbed the details which Robert poured out in full. There were some disclosures that were new to John, and Owen whistled with delighted amazement as he heard them. He and Merton had a venomous hatred of each other, scoring vicious personal points wherever they could. To Owen the urban Merton (Eton and Christ Church) epitomized the Tory types, to whom he referred in his platform speeches as "the rinsings of our society." To Merton the thrusting Owen (Abertridwr Boys School and Workers' Educational Association) embodied all the destructive qualities of the strident demagogue driven by class revenge. "That Minstrel of Malice," he called Owen, in allusion to his adversary's singsong voice, and he had recently delighted his listeners by publicly referring to him as "that morgue of the nation's aspirations."

Both had been fortunate enough to realize really early in life that since all cooperative action starts in the mouth, acquiring dominion over words opens the clear way to power over people. Merton was endowed with an easy eloquence. Owen, because of a slight impediment and because his mother's knee language had been Welsh, frequently needed to pause in search of words, but through diligence he had achieved such command of English that his audience was held in close attention, knowing that out of the silence some sharp-edged phrase was about to be catapulted at the enemy with tremendous effect.

"He deludes his listeners and himself by speaking more clearly than he thinks," he had said with justification after a sparkling speech by Merton had brought the customary "hear hears" from back-benchers, who had not thought at all. He likened Merton's policy for the general election, which was due within the year, to "a phantom pregnancy which would prove to be all windy promise and no fulfillment." The clash of their personalities did little to promote the nation's political interests, but it provided the cartoonists with a mine of material and the public with perennial amusement.

Leaning forward from his armchair, the graying mane, the mastiff neck, and gimlet stare creating a study in astute alertness, Owen listened to Robert's plea for a planned program of carefully controlled research. He nodded approvingly at the cautious proviso about the possible unknown effects and the importance of long trials, but he had no intention of allowing what he called the ritual of science to get in the way of political reality. He believed that far too much deference was being paid to science.

"It's not science, it's discontent that's the root origin of civilized progress," he argued. "Science is only an expression of curiosity, and it wasn't curiosity that drove men out of caves: it was discontent. Apes have curiosity. If they had discontent, they wouldn't still be stuck in the trees."

With that philosophy, such an aggressive politician was not prepared to devote much effort to encouraging science if it could be spent on promoting discontent.

Owen looked at his watch and made it clear that it was time for him to get over to the House.

"You have both done a great service to society in bringing this out into the open," he said as he shook hands with his guests. "You can be sure we shall remember it, Dr. Harvey, if we get into office at the next election, which we certainly shall." Then, as an afterthought he added, "I think there'll be some fireworks about you in the House this afternoon. If you'd like to be there at question time, I'll arrange to get you a seat in the under-gallery."

John looked at Robert sharply but realized that he could no longer coop him up in privacy. If there was going to be a row in Parliament, he could not stop Robert speaking to the other journalists and appearing on television if he wished. The *Daily Dispatch* had enjoyed a tremendous run of exclusivity on the story, and they could not hope to hold onto it forever. Robert was enthusiastic. He had no real idea what the afternoon had in store, but he had never seen Owen in action and seized the opportunity to do so.

"I'll take Dr. Harvey around to your office," John said. "And I'll try and get a seat myself in the press gallery."

John took Robert in unseen by the Ministers' entrance, along the grim passage and through the door marked No. 6, into the Leader of the Opposition's depressing room, with its high-arched windows and its walls hung with prints of long-forgotten MPs. Then, leaving him there to wait for Owen, he made his way to the lower press gallery to pick up his day ticket. As he approached the messengers' desk, the parliamentary and lobby correspondents swarmed around him for news of Harvey. Had he heard about the private notice question? Did he think Owen would be able to force some kind of showdown? There was a strong rumor that Owen has some bombshell he intended to explode that afternoon. The Prime Minister had suddenly canceled a lunch appointment at which he was scheduled to speak. Durrant and Maclaren had hurriedly been called to No. 10. So had Sir Edward James and Sir Frank Butcher.

But John, who recoiled from even the smallest cooperation with rivals, as a slope as slippery as plagiarism, just gave them a half-amused look and pushed open the door leading into the press gallery.

The benches below were filling as he slid into his cramped oak seat to the left of the Speaker's massive chair. Leaning over the balcony, he spotted a few back-benchers, who gave him a smile of recognition, and Maclaren, who cut him icily. Owen came in and slumped down, with his feet on the table, chatting to his deputy. Then just before the Speaker began to call the questions, Merton walked in briskly and sat down by the dispatch box. Though obviously worried, he looked extraordinarily spry for his age. He was not wearing his deaf aid and was reading the order paper without glasses.

Answering the planted question in a strong voice, he said: "The security service has not been misused. A member of the service attempted to make a proper inquiry into a leakage of confidential information from a government establishment. The service was not so much concerned with the particular information in question, but was rightly concerned about the occurrence of any leakage from a defense establishment where extremely secret work is conducted."

As he sat down, Owen was up in an instant. Pointing his finger at Merton and shaking with indignation, he challenged him to explain why the Government had denied that work on SP47 was going on at Porton.

Eyeing his opponent with the arrogance of an eagle, Merton replied in a calm voice, "The statement issued by the Ministry of Science did not deny anything. Its purpose was to put the experiments into accurate medical perspective."

Trying to be heard above the Opposition jeers, he banged the dispatch box and shouted, "I am advised by the Medical Research Council that this work is in the earliest stage and that the utmost caution must be applied in the national interest. These advances must not be exploited without adequate study of all the possible consequences."

This was the moment for which Owen had been waiting. Leaping up he asked, "Is it not a fact that while denying this medical benefit to the public on the grounds of caution, the Prime Minister has been using SP47 on himself?"

Immediately the House was in uproar, with the Tories crying "Withdraw" and the Socialists shouting "Answer! Answer!" The Prime Minister remained seated, as though disgusted by such a suggestion, but Owen went after him. "I have absolute proof that for at least two months the Prime Minister has been using the drug and so has the Foreign Secretary," he announced. "If it was safe enough for them, why wasn't it safe enough for other people in greater need of it?"

It was a question which at the moment Merton could only pretend to treat with contempt. Stalking from the chamber to the sound of angry Socialist jeers and chants of "Resign! Resign!" he moved so vigorously that, for the first time, many of his own followers realized that he seemed to be energized by more than the temporary adrenalin of anger.

Morgan Owen immediately called a conference of the lobby correspondents and told them that he had been given the information by Dr. Harvey, who had quickly found out into whose buttocks those early doses of SP47, requested by Sir Edward James, had been injected. The full facts, including the news that the Prime Minister's much joked-about toupée was real hair, appeared in the late editions of the evening papers.

As Owen had anticipated, the public reaction was intense. There had never been a peacetime talking point of such intimate concern to everyone, from the beauty-conscious typist to the aging duke. The newspapers were deluged with telephone calls, from many who were incensed by Merton's behavior, and many more who simply wanted to get hold of supplies of SP47. The drug's effect on baldness alone was enough to cause a worldwide sensation.

88

Members of Parliament on both sides, representing the powerful interests of British and American drug firms, tabled questions demanding the release of the fullest information. Appreciating the enormous sales awaiting those which could market it first, the firms themselves mounted commercial intelligence operations at all levels. Even Sir Edward James and Sir Frank Butcher were not immune from apparently casual inquiry by eminent scientists quietly serving as consultants to the drug houses. Shirley and the nurses at Porton suddenly found themselves the subjects of close attention by good-looking men who appeared in Salisbury with plenty of money to spend. Some of the most persistent of these suitors were foreigners representing the Italian and Polish concerns which, for years, had made a killing by selling cut-price drugs to the Health Service.

Tory back-benchers, who had been looking for an excuse to get rid of Merton and the other old front-benchers to make way for the younger blood in their own veins, were either horrified or pretended to be. The small group of jealous sparrows, which had long been waiting to peck the canary to death, swelled to a large flock. There were hurried conclaves in the corridors, clubs, and private homes around Westminster, which become the secret meeting places of political assassins on such occasions.

Robert was shocked by the sensation he had caused and realized he had been made use of by Owen.

"These bastards aren't interested in government: they only care about party politics," he complained to Margaret during one of the telephone calls he made each evening to talk to her and the children. But there was nothing he could do: he was caught in a flash flood more powerful than anything he had contemplated. Though his immediate reaction was to escape back to Porton, where, for once, the security shelter would have been welcomed, he was quickly cornered by the television newsmen and submitted to their blandishments in the hope that, when appearing before the public, he could stress the medical need for caution. But the elderly public did not want to know. What they wanted was the treatment. If it was safe enough for the Prime Minister, it was safe enough for them.

Later, Dorothy successfully soothed Robert's distress during her interview, which extended into supper and a flirtatious evening together in the tastefully furnished L-shaped drawing room in Barton Street, while Owen was inciting unrest in the Midlands.

In the succeeding days, Robert was photographed by agencies supplying the European newspapers and magazines and made filmed interviews for American, Canadian, and Australian television. Margaret gave her opinions of the treatment, as well as her impressions of Robert as a family man, which embarrassed him and amused all who knew about his affair with Shirley Howard. Shirley herself refused to talk until Robert returned to Porton, which he did on the Sunday, by which time the newspaper interest had switched to the political crisis.

In a weekend speech given heavy press and radio coverage Owen promised the electorate the quickest possible provision of the drug free on the Health Service. "The moment Labour is in power we will institute a crash program with unlimited funds to pursue this work on life preservation and make its results available to all," he said. "We will soak the rich to pay for it. They deserve to be soaked," he added when the cheers had died down. "The Prime Minister and his wife, Lady Celia, are not the only privileged people who have been getting this treatment while it is being denied to others in greater need of it."

His long hunger for power had so eroded his sense of responsibility that he was not one to moderate his attacks, or his promises, once he sensed he had his audience running with him. He knew that if he achieved office he could always take refuge in the claim that information, previously withheld by the former Government, had delayed the implementation of his word or made it impossible.

Merton and the other Tory leaders counterattacked by denouncing Owen as being thoroughly irresponsible, but nobody over fifty-five and few women over forty wanted to listen. Owen's wife had taken the lead in creating a worldwide cosmetic interest in Harvey's treatment, and this had been followed up in all the women's magazines.

Conservative newspapers did what they could to get some sense of perspective into the situation, but even they could not excuse the vanity of the Prime Minister and Foreign Secretary. The *Times* baldly stated, "Whatever the merits or demerits of SP47 might prove to be, the matter raises the gravest doubts about the Prime Minister's judgment." Sensing the mood of Parliament, Owen put down a censure motion, "That this House deplores the attempt by the Government to suppress medical information which could be of service to humanity throughout the world."

Back in the comparative calm of Porton, Robert wondered what to do about the future. He had received a cabled offer of a job in a big U.S. research laboratory which, with the fringe benefits detailed in the letter which followed, was worth ten times his current salary.

"I think I'm going to take that American post," he announced as he and Shirley were injecting the latest batch of mice in the animal house. "The facilities sound fabulous and the pay is fantastic. Anyway, I'm absolutely sick of being hounded by reporters. Recognition's one thing, but this is intolerable."

"It'll be a damn sight worse in the United States," said Shirley. "The private lives of prominent men seem to be public property there. Nothing's sacred. If you have a medical examination, every detail appears in the newspapers—from the blood pressure to the amount of albumin in the urine."

"It couldn't be worse than it is here at the moment, Shirley. I had four calls from newspapers after midnight last night. California suddenly looks very attractive, at least for a couple of years until all the fuss dies down. As you know, I'm all for extracting advantage out of adversity."

"What about me? Where do I fit in?"

"You're included, of course. You know I couldn't operate without you. They're asking me to take the whole team over. They don't seem to realize that it's only me, you, and a couple of bottle-washers."

"What if I decide that I don't want to go?"

"I'll face that decision when you make it. I don't believe in wasting good computer time on problems that may never exist. Meanwhile, I'm going to submit my resignation to the Medical Research Council."

Next day, Robert told Holmes of his decision, and they prepared a joint letter for immediate publication, revealing the constitution of SP47 and its improved variants. The letter, which appeared in both the *British Medical Journal* and *The Lancet*, did what it could to disclaim any professional responsibility for the wilder statements made about the treatment, which was described as "highly experimental," and stressed the need to be vigilant for side-effects. Both journals carried long leaders deploring the intrusion of politics into medical research. They attacked the Government for its initial interference and Morgan Owen for making capital out of it.

Joseph Greenway, the progeria boy, was presented again by Holmes at a big symposium at the Royal Society of Medicine, with Harvey giving a long paper on the Porton experiments. The Greenway parents sold their tear-jerking story for a big fee to the newspapers, sparing no detail of how they had been sworn to secrecy.

Cornered into counterattack, the Prime Minister concentrated his public relations forces on convincing the nation that Owen had grossly exaggerated the value of SP47 and deliberately underestimated its possible hazards.

Pretexts were organized so that he could be interviewed on television to make the issue appear trivial in comparison with other political dangers facing the country. To curb his treacherous back-benchers, he let it be known through his Chief Whip that if necessary he would use his powers to ask for an immediate dissolution, rather than resign the premiership. A series of by-elections, before the SP47 affair, had shown widespread dissatisfaction with the Tories, who were ripe for replacement after ten years in office. Merton judged that all those MPs with thin majorities would rally round him rather than lose their seats in an immediate election, but the back-benchers were being subjected to tremendous pressure from their constituencies.

Every elderly man and fading woman in the country was impatient for action. The terror of impotent old age, which most normally keep secret to themselves, manifested itself in a mushrooming of Darby and Joan Welfare Societies organized to agitate for the drug. In London a group of influential women, spurred on by the writings and speeches of Dorothy Jordan-Bell, formed a "Youth for Women" movement. It rapidly acquired an enormous membership and it seemed that it would not be long before some of the more wrinkled would be chaining themselves to the railings.

On the night of the censure motion, the galleries of the House were as packed as the benches. In the hearing of the millions watching the televised proceedings, Owen made a savage indictment of the Premier, impugning his integrity as well as judgment, which he described as "a symptom of advanced moral derangement."

Speaking with dignity and deploying all his histrionic gestures— the eyes wide open in hurt astonishment, the assuring smile, the suspicion of a tear—Merton made a spirited reply: "While the Right Honorable gentleman opposite accuses me of judgment corrupted by surfeit of power, it is clear that his own judgment is already corrupted by the sheer greed for it. To find any activity in public life as irresponsible or reprehensible as the speech made by him last weekend, one would have to go back to the time of Titus Oates. It showed he is prepared to play with lives to secure political preferment.

"He has displayed complete disregard of the economic dangers which confront any administration permitting the wholesale use of this drug without strict controls. The Government has gone into these difficulties most carefully. They are very great, and in deciding to take a cautious approach, I ask the House to accept that we acted in the best interests of the country. It is our intention to continue to do so. We shall not be diverted from our proper duty by cheapjack tactics."

Without mentioning the name of Owen's wife, he referred derisively to the Opposition's "squalid effort to drum up a cosmetic vote." He admitted that he had taken the treatment himself, but claimed there was nothing unethical about it because, at that time, there was not enough of the drug available for general use.

"I have no wish to mislead the House," he said. "I felt there was nothing to lose at my age and, in effect, I volunteered as a patient at a time when it might have been difficult to get them."

The Opposition made the most of this admission, pointing out that it was a clear demonstration of irresponsibility on the part of a leader ready for relegation to the peerage. In full cry, Owen, with boyhood memories of exciting nights with a poaching gang of unemployed miners, seized on Merton's well-known addiction to salmon-fishing to compare the Tories—and by inference their leader—to "an old kelt being washed helplessly down the river of events." The best Merton could do in riposte was to forecast that the kelt would return revivified by the stormy sea of the election, bigger and stronger than ever.

As sometimes happens in times of crisis, the mood of the House reflected the mood of the country. There were so many abstentions on the Tory side that the censure motion was carried and the Government was defeated.

In the general election that followed, the Socialist promise of "An earthly heaven, with SP47" proved irresistible, and Owen's prediction that "the ballot box would be the sarcophagus of the Tories' hopes" was amply fulfilled. Labour was swept to power with a 210 majority. The old people and the women were almost solid in their support of a crash program to help them cheat the grave.

In more than fifty constituencies the Conservative candidates failed to secure one-eighth of the total votes needed to avoid forfeiture of the deposit, which, to prune the number of popular singers, disc jockeys, and other comic candidates, who had realized that standing for Parliament was the cheapest form of publicity, had been bumped up to £300. The hundred Communist candidates lost their deposits without exception and in nine constituencies earned the maximum contempt of nil returns. The Liberals finally proved the evolutionary law they had been flouting for years, that when the population of a once-plentiful species has shrunk below a critical level, extinction is inevitable.

Sir Edward James handed in his resignation from the Medical Research Council on the day that the Government fell. In the dissolution honors he got his GBE. Merton did not want the public to think he was being vindictive toward the man who had ruined his career, but neither had he any intention of giving him more than token recognition. So Dr. Robert Harvey was awarded the OBE—three degrees lower in the same order of chivalry. Shirley was unmentioned.

chapter 14

Merton did not accept the earldom which had been forecast by the political pundits. Since, as the daughter of an earl, his wife already had a title, he was, unlike so many politicians, under no pressure from her to acquire one. The luxury of power had become a necessity for him, and he looked with horror at the possibility of a reactivated old age wasted in the House of Lords. He had contested his seat at the election and managed to scrape home, though with a humiliating majority, through the ingrained loyalty of his former admirers and a surge of sympathy for a great man down on his luck.

Apart from Maclaren, who sat for a remote Scottish constituency where the Socialists had stupidly fielded a candidate who was not a Scot, he was the only remaining member of the former Cabinet in the sad rump of his Parliamentary Party, except for Ewhurst and Durrant, who remained sheltered by the perpetuity of the Lords. As he gathered strength and resourcefulness under the continuing benefit of SP47, secured by his doctor on the grounds of medical necessity, he decided that he was the only master mariner aboard a rudderless ship and, with manipulation, could resume the captaincy of such a demoralized crew.

Confident in his own ability and in the certainty that Owen and his crowd would make such a hash of the economy that they would be glad to relinquish office in two years, he set off on his usual holiday to shoot the grouse on the North Yorkshire moors. As he strode the heather and bog moss in the curlew country high above Masham, he felt the best he had in years. He was seeing the birds well without glasses and enjoying the satisfaction of more rights and lefts than he could remember. His departure for the moors caused the usual amusement among the cartoonists, though

Owen's annual holiday with Dorothy, idling on a hot beach in Spain, evoked no critical comment.

As John skimmed through the papers over an early-morning pot of tea in bed, he greatly envied Merton, who was pictured in all of them picking his way to the butts in knickerbockers. He had never appreciated the jibes against the grouse pilgrimage by his colleagues, many of whom considered that time not spent in a smoke-filled pub was wasted.

John folded the papers in the pleasant anticipation that, work permitting, he too would be shooting in a fortnight's time. He was beginning to feel the need for rest as the euphoria of his resounding journalistic success evaporated, with the rapidity peculiar to Fleet Street, to bare the bone-tiredness of unremitting effort and his guilt feelings about his betrayal of Shirley.

Since the political furore, Robert had refused to collaborate, considering John far too dangerous. Shirley would not even answer the telephone when he tried to contact her at Porton and hung up on him when he rang her at her flat. But he had high hopes that she would speak to him that morning because the letter he had sent her three days before read:

Darling Shirley,

To business first. The editor has asked me to approach you formally about the possibility of buying your life story. For a series of four brief articles describing your childhood, how you became a scientist, and the part you played in developing SP47, he offers you £1,500.

I hope you will accept since it would give me the chance to explain certain things to you, which cannot be done in a letter. I deserve this chance, whatever you may think of me. The events which overwhelmed me and disrupted our friendship proved just as irresistible to Robert.

I would be the person delegated to assist you with the series, but if you still find me "untouchable," we could provide another writer. I do advise you to deal with the *Daily Dispatch* rather than any other paper, if you are approached. At least you'll be dealing with a dog you know!

With sincere affection,

John

PS. I will ring you at your laboratory at 9:30 on Wednesday morning for your answer.

Shirley was greatly tempted by the offer on several counts. In the first place anger was never more than a fleeting mood with her. Unlike Robert, who had little forgiveness in his nature and remained vindictive when really hurt, her mind cleaned itself of animosity as a London plane tree sheds its polluted bark. Secondly she suspected that Robert might go off to the U.S. without her, for she had no illusions that he would put her before his career if it came to a straight choice. Though still more in love with him than she had ever been with John, she had become increasingly irritated by his offhandedness, which had been greatly intensified by the demands that fame made on his time and by his too-obvious confidence that she would always be available for him. Further, £1,500 was more money than she had ever seen in one lump, and she also welcomed an opportunity to secure a fairer share of the recognition and to cry caution about the too early use of the drug with which her conscience and professional reputation would forever be associated.

By the time of John's call she was determined to accept the offer, though grudgingly. She intended to make it clear that Mr. Holt had quite a lot of mileage to make up with Miss Howard.

"I can't make this sort of decision over the phone," she said.

"Well, come up to London and let's discuss it over lunch at that Soho restaurant you liked so much."

"I don't know that I care to be seen with you after the way you've behaved."

"I could easily arrange a private room. 'Twould be a consummation devoutly to be wished.'"

"No thank you. And don't go getting any ideas about consummation!"

"I was using it in the French sense. The French use the same word for refreshments."

"Do they? Well, I'll accept the refreshments. Meet me off the 11:33 at Waterloo. And I shall be expecting a pretty groveling apology!"

She remained cool in the taxi when he met her off the train, neat in her mustard-yellow suit and black hat, but thawed when he gave her an unusual antique bracelet in gold, with the motif of two hands enfolding a heart, as a "trivial tribute" for the immense help she had given him in securing the newsbeat of his career. Accustomed to Robert's meanness with material tokens of affection, she was touched by John's thoughtfulness, even though she was suspicious of it.

Under the influence of good wine in a relaxing and intimate atmosphere, Shirley accepted John's explanations and agreed to let him write up the story of her life provided she was able to check the copy, but not without first trying to increase the price.

"If I'm going to make myself cheap, I might as well make myself as dear as I can," she said. "And I want it stipulated in the contract that you'll print my views about the possible unknown dangers of SP47. Robert's insistent about that."

"I'd have suggested it myself if you hadn't," John said. "It can't be repeated enough. My reputation will be as prejudiced as yours if anything goes wrong later. Personally, I don't think Morg Owen will be able to keep his promise of making it generally available in a hurry. But we'd better minimize our liability in case he does."

Over the coffee John let his hand stray onto Shirley's knee hidden by the tablecloth. He was not repulsed, and encouraged by the obvious rekindling of her fondness for him, he did his best to inveigle her back to his flat. But Shirley knew the value of making men wait. She declined his offer of a weekend at the Shooting Box, and when reluctantly agreeing to tape record as much of interest about herself as she was able to remember at his flat, she gave him to understand that she had no intention of going to bed with him.

John regarded that as no more than a ritual rebuff, for women rarely offer much resistance to a man to whom they have previously submitted. Once the barriers of intimacy have been breached, they are not usually restored to their former strength against any amorous assailant, much less against one whose terms of conquest have proved highly acceptable. Shirley was no exception. After four hours of recording the past chapters of her life, she was not averse to making the next as interesting as possible, and after a few gins and some patently genuine expressions of affection by John, she quickly reached the point of no departure.

"Isn't it marvelous," said John, as he slid into bed beside her. "We can legitimately put the whole weekend down to expenses. Fancy being paid for doing this!"

chapter 15

One of the first things Morgan Owen did after being installed as Prime Minister was to make sure that Robert Harvey remained in Britain. He had been quickly informed of the letter of resignation and asked Robert to visit him at No. 10.

"I told you we wouldn't be ungrateful, Dr. Harvey. We have a mandate to provide this drug of yours and as the first move in our crash program we are converting the greater part of Porton into an Institute of Gerontology. I would like you to be its first director and to build up the task force for this great enterprise you've pioneered. I think too that you'll find that we rate your merit a good deal higher than an OBE."

Robert realized that he was hinting at an early knighthood, to which honor he was far from averse. Fellowship of the Royal Society also looked assured, and according to his colleagues the Nobel Prize for Medicine seemed inevitable. He made a spot decision to withdraw his resignation and stay, but seized the opportunity to impose one condition.

"With respect, sir, I am worried about this phrase 'crash program.' Can I be assured that this work won't be rushed forward purely for political reasons?"

"Of course," Owen replied, patting him on the shoulder. "We'll have to be guided by you and the Medical Research Council."

Robert was chauffeur-driven from Downing Street in a government car, feeling highly elated. New levels of life were being opened to him just at the time he needed them, but in No. 10 Owen was far from serene. Reports from the Medical Research

Council and the colleges were urging caution all around. The professional medical journals both in Britain and the U.S. were increasingly hostile to the idea of the crash program. Yet the clamor for SP47 from the public was so strong that family doctors were bombarding the Health Ministry with letters and telephone calls for advice on how to cope with it. When the elixir was not immediately forthcoming on a Health Service prescription form, the family doctors were the handiest target for the national frustration.

Having made a promise on which he could not go back without calamitous loss of prestige, Owen had convinced himself that any failure could not possibly be his fault. He had scant sympathy with the timid logic of his technical advisers who, as was proper, seemed uninfected with his enthusiasm. Confident that all delays could be expedited by push, he told his Cabinet: "These scientists must not let us down on the crash program. To spur them on we'll make them publicly responsible for it."

Within a few days Owen issued a statement from Downing Street announcing the official creation of a National Institute for Gerontology at Porton with Dr. Harvey as director, at the same time gleaning some praise from the Left by emphasizing that the germ-warfare work would be correspondingly reduced. He also announced that Sir Frank Butcher, the Chief Scientist at the Defense Ministry, had been created a life peer and had joined the Government as Minister of Science. In his public utterances Owen had repeatedly referred to the peers as "The Ermine Vermin," but like others before him, he found the Upper Chamber a convenient contrivance for introducing a nonelected man into his Cabinet. Lord Butcher was to set up a much expanded ministry to give greater encouragement to scientific endeavor in general but would have a special responsibility for implementing the crash program on SP47, to which he was to give first priority.

Butcher had always wanted political power but had never been prepared to risk his civil-service career and face the rigors of the hustings, which to him had always seemed a pantomime conducted at a discreditably low intellectual level. When Owen offered him power on a plate garnished with entry into the fat red studbook of the aristocracy, he could not resist it. With such a crushing majority, the Government seemed set for a long run, and being past fifty—he was fifty-four—he could freeze his pension rights. If his political career went sour, he was confident that his past record of achievement, fortified by his title, would command a sufficient number of directorships in the City or some plush post in one of the nationalized industries.

He pondered long over the title he should take. Since the schoolroom "Butch" had stuck to him at the university, he had never been happy with his name. He often thought that its German equivalent, "Fleischer," would have been more impressive for a scientist, just as Casanova would have sounded so much less romantic as Mr. Newhouse, the singer Schwarzkopf as Miss Blackhead, or Verdi as Mr. Green. But for a Socialist politician he decided that Butcher was suitably redolent of strong English meat and solidity.

A former grammar schoolboy from the lovely old market town of Richmond in Yorkshire, who had entered the scientific civil service after postgraduate work at Cambridge, he had achieved international acclaim through brilliantly conceived wind-tunnel research at Farnborough, where he had risen to be director. There, to the surprise of most who felt that a fertile mind was being taken out of production too soon simply to satisfy routine needs, he showed such outstanding ability for large-scale organization that he was rapidly promoted to the four-star job in the Defense Ministry. A consistent part of the political activity, which some of his colleagues considered to be beyond the bounds proper to a civil servant, was his agitation for more scientists in the Government. Now he had his chance to prove his point that scientists could govern and to efface the widespread impression that they were irresponsible meddlers whose insatiable curiosity would eventually destroy the world.

Robert was relieved at the news of Butcher's political appointment.

"At least we have a responsible scientist with a first-class mind in charge," he told Shirley. She nodded approval.

"That should help to keep Owen and the other wild men under some sort of control," she said.

But neither of them appreciated the extent to which political ambition can ravage a man's ideals.

John was also pleased because it meant another friend in a high place. He not only met Butcher through his journalistic work, but they occasionally shot together. Butcher, who had three children and was still educating two of them, had never considered that he could afford to belong to a shooting syndicate. After learning to shoot rabbits as a boy in Richmond, he had become an addict to game-shooting because of its intriguing difficulty and the endless variety of targets offered by fast-flying birds, but he had to rely on friends for invitations and always took part in the huge winter hare drives held by the farmers near Saffron Walden. After meeting him there, John had been able to ask him as his guest on partridge and pheasant drives, and these days in the open had cemented their friendship. In his congratulatory letter John felt privileged enough to warn him, "You will have to toughen up your skin to survive the inevitable Westminster stiletto work from the several Party time-servers who have been hoping for the Science Ministry."

In the rapid expansion of his facilities from the few rooms at Porton, which had been grudgingly provided by the Army Department, always loath to yield a square foot of office space or a rood of land, Robert secured a considerable promotion for Shirley, and he resolved to use this welcome news to offset a really final decision to end their affair. The mental maturity that counseled him to conserve his family life was still prevailing at intervals over the disruptive urge generated by SP47, and he had already tried to exploit the move to Porton as a means of tightening the bands of his marriage.

"We can't lose ourselves in Salisbury as we could in London," he had announced with the nervous smile that craves indulgence, soon after their arrival there. "Someone's sure to see us if we go on meeting here. I'm afraid we'll just have to try to be good."

That decision did not survive the first night they had to stay in London for a two-day conference, and after that they found means of meeting at out-of-the-way pubs in the surrounding villages. But this time he was going to be firm with himself. Now that he was to direct a big staff, for which he was already advertising, his responsibilities were greater and so was the risk that his liaison would be detected.

"I'm sorry it's got to end like this," he said lamely, when they were alone in his office, where Shirley could scarcely make much fuss. "But I think we've both known that it couldn't go on much longer. It's not doing either of us any good. I'm married, and you want to get married. You want children, and much as I love mine, I don't really feel that I want any more."

"What about that somebody else you once threatened to find?" he added when Shirley made no answer.

"Oh, I'm in no hurry," she said, dryly. "The world's full of people."

Once again she had discerned that Robert's pronouncement had emanated entirely from the head and was therefore unlikely to withstand the demands of what is euphemistically referred to as the heart. Her increased salary enabled her to rent a pleasant flat in Salisbury with its own front door, tucked away near the cathedral, and it was not long before Robert was making excuses to call in search of some document or for coffee, with the inevitable resumption of their intimacy.

Margaret for her part was thrilled with the house which the Government had secured as a perquisite of office for Robert and with the status of being the director's wife. The future seemed assured, and she felt she was putting down roots for the Harvey family when she was asked to plant a ceremonial oak tree in the Porton grounds, to commemorate its elevation into a medical institute.

Under the drive which the newspapers quickly called "Butcher's Broom," big clinical trials on volunteers were organized in hospitals throughout the country. The pharmaceutical firms expanded their own research facilities and prepared to move into production. The trials to date had clearly shown that to achieve a lasting effect the treatment had to be continuous. Indeed, there was growing evidence that if the drug was discontinued, the body's time clocks ticked far beyond their normal pace, so that a rejuvenation effect of ten years might be lost in two. The sales prospects for the manufacturers therefore looked brilliant, provided Owen did not nationalize the industry as soon as they had it nicely moving.

A working party chaired by Butcher and loaded by him with coopted talent decided that if the clinical tests were successful, the Health Ministry would make SP47 available under the name of Juvenex in two forms, blue capsules for men and pink for women.

Family doctors would advise their patients on the dosage, the number to be taken daily being graded according to age and physical condition.

Another standing Health Service committee was set up to advise on the selection of patients and the methods of controlling the treatment. The capsules were licensed as having qualified with the safety laws with a haste that seemed suspicious, but the animal and human tests had in fact shown no contraindications. There seemed to be no danger from overdosage because once the aging elements had been cleared out of the cells, any additional SP47 had no effect and was simply excreted. An excess of the drug seemed to be no more injurious than an excess of vitamins, and the odds were that, in time, Juvenex would become regarded more as an essential food than a medicine. Though no effects on growth rate had been reported, the working party decided that its use should be prohibited for patients under the age of twenty-one—it being merely a fluke of circumstance that this is also the age when patients are able to vote.

To ensure firm control, Juvenex was brought under the Therapeutic Substances Act, which prohibited its sale except on a doctor's prescription. Owen was greatly tempted to limit it even further—to a Health Service prescription. He saw that this offered a sure way of ending private practice, which had always been an obsession with him, but he did not want to alienate the medical profession any further at that stage. In the Commons only the voice of Hastings Maclaren was heard in protest against the dangers of rushing such a drug into general use.

"Crash program will prove to be the right term," he thundered. "And the crash will involve millions more than the irresponsible people opposite who are perpetrating this folly."

The impact of these events on Butcher's private life was catastrophic. As a senior civil servant, he had been used to getting back to his home in Farnborough at midnight on two or three nights a week. Now even his weekends were infringed with visits to Chequers, Porton, the new production plants, and other establishments vital to the success of the crash program. He had kept on the house he bought at Farnborough when director there because his wife, Barbara, was caught up in the local social life, in which she exercised her considerable organizing ability, and disliked London. As a hobby she kept Siamese cats, which was immediately apparent to any stranger entering the Butcher household long before any fur was glimpsed.

Few could meet Lady Butcher without being reminded of Napoleon's remark that it was a pity that so many of his generals had married when they were corporals. Eschewing all makeup except for lipstick, dowdy in dress and harsh in intonation, her interests were centered in the Women's Institute, the church, local charities, and her cats. No man could be proud to have her on his arm, but she suited Butcher, who basically despised women. He never ceased to be astonished at the number of expensively educated wives he met who could not multiply seven by eight. He despised them for the way they squandered their share of the gift of curiosity in trivial gossip. Almost always when his efforts to work on the journeys to and from Farnborough were frustrated by the small talk of fellow passengers, women were responsible for the dreary interruptions. He held them in particular contempt for their sexual frailty.

"Aren't you ashamed of your sex when you read of a woman being 'seduced'?" he asked his secretary, who was as dowdy as his wife. "Have you women no will of your own? It's lucky for all of you that men don't undress the minds of the women they meet like they mentally undress their bodies."

Female slavery to fashion elevated his blood pressure even more. When women started wearing long pointed shoes with high stiletto heels, he had never missed an opportunity to explain that the purpose of the high heel was to make the foot look smaller, and having achieved this at severe anatomical sacrifice, the women were now stupid enough to lengthen the toes of their shoes until their feet looked bigger than before. As for the damage inflicted by stiletto heels to floors, carpets, and airplanes—"One and a half tons pressure to the square inch," he had calculated—he considered that criminal. The fact that the heels and most of the fashions were designed by men only increased his poor opinion of the mentality which rushed to embrace them.

A psychologist might have judged that this extreme opinion was a defensive reaction to justify the type of woman with whom he spent his office days and his home nights, and he might well have been right. In his student days when, though short in stature and abrupt in speech, his mind had commanded feminine respect, he had shunned promiscuous friendship as a waste of the time needed to achieve his ambition of wranglership. He consciously decided that he would rather be admired for cold brilliance than loved for warm sympathy. Technical achievement was his substitute for gallantry, and a reputation for being entirely dedicated to the service of study does not commend itself to any girl in search of someone to dedicate himself to hers. Later, though his interests had widened, a fanatical devotion to wind tunnels might have influenced the design of airplanes but was not calculated to further the designs of predatory women. Though he had managed to father three children, what passion there might be in him had never been awakened, and the few women he met when really mature were more than happy to let that sleeping animal lie. If Lady Butcher ever worried about what was really going on when he was missing from home so much, she had no need for concern. But with Margaret Harvey the situation was still very different.

Robert was inundated with requests to lecture, particularly in the United States. American universities tempted him with visiting professorships. An oil millionaire offered him an extravagant fee in return for setting up a research station in Texas. Butcher's insistence that he should be on every important committee concerned with the project made further inroads into his time, and with the proportion of it that he was driven to spend in Shirley's arms, there was little left of "Superdad."

Now that it was certain that Robert was not going to the United States, Shirley had regenerated her interest in him. The prospect of being the second Lady Harvey—or even the first if she moved quickly—intensified the attraction. She had kept her promise not to make use of SP47, but such was the natural disparity in their ages that with Robert's ten-year rejuvenation they were ideally matched on the physical plane. Being cautious, she had not dropped John entirely, but he found that she was becoming increasingly preoccupied with "patients" at the weekends and he was beginning to feel sure who the chief patient must be, though Shirley had always denied any sexual relationship with her boss when John had put fishing questions to her.

If Shirley ever reproved herself for allowing the probability of marriage to sway the balance of her affections, she would no doubt have justified her attitude by claiming that almost every big decision, however altruistic it may seem, is a judgment of probabilities concerned with self-interest. John's immediate reaction was less honest.

"Oh, well, to hell with her! Why should I care what she does?" he commented. But his concern at being deprived of her company intruded into his thinking time, and to his enormous surprise he found himself even prepared to forgo big shooting days in the hope of inducing her to his cottage for the weekend. When this sacrificial offer was rejected, he sought substitution in a vivacious press relations girl from one of the big hotels, all legs and bouffant hair, but he found that for the first time the exhilaration of novelty did not lighten his need for the known.

Margaret, who had been under the treatment for more than a year, had recovered not only her looks but her youthful desires. These remained centered on her husband because they had never strayed, but Robert found there was no going back to the old passion for him. He could not help resenting the sudden appearance of a woman in more active competition with his mistress. He found that the threads of a superficial relationship can be picked up and rewoven into a tighter band, but this cannot be done with an intimacy which has been disrupted either by violent emotional conflict or, as in his case, by the slow attrition of the years. Margaret's personality was not abruptly changed, but somehow it seemed wrong in her refurbished shell. It disturbed a pattern which, after a lengthy struggle, had looked like settling into cozy compromise—a devoted wife, a desirable mistress, professional renown, and the money to put all to proper purpose.

It was not long before Margaret was forced into realizing that there was something dangerously wrong in their relationship. Robert had always displayed the excessive ill temper to minor annoyances that is the mark of the perfectionist, and at first she attributed his increasing irritability, which was really due to his failure to give up Shirley, to his sudden accession to international fame. Robert had proved more than averagely stable over the years, but she knew that no personality could have endured unchanged under such impact of acclaim and publicity. She did her best to be understanding, to take his bouts of temper without retaliation, and made pathetic efforts to win back his interest, but to Robert this resurrection of her ardor seemed unnatural and repellent. The prospect was as unattractive as an unmade bed, and as his irascibility with Margaret increased, the more of his diminished personal time he spent in the mooring of Shirley's embrace.

Events at last forced Margaret to realize that another woman must be involved, and once her suspicion was aroused it did not take her long to realize who the woman must be. In her calmer mood she was determined to avoid any confrontation in the confident belief that the affair would peter out through inanition, but inevitably there came a moment when she could no longer still her tongue.

Throughout their married life Robert had displayed an infuriating habit of disappearing to wash or do some odd job just when a meal was about to be served. Margaret's remark that he suffered from gastroenergitis had become a family joke, but one Sunday, when he decided to make a telephone call the moment lunch was announced, this minor annoyance unlatched the floodgates.

She put her head around his study door and said with venom, "When you've finished calling your mistress, your lunch is ready."

Robert was at once shocked and furious. "What the hell are you raving about?" he asked.

"Don't lie to me," she shouted. "You are having an affair with that bitch Shirley Howard. It's disgraceful. The big director jumping into bed with the hired help. You're old enough to be her father. What do you think your own children are going to think about it when some kind soul tells them?"

By this time the tear glands were in full production and Robert, who hated scenes, could do nothing but stomp out of the house, slamming the door. He did not return until after midnight and slept in another room. Margaret, whose physical desires were strong, again lay awake nursing the fear which drives women to the psychiatrist's consulting room—and to other men's arms.

At that moment eighty miles away in Downing Street another row was in progress. After a late sitting at the House Owen had sent for Butcher to express his dissatisfaction with the delay in the crash program.

"What's holding you up, man?" he asked. "I give you full powers and a task force of scientists to get this thing moving and all I hear are complaints from the Health Minister that twenty-five thousand general practitioners are besieged by dissatisfied customers."

"I'm sorry, Prime Minister, but these tests can't be pushed any faster. The Medical Research Council agrees with me that we are cutting a lot of corners as it is."

"Well, it's your responsibility, but I suspect these scientists are just moving at their own sweet pace. You must bulldoze them along, man. We have a mandate to get this job done, you know. Merton's already beginning to plant questions, and I don't want that arrogant bastard to do any more scoring off me."

"I'll do what I can, Prime Minister, but there are a lot of difficulties."

Owen's rejoinder was the obvious one. "Don't tell me about them. It's results I want to hear about. While we are on the subject of rejuvenation, see if you can rejuvenate the dying art of getting things done."

chapter 16

The weather, which had continued unbroken since before Christmas, was appalling. Thick crusted snow on the fields, sheet ice on the roads, freezing fog on the windshield, but it was so long since Butcher had taken a day off that he was determined not to miss the annual hare shoot at Audley End.

After staying the night at the United Universities Club, near Trafalgar Square, he had set off in his Jaguar while it was still dark. He liked to feel the quick response of two hundred brake horsepower to the pressure of his size seven foot, but the road ice slowed him down as he motored along the A 11 to reach the big barn near Chrishall village where guns and beaters were assembling. It was one of the great sporting days of his year. During six drives over huge fields of rolling plowland and pasture, he stood in a long curved line with about forty other guns while an equally long line of beaters, taken to their starting point by truck, slowly walked toward them, bringing in game from hundreds of acres at a time. There was a break for lunch at the nearby Fighting Cocks Inn, and after the game had been counted, the day ended in a splendid high tea at the house of the farmer who had invited him.

Butcher spotted the Landrover he was looking for and drew alongside it to find Ernest Hobson, his host, talking to John Holt and half a dozen farmers, whom he met there every year. Everything seemed right as he swung his short legs out of his car. A touch of sun had begun to disperse the small pockets of mist still hanging over the white fields. There was the satisfying sound of gun barrels being clipped into stocks. In an accent redolent of the countryside, the head keeper was shouting instructions to a party of beaters as a truck roared by filled with middleaged men with guns and young farm-hands with sticks. Gundogs were sniffing around the few visible clumps of frozen roadside grass and around each other. A few hares disturbed by the noise could already be seen running about aimlessly on the near horizon.

"Glad you could come, Frank," said Hobson, extending a fat hand. "Looks like being a good day. I can't remember when we've had so many hares. They all seem to have come in here since the weather started."

"I can't see what they're eating," broke in a long-nosed farm laborer shouldering an old damascened hammer gun. "I suppose they're digging down to the grass. I shot three yesterday, and they were as fat as butter."

John shook hands with Butcher, and the three of them moved off to take up a stand behind a gappy, wind-pruned hawthorn hedge. It would be some time before the hares started to run, though there were already one or two distant shots from the guns walking with the beaters. John produced a whiskey flask, and they all took a modest swig. "How's it going, Frank?" John asked Butcher as he wiped his mouth with the back of his mittened hand.

"Off the record, bloody awful. This thing needs time. If only Morg Owen could stop fussing about his flaming mandate, we'd all be a lot happier. Your paper isn't helping either with its readers' letters and leaders complaining about the delay."

"I know, Frank. I've tried to get them to plead for caution, but the editor says it's 'too downbeat' when the other papers are crusading for action. We're in the paper-selling business, and what we want are campaigns and news that are 'upbeat.' But surely you can influence Owen with your authority?"

Butcher smiled ruefully. "You don't know Owen. We just supply the footnotes to his text. In the civil service I was used to being overtaken by events. Now I find I'm being taken over by them."

"You're not regretting going into politics already, are you?" Hobson asked.

"Certainly not," said Butcher, who was enjoying handling the civil servants as he had been handled by politicians before. "Don't misunderstand me. It's just that in this particular project the politics are intruding far more than I'd hoped when I took the job on. But I can see now that it's inevitable in a democracy, where the public so often has to be given what it wants rather than what it needs."

A shot down the line signaled the arrival of the first hare. Now they could see a score or more loping toward them a couple of fields beyond. As they moved into their positions about forty yards apart, Hobson shouted, "Don't forget to down any cock pheasants. They've done more damage to my brussels sprouts than the hares."

Within minutes there was a fusillade of shots as the hares approached the line and tried to break through it. John had never heard so much shooting. He was on fair form for him and killed the first four with head shots. Their momentum sent them sliding head over pads to lie still on the snow, with the faint breeze blowing the yellowish fur on their bellies, but as was inevitable with anyone so impatient, and with the hares twisting and turning as they spotted the guns, he hit some of them in the hindquarters. These either stopped quietly in their tracks, sitting up on their forepaws with their ears back to collapse slowly as the blood drained from them onto the snow, or they lay screaming like terrified infants, until silenced by a second barrel.

This hideous noise was offensive to both Butcher and Hobson, who, like most born countrymen, were a strange mixture of callousness and sensitivity. They killed their game cleanly because they could bear to wait until it was really in range and fired at first aim. But both were too discreet to offer John advice and too busy dealing with the hares, which were even running into the line from behind.

Cock pheasants, surprised in the hedgerows, flew over the guns to be shot down or to escape after surviving a royal salute. A few of the many high-flying pigeons fired at flailed down to earth, spinning like great sycamore fruits, but it was the hares that provided the slaughter. The sight of them running in droves to destruction was to recur to Butcher in nightmare and later in more terrifying circumstances.

As the beaters drew nearer, those hares which had chosen to squat rather than run were flushed and either rushed the line or doubled back through the beaters to be picked off by the walking guns. When the shooting stopped, the guns walked out of the line to pick up their game and deposit it by their stands so that the trucks could collect it. Nobody there had ever seen such heaps of carcasses. The first drive had produced nearly four hundred hares, and there were five more drives to come. With three hares eating as much as one sheep, Holt could understand why the farmers needed them shot.

When, in the gathering dusk, they counted them slung by the back legs from poles inside the game trucks, the day's total was a little short of nine hundred. Butcher and Holt tossed braces of hares and cock pheasants into the trunks of their cars, put ten shillings into the cap being passed around for the beaters, and followed Hobson back to his house in Audley End.

The first thing both men did was to telephone their secretaries to make sure no crises had arisen in the few hours they had been unattainable by the instrument which dominated both their lives. In the small farmhouse Holt could not help overhearing Butcher's conversation—not that he tried hard to avoid doing so.

"You tell Dr. Harvey that I say that report has got to be on my desk by midday tomorrow. There's a Cabinet meeting the next day and it's just got to be there." Then there followed some conversation about some other scientific project, which made John suspect that Butcher was interfering in detail which he would have expected to be delegated.

Calls completed, they settled down at the big table laden with cold meats and pies while Hobson's wife poured from a huge teapot. There were twelve men around the table, including the local doctor, the vet, and farmer friends of Hobson. It was not long before one of them asked Butcher whether SP47 would be of any value for animals.

"The Agricultural Research Council is looking into it," Butcher replied. "But at first sight it's difficult to see what use it could be. It doesn't accelerate growth—which is what you want for meat animals. The only value I can see is for giving breeding stock a longer life."

"The Herd Societies won't like that," the vet commented. "And neither will the bloodstock breeders. Remember how they reacted to artificial insemination? If you want to export bulls and stallions, you don't want them lasting forever."

"It'll be no good for racehorses anyway," John interposed. "The Jockey Club would be sure to say it was dope!"

The doctor, a red-faced man who had met Butcher on previous hare shoots, had been waiting all day to say it. "Can I put in a word for the poor old GP? I've had a hell of a time with my patients ever since Holt wrote his wretched story, and it's the same all over the region. When is this stuff going to be ready?"

"The target date for first availability on the Health Service is Easter," Butcher replied, helping himself to another slice of ham. "That was announced by the Prime Minister, and I intend to see that it's kept."

John knew that it would be. He had already sensed that political life was making inroads into Butcher's scientific integrity. He was a fair judge, because the same had happened to him in Fleet Street.

Target dates and crash programs have no place in fundamental medical research, where anticipation can race ahead all too easily into delusion. Butcher's acceptance of them signified a drift from his former standards of scientific discipline. Though still slight, the deterioration in his intellectual deportment brought by just a few months of unchallenged power betrayed itself to a professional observer. This man who had once advised his juniors, "Nobody ever listens himself out of a job," was now little prepared to listen to anybody, and John could well understand why his old civil service colleagues now referred to him as "The Czar of all the Pushers." Even in the intimacy of that convivial table, John noticed an increased desire to dominate the conversation and an impatience with interruption which implied an intolerant reaction to the basic human right to criticize one's rulers. And perhaps most ominous of all, John thought, this man who had been a passionate advocate of argument as a preliminary to prudent action was displaying a definite tendency to declaim rather than discuss.

What had happened was simple and perhaps inevitable. Butcher had been progressively more astonished at the low caliber of the politicians who found themselves in ministerial office after the landslide election. The Chancellor of the Exchequer had once been a railway booking clerk, and still retained the restricted attitude of a man who has spent his life looking out of a narrow aperture. The washing-machine millionaire who had become President of the Board of Trade could have sold paternity clothes to expectant fathers, but his brash, bulldozing manner was ill suited to any office demanding diplomacy. The former schoolmaster who had risen to be Defense Secretary could not help treating his Chiefs of Staff like prefects. The only previous association with the problems of agriculture which could be claimed by the Minister of Agriculture, Fisheries and Food was the weekly purchase of cracked maize for a few backyard chickens. Though the trade union men had a native shrewdness, they, too, seemed unable to think on a broad front. Even Owen was proving disappointing as an administrator. In this milieu it was natural that Butcher should feel it incumbent not only to remain in office, but perhaps to take on even greater responsibility.

Throughout his service in the Defense Ministry, he had hated the Foreign Office, which was always finding some objection to his plans. He was dying to apply "Butcher's Broom" to the cobwebbed corridors of that extraordinary Old Boys' Club. And when he looked around him in the Cabinet room he saw no reason why he might not get the chance. The Foreign Secretary was an elderly time-server certain to go in the first reshuffle, and the other aspirants were scarcely intimidating: but first he had to impress Owen with his handling of Project SP47.

As John eyed him, so much enjoying the deference being paid to his position, he was reminded of Lord Acton's comment on power. Butcher was an integral part of the power structure, and his judgment was being corrupted by it. When he had been a civil servant, he had defended the ponderous Whitehall machine when John had criticized it by saying, "Its inertia is its saving virtue because it limits the damage that incompetent rulers can do."

Now John was hearing complaints from other civil servants that he was by-passing the machine. What Butcher would have told him, had John been ill-mannered enough to ask for an explanation, was that ministers, ludicrously overloaded with responsibility, have no time for thinking about scientific standards when they have so many decisions to take. As many had discovered, painfully, before him, government had turned out to be more concerned with priorities than with principles.

John wondered how much further down the slope he would be at the next hare shoot in a year's time. Would he be too grand to come? Almost certainly. The picture he projected was of a hustling careerist, vain, peremptory, an inveterate pressurizer, now chronically infected with the ungovernable urge to govern other people.

Fifteen hundred miles away in Moscow, and only one hour by supersonic jet, the same subject was being discussed around another table, but in a very different atmosphere and context.

chapter 17

In a conference room of the Kremlin, carefully selected experts from the Academy of Science, Medical Institutes, the economic ministries, Gosplan, and the Central Committee were considering the pros and cons of introducing the Russian variant of SP47 into the Soviet Union. This was their twelfth meeting prior to preparing a full report for consideration by the Presidium of the Central Committee.

They had no lack of evidence. Weeks before John and Morgan Owen forced the news into the open, Soviet scientists had analyzed the SP47 capsules provided by Fayverdale and secured further information from Porton, which had been a prime target for infiltration during its long service as a germ-warfare station. The main Soviet agent there, a British Communist clerk in the registry, had secured access to the secret reports on human patients and animals and passed on microfilms to the official in the Hungarian embassy who controlled him. From then on several polyclinics in Russia had been hard at work on confirmatory experiments and human trials.

The results had been so dramatic that preliminary reports were quickly presented to the Presidium, where they raised the particular interest of Maxim Turganov, who had retained unchallenged power in the key positions of Premier and First Secretary of the Central Committee of the Communist Party for the last seven years.

A young-looking fifty-seven, Turganov was out of the run of Soviet dictators—over six feet tall, ever ready with a smile on his flat Ukranian face, his prominent ears giving him an extra look of boyishness. A compulsive worker, who feared the corrosion of even the briefest idleness, he was the first Russian leader to begin his working life as a career diplomat, and after early service in the Soviet embassies of both Britain and the U.S., he spoke English well.

More intellectual than any of his predecessors since Lenin, he had been successful in promoting what he called "The Philosophy of Most Effort," the belief that in a Socialist society work is its own reward through the personal sense of achievement it generates. He was convinced that "the strain of modern living" and "the need to relax" are among the most dangerous myths of the twentieth century. A study of world history had satisfied him that past civilizations had never perished from excessive mental or physical exertion by their citizens or slaves. They were rotted away by indolence and prodigal living, which he saw, with some satisfaction, to be potent threats to the West. At his insistence the cartoonists of the satirical *Krokodil* and other magazines never ceased to project capitalist society as being doubly trapped in its leisure and in its fat.

Turganov found strong support for these beliefs from his medical advisers, who attributed the steady increase in heart disorders and mental troubles to lack of physical endeavor. With the rapid rise in material living standards in the Soviet Union, he sensed the need for some other form of fulfillment rather than the accumulation of domestic hardware. It was far from easy to convince even dedicated young Communists that work is the meat in life's sandwich, but by subtle propaganda he had substantially increased productivity in the factories without a corresponding rise in wages.

His inclination was to keep to the expanded liberal tradition first promoted by Khrushchev, while exploiting every lesion in the Western alliance, but as a dedicated Marxist-Leninist he was prepared to zigzag as the situation demanded, in pursuit of the ultimate objective of global Communism. By that, he meant the Russian brand, for though he and Marshal Ho Cheng had recently exchanged visits between Moscow and Peking, the wedge of ideological conflict was in as deep as ever.

The implacable Chinese dictator had forgiven neither the Russians' prudent refusal to supply their more numerous neighbors with long-range missiles, nor the continued affront of being reminded by Turganov that nations without such striking power were second class. The Chinese had managed to explode a few nuclear devices, but deprived of all Soviet aid, they had been unable to build up the industrial strength and electronic sophistication to produce an operational force of nuclear-weapon-carrying missiles. There was also the humiliation of the repeated Soviet refusal to return Outer Mongolia and that large slice of Eastern Siberia which had been part of the Manchu Empire until the Russians seized it in the nineteenth century. Regarding himself as the only genuine exponent of world revolution since the Russians had become so rich and fat, Ho Cheng was outraged by Turganov's image of China's Communist role as being no more than a tail to the Soviet kite, and was dedicated to reversing it.

The prospect of an extension to the expansive phase of his life through the drug, which had been declared safe by the Soviet researchers, had particular appeal to Turganov, who was naturally desirous of achieving the maximum progressive change in his lifetime. But when, a few weeks later, he studied the final reports of his advisory committee, he and the rest of the Presidium came to precisely the same conclusion as the previous British Government. Most capital discoveries have potentialities for good and evil, and in this case the balance came firmly down for evil from the viewpoint in Red Square.

Turganov was horrified by the prospect of what he called "Panjuvenescence"—the eventual situation where the entire population would be youthful and remain so indefinitely. Whether he forced retirement so that the young could succeed to their Socialist inheritance, or whether he reduced working time all around so that all could remain employed, he faced the predicament he feared most—a catastrophic expansion of leisure.

With one-seventh of the world's land surface at his disposal, he was the least menaced by an internal explosion of population, but he was terrified of an explosive increase in barren time. The steady introduction of automation, which he had been able to delay but not prevent, had already produced the five-hour day. To some extent his planners had managed to offset the threat which idle hands and minds will always pose in a rigidly controlled society by ensuring that most workers had to spend at least ten hours a week commuting to the overgrown cities and new towns. But the State had reached saturation on what it could do in the way of welfare centers, workers' holiday camps, parks of culture, riverboat tours, and other instruments of mass sedation.

The Spartan Turganov had a passionate devotion to discipline. To him the undisciplined mind was like an unfenced steppe over which ideas rage as a riotously as stampeding cattle. Discipline sets up the fences so necessary to constructive action, and the picture he foresaw of long lingering youth was accompanied by a dangerous decline in the national compliance. The widespread use of SP47 might dislocate the bone structure of the State simply for the benefit of the individual.

In spite of their belief that Communism has nothing in common with capitalism, the thirteen men and one woman of the Presidium found that their economic objections to a rapid increase in lifespan were the same as those discerned by Merton and his Cabinet. Indeed, they realized that their brittle political structure was far less capable of accommodating to such a fundamental change than Britain's.

"I put it to you, comrades, that for the foreseeable future this unnatural development, so greedily embraced by the capitalists, could do nothing but harm to our glorious socialist State," Turganov pronounced to the Presidium.

With some relief the Deputy Prime Minister responsible for industry immediately agreed, pointing out that a sudden increase in the labor market would bring chaos to the next two five-year plans. The resetting of output targets and the reallocation of manpower posed stupendous problems of administration.

The Minister for Agriculture reminded his comrades of the knife-edge of famine on which they already lived, because of an always possible failure of the Siberian crops on which, they knew, they had become too reliant.

It remained to Anatoli Belitsky, the astute Foreign Minister, to make the full political point which was in the minds of all of them —that where the nuclear bomb had failed to resolve the struggle for world leadership by becoming unusable, the population bomb might well succeed.

"Comrades, both Marx and Lenin insisted that capitalism contains the seeds of its own destruction, and it has been some surprise to all of us that these seeds have taken so long to germinate," Belitsky said. "Capitalism, as we know, has proved more resistant to its inner decay than had been imagined. But to me, this unstable new situation in the West is surely the result of one of those inherent contradictions in capitalism which, as Marxism-Leninism predicts, only needs to be allowed to express itself fully for disaster to ensue. The British government clearly saw the threats to the survival of the capitalist state it serves, but such was the weakness of its structure that it was powerless to prevent what it foresaw as a disaster because of the impossibility of infringing what it calls 'Personal liberty.'

"The weakness of capitalism lies in the liberty needed to support it, as the weakness of a wineglass is in its stem." Belitsky poured himself a drink of water to give time for his simile to be appreciated, then continued. "We know from our deliberations today that in this case history will judge this liberty to have been license—a license to commit national suicide. Fortunately, our beloved people can be spared this danger. We do not give them freedom to starve and we shall not give them freedom to destroy themselves or their heritage.

"It seems to me, comrades, that our path is clearly defined by dialectic," Belitsky continued, adjusting his rimless glasses. "We must take the most rigid precautions to keep this evil drug out of our happy land and let it do its work for us on the other side of what the imperialists call the Iron Curtain. Even that barrier, so wisely erected by our predecessors against the infiltration of counterrevolutionary ideas, may now play a dominant role in our destiny. For we must not be so unrealistic as to forget that the temptation of longer life would be a difficult one to resist for many of our weaker comrades. We must ensure that they hear nothing about it."

Belitsky's argument was quickly approved as policy by Turganov and the others, who had experienced the usual mixture of annoyance and satisfaction at finding their original thoughts crystallized in someone else's telling words, and the Minister for State Security was given the responsibility for ensuring that the drug and any further public knowledge of it was kept out of the Soviet Union. But since committees are the same the world over, this one ended in some degree of compromise. It was decided to continue the basic research into the potentialities of the drug but to restrict its use to a small number of people who would not be told what they were being given. From the results, which would be analyzed over a long period, the effects of its general use could then be more accurately extrapolated. Human nature also being what it is, irrespective of geography, Maxim Turganov saw to it that he was one of the few—and the only one of the Presidium—selected to take it. At fifty-seven, he was highly sensitive to the fact that the high tide of life is brief, and was desperately anxious that a few more of his marks should remain on the sands when it ebbed.

There was no difficulty in justifying his decision to make a medical exception of himself. Vanity was one of the pockmarks of power which he had not escaped, and he had convinced himself that the national programs would suffer if they fell too early under the control of the thrusting and too inexperienced Belitsky.

Unlike Merton, he was at no risk of public censure. There were no Parliamentary questions in the People's Democracy and no Morgan Owens or John Holts to get in his hair.

The Minister for State Security lost no time in putting his instructions into effect. Foreign newspapers, even including the *Daily Worker*, had been banned, as a precaution, from the time of the Merton crisis. A strict censorship of press cables and telephone messages was reintroduced. The corps of foreign journalists dwindled to eventual extinction, as applications for visas and permits lay conveniently forgotten in the Cambrian layers of officials' in trays. Visits by foreign tourists, progressively encouraged over the previous fifteen years, were first made difficult through visa delays and then made impossible. The movement of scientists in and out of Russia was forbidden. A subtle propaganda drive to discredit "Western" medical science as inferior to the Russian brand was introduced, rising to a level of bitterness reminiscent of the long-forgotten Lysenko genetics controversy. And this time it was also directed, with even greater scorn, at Chinese science, which was projected as a pitiful attempt by a nation of coolies to compete in fields hopelessly beyond their technical and intellectual capacities.

The restrictions were imposed with particular ruthlessness in the satellite countries. Extra fortifications were added to the brutal barricade of barbed wire and minefields stretching two thousand miles from Austria to the Baltic, and, though less continuously, along the Soviet-Chinese border. Mutilating booby traps operated by photoelectric cells, television eyes, and other refinements that made the medieval mantrap seem benign were set up along the frontier between East and West Germany, where the pull of blood relationship might overcome submission to authority. The Berlin wall was electrified. Few, except border guards themselves, made successful escapes. There were savage shootings and other sordid incidents given maximum publicity in the West. At Marchegg on the Austro-Czech-Slovak border, a four-year-old boy strayed across the agreed boundary, and his mother was too frightened to go forward to bring him back. The Communist border guards simply watched while he walked onto the minefield, where he was blown to bits under his mother's eyes.

Such events received no mention in *Pravda* or *Izvestia*, but the domestic restrictions demanded some acceptable explanation. The inevitable solution was to present each of them via the rigidly controlled newspapers and radio, as an unfortunate precaution necessitated by new warlike moves by the West. Since the test-ban agreement, negotiated back in 1963, there had been a gradual reduction of East-West tension beneficial to both sides and to the neutral nations. So the new truculence was misinterpreted by the Western ambassadors in Moscow and by the newspaper "Kremlinologists" in the West as the result of a Party upheaval, in which the aggressive Red Army generals, headed by the impassive Defense Minister, Marshal Volkoff, had triumphed over the liberal policy of Turganov, who could be expected to be demoted to the managership of a Siberian power station at any moment. As the months passed, though Turganov remained in the key positions, all the old suspicions of Soviet military intent were resurrected.

In China, the official reaction to SP47 was somewhat different but the result was the same. Since the young and uncompromising General Ho Cheng had seized power, soon after the death of Mao-Tse Tung, it had become admitted as public policy that the grossly excessive population was a detriment to progress. Any development that threatened to negate the birth control program, which was just beginning to be effective after a prodigious effort against ingrained ignorance and habit, was anathema to the more progressive, if more repressive, regime. So the government decided to exercise strict control by similar methods to those adopted by the Russians. Inevitably, a black market in the drug began to operate through Hong Kong, but this was ruthlessly suppressed by shootings—which further exacerbated the renascence of tension between East and West.

India, too, which had managed to remain out of the Communist camp and was beginning to reap the benefits of a contraceptive program pushed forward against rocklike religious opposition, also decided to exercise control, though with mixed success.

In Europe, the United States, and all other countries where liberty was assumed as an inalienable right, the equivalent of Juvenex was made available either to all or to all who could afford to pay for it.

chapter 18

The effect of mass medication by SP47 was most quickly observable in the business-lunch restaurants and clubs where the proportion of fat men magically declined. The drug rapidly raised the body's metabolic rate so that the accumulated fat of middle-age sloth and indulgence was consumed by internal fire of youthful intensity. The feeling of well-being and added vigor accompanying the loss of surplus weight enhanced the rapture which men and women were experiencing from the marked improvement in their looks, except in the case of those few like Dr. Holmes, who had been nondescript until age had endowed them with an air of distinction. In the general euphoria Dr. Harvey was hailed as the greatest benefactor of all time, a triumph in which Morgan Owen and his administration were given their full measure of acclaim, even by people to whom the word Socialist had been a term of abuse.

The undertakers did not suffer too severely during the first few months after Lord Butcher achieved his target date and capsules of Juvenex became generally available on doctor's prescription. There was a substantial backlog of people already too frail and internally damaged by disease for the drugs to be of any benefit to them, but as these died off the number of funerals became more and more restricted to those whose lives were ended by accidents, and these were not nearly enough to support the five thousand men who had so far made their living through the dying. After the conquest of the virus diseases back in the nineteen-sixties, they had managed to survive by increasing their fees to something like the exorbitant American scales after an advertising campaign had persuaded enough Britons that they had been inflicting hardship on their relatives too long by burying or cremating them unembalmed in unsprung, unquilted coffins, but they could not hope to repeat that tactic.

The insurance companies also experienced a chill breeze as people began to feel less pressure to insure against their death or retirement, but this fall in business was soon made more than good by the growing demand for home loans.

It was a year before the housing shortage began to be a subject of national concern. In the past about a hundred thousand houses had become vacant annually through the deaths of their owners, and these now looked as if they would remain occupied indefinitely. It was clear to the Housing Minister that the only expedient would be to build temporary prefabricated homes designed to last ten years but in the nature of political promises intended to be in use for twenty.

A growing number of young couples were forced into living with their parents, and this situation, always a potent source of friction, was enormously exacerbated by the problem of coping with the old people who were recovering their vigor. Thousands of men who had settled into the routine of retirement, accepting its restrictions along with its recompenses, experienced a resurgence of energy and appetites which had to be converted into activity of some kind. The disparagement of self-esteem that accompanies normal aging disappeared, and old men regenerated their faded pride in their appearance. Many were imbued with the drive to reenter the realms of productive work, and suffered profound frustration when they found the doors barred to them. Those who attempted to sublimate their excess energy in golf soon found themselves killing most of their time at the nineteenth hole.

Wives who had readily embraced the calm of sterility that follows the menopausal storm suddenly discovered that they were distressingly fertile. Men whose essential hydraulics had long since ceased to respond to the hunger of their eyes, and who for years had enjoyed their release from the bondage of desire, quickly disproved the commonly held fallacy that there is a preordained limit to the number of occasions on which a male can demonstrate his virility. So after the pharmaceutical manufacturers, the abortionists were the first to benefit from Dr. Harvey's great advance. But many hundreds of children were born to elderly couples and elderly spinsters, in that first year of the widespread use of Juvenex, creating havoc in private homes and a new problem for the almshouses and adoption centers.

A few years before, when the British Medical Association health magazine *Family* had offered a prize for the oldest attested mother, a woman of fifty-five had won it, but headlines like "Great Grandmother of Eighty-four Has 8-Pound Son" were becoming common. To the younger people the birth of so many children to the old seemed disgusting. Men of sixty who were grandfathers were finding themselves with a baby brother. Great uncles were younger than their great nephews, sons were younger than great-grandsons, and wills were being changed with consequent family discord.

There was a further disturbing development, which had been quite unforeseen, that threatened to throw society out of emotional balance. This was a sudden increase in the proportion of baby boys to baby girls. Scientists had long suspected that, for some quite unknown reason, about 130 boys are conceived for every 100 girls, but so many male conceptions miscarry that the proportions at birth are down to about 106 boys to 100 girls, and this is leveled out further by the higher rate of infant mortality among males. Now it seemed that Juvenex, circulating in the pregnant woman's blood, was preserving most of the male embryos that had previously died. If this continued, it foreshadowed a huge surplus of men, a high scarcity value for women, and the prospect of a steep rise in homosexuality, though the last was likely to cause little public concern since Owen's administration had relaxed the laws and social objections to masculine malpractice.

At that stage the only move by the Government, which was reluctant to interfere with the most personal of remaining liberties, was to award a block grant to the Family Planning Association and to step up propaganda to encourage birth control, but such gestures were powerless against an impulse to mate, which had never been so imperious in so many homes.

What Hastings Maclaren called "the pestilence of procreation" was the first widespread threat to survival over which every responsible adult could exert control. With wars, with the build-up of nuclear arms, with recessions, the people could blame their leaders and claim, with justice, that, short of revolution, they could have wielded little effective influence. Yet with their own fertility so obviously menacing their living standards, as well as those of their children, they put their immediate need for sexual satisfaction and their long-term need for children first. The scientists offered a sure protection against the threat of excessive reproduction, but too many millions throughout the world declined it.

Soon almost every established marriage was complicated by the mental readjustments necessitated by the rapid physical changes in husbands and wives. Some couples found their more youthful appearance and increased vigor mutually more exciting. Marriages about to expire from inanition were revivified, but there were many more consorts who found the readjustment painful or impossible. Some, who over the years had built up a smoothly working relationship, now found themselves as mutually abrasive as two sheets of sandpaper. Other unions, accepted by both partners as permanent because no alternative was ever likely to present itself, were menaced by the subtle realization that suddenly time had become available in which to make a successful remarriage. The sixty-year-olds no longer considered themselves as too old for divorce, and the reawakening of their sexual drive intensified the tendency toward break-up. In the face of such an unexpected situation to which society had not been given time to condition itself, the bedrock in which so many families felt their future was securely anchored proved as friable as pumice.

In the first two years of Juvenex the mortality for marriage nearly doubled, and since the obituary columns were almost empty, the *Times* replaced them by daily divorce columns—"Fraser—Clifford and Jessica, formerly of Hereford, on November 29th at the Law Courts, London, the marriage was dissolved. Aged 16. No letters please." As usual, the law, with all the inertia of its machinery, lagged far behind society's requirements for shedding the marital load, and the courts could not cope, thereby intensifying the frustration of those anxious to unshackle themselves.

A few MPs tried to introduce private members' bills to expedite the divorce procedure, but the Government was too busy trying to cope with the early effects of the drugs in industry and business. Top executives scheduled to retire at sixty-five had lost all resolve to do so. The numbers of those who took advantage of their increased vigor to enjoy an active retirement was minute, compared with those who decided that they need not retire after all. Having found that their failing grasp of the reins of control was suddenly strong and supple again, they lost all desire to release them.

So in factories, offices, laboratories, in almost every habitat of employment throughout the Western world, promotions were brought to a halt and the young, ambitious worker faced unshiftable roadblocks in the way of his advancement. Youth's high-pitched cry of "Make way there" was drowned by the more authoritative response of "Hold back." Before the conflict between youth and age had become fierce enough to threaten the whole structure of society, the elderly took some satisfaction from reversing the insult of retirement, which the young had previously inflicted on them.

It was not only that the old men were refusing to make way for selfish reasons. They were fully justified in hanging onto office because their combination of long experience and renewed vigor was overwhelming in straight competition. The younger, who in the past had depended on their stronger drive and bolder outlook, were outclassed by men who could match those qualities and could offer wisdom and experience as well.

The top executives could hardly force compulsory retirement on their employees while avoiding it themselves: nor did they want to get rid of the tried and trusted men below them who had suddenly acquired additional value. Only in the civil service and other organizations, where tradition was so entrenched that geological time was needed to wear it away, was retirement at sixty-five rigidly maintained, and even there, the men at the top were making more and more exceptions of themselves.

As the dead men's shoes remained filled by agile feet, the surge of back-pressure in the employment current quickly made itself felt at the source. For every man or woman who did not move up, there was one less job for a school-leaving boy or girl. Youth was still thrusting to be served, and as Robert's nineteen-year-old son, Paul, put it in a hurtful letter to his father, the service seemed like being interminably interrupted.

"I like the work in advertising," he wrote from London, "but the future look absolutely stagnant. There's no movement inside the agency or much hope of transferring to another. The fogeys at the top look like being fixtures as permanent as the gargoyles on Notre

Dame. A few of us were talking about it over lunch yesterday, and I must say that your name came in for some pretty harsh abuse—and I got the backwash. I thought that being your son was going to be a help, but as far as the younger people are concerned, it will pay me to keep quiet about it."

At all social levels natural rights of inheritance were threatened. Few normal people consciously want their elders to depart, but neither do they want them to outstay their occupancy. The assumption that property and privilege are held only in relatively short leasehold had always been fundamental to civilized living. From the sons of the smallest shopkeepers to the heirs of the great estates, millions began to realize that this assumption was no longer warranted. In the general moral disarmament the romantic notion that "any man's death diminishes me" could not survive the material fact that so many were impatient for somebody's death to increase them.

Of the three basic requirements for a tolerably satisfying life—someone to care, somewhere to live, and something worthwhile to do—the last two were immediately threatened for thousands by the rise in unemployment, and since love is usually limited by the duress it can take, so, indirectly, was the first. The economists warned that a massive increase in unemployment was inevitable, with all the perils of its quicklime corrosion of morale. The trade unions, too, were vocal in this regard, but their leaders, who tended to be at least in their late fifties, were noticeably reluctant to urge the Government to legislate for compulsory retirement.

"I believed I was going to be faced with the headache of too many jobs for too few men, but instead I've got the heartache of seeing too many men chasing too few jobs," Owen said despondently to his wife.

The first observable result of these assaults on the rights of maturing man was an increase in crime. The undertow of teenage resentment expressed itself in a wave of violence that spread from the dance halls, jazz clubs, and streets and even reached into the schoolroom. Newspaper reports of incidents in which teachers had been attacked in their classes by unruly boys had made little impact on Robert until Simon's headmaster telephoned to inform him that his son was being questioned by the police. A gang of fifth-formers had beaten and kicked an elderly master at night, and though nothing was ever proved against him, Simon, a talented but somewhat neurotic child, was among the suspects.

The current successors to the Mods and Rockers, the mid-sixties gangs of youths and girls who invented the game of swooping on seaside towns on motorcycles, to fight and destroy property for the fun of it, called themselves Georgians and Martians. The Georgians sought sartorial inspiration further back than the earlier Teddy Boys and had adopted the fancy waistcoats, cravats, knee-breeches, and buckled shoes of Regency days—garb quickly provided by the East End sweatshops. The Martians owed their name to their quilted protective motorcycling suits and bulging crash-helmets fitted with built-in transistor radios so that not a moment of jazz need be missed. Their excesses stole the headlines, especially when the Government had to ban the sale of sword-canes after the Georgians revived the practice of dueling at dawn, but the Home Office was even more shocked by the unprecedented rise in "white-collar" crime—fraud, embezzlement, forgery—by middle-aged men, many of whom had no previous offenses.

A further symptom of this frustration was the resurgence of anti-Semitism, directed particularly against Lewis Rosenfeld, who had originally financed the research resulting in Juvenex.

In Parliament, the muted voice of the Tory minority, with Hastings Maclaren as its most persistent spokesman, called for repressive measures.

"I warn this House that unless action is taken now to withdraw this unnatural drug from general use, we shall see all belief in the sanctity of human life eroded within this decade," he declared, stabbing the air with his bony finger. "We are spawning a generation of hardened thugs, to whom the constraints necessary to a civilized life mean nothing. Through denying the satisfactions of work, which are the main source of self-respect, we face a complete breakdown of law and order and we are doing nothing to prevent it. It was my view that this witches' brew was an evil defiant to God's purpose when it was first drawn to my attention when I was Minister of Health three years ago. I suspect I may be alone in this House as having resisted the temptation to embrace this evil myself," he said, looking around the quarter-filled benches sanctimoniously.

"This crisis in crime is giving us just a glimpse of the disasters to come—disasters which the previous Government foresaw so clearly and tried to prevent. Knowledge is not self-regulating. Science is not automatically producing the solutions to the new problems its discoveries present. I urge the Government to exercise control not only of this menacing youth drug but over all the advances with which the mind may not yet be fitted to cope. What is happening today convinces me that some censorship of science is essential."

Unfortunately, by this time Maclaren had become regarded as something of a Bible-punching crank both by Parliament and by the public, for whom rigid recitude has little appeal. The cartoonists portrayed him as a modern John Knox whose hellfire demons had white jackets instead of red cloaks and test tubes instead of forks. Owen derided him as having "frost in his belly." Only the Home Secretary, who was burdened with the problem of overcrowded prisons, and John, who had made his peace with Maclaren and was listening in the press gallery, heard the speech with sympathy. Owen and the rest of the men whose office had been confirmed by a further General Election had been too long attached to the view that criminals are mentally ill or suffering from social deprivation to give the police and courts additional powers. All they did was to set up a commission, composed mainly of psychiatric vivisectors of the criminal mind, who could offer no more positive action than to go on scratching like chickens in the deep litter of repressed experiences.

Nevertheless, it was Maclaren's insistent condemnation of the drugs which forced the Church into its first major pronouncement on them. Hamstrung by its obstinate battle against birth control, the Church of Rome was powerless to do anything but welcome the additional members of her faith, however late their arrival, though the social outlook for overcrowded Italy was grim indeed. For the Church of England it was easier. From the Palace of Lambeth, the Archbishop of Canterbury issued a measured statement condemning the general use of the drugs as an unnatural interference with God's intentions. Preachers were enjoined to point out from the pulpit the grand purpose of death in the Divine ordinance, but the Archbishop was in some theological difficulty in drawing any distinction between the accepted use of God-given drugs like penicillin, which preserved life, and the satanic Juvenex, which postponed death.

His embarrassment was even greater when the atheistic Morgan Owen—"Some of my best friends are Christians"—arranged for the newspapers to be quietly told that the reason the Archbishop had not been seen in public for so long was because he had been taking Juvenex himself.

Owen had been lost to religion from the day that the village preacher announced as his text "Blessed are the meek: for they shall inherit the earth," and young Morgan commented, too audibly, "Yes, six feet of it." The preacher, who carried great weight in the community, had never ceased to ridicule and harry the boy, creating in him a lifelong antipathy toward all clerics. But even without the Prime Minster's hindrance, the archiepiscopal utterances were bound to go unheeded. Extended life in this world was infinitely more attractive than the unproved prospect of eternal life in the next. So the rejuvenating capsule became the modern sacrament, and the more remote that death was made to seem, the emptier the churches became. Evangelical drives for a "great spiritual revival" and stopgap gimmicks like pop religious music and even the introduction of the shake, the blue beat, and other dances static enough to be possible in a pew, had no influence on the swelling numbers of sinners. As Morgan Owen put it—prudently in private conversation—"It's no coincidence that the bulk of every congregation is composed of those who suspect that their call to account may not be long delayed."

He believed that in Western civilization the fear of death has always been at the root of religion and that immortality was invented to keep alive the essential day-to-day assurance that we shall be here tomorrow.

By the fluke of their strange creed, only the strict adherents to Christian Science were immune to the lure of the longer life, and even some of those resolved the difficulty by joining the general trend to regard Juvenex less as a medicine than as a welfare food, to be tossed down with the orange juice and cod liver oil.

These events were closely paralleled in the rest of the free world, where elected governments found it impossible to interfere with what had quickly become a right as inalienable as daily access to cow's milk, and no more artificial.

The nuances of national pathology were reflected in the scale and nature of the reactions in the different countries. In the U.S., where nearly two millions who should have died each year failed to do so, crime was more violent, with proliferation of protection rackets, gang warfare, and graft. The Negroes took the brunt of the exasperation. Membership in the Ku Klux Klan soared, and fiery crosses burned almost nightly on the hills of the southern states. Lynched bodies hung from trees, and many of them were white, for movements like the Black Muslims had organized Negro resistance.

In South America there were still more revolutions; in India yet more beggars; in Sweden even more drunks. In France, where prolonged exposure to political instability had immunized the public against warnings of chaos to come, the material difficulties created by the youth drug were more than offset by the increased bonus of lengthened libido. In West Germany, where the channeling of spite toward the Jews swelled to its former virulence, there were more secret meetings of incensed young patriots in beer cellars.

All that the British government did was to set up committees and introduce piecemeal measures to blunt the impact of the immediate problems. The U. S. President provided increasingly bigger unemployment benefits at the expense of foreign aid and other expenditures. The South American dictators introduced martial law. The Indian government appealed for help both to the Russians and to the West. The Swedes brought in a new rationing system for alcohol. The German Chancellor denied the existence of any underground political activities. In France, President Artois stumped about his country singing the Marseillaise.

All then drove on, for the time being optimistically, down the dual highway toward destruction.

Item by detailed item, these social developments were relayed to Moscow by the Soviet embassy staffs in the meticulous routine reporting, which is one of Communism's most indelible brands. As Maxim Turganov, now looking and feeling ten years younger himself, studied the summaries with satisfaction, he felt genuinely grateful to live under a political system where any such incipient chaos, conceived in the name of individual freedom, could be quickly aborted by unchallengeable authority.

chapter 19

Sir Robert Harvey quickly joined the ranks of those to whom every day is one thousand four hundred and forty mortgaged minutes. He was working continuously in overdrive, a slave to the telephone, his creative time consumed by administration and committees, his leisure by shop-talk lunches, ceremonial dinners, and the international scientific conferences, which spawned themselves out of his original discovery like bacteria spreading in a culture dish. Even his fellowship of the Royal Society ate further into his freedom. The awareness that he now had additional active years ahead did not reduce the pressure of the day's demands for him or for any other self-driving executive, for whom overwork was a drug of addiction.

For years, Robert had based decisions on how to allot his time on the simple four-point guideline—duty, pleasure, cash, or merit. When requested to do something demanding time, he had asked himself, Is it my duty? Is there any pleasure in it? Is there any cash? Is there any merit? If the answer to all these questions was negative or marginal, he declined. Now demands on his time were so relentless that he was tending to cut out activities involving pleasure alone. As Shirley, who was loaded with more and more of the experimental work, was finding out, there is nothing like a full professional diary for keeping a man out of mischief.

By this time, under the impact of irritability, increased by his efforts to stretch out the day by cutting down on sleep, Robert's marriage was being held together by little more than habit and concern for the children. After the first time that Margaret had made it clear she knew about Shirley, Robert had decided that in view of his professional responsibilities, his enhanced social position, and the children, he would really have to sacrifice his mistress. Once again he levied the resolve to tell Shirley that their love affair must finish. And once again, instead of creating a fuss, she was cunningly sympathetic. They avoided meeting outside the laboratory for a couple of weeks, but Robert's carnal demon commandeered its full share of the urge generated by the Juvenex, and the solemn sacrificial decision quickly degenerated into an agreement that they would have to be even more careful where and how they met. But once Margaret's suspicions had been aroused she became sensitive to nuances of misbehavior that would normally have escaped her attention. Robert kept up the pretense of fidelity with the affectionate kiss as he went off to visit his mistress, and though his wife was basically opposed to bringing down the mellowed edifice of their marriage, she found there was a limit to the length of time she could knowingly live with Judas. The streak of cruelty in most men and the capacity to irritate present in all women were mutually reinforcing, leading to vitriolic rows which steadily etched into the remnant of belief that divorce was not for them. What for years had been unthinkable was rarely from their thoughts.

The public attention paid to Margaret, as the wife of a great scientist, roughened the relationship still further. As Lady Harvey she was in demand to open fetes and preside on boards of charities. Having been in the domestic background so long, she reveled in describing in newsprint and television interviews the difficulty of being married to an illustrious innovator.

"Lady Harvey, I would like your views on woman's role as the wife of a famous scientist," Margaret was asked on television by a waspish woman interviewer intent on snaring her into commenting about Shirley, to whom the gossip columnists had been making pointed allusions. "As a woman who is not a scientist herself, to what extent do you think you have contributed to your husband's enormous success?"

"To such an extent that I think that his research papers would have been more informative if they had been signed 'By R. Harvey, M.D., with indispensable support from Margaret Harvey,' but if this sort of tribute ever occurred to a scientist, I've no doubt it would be ruled out as an unprofessional intrusion of sentiment."

"Did his research reports record the fact that you were his first human guinea pig for Juvenex after he tried it on himself three years ago?"

"Not by name. I was simply listed as 'Subject No 2.' "

"That does seem unfair, Lady Harvey, especially as so much credit has been given to his assistant, Dr. Howard," the interviewer added smartly.

"Miss Howard, really," Margaret said with a disparaging look. "She's not a real doctor—not medically qualified, you know. Just a Ph.D."

"Lady Harvey, one of the newspapers quotes you as saying that your husband is very untidy about the house. Isn't it strange that a man with such a tidy mind should have untidy habits?"

"Oh, he's got a two-tone temperament in many ways," Margaret replied, warming up to the theme of the program, which was called "Speaking Frankly."

"Which other ways?"

"Well, like a lot of scientists, he has a genius for understanding nature and an outsize capacity for misunderstanding people."

"Finally, Lady Harvey, as a mother of three children, what do you think about the increase in the divorce rate which is being attributed to your husband's discovery?"

"Oh, it might not be such a bad thing. Two or even three marriages may be needed to rub the rough edges off some men."

Such indecent exposure of his character defects infuriated Robert, but they were but a prelude to the embarrassment he suffered when Margaret sold her story to a Sunday newspaper as much to spite Shirley as for the £6,000 she received.

Inevitably, these changes in her life brought her into contact with men. She had responded exceptionally well to the treatment, having had it longer than any other woman, and her physical desires were strong again. So it was not long before Robert's flagrant inattention and her increasing exposure to the flaying edge of his tongue brought its result.

While having greater need of Shirley to smooth out his emotional peaks, Robert was finding himself caught up late in London so often that though, by nature, he was an unclubbable type, he was spending more and more nights in the severe celibacy of the United Universities Club.

It was on such an evening, in early November, that he was sitting alone in the smoking room reading the *Times* over a nightcap when Butcher walked in. It was a moment for mutual congratulation, for a few hours previously, the teletype in the hall had tapped out the announcement that in a major reshuffle Butcher had been appointed Foreign Secretary.

Owen had realized the advantage of having the heavily burdened Foreign Secretary in the Lords, where he was freed from constituency duties and Parliamentary questions, and Butcher had made a fine public reputation through his administrative triumph with the Juvenex project.

This well-anticipated change followed only two days after the official confirmation that Robert and Shirley had been jointly awarded the Nobel Prize for Medicine. For the past twenty years the Swedish award committee had shown an increasing tendency to give the prize to a team, and since all Robert's major papers had been jointly signed by Shirley there was no way of awarding the tax-free £20,000 to him without including her. Further, the committee was keen to nominate a woman to buttress the general façade of sex equality.

Robert was still churned up by the destructive verbal battle with Margaret, that had followed her realization that Shirley would have to go with them to Stockholm to receive the prize and gold medal from the hands of Sweden's king. In her anger at Shirley's elevation to a degree of fame she believed to be quite unmerited, at the sharing of the money, and at the prospect of having to put on a gracious act in front of so many people, she had declared that she would not go with him, and with no more constructive comment than "Then bloody well stay away," he had stamped out of the house at Porton enervated for the day, and later made the few fog patches an excuse to himself for failing to go home.

After the handshake Butcher, who was in a more mellow mood, asked, "Is anything wrong? You looked terribly fed up when I came in. Derek Hewitson will be looking after you as Minister of Science now, but don't hesitate to approach me if there's anything I can do."

Robert had no wish to discuss his private life, but needing to talk with somebody, he turned the conversation to the first convenient question, "Well, Frank, how do you feel about achieving so much ambition?"

Butcher paused to take off his spectacles and polish them (for Juvenex could not remedy short-sightedness)."It's exhilarating tonight, but I'm afraid that all my life I've found fulfillment as elusive as a wisp of snipe. And I've no doubt this will turn out the same way. Even the thrill of being called to the Government and being given a peerage was extraordinarily fleeting. The sort of success we've achieved has demanded such effort that I really feel there ought to be more reward inside, if you see what I mean."

"Perfectly, Frank. I'm surprised to find we're so similar, but then maybe every compulsive worker's the same. I was thrilled at getting a knighthood, but the lift was very temporary. Now I know that even the Nobel Prize, which until SP47 turned up was never more than a wild dream for me, will give me no permanent feeling of satisfaction inside. I know I'll just flog on under the illusion that the next success will bring some peace of mind."

Butcher shook his head. "You know what the Americans say. Peace of mind is for the birds. Anyway, I'm convinced it's not for the likes of us. Our trouble may be that because we both started poor we developed a habit of work which we can't give up without feeling guilty about it. I didn't dare fail an examination at the university, because I knew my parents could never afford to keep me there if my scholarship was withdrawn. So I did nothing but work, and have never been able to stop. Since then I've always been haunted by the fear of losing my job, no matter how much real security I acquired. Odd! I suppose it's a legacy from having poor parents who used to worry about it. I think it's one of the things that made me a Socialist."

"There's no doubt, Frank, that all success does in the end is put you on the treadmill of more work. I may be a bit depressed tonight, but life just seems to be Mount Slog, rearing ahead with an endless succession of false tops and no time even to look at the view."

"Oh, cheer up, it's not that bad," said Butcher, pressing the bell for more drinks. "But this Foreign Office job is certainly going to mean more work for me, though how the hell I can pack more in, God knows."

"I suppose it'll mean a lot of social life, too. I'd hate that."

"I'm afraid there's no dodging it. I've had a taste of it tonight at the Russian embassy. I've just come from the October Revolution Party—which for some reason they always hold in November. I can see that going through the motions of being friendly, when they've reverted to calling us jackals and lickspittle lackeys of the Americans, is going to be quite an exercise. The whole place was seething with so-called diplomats, who are almost all intelligence agents posted here to subvert and destroy us. Of course, the fellow-travelers from Westminster were all there, pawing over the Ambassador to get the next free trip to Russia."

"I've never been to the Russian embassy or met many Russians for that matter," Robert interposed. "You see they even stopped Vladimirsky, their best nuclear physicist, from accepting the Nobel Prize for physics because it would have meant his leaving the country."

"Oh, they'd never invite you, Robert. They have to go on pretending that you and your youth drug don't exist, though how long they can keep it up I don't know. However, I noticed that the Russian Ambassador seemed to have more hair than last time I saw him. By the way, I spotted your very attractive partner there— Miss Howard, or is it Dr. Howard?"

"Doctor. She's had her Ph.D. some time, and she'll get her D.Sc. soon and almost certainly her FRS. Even the fuddyduddies in the Royal Society can hardly keep her out with the Nobel Prize. She's quite ambitious, you know. She wants a chair, and I've no doubt she'll get one."

"Well, she was there with John Holt from the *Daily Dispatch*, so presumably he'd taken her along. The place was creeping with journalists."

Robert could not help looking surprised. Shirley had told him she would be staying down in Salisbury until the weekend to avoid being pestered by journalists, and instead she was out in London with the most notorious one of them all.

Feeling that this deception was all he needed to round off a really appalling day, Robert bade Butcher good night. Though neither was yet aware of it, the day had been a critical one in the private lives of both of them.

138

Like most Cabinet Ministers and Opposition leaders, Butcher had attended the party at the Russian embassy in Kensington Palace Gardens in line of duty. As he joined the queue waiting to shake hands with the Ambassador and visiting Soviet generals, he eyed the flattering head-and-shoulder painting of Turganov above the grotesque marble chimney-piece with its artificial fire. The wide-apart, brown eyes seemed to be gazing wistfully toward the landing, which accommodated the full-size portrait of Lenin, the only Russian whose character seemed immune to assassination. The first person he had noticed on entering the long room, where a hundred people were crushed around the tables crammed with food and drink was the tall figure of his House of Lords colleague Lord Fayverdale, who, as usual, was accompanied by a particularly beautiful woman.

Butcher, whose personality had expanded with his environment, was still generally immune to women, in spite of the stimulant effect of the product to which he owed his promotion, but as Fayverdale introduced him to Miss Diana Douglas, he not only noticed her fine head with its arch of blonde hair framing a face of compelling remembrance: taking in the full inventory of her physical and psychic presence, he was also conscious that she was the most beautiful entity he had ever seen, man-made or God-made. For the first time in his life, he experienced that strange polarization which interconnects some personalities on sight, like lines of magnetic force.

"Diana is beautiful, isn't she? And very dedicated to being a woman," Fayverdale said languidly, sensing Butcher's obvious reaction. "I tell her she owes it all to the Juvenex you provided. Maybe she'll tell you how old she is—which she won't tell me—while I get us all some more vodka and caviar. With all these gannets at it, we'll be on cheap red wine and chipolatas before we can say 'Karl Marx.' Excuse me."

Left alone for a few moments, which merged into minutes, as Fayverdale talked in Russian to the Soviet naval attaché by the buffet table, Butcher experienced an extraordinary sense of ease with Diana. The awkwardness he felt with most women seemed to dissipate, and he noticed that she was not so tall that she accentuated his own lack of inches as so many did.

"It's easy to see that our Soviet friends are still not allowed to use Juvenex. Every bald head in the room is on Russian shoulders," he said, leaning toward Diana to be heard above the background murmur. "Perhaps they console themselves by saying that each day they look a little more like Lenin."

"Their heads still seem to be pretty productive inside, though," Diana remarked, putting down her empty glass. "Those I've talked to seem very sharp."

"Oh, I know I'll have to keep my wits about me when I'm dealing with them, Miss Douglas. Why we all come to celebrate their wretched Revolution when these people bode us so much ill I can't think. I'm supposed to be here in the interests of diplomatic relations, but there are hardly any left. Still, if we were to restrict diplomatic relations to countries with internal policies we admire we should soon find ourselves alone. Tell me, what's your interest here?"

"Well, I just came along with Tony Fayverdale really, but I am interested in left-wing politics and even more in left-wing politicians," she added provocatively. "Is your wife here?"

"No. My wife's in the country. She prefers cats to Russians."

"Which do you prefer?"

"Neither. Frankly I dislike cats, but I see now that they may have served some purpose in my life. If I could learn to coexist with cats for the sake of domestic peace, I can learn to coexist with Russians."

Diana laughed. "Yes, I see they have something in common. They are both quick to show their claws when it suits them, and you can never tell what's going on in the heads of either."

As he watched enraptured, Butcher noticed that Diana was one of those rare women with a double smile. In normal merriment her mouth expanded in what seemed to be an ultimate smile, but when she was especially amused or happy, her upper lip arched itself into an additional curl, a most intriguing expression, which she could also feign.

"Regrettably, I have to circulate," he whispered, seeing the Ambassador with Dorothy Jordan-Bell in tow, bearing down on him. "I would like to find out just how left-wing you like your politicians and whether I would qualify as 'interesting.' Perhaps we could discuss it over dinner some time," he added, amazed at his audacity.

"I'd love to, so long as it's not in the country. I like to think the country's there, but I'm conditioned to concrete and allergic to mud."

"I shall be moving into the Foreign Secretary's residence in a few days' time. I'm determined there are going to be no cats there, so I don't suppose I shall be seeing much of my wife. Perhaps you would dine with me there?"

"That would be delightful. You can ring me at my flat, or if I'm not there, you can always contact me through Tony," she said invitingly as Butcher was led away into the grim conservatory, with its spiky evergreens and hanging Aladdin's lamps.

"How did you get on?" Fayverdale asked, after his deliberate delay over getting the drinks.

"Couldn't have been better. Odd little man, pompous, opinionated, but amusing and obviously very bright. He soon made it clear that he's burdened with a clog of a wife. I think I could bring quite a lot out of him that he doesn't know exists. Anyway, he's already asked me to dinner."

"Absolutely splendid, dear girl," said Fayverdale, lifting his vodka glass to the toast position. "A pushover, I would think." He was most anxious to please his masters since they had increased the value of his diamond concession, following his success in securing the SP47 capsules.

Diana was forty-five, according to Somerset House, but had never looked more than thirty-five, and under the influence of Juvenex had the unblemished freshness of a girl in her early twenties. With this allure she coupled a high intelligence quotient, fortified by much intimate experience of the ways and weaknesses of men, who provided her main time-filling activity. She made some money through modeling but lived chiefly on alimony and on the "hospitality" she received from friends like Fayverdale. Her view about men was that all were animals but some were more animal than others and that these were her rightful prey. Combining the bloom of youth with the refinement of experience, she represented the new breed of women with an unprecedented array of appeal potentially capable of giving them a degree of influence over men of affairs never possible before. Throughout the free world, such middle-aged women were glowing again in all their girlhood coloring, and the men, revivified in their masculine way, were responding to this unprecedented charm, which was pristine yet mellow, like an old master that has achieved esteem through age and is suddenly permitted to regain its easel beauty by the cleaner's art.

Since being seduced at sixteen, Diana had never stopped wondering what all the fuss was about. The extent to which intelligent men were excited by a glimpse of a garter being pulled down across six bare inches of thigh or by the cleft between her breasts never ceased to astonish her. Their interest could be diverted from almost any task by the chance sight of a girl in her underclothes, when they were seeing something they shouldn't, yet a body in a swimsuit, displaying far more, hardly merited a second glance. Surely they deserved to be exploited—an inference that, in successful practice, led her to the conclusion that money is the fruit of most evil. She had never once asked for money from her admirers but quickly insinuated the message into their skulls that—to use the Harley Street euphemism—her favors should attract a fee. To such a siren, Juvenex was proving a double blessing. It enhanced her personal charms and strengthened her chief allies, the demon riders.

Though Fayverdale had still not been asked to do anything dangerously illegal to demote the national interest, he was on a slimy descent and soon found himself required to utilize other creatures as venal as himself to secure information and create scandal. Of these Diana was his latest find. He had taken her to the Russian embassy party in the hope of introducing her to some minister who might prove responsive. Butcher, of course, had been on his list, but he had never imagined that it would prove so easy to ensnare him.

"Surely the power of the devil lies in the privy parts of man," he said cynically, quoting some source he could not recall.

"Oh, I hope I've something more than sex to offer," said Diana, who prided herself on the mental treasury she had stocked with much effort over the years. "We're going to discuss left-wing politics."

"Not for long, I predict," Fayverdale replied. "I saw that lecherous look in his eye."

At that moment Dorothy Jordan-Bell drifted by with John and Shirley, who was being congratulated on all sides, except by the

Russians who pretended to know nothing about her success even when told about it. John was regularly invited to Russian embassy functions by the Soviet press officers and service attachés with whom he kept in touch, in the hope that they might one day be useful, though years of dull lunches had produced nothing but unprintable propaganda.

Dorothy stopped for a word with Fayverdale, with whom she had enjoyed a desultory romance when they were both much younger.

"Have you tried the champanska yet, Tony?" said Dorothy, holding up her glass. "It gets better every year. Still a bit smoky, but drinkable."

"Dorothy used to be a hot number," Fayverdale volunteered ungallantly, as he watched her drift out of earshot, her bottom, which had a life of its own, giving her dress a delightful sway that would have seemed tarty on anyone less elegant. "I wonder what she does now for sex. I would think that Owen is only interested in power and the sort of attention she requires takes time. She wouldn't be the first woman in No. 10 with a lover. It would be interesting to know if she indulges. That's a high-priority theme you might prod your Butcher-boy about later."

After they moved on to see who might be in the other crowded rooms, Shirley asked, "What was the scent that girl was wearing? It smelled delightful."

"Essence of Bitch, I should imagine," replied Dorothy, with whom the encounter had been a matter of loathing at first sight. "I wouldn't run the risk of incurring her friendship."

Diana was about as transparent to other women as the seethrough nightgowns Dorothy wore to stimulate Morgan Owen's reviving interest. The attractive clothing most women wear and their heroic cosmetic endeavors are intended to give at least a nudge to the baser instincts of the man in the street or the man at the party as well as the man in the boudoir. Yet they react with moral indignation toward the woman who becomes so blatant in flaunting her charms that they sense that, with her, sex might have lost its amateur status.

Diana's reaction to Dorothy made the distaste mutual. "I agree she's the most elegant Second Lady that Britain has ever had, but it's easy to see who's wearing the pin-stripes in No.10," she observed to Fayverdale.

There was some truth in the remark, but it had much wider application than to Downing Street. As the shedding of the years made the men seem more boylike than ever, the maternal feelings resident in all women, except the mentally warped, intensified, and the degree of matriarchal domination to which husbands traditionally submit was strengthened.

The awareness of this enabled John to persuade himself that there might be some recompense in having lost Shirley. His desire to monopolize her had become compelling from the moment she had decided to make it obvious that her marital ambition lay with Robert, and a future totally deprived of her companionship had looked as bleak as a slate quarry in the rain.

He had sent her flowers, boxes of stockings, and Romeo and Juliet in tooled red leather, inscribed on the flyleaf "To my own Dark Lady. I was going to write all this myself if Shakespeare hadn't hogged the language." When he thought of possible compliments that he might pay her, or heard gossip which would keep their conversation interesting, he noted it in his diary, an effort he had never been prepared to make for anyone before.

The penalties of freedom had suddenly seemed so severe that he had been driven to his first proposal, though he couched it in terms which gave her the opportunity to ignore it as a jest, if she chose.

"I see some electronics firm has programmed a computer to give guidance to engaged couples," he said, as they sat in the firelight with brandy balloons at the Shooting Box. "They fill in questionnaires and the machine sorts out the sentimentality from the qualities that matter and then gives a verdict on whether a couple is temperamentally suited. It works on the principle that two people are more likely to be honest with the machine about their personality weaknesses than they are with each other. Why don't we go and try it?"

Shirley had laughed and replied, "We know each other's weaknesses too well already." Then, to change the subject, she had added, "I do love it here: it's so peaceful."

John had jumped in with, "It's yours if you'd like it," but regretted being so impetuous when it brought nothing more welcome than, "You make it sound very tempting, but it's too far away from my work and I couldn't give that up."

After this rejection John had sublimated his frustration by de-
luding himself that really he was very happily unmarried, in view of
the increasing subservience to women that he sensed among his
colleagues and contacts. On the infrequent occasions when Shirley
spared time for him, she was still prepared to demonstrate her
affection, and though he deeply resented sharing her, he consoled
himself that there was some relief in being on a basis where her
fruit could be sampled without day-to-day responsibility for its cul-
tivation. Further, he reflected, he had been too successful with
other men's wives to entertain much hope of fidelity in one of his
own, and however dispassionately he might look at sex in conversation, the highest fidelity would be required of Mrs. Holt.

He had invited Shirley to the Soviet party because the invitation
was addressed to Mr. and Mrs. Holt and he felt that she would be
sufficiently interested in seeing the Russians "at home" to accept.

"Pity I had to change it," John whispered as he showed her the
invitation card altered to "Mr. Holt and Dr. Howard" before
handing it to the official who was announcing the guests.

After driving Shirley to Waterloo station early the following
morning, John returned to his flat to efface her traces before the
char arrived. Removing the shakings of her powder puff from the
washbasin and pocketing two stray hairclips, he remarked to Scoop,
who followed him from room to room with such adoring eyes,
"We're all right, aren't we? It would take a phenomenal wife to be
better than none."

chapter 20

With her life story in every newspaper and magazine and with
inescapable interviews on television and the newsreels, Shirley
quickly became something of a latter-day Madame Curie, a compliment enhanced by the fortune of being photogenic to a degree
which exaggerated her quota of glamour.

Margaret wanted to withdraw her impulsive refusal to accompany Robert to Stockholm for the Nobel Prize ceremony, especially when he made some effort to induce her to change her mind, but her pride was too swollen by its injury.

When Robert and his mistress stepped from the plane at Bromma airport on that bitter day in mid-December, the newspaper and television attention was terrific. They were treated like visiting royalty—not only because they had won the Nobel Prize, but because of the special appeal of their discovery in a country where youthfulness and body fitness are worshiped to a degree unparalleled since Ancient Greece. As she followed him with a few words into the out-thrust microphones, Shirley felt it could only be a matter of short time before their partnership became full and legal. Robert, too, realized that he was increasingly in need of the emotional refuge she provided.

Shirley had lied to him when he had questioned her about the Soviet embassy party, claiming that Holt had rung her up at the last minute and that she had gone purely out of interest to see how the Russians behaved. She insisted that she had caught a train back to Salisbury immediately after the party and the fact that she had been back in the laboratory early the following morning supported her story. Robert did not press her too hard on discrepancy of detail because he did not want to create more emotional turmoil for himself by disbelieving her, or force another showdown over the furtiveness of their relationship, with which Shirley was becoming increasingly impatient.

As they sped in their chauffeured limousine along the snow-plowed roads toward the splendor of the Grand Hotel, Robert looked at the tight program of lectures, receptions, and parties which had been drawn up for him.

"I can cope with the academics, all right," he said, "but you'll have to help me out with the small talk at the receptions and especially with the press conferences. You're good at handling newspapermen," he could not resist adding, with a smirk.

"Don't worry, darling. I'll help you," said Shirley, who had learned that it rarely paid to nibble at such dangerous bait.

As Margaret watched Robert and Shirley arrive at the airport on the Eurovision TV at Salisbury, she did her best to hide her distress from Angela and Simon, who were at home, but when the smiling, fur-clad Shirley, whose aura of competence and femininity showed up well in color on the screen, began to tell the world how pleased she was to be in Sweden and what a privilege it was to work with Dr. Harvey, she could scarcely refrain from kicking the set. She flung her tapestry-work on the floor and hurried upstairs to her bedroom to give way to a near-hysterical outburst of anger, self-pity, and indignation. When the excess energy was spent and only the inner heaviness remained, she decided that the confrontation with "that slut Howard" which she had carefully avoided had become a matter of urgency. She was rehearsing the scathing commentary she intended to make as soon as the paramours had returned when the telephone rang. It was Lady Butcher.

"Frank and I are having a house-warming tomorrow night," she said. "We intended to ask you and Robert but thought you'd both be in Stockholm. When I saw you weren't there on the television I thought you might like to come. I wish you would. I can't think why Frank has suddenly become interested in parties. You know how he used to hate them. He even used to resent it when I wanted a few of my Women's Institute friends in with their husbands. But he says it's something we have to do now. Do come. It'll be such a help to have somebody here I know."

Margaret, who had met the Butchers many times when Frank had been Minister of Science in charge of the Juvenex project, was not particularly fond of the organizing Barbara, but at that moment she badly needed taking out of herself, and was grateful for the chance of securing the temporary relief which, she had found, accrued from putting a few miles between herself and the geographical focus of her anxieties.

"I'd love to come."

"Fine then. Seven o'clock. Number One Carlton Gardens. Take the lift on the left. The messenger on the door will show you."

With the luxury of good servants, Margaret had no difficulty in leaving the children for the night. Feeling that a little indulgence would help to restore her shattered morale, she booked a room at the Savoy and arrived there after lunching on the train.

As she entered the rather drab furnished flat which the government provides as a London home for its Foreign Secretary, Margaret was met by Barbara, who had made a pathetic effort to look attractive. Lady Butcher had been one of those unfortunate girls who had never really bloomed, but by-passed youth into a permanent seedy stage. Not even Juvenex, which she had been taking like almost everyone else, could do much for her full-bottomed form. Her brittle hair drawn back to a bun, in which the pins were carelessly concealed, accentuated the hard line of her mouth, and her dress sense was too poorly developed to enable her to avoid loudly clashing colors.

"Thank heavens you could come, Margaret. I hardly know a soul," she confided. "Come over and say hello to Frank."

Butcher was by the fireplace talking to Diana Douglas, who was the main reason for the party. No opportunity to invite her to the flat privately had presented itself because his wife had taken possession to get the place in order, and, in any case, as he had shaved in the light of the bathroom mirror on the morning after the Soviet party, he had felt diffident about following up his meeting with such a beautiful creature for fear that he might be rebuffed. Being laughed at was something he had never been able to tolerate.

He had invited "Lord Fayverdale and lady" in the hope that he might bring the woman who had been the first since his courtship to insinuate herself into his unromantic mind. As soon as Butcher had introduced Margaret to Diana, the predatory Fayverdale drifted away from the dull dowager with whom he was saddled to secure a close-up of the new arrival. When he heard it was the great Sir Robert Harvey's wife and that she was there alone, he quickly inveigled her away to a spare settee, much to the appreciation of the host, who was making the most of his conversation with Diana. Fayverdale had an unerring nose for scenting out an unhappy woman and a practiced gift for making her feel that her problems not only mattered to him but were, at that moment, his most vital concern.

Sensing a contact of value as well as a fresh female of considerable charm—for even without the incitement of Juvenex he had always been slave to the masculine illusion that the next conquest would be surpassing—he devoted more attention to Margaret in one hour than she had experienced in the past year from Robert, who had always been stingy with his compliments.

Margaret was entranced with the conversation of her elegant

148

companion, peppered as it was with some spontaneous wit but far more like changeling *bon mots* he could safely pass off as his own with such a naïve listener.

"Ah, Lady Harvey, I do feel for you, being married to such an expert," he had said on meeting her. "The acknowledged expert is the modern tyrant. He brooks no opposition."

To Margaret, who had never won a verbal argument with Robert in her life, this remark seemed extraordinarily perceptive.

"And what are you expert in?" she laughed.

"Oh, I'm just expert in being a bachelor. A somewhat misunderstood bachelor."

He was never slow to let it be thought that he was lonely in spite of his numerous acquaintances.

"I'm much more despondent than you'd think," he told her. "Everything may look calm on the surface, but you've no idea what goes on under the duckweed."

"You look pretty gay to me, Lord Fayverdale."

"Actually I'm a melancholic by nature, perhaps because of the formative years I spent in Russia. It takes the form of feeling convinced that I'll come to an early and violent end. Like Julius Caesar, I came into the world by the quickest route—a surgical birth. I suspect that, like him, I'll also be shown the quickest way out of it. So I make a deliberate ploy of enjoying it as much as possible while I can. You never know what Freddy Fate has tucked away in the pipeline."

To his inquiries about her absence from the Nobel Prize celebrations, Margaret responded with a few lines between which he had no difficulty in reading the true reason.

When their bustling hostess split them up, as invariably happens to two people who seem to be enjoying their conversation at a cocktail party, Margaret lost only the minimum decent interval in getting back to Fayverdale's company and found herself warmly welcome.

"Thank God you've come back. I was getting bored stiff," he said as he took two more glasses of champagne from the waiter. "I shall be taking Diana home. Can we drop you off somewhere?"

Margaret was delighted with the solicitude and suspected nothing as Fayverdale spoke quietly to Diana, after rounding her up from Butcher's company.

"Darling, I'd say, by the look on his face, that you're all set to be the most influential courtesan since Diane de Poitiers," he said.

"You flatter me, Tony, though not half as much as he does. Incidentally, you seem to have found an admirer yourself."

"Yes, and she could be a valuable one, so I fear we'll have to change our plans."

When they were seated in Fayverdale's car, he turned to Margaret and said, "We have to go round the mulberry bush because of the one-way traffic. So do you mind if we drop Diana first? She lives quite near, off Buckingham Palace Road."

As Margaret was in no mood to be on her own, she was pleased to hang on to his company as long as possible.

"Are you sure you had enough to eat at the buffet?" Fayverdale asked after Margaret slipped into the front seat beside him when they had decanted Diana at her door at 10:30 P.M. "Or would you like to have some supper with me somewhere?"

"I couldn't eat a thing."

"Well, it seems early to turn in if you visit London so rarely. Let's go and have a drink at a funny little club I know. It might amuse you."

Margaret was so bubbling with the effervescence which champagne seems to inject into women who don't see much of it that she was game to go anywhere.

Fayverdale was a member of more than a dozen nightclubs grading from the smart and decorous through the semi-nude and noisy to the downright indecent. He was adept at choosing the right club for the right person and felt that in his companion's current mood, the Roaring Forties was just the place. Margaret had never heard of it.

Sitting at a table which had often been used by Robert and Shirley, Margaret and Fayverdale talked and danced their way through the details of her threatened marriage and through another bottle of champagne and by 1 A.M., when he judged it was time to go, she was decidedly unsteady.

"I really can't take you back to the Savoy like that," he said, after she had apologized for drinking too much. "It's my fault really for letting you. Come back to my place and I'll brew you some strong coffee."

Margaret was in no condition to argue about geography, and she was soon being half held up in the lift to Fayverdale's flat in Mount Street.

Margaret had little recollection of how she had got there when she found herself in Fayverdale's bed next morning. She was ashamed and furious with herself, for in the past months whatever retaliation she had threatened in her mind, she had always managed to recoil from contact with the flesh of masculine passion quickly enough to preserve her option on the legal interpretation of fidelity. But Fayverdale, who had awakened her with a coffee tray set in the kitchen by Kopec, who always effaced himself on such unplanned occasions, was so gentle and solicitous and, as always, had been so artful at disguising pedestrian lust as consuming passion, that she began to see the exciting side of her escapade.

The waking circumstances, which would have seemed sordid in the airless confines of a cluttered two-room flat, could be written off as sophisticated in the elegant modernity of a spacious Mayfair apartment, and Margaret was not committing any crime which had not been inflicted on her many times. As her seducer expressed it when she began to fuss, as he climbed back into bed beside her, "Is it likely that *both* those single rooms so studiedly booked in Stockholm were occupied last night? You haven't done anything you weren't driven to by neglect. Nature abhors a sexual vacuum, my dear, and it's not only fruitless but dull to fight too hard against nature."

"No family would survive if women didn't fight against it!"

"How rewarding has the struggle been in your case?" he asked, stretching luxuriously. "No, my dear, we're all powered by drives we can try to steer but we can't ignore them. I've come to the conclusion that some degree of promiscuity is one of the constants of nature, and it's time we fitted it into our formula for civilized living."

Margaret knew far too many couples whom she believed to be mutually faithful to agree entirely, but by the time she left his flat after midday, she had been skillfully convinced that for years she had been a martyr to monotony.

"No regrets?" he asked as they drank a parting sherry.

"No regrets. Really," she smiled.

"That's the girl. You know, an efficient self-excusing mechanism is essential to every man and woman outside the religious orders. To err is human, and we can't all go about in hair shirts."

chapter 21

The haunting quality which many men found in Diana Douglas certainly haunted Frank Butcher. He could not bundle Barbara back to Farnborough quickly enough, and fortunately for him, his wife was equally anxious to get back to Prince Phumiphon, her chief Siamese stud cat, and his numerous offspring.

Diana was due to dine with him alone only three nights after the housewarming, and Butcher found that the prospect was intruding so much into the perusal of his Foreign Office papers that it was a matter of some national urgency that he should come to grips with it, and with her, without delay. Through the faithful courier, Kopec, Fayverdale had reported the assignation to his Soviet controller, a so-called Second Secretary named in the Foreign Office list as Leonid Yarochetsky, and it had been received with acclamation, though Tony had recently sensed a growing impatience with his efforts.

"You must get the photographs as quickly as possible," Yarochetsky had said peremptorily when he and Kopec bumped into each other by arrangement in the Whale Room at the Natural History Museum. "And warn The Doctor that we may require The Nurse to plant a small object in Lord Butcher's bedroom. Do you know if there is any exposed iron on his bedstead?"

"How would I know that?" Kopec protested.

"Then get The Nurse to find out," Yarochetsky said sharply, emphasizing with his eyes that the Soviet government did not distribute its largesse for nothing.

Yarochetsky, who had spent three years—one of them as an instructor—in the espionage school in Moscow, had good reasons for asking his odd question. The electronics experts involved in the colossal effort which the Russians invested in subversive activity had devised a most ingenious gadget which could relay the speech in a room without need of wires or any of the other appurtenances of "steam-age" eavesdropping. By means of transistors and other miniaturized devices, a microphone, a transmitter, and a minute battery had been accommodated in a hexagonal plastic case that looked like the head of a bolt when attached by a tiny magnet to an iron bedstead. A receiver in a parked car outside, or in a hired flat nearby, recorded the conversation of the bed's occupants and monitored any late-night telephone talks.

Fayverdale, who knew none of these details, nevertheless realized that for the first time he was being required to involve himself in something dangerously illegal, but when he demurred Yarochetsky made it plain that the alternative to cooperation would be far more unpleasant than mere loss of his diamond concession. He could not think how he was going to explain the requirement to Diana, who was even more concerned about remaining on the right side of the law. So he decided, at that stage, to do no more than ask her to find out about Butcher's bed and to plead mystification about the purpose of the information.

"They're odd fish," he said, shrugging his shoulders when he told her what was needed. "There seems to be someone in Moscow who collects useless information. You'll probably be asked to find out his size in collars next. Anyway, you can be sure the Foreign Secretary's bed isn't on the secret list."

Diana had no difficulty in answering the query. With his sense of value distorted by the novelty of infatuation, and his susceptibility to enticement heightened by Juvenex, Butcher was so excited that he could not get the dinner over quickly enough, and after less prompting than Diana had anticipated with such an inexperienced admirer, he had managed to escort her to the connubial couch. There she submitted responsively to his superficial embraces, but after edging her fingertips below the box mattress until she could feel the cold hardness of iron supports, she resisted his more intimate advances.

"I like you very much, Frank," she whispered as he lay in the darkness almost whimpering with tension in the warmth of her arms. "But I can't stay here long because both the messenger on the door and that policeman who's always there in the street will see what time I go. I'm very averse to being made love to in a hurry and then being sent home. That's not the way I see us at all. Leave it to me and in a few days I'll arrange something more convenient. I'll be worth waiting for," she added, stroking his hair, luxuriant after nearly two years of stimulation by Juvenex.

It had taken him so long to find such a woman that he was too scared of offending her to argue.

"You do promise to see me again soon?" he begged, as she renovated her makeup prior to leaving. "Of course, darling," she answered as she dropped her lipstick into her evening bag and gave him an affectionate hug. "Give me a ring at about ten-thirty tomorrow."

Butcher, who had sent roses to Diana's flat on the afternoon of their next meeting—the first time he had ever sent flowers to a woman—was surprised to find that she was not taking him back there after they had finished their dinner at the Mirabelle.

"Tony's out of town and I've borrowed his flat for the night because mine's being decorated and it's all upside down. He won't know you've been there," she added, sensing her escort's concern.

"What about the servants?"

"There's only Kopec, Tony's man, and he's away with him."

He was so ensnared by Diana, who was tastefully gowned and jeweled, that he didn't care where they went so long as it was soon.

In the ecstasy of an embrace remote from anything he had experienced, he poured out his desire. Diana felt so pliable and feminine compared with the awkward rigidity of his wife, and the elation at being in possession of such a woman, after the superficial encounters to which he had become accustomed, intensified his excitement. The charm of daintiness was a new experience in itself for him, and the provocative way she had undressed had been in such contrast to Barbara's labored uncorsetting. Both women regarded their underwear as functional, but whereas Barbara's was selected entirely to keep her own animal heat in, Diana's was designed to generate it in someone else.

154

"I used to pride myself on being master of my emotions," Butcher said as he relaxed in a suffusion of satisfaction. "But when I'm with you they take over."

"Never mind, darling," Diana said as she switched on the bedside lamp and lit cigarettes for both of them. "It's a prudent politician who displays his strengths in public and his weaknesses in private."

It was, in fact, far less private than Butcher imagined. Kopec was enjoying his work in the infrared laboratory on the unseen side of the see-through mirror.

"You're a dangerous woman, you know, Diana," Butcher said as he dressed next morning. "After you nobody else could be any good."

"Thank you, darling, that's a nice compliment," she responded drowsily from between the sheets. "But don't you go trying anybody else because you might be wrong."

"What moth would bother with a candle if he could embrace the sun?" he asked as he bent down and kissed her good-bye.

"You sound as though you think you're going to get your wings singed."

"I suppose all illicit lovers do in the end," he answered prophetically. "Well, back to governing the people, my precious," he joked as he left to call a taxi.

" 'Bye, darling, ring me soon," Diana replied, snuggling down in the satisfying assurance that the Secretary of State for Foreign Affairs had lost the power of governing himself. As for her attachment to him, it was about as incidental and unsubstantial as the condensation trail being made by the superjet bringing Robert and Shirley back to London.

Conscious of the distressing scene which Robert undoubtedly faced with Margaret on his return, they had escaped into reminiscences of their stay in Stockholm during the journey home, and had to leave unsolved the riddle of why Swedish men are so dour while the women are so gay when their plane touched down at London Airport.

Robert had cabled the time of his expected return. But Margaret was out when he arrived back home in Salisbury. Instead she was parked close by Shirley's flat, and after giving her time to put down her bags, rang the bell.

"Oh, come in, Margaret. I was expecting you," Shirley said, trying to hide her embarrassment on opening the door to her caller.

"So this is the love nest where my husband works so late so often," Margaret said, surveying the comfortable living room. "Do you mind if his wife sits down?"

Shirley motioned her toward the settee.

"I suppose you are aware that I've been having you watched," Margaret lied. "I know all about your affair with Robert, who's old enough to be your father, however young he may look. You know there's a name for women like you."

"Look, Margaret, you'd better get used to the fact that Robert and I love each other. Neither of us sought it out. It just happened, and there's nothing we can do about it."

"You talk like a teenager, but then that's about what you are. I've spent twenty-three years with this man and borne him three children, and I know a great deal more about his mind than you do. This is just a stupid infatuation on the part of both of you."

"It so happens that I've worked with Robert now for eight years, and in that time he's probably spent more time in my company than in yours," Shirley replied quietly.

"I'm beginning to realize that."

Shirley blushed. "I was thinking of the lab. Anyway, wherever we've been, I've probably had to sustain him through as much disappointment and bad temper as you have. And I do feel I've contributed as much as you to his success."

"My God, that's rich, after the way I looked after him through all the years when he was nobody."

"Maybe, but Robert once said a wonderful thing to me that I've never forgotten. He said that I served him as a mental trampoline —that in my company his ideas and his ambitions leaped higher than they'd ever been able to before."

"Pity you didn't keep it on that plane instead of becoming a mattress."

"There's no need to be coarse. But if you want it put bluntly, you may have fed his babies but I fed the rats, and it's those that have made him famous."

156

Though there could be no doubting the truth of Shirley's point, the equating of her children with rodents was more than the outraged wife could take.

"Don't you dare mention my children, you slut," she shouted.

"I'm truly sorry about the children," Shirley said quietly, determined to keep her temper. "But people do change, you know, especially now."

"Robert has certainly changed since he got involved with you," Margaret said, repressing tears with difficulty. "He used to set such store by honesty, and you've made him into a cheat and a liar."

"I've hated the deception, Margaret. You might not realize it, but this situation is worse for a woman who's in love with a married man. She *knows* that after they have been together he's going to another woman's bed. At least you've been spared that for a long time."

"Thanks very much, I do feel for both of you," Margaret retorted, resolved that whether she was happy with Robert or not, she would see that Shirley never married him. "I've devoted the best years of my life to him, and he owes me some allegiance, apart from the children."

"I'm afraid the 'best years of your life' idea doesn't have much meaning anymore. You know, there's time available now for all of us to take stock and start again. We needn't be stuck with anyone. In fact, living happily 'ever after' is soon going to seem far too long."

"Well, I can see it's no good talking to anyone so immoral," Margaret said angrily, drawing on her gloves. "But at least you know what I think about you. And you can abandon any highflown ideas you might have about becoming Lady Harvey."

A less practical woman might have broken down after Margaret had slammed the door, but Shirley's response was to make an immediate phone call to warn Robert what had happened.

When Margaret walked into her living room, he was standing by the fire with his back to her in a mood that was a mixture of anger at her intrusion into Shirley's flat and embarrassment at the full exposure of his behavior. As he turned, reluctantly, to face her, she could do nothing more resolute than dissolve into uncontrollable tears. In the comfortable atmosphere of their long partnership, surrounded by objects they had collected over the years, each with its evocative association—their modest wedding presents, the antique marriage jug, which Robert had patiently repaired after the children had broken it in a scuffle, the rose-pink oil lamp they had found together in the junk shop behind Leicester Square, the inlaid mahogany spinet, and their other more valuable acquisitions which had seduced them beyond what they could really afford but had continued to give them pleasure long after they had forgotten the price—he suddenly could only feel sorrow and shame for the distress he had brought his wife. He put his arms around her as she sobbed on the settee, and they sat in silence for several minutes, neither knowing what to say.

"What are we going to do?" Margaret asked eventually, dabbing her eyes.

"I don't know, dear," Robert replied quietly. "I'm sorry to have hurt you, but it will all work itself out somehow. I suppose every marriage ought to have a state-of-the-union survey each New Year, and I'm afraid we've just let things drift too long. It's my fault, but let's do nothing in a hurry. I know we should both put the children first. Make some coffee, and then I must go up to the Institute. We'll talk about it all tonight when we both feel less upset."

Robert was anxious to get out of the house, but his excuse was genuine. A disturbing medical development which seemed to be caused by Juvenex had come to notice a few months previously, and the report of a full inquiry into it was waiting on his desk. The statisticians had discovered a substantial increase in fatal cases of coronary thrombosis, which had been expected to decline. Preliminary investigation had pointed to a simple cause. The victims seemed to be mainly men who had been in the most dangerous decade of forty-five to fifty-five and had already been suffering from silent coronary disease when they began taking Juvenex. The increased general activity of their bodies, stimulated by the drug, had put an excessive strain on their weakened hearts. To check this interpretation the Health Ministry had carried out a large-scale postmortem survey and the results, which fully confirmed the suspicion, had become available during Robert's absence in Sweden. He had to become conversant with them before taking part next day in a meeting of the committee convened to advise the

Government on the nature of the public warning, which clearly had to be issued.

It was a one-generation problem because there was every sign that the people who had taken Juvenex since they were young would be protected by it from heart-weakening disease. But this was small recompense to the victims, who included Sir Edward James, the former Secretary of the Medical Research Council, and Geoffrey Carslake, the former Chancellor of the Exchequer, or to their relatives, who naturally blamed the drug.

As he drove out to Porton in the loneliness of his car, Robert decided that somehow he and Margaret would have to stick it out together at least for a few years, until Simon was better fitted to withstand the mental bruising of a broken home. Who was to know? Perhaps by that time his affair with Shirley might have consumed itself. Margaret's considered opinion was the same. She realized that her bitterness would help nobody, least of all herself, and on the rebound of relief at having put the confrontation behind her, she argued herself into believing that she and Robert could make a fresh start built, perhaps, on a sounder mutual understanding. After all, she convinced herself, attaching all importance to fidelity is only a state of mind, and she had her undeclared experience with Tony Fayverdale to demonstrate how difficult it can be to avoid seasoning the duty-free diet of marital love with a contraband alternative.

Over some days, which included Christmas, the Harveys worked themselves into a state of euphoria at having refound each other, but the stark facts of their altered lives soon began to reassert themselves, and both realized that when the forward path of marriage had proved to be so difficult for them, to reverse down it would be impossible.

They both knew that the wisest course was to keep their conversation off the subject of the infidelity, but night after night, and often at the sacrifice of sleep, they returned to it. Neither could resist the temptation to talk about it, to inject into any casual discussion remarks or topics which led them back to their pivotal problem, with the inevitable invective and spiteful comment.

Their first major relapse came after a particularly pleasant evening with friends when, as they were driving back, Margaret raised the question of Shirley's future. She had read that Shirley had been offered a professorship by an American university, the news having been given special prominence as a further unspeakable attempt to lure Britain's best brains with dollars. Shirley had been quoted as saying that she was greatly tempted but did not see how she could leave the research on Juvenex now that Sir Robert Harvey was so dependent on her.

"Couldn't you encourage her to go, darling?" Margaret asked. "Even if only for a couple of years. Wouldn't it be best for all of us?"

The curt evasiveness of Robert's response was so eloquent of his continuing attachment to his mistress, whose charm was enhanced by the maturity exuded by success, that Margaret realized that unless Shirley was physically removed from the microclimate of her daily life, the memory of the affair would remain erosive even if Robert was managing to keep his hands off her, which she doubted. As the weeks passed, she became increasingly certain that, short of murder, the only way she could rid herself of Shirley would be by ridding herself of Robert, too.

Robert had become convinced, even more rapidly, that any magic in their marriage had been dissipated forever and that the best they could hope for would be a sexless companionship. "Sex without love may be played in a minor key, but love without sex is a dirge," he had said in one of his aphoristic moods. Nevertheless, he felt he could face this situation with Margaret and believed that she too might be content with it, but her need for physical satisfaction had been more strongly aroused by Juvenex than her husband appreciated.

She had resisted Fayverdale's telephoned temptations, but once she had satisfied herself that Shirley had resumed the role of mistress, she opposed him no longer.

Had Robert applied his biological insight more perceptively to his wife's problem, he might have foreseen in time to prevent its consequence that, under a strong enough masculine breath, such a slow-burner could suddenly flare into incandescence.

chapter 22

The sudden awareness that death had been pushed away made rapid inroads into the sanctity of life, a concept that had commanded homage for many centuries, but which had been generally accepted in practice for less than one. This degeneration germinated unnoticed in the public subconscious but soon erupted into wondering about the sense of campaigns to keep death off the roads or reduce infant mortality when the threat came from too many living.

In the ensuing summer, which was hot for a climate where the sun normally tires so easily, the irritations of overcrowding generated still more crimes of violence and pointless acts of destruction. In a spate of vandalism, pylons, power stations, rolling stock, and naval vessels were sabotaged by people with no other motive than irrepressible exasperation. There was even an attempt by a gang of "Martians" to explode a homemade bomb in the Channel Tunnel. As a result, security guards with savage dogs were mounted at important installations, adding to the oppressive atmosphere of expanding state control.

Murders, which rose to a level never seen since the nineteenth century, included many premeditated to expedite inheritance. For all classes of homicide the death penalty was reintroduced, not for its deterrent value but on the conscious principle that an overcrowded state was not prepared to bear the expense and trouble of keeping such antisocial people alive.

Once this had been accepted, those who had been trying for years to bring back flogging found their opposition weakening. There was open support for the extension of capital punishment to rape, criminal assault on young children, and other crimes arousing strong public indignation.

A commission of judges and other legal experts was set up to review the whole question of terms of imprisonment, because even a ten-year sentence was obviously much less of a deterrent if the culprit was to emerge looking and feeling no older and with plenty of full life left in front of him. Their recommendation, after six months of ponderous brooding, that life imprisonment should mean sixty years, shocked few people, especially as even longer sentences had long been common in the United States.

The legal experts referred back to the Government the interesting possibility that life-sentence prisoners might reasonably be denied Juvenex, as being perhaps a more effective deterrent than mere imprisonment. In their learned opinion this was a matter more for medical than legal authority. They had to consider the issue because Juvenex had been denied from the first to prisoners who were in jail at the time of its introduction, and those who were still there had never been given it. The drug was under the control of the prison doctors and they could see no more reason for prescribing it for fit criminals than for giving them vitamin pills, particularly as it aggravated the problem of coping with the convicts' sexual deprivation. (The latter complication was also inflicted on abbots and mothers superior, who had to decide whether a reduction in life-span was a less exacting and more exalting penalty for their subordinates than an increase in inflammatory desire.)

The opportunity of using general withdrawal of the drug from persistent criminals as a deterrent was quickly lost by the establishment of a prison black market in Juvenex smuggled in by guards, bribed by the relatives of wealthy convicts, who operated a monopoly inside the prisons, as they had done for years in tobacco. So those prisoners who had been taking the drug before conviction were officially supplied with it, and refusal to swallow it replaced the traditional hunger strike protest against cell conditions. At first, the strikers were force-fed with the drug, but the Home Secretary soon took the popular decision that it was no business of his to prevent criminals from accelerating their departure from an overcrowded world.

The next overt sign that this inhumanity in common opinion had insinuated itself into the minds of the nation's governors was the almost unopposed passing of a bill to legalize euthanasia at birth for malformed children, with the parents' and family doctor's consent. The bill was introduced ostensibly in the interest of the children, but covertly to satisfy the protagonists of eugenics, who had long been clamoring for the elimination, at least from the breeding stock, of individuals who might perpetuate their defects in succeeding generations.

These crusaders had already secured legislation to permit the compulsory sterilization of the "unfit to breed." Now they were urging that Juvenex should be withheld from the mentally defective and seriously deformed. Even their opponents, who still considered it wicked that such individuals should be painlessly eliminated, found it difficult to justify the deliberate prolongation of their lives. A spirited opposition by Hastings Maclaren, who described eugenic control as "nothing less than the application of a selective weedkiller to humanity," attracted little political support.

"You are writing the most degrading chapter in the history of human error," he warned the apathetic House of Commons. "This is only the beginning of a demand for the elimination of anyone who might be considered unfit to survive by some impersonal judge or other. How long will it be before we are asked to legalize the murder of illegitimate children and the mentally sick?"

Maclaren sensed in this growing support for euthanasia an atavistic reaction to the unspoken fear of famine. In primitive communities culling of the young and infirm had been the accepted answer to the threat of food shortage, and he could see little evidence of much decline in man's ferocity. Though most foods were still available in Britain, fats and meat were rationed and were shooting up in price, and it was becoming obvious in the poorer parts of the world that in spite of the production of revolting substitutes from oil and plankton, humanity was threatened far less by the abundance of guns than by the shortage of butter. In the House of Lords, the chief physician to the Royal Household expressed the views of a powerful section of his profession when he urged the application of euthanasia to children and adults who had suffered such severe brain damage as to make them little more than cabbages.

"To keep such fragmentary creatures alive requires the services of expensive teams, working almost around the clock to sustain a parody of life," he said. "No purpose is served in prolonging living in circumstances where it is really no more than prolonging dying."

John, who still saw Maclaren through his thalidomide work, in which he had also managed to involve Shirley—an asset to any medical committee with her cachet of the Nobel Prize—gave him what support he could with articles and leaders in the *Daily Dispatch*. But it was not long before Euthanasia Boards were set up by the local authorities, and these soon took on the additional task of issuing certificates for the compulsory sterilization of adult mental defectives and congenital cripples. Shortly afterward, abortions by request for unmarried women became legalized for the first time in Britain—again without much opposition, even from the Church. This was quickly followed by the extension of the law to include any unwanted pregnancy. The Government set up a family-limitation service inside the health scheme, providing welfare contraceptives free through family doctors and clinics, and at a nominal price through subsidized slot machines. Compulsory instruction in birth control methods was introduced into the schools.

Money allowances for children, originally brought in to boost the birth rate, were withdrawn along with income-tax benefits. The legal age for marriage was raised to eighteen and then to twenty-one with growing pressure to increase it further. There was financial inducement to infertility through special tax concessions to bachelors and childless couples. The Government's anti-smoking drive lapsed quietly into desuetude.

The general hospitals were almost empty, except for the accident wards, but there was much more neurotic illness, which showed itself in a steep rise in the suicide rate. Even in Ireland, where suicide had always been rare, there was a marked increase in the urge for self-destruction, which in the other countries was being described in the medical literature as "a social disease now reaching epidemic proportion."

The change in attitude to life and death had come too suddenly for many middle-aged people to adapt themselves to it. The drug rejuvenated their cells but could do nothing to elasticize rigidity of thought. Whatever neuroelectric mechanism is involved in fixing attitude in the middle-aged brain, it seemed to be proof against interference by Juvenex.

Young people were showing progressive nervous symptoms of

164

frustration and anxiety engendered by the prospect of being permanently held down by the old. There was a surge in dope traffic and a sudden germination of sleazy clubs with their concomitant increase in vice and crime. As commonly happened before in times of religious decline, there was an enhanced interest in the magic arts. Clairvoyants, fortune-tellers, astrologers, purveyors of amulets and lucky charms, specialists on flying saucers and other self-appointed sages, who batten on the superstition generated by insecurity, flourished as never before. Though doctors had been advised not to prescribe the drug for healthy patients who were still growing, there was a strong demand for it from adolescents who craved the kick of its sex hormones—a demand quickly satisfied by jazz-club and coffeehouse pedlars, who dispensed Pink Peppers and Blue Boosters from their inside pockets, as they had once exploited the "purple hearts" tranquilizer craze. Georgians and Martians washed them down openly in top strength as a joint advertisement of their contempt for authority and chastity. Unconforming introverts swallowed them in secret, with the result that Simon was caught by his horrified father tiptoeing out of the maid's bedroom at 2 A.M.

The Government, which became more and more authoritarian as the necessity for control increased, gave grants to youth clubs and youth hostels to absorb the excess energy of the unemployed. It encouraged the building of new municipal centers providing free entertainment in the shape of cinemas, dance halls, skating rinks, and bowling alleys, but the hangover of emphasis on the value of honest work and achievement was too heavy for so much leisure to prove satisfying.

Efforts to channel this energy into higher education were even less successful. The school-leaving age had been raised to eighteen with funds switched from retirement pensions, which had been greatly reduced by the introduction of a tough means test, but except for the relatively few academically minded, the impatient teenagers felt that eighteen years was already a big enough slice of time to devote to preparation for living. And the longer that young men and women remained students, with time and opportunity for discussion, the greater became the risk that they would become revolutionary demonstrators.

This was again brought home to Robert by the behavior of Simon, who was in his first year at Oxford. Simon, who had been forced into growing a straggly beard by the same personality pressure which would have made him shave in a bearded community, had not been in college for more than a week before a posse of older undergraduates threw him in the river as an expression of their distaste for all things associated with his father. As the months went by, he compensated for this antipathy by speaking out so forcibly in public against the repression of the young by the artificial old that Robert was warned that unless his son could be induced to moderate his attacks on his elders, he might have to be sent down.

Just as the increasing affluence of society had always induced more people to take their lives, it became apparent that earthly paradise becomes less attractive to some people when they know they have longer to enjoy it. The too-examined life so often proves not worth living to the overly introspective, and the provision of more time to examine it was reflected in an increased demand for barbiturates, more and more of which were consumed in deliberate overdose.

In this decline of moral values, the life expectancy of the average newly contracted marriage slumped still further. Even in pre-Juvenex days, many couples had found that love was perishable, so that their union wore out after twenty years or less. Now, with the prospect of extended life, the deliberate practice of what the Church decried as "consecutive polygamy" gradually became socially acceptable. At the altar rail, more and more mentally modified their marriage vow to read "until death or boredom do us part." Of course, the general acceptance of consecutive polygamy, which had previously been a perquisite of the rich, necessitated a relaxation of the monstrous alimony law, which had too long enabled the able-bodied woman to exact a lifelong penalty for a man's adolescent error of judgment.

Though the Church considered that consecutive polygamy smacked less of promiscuity than the concurrent polygamy practiced by infidels, it favored neither, and was waging a lively rearguard action to maintain its grip on marriage as a sacred institution. Largely through the drive of the Archbishop of Canterbury, the campaign was forcefully promoted with addresses to captive audiences in tube stations, fireside talks on television, doorstep sermons by itinerant curates, and blanket use of the new talking billboards, which the Government had licensed to proclaim advertising slogans vocally as well as visually to secure more money for its enormous dole bill. But in spite of the example of the Primate, who had registered the birth of his eleventh child to the same wife at the age of seventy-three, it was clear to the far-sighted that the legal sanction of divorce by mutual consent was only a matter of short time.

Juvenex could not be withdrawn because animal tests and the few cases of humans who had ceased to use it for special reasons showed that all those millions who had taken it for more than a year would age rapidly, and these included the Cabinet Ministers who would have to take the necessary legislative action. Owen concentrated his energies on solving the social problems, setting up special advisory committees of the country's best brains, but they could do no better than recommend piecemeal remedies, so that stopgap benefits were offered with one hand, while stringent restrictions were clamped on by the other. The same problems were tackled in basically the same way throughout the rest of the free world, with substantially similar results.

In India, Southeast Asia, and Latin America, where the populations rocketed because of the previously high death rate, millions were more underfed than ever, and starvation became a partial solution to their problem. Money which should have been spent on farm machinery, fertilizer factories, and long-term land improvement had to be used to import what food was still available. The U.S. and Canada had a surplus of grain but they could scarcely cover the bottom of the cavernous breadbasket held up by the rest of the world. Advances in agriculture were managing to cope with the extra demands in most European countries, though water shortage was a serious problem, but in Britain the steadily increasing imports were creating a trade gap that could not possibly be bridged by industrial exports.

Immigration to Britain, even from the Commonwealth and Eire, was harshly restricted, and as the economic consequences grew and the shackles of authority were forged more strongly week by week, the queues for emigration to Canada, Australia, and New Zealand lengthened. The application lists for emigration to these places were soon declared closed, for there was a limit to the rate at which comparatively empty countries could accept the overflow of the world, without disrupting their own economy, and the governments there realized that they would soon have a population problem of their own. The British Exchequer was prepared to speed the departure of emigrants with free travel and other subsidies, but there was soon nowhere to go.

Robert had continued to hope that these social difficulties were the teething troubles of a new age, to which the human species would quickly adapt itself and eventually remedy by intelligent action. But as the months passed and the problems intensified, he became more and more despondent and began to wonder whether his dream that people would become wiser through the bonus of more creative years would ever be realized. With his growing feeling of personal guilt for the worldwide problems he had caused, he repeatedly sought reassurance from his colleagues and particularly from Shirley.

"God knows, I did warn them to take it slowly, didn't I?" he asked her. "But they'll still blame me for the mess in the end. And I suppose they'll be right. I know I should have fought harder to prevent its premature use four years ago."

"It's not your fault, darling," Shirley reassured him. "And all these teething troubles will soon be sorted out."

"I suppose it's early days. But, you know, I've been wondering whether three score years and ten is an adaptation to human needs that has taken millions of years to settle and can't be interfered with without causing internal conflicts we didn't bargain for. Lifespans vary from species to species so much that maybe they are as nicely adapted to their purpose by natural selection as the muscles of the human hand. After all, why should the mouse live only two years and the elephant seventy unless there's some vital reason for it?"

"Yes, but man is different, because through intelligence he should be able to mold his environment to suit any new conditions," Shirley replied. "He doesn't have to wait for natural evolution. He can accomplish the change quickly by artificial means."

"Well, it doesn't look as though he can, does it?" said Robert gloomily. "But surely the eventual impact of millions of memories in which experience has accumulated and can still be applied with precision must result in more wisdom. After all, what is wisdom if it's not based on the brain's ability to store information, cross-link it, and then serve judgment?

"Oh, surely there's more to it than that, Robert. There's the humane components of wisdom, like kindness and pity." She paused thoughtfully and added, "I wonder if that's the answer?"

"If what's the answer?"

"That by diminishing physical suffering, Juvenex has also stunted compassion and without compassion people can't really be wise, however much knowledge they have."

"I suppose there might be something in that, Shirley. God knows, compassion's in short supply these days. It has to be stimulated like any other human reaction and it's suffering that stimulates it most. But I still believe that the human race must benefit from having more information in its communal head and more time to use it."

In the field of technical progress the effect of longer mental productivity was definitely apparent. The capacity for ingenuity in electronic computers and automation devices was rapidly enhanced, but the hope that they might help man to happiness had not materialized. They could solve his sums but could not resolve his conflicts.

Repeated outbreaks of machine-smashing by latter-day Luddites underlined the steady encroachment of the robots on man's right to work, but when governments tried to delay it they found that the complex machines exerted an irresistible pressure, forcing them into illogical action more in the machines' interests than in man's. The plans for an exorbitant monster had only to be printed for its manufacture at the taxpayers' cost to be inevitable. In Britain the first dramatic symptom of this triumph of ingenuity over wisdom had been the 1962 decision to build a fleet of supersonic airliners. The machines were unwanted by the airlines, which were already overloaded with expensive airplanes adequate for many years of service, unwanted by the passengers, who were content with six hundred miles per hour, dreaded by the grounded public who faced a life punctuated by sound-barrier bangs, and desired least of all by the Government, which would have to sell them at a huge loss. Yet the machines were made, not only by Britain but by Russia and the United States, where, under the prodding thrust of the re-elected Brandenburg, invention had become an even more prolific mother of necessity. In those countries the cost of the missile race to land men on the moon had been far more crippling and brought the winner nothing but prestige. Yet the loser was already spending even more on a bigger rocket in the compulsion to be first on Mars.

The common use of electronic computers for assessing rents, rates, and taxes was leading to many anomalies and hardship cases, but the cost of injecting them with something nearer humane judgment was deemed prohibitive.

The incursions of mechanization into freedom had come a long way since the parking meter.

Only behind the Iron and Bamboo curtains, where the drugs were successfully kept under rigid control, did there seem a chance that reason might keep pace with the menacing hardware. Even there, the regimes had run into a difficulty created by Juvenex. The effect of the drug was making itself felt throughout the world of sport. The Moscow Dynamos and other crack teams were no match for the British and European sides, fielding veterans who steadily increased their skill without losing their speed or endurance. In the Olympic Games held in Peking, the Communist contestants, who were not allowed to mix socially with any Westerners, were hopelessly outclassed in the Marathons and other long-distance events and in the arts like fencing and horsemanship. Even in chess they were being defeated by men who would normally have been surpassed by younger minds.

The Soviet and Chinese reaction to this situation was direct and honest. They independently announced that they had discovered that all the Imperialist athletes were using dope, which no clean-living Communist would do, and withdrew from all competitions.

As Robert was driving past Horse Guards Parade on his way to the Athenaeum, the members of which, thanks to his discovery, had become more animated than at any time in the club's history, he was held up by a noisy procession wending toward Trafalgar Square. Its ingredients were the counterpart of the compulsive demonstrators who had made up the extinct Committee for Nuclear Disarmament movement—teenagers with an inborn urge to create a nuisance, adults needing an excuse for exhibitionism, some genuine reformers, a few clergymen and scientists, and many Communists.

Their banners bore the initials CNA, which stood for Committee for Natural Aging. Their badge-symbol was a lamb—an ingenious device, for it not only represented real youth but had a religious flavor. Their main slogan was "Ban the Pill," and they put the letters GY after their names to signify that they were Genuine Young in contrast to the fake youth of their elders.

In London their marches began from the Health Ministry headquarters at the Elephant and Castle, taking them via Westminster Bridge past the Houses of Parliament where they chanted their slogans, but as Owen, the arch-democrat, would not allow the peace of Downing Street to be disturbed, they were diverted around the back of the Horse Guards even though this meant that for a few yards they trod the Mall in view of Buckingham Palace. The Institute of Gerontology at Porton was the place they preferred to besiege with sit-down demonstrations outside the gates and assaults over the security fence, but it was a little too far from London to serve as a general rallying point, as Aldermaston had done in the day of its denigration.

This was the first organized group representing the young people who realized that they faced indefinite frustration at the hands of what they called "the undead," who in their opinion were a far more menacing component of the population spiral than the unborn. Its aims particularly appealed to the girls, who were being made to feel perpetual children by middle-aged and elderly women whose looks were no longer a fading asset and for whom "well-preserved" had taken on a quite different meaning. Many girls of twenty attempted the pretense of being forty-five, even to the extent of carrying forged birth certificates, but even with this artifice it was difficult for the genuine young to get a good secretarial post, because the little riches in the infinite room of their minds did not delude many men in search of the satisfying combination of beauty and matured understanding. Frank Butcher was far from being the only man of influence to be under petticoat domination.

At first, the effects of this matriarchal surge were scarcely noticeable in Britain, where the women had much leeway to make up,

171

but in the United States the increased ascendancy of female influence was rapidly apparent. In most families the hen-peck domineering was purely domestic, since the wives had little desire to interfere with the sources of their husbands' income, only with its dispensing: but in the White House and to some extent in Downing Street, the rule of women had far-reaching consequences.

The main drive behind the CNA came from an eighty-year-old scientist, long elevated to the peerage as Lord Questing, whose life had been dedicated to warning about the dangers of overpopulation. His rallying cries like "The twentieth century plague is people," "Mouths are more menacing than missiles," "Is it to be standing room only?" had been adopted as slogans for the peeling plastic banners carried by his new disciples, who revered him as one of the few old men in the country to look his age, for, faithful to his principles, he had declined to take Juvenex and fathered no children. His unwelcome prophecies of doom had been repeatedly frustrated by the agricultural scientists, who, in the West, had managed to balance reproduction with food production, but since Harvey's innovation, the population bomb was ticking so loudly that they looked like being fulfilled. And Questing missed no opportunity of standing on platforms or sitting on pavements to tell the world "I told you so."

The CNA movement had soon spread to the United States where it was known as LENA—the League for Natural Aging—because of the public relations officers' insistence that it would not catch on unless its initials formed a word. LENA attracted such an enormous membership of Negroes that it was often impossible for the exasperated police to decide whether the bodies blocking the roads and sidewalks were demonstrating for the rights of youth or the rights of man. But the distinction was academic, for the standard treatment had become the same for both—rough handling, then the firehose, tear gas, police dogs, and, as a last resort, shots over the crowd that sometimes found their way into it.

In both countries the movement was a natural target for the Communist Party, which had maggoted its way in at the founding meetings and in Britain, by zeal and persistence, had secured organizing control. The rally in Trafalgar Square, with its cadre of young Parliamentary candidates, who were not all pop singers in search of publicity, was to clamor for compulsory retirement at seventy. Lord Questing was there to speak in his croaky but effective voice; a canon from Canterbury Cathedral; a left-wing Socialist, who battened on any chance to show how rebellious a rebel he was; and a backbench Tory who missed no occasion for attacking Morgan Owen, were also to address the multitude. The fact that the Tory MP was openly taking Juvenex himself seemed no more anomalous to him than the position of the numerous Socialists who were taking profit out of capitalist enterprises. His argument was the stock answer trotted out by Socialist millionaires for half a century—"You can't abstract me from the system in which I'm forced to live."

As Robert was eventually waved on past the noisy rabble, he mused with transient satisfaction on how extraordinarily young all the policemen were looking.

chapter 23

At the individual level the Russians extended their subversive activity in every stratum of society from the not-working man to the nonworking aristocrat. Incited by Fayverdale, who was under hustling pressure from Yarochetsky, Diana Douglas had continued to feign infatuation with the Foreign Secretary, and he had continued to return it with the genuine emotion, but now some more positive action was needed from her.

"The Radiotherapist brought something for you this afternoon," Fayverdale said casually as they were sitting in his flat in the early evening.

"What radiotherapist?" she asked, looking puzzled.

"Oh, I thought you knew. That's what Our Kensington Friends call Kopec. It's all part of their cloak-and-dagger service," he said, passing her a small jeweler's case.

Flicking open the lid expectantly, Diana was disappointed to find that nothing more exciting than a hexagonal piece of metal about half an inch wide lay on the blue satin lining.

"What on earth is it?" she asked.

"I haven't the faintest idea, my sweet, and I've learned that it's pointless to ask."

"But what am I supposed to do with it?"

"That's easy! All you have to do is place it gently on one of the iron supports under Butcher's bed. It's a magnet so it'll stick there of its own accord."

"Look Tony, I don't like this," she said, closing the case and handing it back. "It could be an atomic bomb or something. I don't want anything to do with it."

"I assure you it's not a bomb. They're clever at miniaturization, but they can't make them that small. But whatever it is, my dear Diana, I'm afraid you've no choice but to do what Our Kensington Friends ask. You've been taking their money for years and you're old enough to know there's nothing for nothing in this life."

"But you promised me that I'd never have to do anything illegal, and I'm sure that this is."

"I can't see how," Fayverdale replied impatiently. "But in any case I advise you just to get on with it. Our Kensington Friends have always been very agreeable, but I wouldn't fancy them much if they were really upset."

"What do you mean?"

"I mean they could make life very unpleasant for both of us if we frustrate them over a trivial matter like this."

"I don't think it is trivial, but anyway, what could they do?"

"Well, to put it crudely, they've shopped people before when they've ceased to be useful or become uncooperative. Klaus Fuchs would never have been suspected if the Russians hadn't deliberately tipped the Americans off about him."

"But he was a spy. I've never done anything like that," Diana said indignantly.

"That's a matter of definition. MI5 might think you qualify."

"There's no proof that I've ever done anything wrong, Tony, and you know it."

"I assure you that Our Kensington Friends could produce plenty of proof if they were driven to it. They're a lot more resourceful than you seem to think."

174

Fayverdale gripped her hand as she picked up her bag as though deciding to leave.

"You know about the Polish freighters, don't you?" he said, narrowing his eyes. "The ships that slip away in the night from the London docks—sometimes with people on board who don't really want to go. I don't think you'd like Moscow. Especially now," he added, deciding to turn on the maximum pressure.

"Why especially now?"

"Because there's no Juvenex behind the Iron Curtain, and you know what happens to people who stop taking it. In your case Dorian Gray wouldn't be in it!"

He picked up the jeweler's case and put it into Diana's hand.

"And don't think you can get away with just pretending to plant that little object. I can assure you Our Friends will know immediately whether you've carried out their mission honestly or not."

Diana's hand was trembling as she dropped the case into her bag. It was the first time Fayverdale had threatened her.

Her fear persisted even after repeated examination of the gadget in her flat convinced her that it was no more than a piece of metal covered with polished plastic, but to her surprise it quickly evaporated once she was with Butcher and she found it was so easy to carry out her task undetected while he was in the bathroom. She was well rewarded for her effort, not only through Fayverdale but by her victim, who had fallen completely under her domination. He never stopped buying her expensive presents in the belief that this would keep her from straying from him, and she found she had no difficulty in borrowing substantial sums from him on behalf of mythical impoverished relatives. The appetite she had awakened proved to be as self-reinforcing as any other, and when he was with her, his body, over which she exerted such control, usurped the command of his mind so that he was either blind to all the halt signs or resolved to ignore them.

Diana was as expert in hiding emotions as she was in feigning them, but her anxiety mounted beyond concealment as Fayverdale began to press her to secure information from her lover. At first she was asked to report nothing more dangerous than the dates of meetings and forthcoming visits which he confided to her, but she was soon enjoined to angle for information of a more valuable nature. She had been concerned about the presence of a beggar operating in the unlikely area of Carlton Gardens, but as Fayverdale pointed out, there were beggars all over London as a result of the unprecedented unemployment. In this regard she was the more perceptive. The security authorities had not been entirely dormant, and the beggar and his colleagues, including the policeman on the door, had been building up an interesting dossier on the movements of both Lord Fayverdale and his accomplice.

The first that Butcher knew about it was a visit from the secretary to the Cabinet who warned him, with the deference due from a civil servant, that the security authorities were interested in the lady with whom he had been spending so much time. It was suggested that the Foreign Secretary should agree to a brief visit from the Director General of the Security Service.

"This is a rather embarrassing situation for both of us, Minister," Sir Roger Black began deferentially, when he visited Butcher in the Foreign Office. Then, reverting to the inquisitorial manner he had acquired when practicing as a barrister before joining "The Firm," as MI5 was known, he continued: "We are concerned about the behavior of your friend, Miss Diana Douglas. Frankly, we think she is being paid to collect information and particularly to subvert important people. We suspect that both she and Lord Fayverdale are involved in reporting to Soviet bloc intelligence on VIPs with the eventual object of blackmailing or disgracing them."

"I just don't believe it," Butcher said in astonishment. "What's your evidence?"

"You'll appreciate that I can't go into details, but we have some information from a reliable source inside one of the embassies. There's no evidence of anything illegal—yet."

"I've known them both for over a year and there has been nothing suspicious in their behavior whatsoever, Sir Roger. I realize you must take all precautions, but I'm sure you are on a false trail—certainly with Miss Douglas."

"With respect, sir, I must disagree," said Black, shifting uneasily in his chair. "I'm sure you'll appreciate my embarrassment, but I must ask you whether she has at any time attempted to secure any confidential information from you?"

"Most definitely not."

"Well, that's reassuring, sir. But in the circumstances I must go through the motions of advising you to break off the association, though we'd be grateful if you could do it in such a way that her suspicions are not aroused. You can always plead pressure of work. I understand that you are going away shortly to the Middle East in connection with the Central Treaty Organization. I put it to you that you might make it clear that you don't want to renew the association when you return."

"And I put it to you that I have no intention of doing anything of the kind," Butcher replied testily. "I must be allowed some private life. But in view of what you say I'll be on my guard, and I'll let you know the moment I suspect anything."

"There's just one thing more, sir, I feel I should tell you," Black said as he moved to leave. "The Prime Minister has been informed that I was coming to see you. That, of course, has been routine ever since the Profumo affair."

"I understand," snapped Butcher, realizing that Owen must at least have been told that he was having an illicit affair with Diana.

Butcher was loaded with work for his forthcoming visit in two days' time to Cyprus. The Cyprus government was insisting on the removal of all British nuclear weapons from the island, in defiance of an agreement still in force, and this could well result in the break-up of the Central Treaty Organization. Pakistan and Iran, which were both uneasy members, would feel themselves deserted if the deterrent weapons were withdrawn from the area, and the Russians, who had been trying to disrupt CENTO for years, were already making the most of the situation with tempting offers of military aid. If Iran could not be held within some Western common-defense bloc, the RAF would be unable to secure the right to overfly Iran, which was the only quick military path remaining to the Middle and Far East since Arab nationalism had closed the air routes over Libya and the Sudan. Much depended on Butcher's forthcoming talks with the Archbishop who virtually ruled Cyprus and with the political leaders of the other countries concerned. But he had to see Diana without delay. So, pleading indisposition, he sent his Minister of State to represent him at an important dinner with a visiting Nigerian dignitary, so that he could dine with her.

Whether in anticipation of the presents she hoped he would

bring her from his tour, or at the prospect of being rid of him for three weeks, she was in a particularly affectionate mood, and Butcher's doubts were quickly dissipated.

He tried to pump her a little about Fayverdale but all she had needed to do to stifle that issue was to remind him that they had little time left together before his departure, when he would be sorely missed. The man who once had spared no time for dalliance had become so dependent on her that she had only to tempt him for all normal caution and resistance to evaporate.

Butcher had raised the matter of Black's visit with Owen, but the Prime Minister had no wish to pursue it immediately before his Foreign Secretary's vital mission and behaved as though he was not seriously perturbed. Immediately before setting off, Butcher tried to telephone Diana using the private line in his bedroom but found it was out of order. The Post Office officials were not surprised when the fault was reported to them. On instructions from MI5 they had deliberately put it out of commission to give the security authorities a reason for introducing two skilled searchers into the Foreign Secretary's bedroom and the other rooms where there were telephones. By the time Butcher's airplane had touched down at Akrotiri air base, the two "Post Office technicians," working silently because their speech would have been overheard, and found what they wanted tucked away in the angle of his bedstead.

At MI5's London headquarters, the location of which is known to the Russians but is secret from the public to spare its operators from the stare of the curious, Black and his deputy director pondered on what they should do. A defecting diplomat in the Hungarian embassy had given them the lead, which had made them suspect that information was somehow leaking from telephone calls made by the Foreign Secretary from Carlton Gardens.

A scrambler device made the telephone line itself untappable, but much could be learned by an intelligence analyst from Butcher's half of the conversations, which had all been overheard, and occasionally the conversation from the other end filtered through the earpiece loudly enough to be detected. Now that they had the proof, they had to decide how to use it. The security men had left the device where it was because they knew that the Russians could have detected its removal by its failure to transmit the noise of the servants cleaning the bedroom, and they were anxious to avoid alerting them to its discovery.

"I suppose M15 want to make the usual use of the bed microphone," Black said to his deputy, a recently retired major general.

"Yes. I was over there this morning. They've got some misleading guff they want to feed in to cast whatever doubt they can on the information that's been picked up before. Either they'll have to get Butcher to do it or get someone to imitate his voice."

Black grunted, pushed the stock dossiers on the two suspects to one side, and turned over the pages of the summary, which included the fact that five years previously he had decided that no surveillance of Fayverdale was needed.

"All the servants have been checked," he thought aloud. "They are hand-picked and have been there for years. It must be the Douglas woman. Everything fits. Her relationship with Fayverdale and his connections with the Soviet embassy. We've now examined his bank balance. All that money from the diamond concession for which he seems to do nothing!" He paused to tap the ash out of his pipe.

"Well, the PM will have to be informed of this development today," he said to his deputy. "We'll leave it to him whether he sends a message to Butcher, but I shall advise him against it. Meanwhile, we must make a search of the Douglas and Fayverdale flats. The telephone trick doesn't work with them. If the line is being repaired, they always stay in the room—clearly on instructions. We'll just have to do a break-in and entry job."

"Green's the right chap to put in charge of that exercise," the deputy said.

"Okay. Now we must think about the consequences of interrogating the Douglas woman if we find anything more incriminating. If we break her down, she might tell us so much that we won't be able to avoid arresting her. That'll mean publicity, and the PM may want to avoid that. You know, it's at times like this that you realize how hamstrung we are by the regulations. The public just wouldn't believe it if they knew how powerless we are. They read so many spy novels they think we can do anything." Black took out his tobacco pouch. "Sometimes I wish they were right," he sighed.

Because of the delicacy of his mission, Black entered No. 10 by the back way when he went to see the Prime Minister. Owen was deeply shocked by the news but hardly needed Black's advice in deciding what to do. He rose abruptly from his chair and paced the room for a few moments. "I don't have to explain to you the political repercussions of an open scandal revealing a Cabinet Minister to have been the dupe of a woman spy, especially when he also happens to be the Foreign Secretary and it's well known that the Foreign Office runs the British Secret Service," he said. "I can just picture the reaction of some of those Senators in Washington, especially those who know about the new agreement on interchange of information on anti-submarine warfare. By the way, I hope you haven't told the FBI anything about this affair?" he asked with sudden apprehension.

"No, Prime Minister," Black replied with a self-satisfied look. "I felt this was a case where our normal channels of liaison might be blocked for once."

"Thank God for that. We shall have to stifle the whole business," said Owen. "In the national interest," he added, identifying it with his own. "I'll talk to Lord Butcher when he returns. Can you cope with this woman and Fayverdale without precipitating publicity?"

Black reassured him that in counterespionage work this was common practice.

"I think it should be reasonably easy to control the activities of both suspects without their knowing it, Prime Minister. Of course, it might eventually be necessary to frighten them out of business by letting them know they're under suspicion. That's something we'll have to decide when we know more about them. I'll let you have a report in a day or two."

Owen congratulated Black on the efficiency of his department, and at the end of their meeting both felt relieved that such a potentially dangerous penetration had been countered so promptly. It had been a fine piece of work by MI5, but as the next twenty-four hours were to show, it was several weeks too late.

chapter 24

The examination of Diana's flat, carried out during the three hours she was safely immobilized in the hairdressers', produced little of interest beyond some compromising notes from Butcher, which the security men removed, and the search of Fayverdale's apartment carried out at the same time was even less rewarding. Because of Kopec's services, Fayverdale had never been encumbered with the radio transmitters, code books, one-time pads, invisible inks, or any of the other incriminating paraphernalia of the professional spy, and during the previous two days his Kensington Friends had removed all their equipment without giving him any reason. They had replaced the transparent mirror with a real one, but since there had been no time to brick and plaster the hole behind, it had been covered only by a tapestried panel, and Green had little difficulty in deducing what had been there before. He also detected that a hole big enough to conceal a microphone had been bored behind a wall-plaque bearing Fayverdale's coat of arms, which he zealously noted in his report as carrying a motto reading, when translated, "We are not born for ourselves alone but for the whole world."

Acting under instructions, the flat was left in a sufficient state of disarray to make its owner realize that it had been visited by intruders looking for a particular kind of loot. Black hoped that by this maneuver Fayverdale and Diana would be scared into inactivity and that their Soviet controller, who had not been identified, would leave hurriedly for Moscow. His hope was to be realized but hardly in the way he had anticipated.

Hours before Black's agents had forced the lock on Fayverdale's apartment, Yarochetsky had packed his bags, ready to catch the Polish freighter sailing from Tilbury Docks that night. Before doing so, and acting under direct orders from Moscow, he had prepared and posted identical registered packages addressed to Dorothy Jordan-Bell, Lady Butcher, Julian Merton, and the editors of the Communist newspaper in Cyprus, *L'Humanité* in Paris, all the national dailies in London, and several New York and Washington papers.

Dorothy was having her tea and toast in bed when the morning papers and her mail were brought up to her. Wiping the marmalade from her knife on her napkin, she slit open the registered packet to receive the biggest shock of her life. The contents consisted of six glossy, well-focused prints showing the Foreign Secretary in the most compromising situations with Diana Douglas. Both were so easily recognizable that neither could pretend it was somebody else. The pictures had been carefully chosen so that while some were only fit to be sold surreptitiously on the Paris boulevards, others were printable by an editor with no inhibitions. Dorothy leaped out of bed and ran with them into the next room, where her husband was already busy with the contents of his red boxes.

"My God, look at these," she said. "Who on earth do you think sent them? And why to me?"

Owen could hardly believe his eyes. He wanted to think they might be fakes. The Russians had been circulating fake documents intended to blacken the characters of governments and public men in this way for years, but he could not help feeling that those in his hands were all too genuine after the information the Director General of MI5 had given him previously. He reached for the telephone.

"Get 'DG' round here as soon as possible," he told his secretary. "And cancel my appointment for 10:30."

A few minutes later Merton also reached out from his bed to cancel a morning appointment. He had gazed long and hard at the photographs, and with memories of a previous Conservative Premier whose reputation had been roasted by the Socialists because of the sexual diversions of one of his Ministers, he saw in them the means of satisfying personal and party revenge.

Within hours the pictures were being passed around at every morning conference in Fleet Street, and the guffaws were soon being echoed throughout Whitehall. Because of the shackling libel laws, no Fleet Street editor dared print even the less indecent photographs, but after inquiries all decided to carry front-page stories linking Butcher in a scandal with the beautiful Diana and hinting at his resignation.

The message from Downing Street to Butcher in Nicosia reached him only minutes before the embarrassed High Commissioner with whom he was staying drew his attention to the anti-British Cyprus newspaper, with two of the photographs showing him in bed with Diana spread across its front page. He could not understand how they had been secured, but the immediate telephone call he made to Owen soon explained that.

"I need your resignation and I want it by tonight," Owen said after his brief cross-examination, with Black listening in.

"Surely I must be given a chance to explain things more fully first."

"You'll get that all right. I want you back by this evening. Your transport's already fixed."

"What about the conference?"

"To hell with the conference. You'll have to postpone it. The crisis is here right now, thanks to your bloody folly."

In the dowdy room that had once been Morgan Owen's, Julian Merton, Hastings Maclaren, and other senior members of the Shadow Cabinet gathered to discuss their battle plan for exploiting the situation. Since further publicity was inevitable, they had no inhibitions about exacerbating the national ignominy, but these would have been submerged anyway in their vain conviction that the nation's interest would best be served by driving the Socialists from office by any means. As for Butcher's ignominy, they gave it no thought. The principle that a man must not be hit when he is down has never applied to political opponents.

"Well, gentlemen, my information is that there's much more in this Butcher business than a sordid sexual affair," Merton began. "Apart from the calamitous damage likely to follow the breakdown of the Cyprus discussions, I can assure you, within these four walls, that there has been a real security risk and almost certainly actual breaches of security. So let us focus our attack on that issue— security. The Prime Minister has brought the entire administration into disrepute by appointing as Foreign Secretary a man with serious defects of character. He should be made to resign for displaying gross lack of judgment!"

"I agree, Julian," Hastings Maclaren interposed, drumming the table lightly with his fingers. "But we shouldn't ignore the moral implications. Without the immorality, there would have been no breach of security. We shouldn't miss any opportunity to charge this Government with responsibility for the immorality which has spread like a fulminating infection in the community ever since they gained office six years ago."

Maclaren's point was undeniable, but with mental shudders at their own secret lives, which were as full of dark corners as a painting by Rembrandt or Caravaggio, most of the men around the table supported Merton's plan for concentrating on security.

"It's agreed, then, that we shall press for a public inquiry into the security aspects of the Butcher case, first through the channels of the newspapers and television and then in the House," Merton concluded. "We can decide now who will do the public talking. I propose to say nothing myself until I have seen Owen in private."

Meanwhile, Butcher had been smuggled back to England in an RAF plane officially scheduled, as a cover plan, to touch down at Lyneham, in Wiltshire, where journalists and cameramen were assembled, but which was diverted to Abingdon, thirty miles away in Berkshire, so that the Foreign Secretary could be hustled by helicopter to Chequers, the country retreat provided for the Prime Minister, where Owen was awaiting him.

Realizing that he was politically ruined, Butcher made a full confession about his imprudent affair but was still adamant that Diana could have known nothing about the photographs.

"I know this woman, Morg: whatever else she may be, it's unthinkable that she could be a spy," he insisted as they sat around the fireplace in the disarming atmosphere of the long gallery with its mellowed portraits, stained glass windows, and leather-bound books. "It's that swine Fayverdale you want to be after."

Even Black, who had also been called to the Elizabethan elegance of Chequers, found difficulty in making Butcher accept his picture of the Fayverdale-Douglas relationship. Butcher had been asked not to communicate with Diana before the Prime Minister had spoken to him, and on Black's advice he was not to be in-

184

formed at that stage of the discovery of the listening device attached to his bed.

"How did these photographs come to be taken, Lord Butcher?" Black asked.

"I haven't the faintest idea. Obviously they were taken in Fayverdale's flat on the one night we stayed there. But I'm damned if I know how."

"I must ask you a very embarrassing question, Lord Butcher," Black said. "Your answer is vital to our future action in this case. Did you willingly pose for these photographs for sexual gratification, either to please Miss Douglas or yourself? It's been done before, you know," Black added hastily, as Butcher narrowed his eyes in disgust. "And by prominent people!"

"I assure you that neither I nor Miss Douglas could possibly do anything so sordid. The whole idea's revolting."

"I agree, Lord Butcher. But you do see, don't you, that it would have been a more satisfactory explanation from our point of view. The alternative—that the pictures were taken surreptitiously by some foreign agent for subversive purposes—is infinitely more damaging politically."

"Maybe, but I'm sorry I can't oblige you," said Butcher wearily. "I've told you all I know. I've never given Miss Douglas any secret or confidential information, and she has never asked for any or displayed the slightest interest in that direction."

Owen, who had been listening with particular intensity to this exchange, decided to end the interview.

"Frank, I don't doubt that DG is as convinced as I am that you are entirely innocent of any breach of security. But you'll have to resign, and your letter must make it clear that you are doing so because of the moral scandal over Miss Douglas. We'll draft it together, then we can issue it to the press with my letter of acceptance. If we get it over quickly and avoid any suggestion about security, the public will accept the whole affair as just a human weakness. Most of the Opposition front bench will be too conscious of their own private misdemeanors to dare to make too much of it. I also intend to shut Merton up by taking him into our confidence to some extent. It'll be like putting a muzzle on a mouse, but it might help."

Butcher did not need pressing to stay the night at Chequers. He had little desire to encounter the frustrated newsmen lobbying his homes in London and Farnborough and still less to face the formidable wife who would undoubtedly divorce him as soon as she knew the full truth.

The moonlit roads were sparkling with the night's first crystals of frost as Owen and Black were driven back to London in the Prime Minister's limousine. As they passed through Amersham, where lights were showing in bedroom windows, Owen reached forward and shut the double glass partition separating them from the chauffeur.

"Well, what do you propose to do about Miss Douglas this time, DG?" he asked in a tired voice.

"We can't avoid interrogating her now, Prime Minister. I suspect she was just a paid dupe for Fayverdale, but it's conceivable that she's part of a bigger network, and we must find out who her other contacts are."

"I agree. We want every bit of information we can get about the bitch. I'm going to be pelted with questions in the House, and there's sure to be a debate. What about Fayverdale?"

"We'll have to be very careful how we handle him. He's not publicly connected with the case at all yet, and there's no evidence against him that we could bring into court. And he is a member of the House of Lords."

Black paused to reposition his bowler hat on his knees and added quietly, "I take it you don't want Butcher in the witness box if it can be avoided?"

"Christ, no! I can't think of anything more dangerous," Owen said, sitting up sharply.

"Then I must point out, sir, that if this woman breaks down and names confederates we might have no option but to arrest her, and then Butcher would automatically be called at the trial. We should, of course, insist on holding most of it in camera, but it's surprising how the courts leak."

"Wouldn't contempt of court keep it out of the papers?"

"In Britain, yes, but not in the United States."

"I see the New York papers are already recalling the Vassall case and others where compromising photographs were taken by Russian agents for blackmail purposes."

"It's nothing to what they'll do if they get hold of the full story, Prime Minister. They always forget their own traitors when we have one. And they've had some stinkers! Incidentally, I need your advice about how much we should tell the American security authorities now."

"What do you think?"

"I think we should tell them everything. If we don't, and they find out, it'll ruin our liaison with them for good."

"What level should we do it at?"

"Let me soften the impact by first giving the information to the FBI representative in London. Then you can follow it up a few days later with something in writing."

"I could wring Butcher's neck for getting us in this bloody mess," Owen said, rubbing the condensation off the window.

"So could I, Prime Minister. The Firm'll be blamed for it all again. We always are."

"I'm the one who'll suffer personally if there's a security scandal, DG," Owen said sharply. "The public doesn't even know your name, and the newspapers are forbidden to mention it. You can go on hiding behind your initials!"

Black just grunted and pretended to look out of the window at a passing car. After a few moments of silence, Owen said, "I was thinking about your interesting suggestion to Butcher that the photographs might have been taken as part of some sort of sexual orgy. You know, that wouldn't be a bad story to put around."

"How do you mean, Prime Minister?" Black asked ingenuously.

"Well, you must have channels for planting that sort of story with the press. Try Holt on the *Dispatch*—he might buy it if he was satisfied it came from an official source. We've misled the press often enough before in the national interest. We did it today over Butcher's arrival. Even if the papers won't bite, surely you could get the rumor spread about?"

"Butcher might deny it through his lawyers."

"Butcher can do what the hell he likes. Nobody's going to believe him. His reputation's ruined anyway, through his own stupidity. He can sacrifice a bit more of it in the national interest."

"It's irregular, Prime Minister, but I agree that the national interest must come first."

Realizing that his message had been registered, Owen said, "On balance, then, can I take it that you still think we might suppress the security implications?"

"I think there's a better than even chance of that, PM," said Black, smiling reassuringly.

But as next morning's newspapers were to prove, his confidence was again unwarranted.

About the time that the disgraced and dejected Butcher was trying to explain his behavior to his wife, John Holt was sitting in his office in the *Daily Dispatch*, wondering how he could best contribute to the big story of the Butcher scandal, which every paper was trying to build up for use that night. His personal intimacy with Butcher, and the fact that he had met Diana at the fateful Soviet embassy party, made him a key figure in the team working on the assignment. Since Butcher had not been traced, John was being held in the office so that he could be rushed to see him the moment he was located. As the hours passed and efforts to find Diana and Fayverdale had also failed, he was typing out a stopgap feature on "My Friend Frank Butcher." It was going badly because he knew that there must be a better story to write if only he could find it, and had just remarked to his secretary that the words were flowing like cold treacle, when his telephone rang. The voice was anonymous, the intonation foreign, and the brief message so electrifying that he raced around to the editor's room with the news. A few inquiries confirmed both the information and John's hunch that his hours of patience with his Soviet embassy contacts had at last paid a rich dividend.

The banner headline in the first edition of the *Daily Dispatch* rushed to Morgan Owen and Sir Roger Black at midnight was all they needed to see to realize that their plan for suppressing the security scandal had been skillfully scuttled.

"Peer Flees to Russia" it announced in huge type. In the story below, which appeared under Holt's name, almost all the most damaging details were there:

Lord "Tony" Fayverdale, 42-year-old son of a famous diplomat, has fled behind the Iron Curtain on the eve of an MI5 inquiry into the scandal involving Lord Butcher, the Foreign Secretary.

He left at the same time as Leonid Yarochetsky, a Second Secretary in the Soviet embassy. Both men are believed to have been smuggled aboard the Polish freighter *Gomulka*, which left Tilbury docks two days ago. Inquiries in Amsterdam indicate that two men answering to the descriptions of Fayverdale and Yarochetsky boarded a Soviet Aeroflot jetliner bound for Moscow there yesterday.

A Soviet embassy spokesman confirmed that Yarochetsky had been recalled to Moscow and would not be returning, but disclaimed any knowledge of Lord Fayverdale's whereabouts.

Miss Diana Douglas, the beautiful blonde involved in the Butcher scandal, is also missing, though there is no evidence that she has left Britain.

The disappearance of Lord Fayverdale, who is the son of a former ambassador to Moscow, will strengthen the Tory leaders' determination to insist that national security has been infringed as a result of the Butcher affair.

Miss Douglas is a close friend of Lord Fayverdale, who derived most of his income from a Soviet diamond concession.

Last night, inquiries revealed that his luxurious flat in Mount Street had been raided by detectives or security officials a few days ago.

It now seems certain that this flat was the location of the compromising photographs of Miss Douglas and Lord Butcher which were published in a Cyprus newspaper while the Foreign Secretary was engaged in vital defense talks there and led to his recall by the Prime Minister.

Security officials suspect that the photographs were taken surreptitiously by Soviet agents, probably through a trick mirror, and circulated by them deliberately to discredit Lord Butcher at a critical time.

Britain's hopes of continuing to base nuclear bombers on Cyprus have been seriously diminished, following suspension of talks with the Cyprus authorities.

U.S. reaction to this development is likely to be severe in spite of several recent defections by American officials.

Then followed a list of British defectors to Russia going right back to Harold Philby, Burgess and Maclean, and Pontecorvo.

Among the many of Fayverdale's friends who were sickened when they read this story, none was more terrified than his former mistress, Coral Carslake, but she need not have been afraid, had she appreciated the patience which keeps the Soviet intelligence machine geared to political purpose. The men who compile the card index of defamation would never have been prepared to use their valuable pictures of her while she was no more than the widow of a politician who had died out of office.

Over a quick snack lunch in the St. Stephen's Tavern, in Westminster, John passed on all his firsthand information to Maclaren, who, as a practical politician, was more concerned with opportunity than with recrimination, and regarded Holt's last disclosure as fair recompense for his original disservice to the Tories. That afternoon, at a meeting of the Shadow Cabinet, the Conservatives decided to force a censure debate over the scandal. At a meeting of the real Cabinet, it was decided to forestall this by announcing the setting up of a tribunal to investigate both the security and moral aspects of the whole affair. This, Owen argued, would take some wind out of the Tory sails and give the public time to get bored with the issue.

The police were alerted to look for Diana, the port and airfield authorities being warned to watch for her possible escape, but while Black was wondering whether in fact she was already out of the country, she was discovered by a local detective in Market Harborough, following a tip by a waiter in the hotel where she was staying under an assumed name.

In his message to the Red Army Colonel in charge of Intelligence at the Soviet embassy in London, the Director of Military Intelligence at "The Center" in Moscow had spelled out Yarochetsky's instructions:

Reference No. 227.
1. Urgent that The Doctor is brought here for conference immediately.

2. The Nurse will render better service where she is.
3. Ensure that The Radiotherapist gets the high-voltage treatment.

Director

The Colonel had no difficulty in deciphering the Director's skillful purpose. Fayverdale was not to be left behind, partly because he knew too much but mainly because his escape would cause a much bigger sensation and bring the British security authorities into greater disrepute than would his arrest. Diana should be made to remain because she knew hardly anything about the espionage situation at the Soviet embassy and her possible arrest and trial would spice up the sex aspects of the scandal. As for Kopec, he knew so much that he was to be taken aboard the *Gomulka* at gunpoint and kept there.

Yarochetsky had given Fayverdale only half an hour to pack a briefcase, warning him that he would undoubtedly be arrested on the following day, when the photographs were due to appear in the Cyprus newspaper, and he had been instructed not to contact Diana. Fayverdale felt he had no alternative. The clerk at Porton who had provided information about Juvenex to the Russians, as well as many defense secrets, had recently been given fifty-five years.

Black and his department were under heavy assault in the newspapers for yet another blunder. Fayverdale had been under continuous surveillance but this had been relaxed after the search of his flat. Instead of a surreptitious watch, involving about eight field agents relieving each other around the clock, a man was posted in an obvious position at the entrance to the block in which Fayverdale lived, as a further means of scaring him out of activity. When Fayverdale failed to emerge for several hours, his presence in the flat was confirmed by making occasional "Sorry-wrong-number" check calls. What the watchers had not realized was that the man who answered the telephone in the flat in Fayverdale's name was someone else placed there by Yarochetsky. When this man had finally emerged from the flat, he went unrecognized, as just another resident in the block.

All the old security incidents, including those in which MI5 had done rather well in arresting spies, were dragged out and presented as a saga of resounding success by the Russians against a comic opera outfit that hid its appalling inefficiency under the convenient blanket of security.

So Green and another of Black's ablest operators were sent to cajole enough out of Diana to justify the issue of a warrant for her arrest by the local police. Then she could be brought back to London, where she could be interrogated in the privacy of one of the Brompton Road flats kept for that purpose by MI5, with all the aids such as bright lights, deprivation of sleep, snap questioning in the middle of the night, and the latest truth drugs, though really strong-arm methods were still forbidden for women suspects, in spite of the steady brutalizing of society.

Diana was in the bath when the receptionist announced that two men had arrived to see her, and she kept them waiting for almost an hour while she lay back in the water, frightened but composed enough to recall the advice which Fayverdale had passed on during one of her apprehensive evenings after she had planted the hearing aid.

"If anyone tries to question you, just remember the lesson of Klaus Fuchs," he had said, wagging his finger at her. "They could never have even brought him into court if he'd kept his mouth shut. He was convicted entirely on his own confession. Even when MI5 have hard evidence, they often can't bring it into court because it would prejudice their secret methods or their contacts. Half the time they rely on their suspects to convict themselves during interrogation. If you persist in saying nothing, the interrogation can't even begin."

So Diana knew exactly what she was going to do by the time she went down to the hotel lounge, looking unconcerned and very beautiful. After all, she assured herself, however professional her visitors might be, they were only men. And in the management of men she was no amateur.

"We're making some inquiries and we think you might be able to help us," Green said disarmingly, after showing his credentials. "It's very confidential and it's rather public here. It would be more convenient if we could talk in our car outside."

"I'm sorry, but I never get into cars with strange men," Diana said with a prim smile, motioning them to the furthest corner of the lounge.

"It's about Lord Fayverdale that we think you can help us," Green said as he stood his heavy briefcase on an empty chair.

"I'm afraid I've no intention of helping you at all. I wouldn't dream of saying a word without my lawyer present, and I doubt if I'd say much then."

Alternating friendly courtesy with frosty curtness, Green emphasized the chance he was giving her to clear herself of complicity in Fayverdale's disappearance and dropped dark hints about evidence in his possession, but she resisted all his blandishments.

"Lord Fayverdale has done nothing illegal in leaving the country, so there's simply nothing to discuss. Good day, gentlemen."

As Green watched Diana's shapely legs disappearing up the stairs, he picked up the briefcase containing the tape recorder he had set in motion to record the interview and flicked off the switch with annoyance.

"I'd give a lot to see just how composed she is right now," he said, as Diana locked her bedroom door and leaned heavily for several seconds against the inside of it.

Driving back despondently to London, he analyzed the reasons for his failure, in anticipation of the grilling he faced from "DG," to whom he had already spoken briefly on the telephone.

"The trouble is that woman's got no moral sense," he remarked to his junior colleague after a long silence. "It's the amoral spies who operate purely for money who are the hardest of all to break down. They don't feel they need to justify their behavior. There's no burden on their consciences that they have to unload. They're not consumed by any political fire you can stoke up. You can't humble them and you can't appeal to their patriotism. All you can do is try to trap them with facts, and in this case we were hamstrung. I had a strict injunction not to mention the microphone found on the Foreign Secretary's bed, which is the only hard evidence we've got, and 'DG' repeated it when I talked to him just now. How the hell can they expect us to get results when they send us out with our hands tied behind our backs?"

Morning and evening Butcher scanned the papers for news of Diana. There were scores of pictures of her snatched by photographers after her return to London, but she was as peremptory with journalists seeking interviews as she had been with MI5. Butcher was still convinced that, at the worst, Diana had been the unwilling dupe of Fayverdale, who was the real villain. Unable to contact her by telephone, because she had changed her number to avoid the newspapers, he had written:

My Beloved Diana,
You must let me see you if only to assure you that I do not hold you in any way responsible for what has happened. I know that you are incapable of doing the terrible things I have been urged to believe about you. But I wouldn't care now if they were true, for I find that I value your love more than my reputation.

, Barbara is divorcing me and citing you as co-respondent. I have tried to talk her out of it and offered to provide her with other evidence to save you further distress, but she is determined to be vindictive.

You are all I have left now, and though without you life might prove too empty for me to continue with it, with you I know it could be satisfying and worthwhile. The public memory is short, and my disgrace will soon be submerged by the tide of more important events.

The suffering of the last few weeks has intensified my love for you so it is most urgent that I see you without delay. I am hiding away with a loyal old colleague from the Ministry of Defense in London, so please write to me at my club, where he calls every day to pick up any letters.

Yours, in desperate need of you,
Frank

Diana did not reply for she despised him almost as much as she hated Fayverdale for the mess that she was in.

Unemployed, professionally disgraced, and socially ostracized, the butt of a thousand coarse jokes, Butcher had no idea what to do in the future and cared less. For Diana the future turned out to be much rosier. After a week of bargaining by an agent, she signed up to sell what was to be called "My full confessions" to a Sunday newspaper for £25,000. The story, which the ghost writer eventually extracted from her, denied the espionage innuendo but made up for it in saleability by exaggerating the sexual details of her affair with Butcher. Placards announcing articles like "My Nights in Carlton Gardens," "The Butcher I Knew," and "Sex and the Secretary of State," were hardly calculated to help a ruined man, who faced a future far more demoralizing than in pre-Juvenex days.

Formerly a man in his sixties had at least the compensation that he would not have to live long with a demolished reputation, but Butcher was physiologically a man of forty-five, and apparently likely to remain so provided he went on taking Juvenex. The sheer problem of securing employment at a time when jobs were so scarce looked insuperable. He was highly specialized and psychologically incapable of returning to laboratory work even if he had been still fitted for it. Owen had intimated that an exception would be gladly made in his case if he wished to emigrate, but the prospects abroad seemed even less promising than those at home. Fleetingly, Butcher had contemplated suicide as the simple solution, but he was basically too stable to commit it. He realized that he could shorten his life simply by ceasing to take Juvenex, if he found things intolerable.

Fortunately, though charity was perhaps at its lowest ebb since pre-Christian days, there was one man who was anxious to come to Butcher's aid. This was Lewis Rosenfeld, who had been given the title of Viscount Rosenfeld of Hampstead for his philanthropy and in particular for his early support of Robert Harvey's experiments. Owen felt that this was the least he could do to demonstrate his profound disapproval of the anti-Semites, who had chosen Rosenfeld as a particular target.

Rosenfeld decided to offer Butcher a seat on his board for three reasons. First as a gesture of defiance, for the anti-Semites had even suggested that Butcher, who had been the means of making Juvenex available for all, was a Jew himself: secondly because, having experienced a particularly tough childhood, he was something of a collector of lame ducks: thirdly because he recognized in Butcher an outstanding administrator and project chief who could be picked up cheaply. Rosenfeld had never had difficulty in securing able men to control his factory machines, but had found that men who are really expert at handling people are far too sparse to be missed. So on the day that the tribunal report and the subsequent Parliamentary debate completely cleared Butcher of everything but moral turpitude, he made his offer.

Realizing that most City boards would be barred to him, probably for life, as he lacked the Old Etonian tie which has served as a lifeline to so many drowning careers, Butcher accepted it. So, soon, the man who had decried stiletto heels was in charge of the footwear side of Rosenfeld's business, which was the mainstay of the nation's chiropodists.

Robert had been more astonished than most at the revelation of Butcher's private life.

"What a fool," he commented to Margaret. "What a fool. Public men just shouldn't get themselves into such a dangerous position."

He was impervious to Margaret's sarcastic stare. He would have argued that his infidelity was quite different since he believed he knew all about Shirley's background and, in any case, he was not responsible for state secrets.

He and Margaret were still just managing to hold together, and they might have carried on in armed neutrality, avoiding the legal confession of incompatibility for several years, if Yarochetsky's successor had not been ordered to take a hand.

There were two important-looking packages on the table when Robert came down to breakfast. The one he opened first was from the municipal authorities in Madrid and contained sketches of a statue they proposed to erect in his honor as they had done for Alexander Fleming after his penicillin had cut the mortality rate among gored matadors. It also requested his opinions on possible inscriptions for the plinth. Robert passed the sketches to Margaret and read out the florid attributes, "The implacable enemy of death," "Redeemer of youth."

"And here's some awful play on Omar Khayyám about keeping youth's sweet manuscript open. God, how appalling!"

The second package into which he slipped his tableknife had a Hampstead postmark but was otherwise identical to that which had been sent to Lady Butcher, including the photographs and the postures, except that the participants were Fayverdale and Margaret. As Britain's best-known scientist, Robert was a particularly prime target for discredit on the Soviet list, and since scientists who married Communists were automatically barred from important government posts, it followed that publicity connecting his wife with a security scandal would cast serious doubt on him.

Like many habitually unfaithful men, Robert was not conditioned to be at the receiving end of infidelity. Enraged that his reputation had been imperiled, he stormed and fumed as though he had never been guilty of any indiscretion.

"Supposing these have been sent to a newspaper, like Butcher's," he shouted, waving the photographs in Margaret's face. "I'll never be able to hold my head up again."

To which all Margaret could do was hang hers down.

He soon had proof that his fear was justified. Reporters instructed to confirm the identity of the woman in the photographs were soon ringing up to ask if Lady Harvey had been a close friend of the missing Lord Fayverdale. All the newspapers had been looking for reasons to keep the Fayverdale sensation alive, and nothing had been heard of him since his disappearance. Direct inquiries in Moscow were impossible, since all Western correspondents had been withdrawn, and, as was standard practice in security matters, the British embassy in Moscow and the Soviet embassy in London would say nothing. Two of the photographs simply showed Fayverdale and Margaret standing together in his flat, and the newspapers were delighted with any new picture of the missing spy, especially when coupled scandalously with the wife of a famous man.

MI5 were equally curious, and Robert felt that, in this case, he could hardly afford to be as offhand with the agent who came to see him as he had been before. Black was quickly satisfied from the agent's report that Margaret had no complicity in the security side of Fayverdale's life and was able to reassure them that because of the restrictive libel laws, the British newspapers would be unable to print the pornographic pictures or hint much about them. To strengthen his defenses in this regard, he advised Robert to consult a lawyer and to issue a confidential warning notice to editors over the wire service of his determination to sue if given grounds, but nothing could stop the news from spreading on the gossip circuits, and Margaret ceased to receive invitations to open hospitals and charity bazaars.

When she had recovered from the initial shock of her exposure and the natural reaction of self-justification asserted itself, she decided she had no more to be ashamed of than her husband and said so. But Robert's overload of masculine pride had been shattered, creating an obstacle in the path of forgiveness that would take years to remove. He might soon have forgiven his wife had she been convicted of shoplifting, a crime against somebody else, but adultery was a crime against him. Furthermore, by nature he was not among the few who can easily pardon those they have injured or to whom they are beholden.

Both recognized that their alliance was wrecked beyond salvage. Even the ligaments that bound them through the children were atrophied. The children had been home for Christmas but were all away again. Paul was working in London. So was Angela, who, through the influence of Dorothy Jordan-Bell, had started work as a junior assistant on a fashion magazine. Simon was in his second year at Oxford.

As the house in Salisbury was tied to Robert's job, it was Margaret who moved, and he made only a token effort to stop her and none to bring her back. He could hardly import Shirley at that stage, but it was understood that once a divorce was arranged, they would be married.

In the days that followed Margaret's departure Robert assured himself more and more that he was less and less to blame. She had been the one who had left. She had been the quitter. It was she who had deserted the home and created the problem of explaining the break-up to the children. It did not occur to him at that stage to consider how much his Juvenex might have been responsible both for his inability to resolve his conflict of loyalties on the side of sound sense and stability and for her out-of-character infatuation with a philanderer like Fayverdale.

His good-riddance determination to rub Margaret right out of his life was reflected in the sudden death of the commemorative oak tree she had planted in the Porton grounds. The shrivelling of its buds, which was inexplicable to the gardener who reported it, posed no mystery to Robert, who had soaked its roots with a bucket of weedkiller poured out in the darkness.

"Dig it out, we won't bother to replace it. And bring the plaque to me," he told the gardener.

Yet though he spent more and more time in Shirley's flat, he was surprised to find how much he missed the woman he affected to despise, when in the loneliness of the home she still haunted. A compelling memory, which is the attribute of most innovating scientists, in contrast to the caricature of the absentminded professor, has its penalties. To mitigate them, Robert went through the motions of asking himself what he would be doing during despondent moments had Margaret still been at home.

"I should be traveling in this train—alone; going to this meeting —alone; working in this study—alone."

But the emotional forces which ensure survival of the human species have seen to it that severance of the marital cord shall be much too painful to be cured by such simple balm.

chapter 25

On a crisp March morning Robert was standing by his office window staring dejectedly at the plovers wheeling over the long, rolling fields. He was desperately concerned about the social developments, for which he felt himself responsible, and deeply unhappy over the break-up of his marriage. In spite of Shirley's solicitude, he had found himself virtually emasculated by the emotional turmoil, which was continuing much longer than he had expected. It was becoming obvious, too, that the children, who seemed to have accepted the sundering of their home without undue fret as a situation commonplace to the time, had been hurt by it, and the news of Margaret, who was sharing a flat with Angela in London, was distressing. She had reacted in the usual manner of lonely people with a wish to escape, and was drinking too much in sordid little clubs with sordid people who were alien to her character, and however tough Robert pretended to be, he could not bear to see anyone, least of all the mother of his children, in despair. He had just received a letter from Angela which read:

Dearest Daddy,

A group of us went to supper at the Looking Glass last night and Mummy came in with some awful man who looked like a dago. She was drunk and made a dreadful exhibition of herself on the dance floor. It was terribly embarrassing because at least two of the boys with us knew who she was, though they pretended not to. I was so ashamed that I just had to get up and leave.

Mummy still hadn't come home when I left for the office this morning. I'm dreading going back tonight. In haste,

Love,
Angela

As he was wondering whether he would have to go up and see Margaret, he received an anxious telephone call from Dr. Holmes at the East End Hospital.

"I've had the Greenway boy back in hospital for some X-ray treatment for a skin condition on his knee, and a most disturbing thing has happened. There's been a complete breakdown of the irradiated tissue. I'd like you to come and see it."

Robert had one of his numerous committee meetings in London the following day and arranged to call in at the hospital. Joseph, now nineteen, looked normal for his age, except for being rather short. Holmes reminded him who Robert was, then turned down the bedclothes, arched by the steel cage underneath, to expose the patient's knee. The entire area that had been exposed to the X-ray beam could only be described as having gone rotten. The overlying skin and surrounding muscle had collapsed, and the bone of the kneecap was showing.

"What do you think?" Holmes asked after he had taken Robert into his office.

"I suppose there's no possibility that it was caused by an overdose?" said Robert.

"It was the normal dosage for the purpose and there's no signs of any burn, but it certainly seems to have been a catastrophic overdose for Greenway," Holmes commented. "The only explanation I can think of is that your drug eventually makes the cells more sensitive to radiation."

"Christ! I hope you're wrong! But I suppose that's possible,"

200

Robert said, tilting back his chair and staring at the ceiling. "Some substances, like cysteine, make cells less sensitive to X-rays, so presumably others might make them more sensitive. It's also well established that radiation reduces the life-span of normal cells. But this is something of a different order. We ought to find out whether any of the radiologists have had any similar experience and I'll get some experiments going. I hope to God that this is just an individual reaction."

Robert's inquiries quickly brought to light one incident that looked similar. A sixty-five-year-old woman who had taken Juvenex from the time it became available had died while undergoing X-ray therapy for a lung malignancy. The postmortem had revealed a strange cellular collapse of the lung tissue.

Without delay, he arranged for Shirley to return temporarily to St. Patrick's because there were no X-ray facilities at Porton. He needed to know as quickly as possible what happened to white mice, which had been kept youthful by Juvenex, when subjected to varying doses of X-rays. Had he been aware that Shirley was still carrying on a desultory affair with John Holt, he might have made arrangements to send her to some center of medical research other than London.

On the day that Shirley returned to her old laboratory, Morgan Owen called a Cabinet meeting to discuss a political emergency. On the see-as-you-talk TV picture-phone from Washington, President Brandenberg had told him, "I have indisputable evidence from the Central Intelligence Agency that the Russian nuclear testing ground at Novaya Zemlya is being refurbished with great activity."

"What do you think they're up to?" Owen asked, noting, as he watched the small screen on his desk, that the Presidential face seemed more boyish than ever beneath the severe crew cut and more tanned than usual against the gleaming white shirt with the button-down collar.

"I've discussed the situation with the National Security Council, and the considered view is that within a few weeks the Soviets will make some excuse to break the test-ban agreement, just like they did in 1961, and stage a new round of tests in the atmosphere. We know they have several nuclear weapons of novel design, including one showing particular promise for inactivating our long-range missiles in their silos."

"What do you propose to do?" Owen asked, catching sight of the gold-fringed edge of Old Glory standing on the President's left.

"I just can't be caught short on this, Morgan, so I've ordered preparations for testing to be put in hand at the Pacific Proving Ground, so that we can begin immediately after the first Soviet explosion. I propose to warn Turganov of this in a note."

Owen was highly suspicious of the move. He knew that the President had been under relentless pressure from the armaments firms, from the Senators and Congressmen who supported them, and from the weapons scientists, who all wanted to restart nuclear testing in the name of essential progress for the defense of freedom. The U.S. undoubtedly had several new missiles and other nuclear weapons that could not be further developed without atmospheric explosions.

"Wouldn't it be better to talk to Turganov on the hot line and avoid sending him a note? He'll only publish it and use it against you."

"We've gone into that and we'll come out cleaner on the historical record if we send a note," Brandenberg replied crisply, nervously fingering the framed motto he had kept since his student days—"The difference between a groove and a grave is only a matter of depth."

Since the Nassau agreement of 1962, which had permanently downgraded her status as a nuclear power, Britain had ceased to wield much influence with the U.S., and the possibility of using the technical secrets of Juvenex to secure new political concessions, as suggested by Lord Ewhurst, the former Foreign Secretary, had been sacrificed in Owen's rush to discredit the Tories. Further, Owen could not but agree that there had been a sinister stepping up of the propaganda war of hate against the West in recent months, due, in some degree, to the ever more repressive measures needed in Russia and China to hide the existence of the anti-aging drug from the masses. Through self-reinforcing fear, both sides were being driven to increase their military preparedness.

Maxim Turganov was waiting impatiently for the President's note. He had seen to it that good intelligence of the Soviet test preparations would leak to the U.S., and he was ready to take action as soon as the American Ambassador handed the inevitable document to him in the Kremlin.

The note drew Premier Turganov's attention to the grave danger that would confront the world if the Soviet Government broke the solemn test-ban agreement. It stated that the U.S. had indisputable evidence of massive preparations for a round of atmospheric tests. It stressed the medical dangers from nuclear fallout, which might afflict future generations, and warned that the Soviet Government would bear the blame in history if the U.S. was forced to resume atmospheric tests as well.

Turganov lost no time in putting his propaganda machine into action. *Pravda* printed the confidential note in full, with a long editorial, claiming that it was a typical Western imperialist trick to excuse the resumption of tests by the U.S. and put the blame on the peace-loving people's democracies. Moscow radio took up the theme.

"The capitalist armament makers and imperialist warmongers have forced the U.S. President into agreeing to break the solemn test-ban treaty for which the Soviet leaders worked so hard," the announcer thundered. "The peace-loving peoples will not be deceived by such a despicable maneuver. The official answer to President Brandenberg's impudent note will be given within twenty-four hours."

The official answer proved to be a thumping nuclear airburst over the Arctic proving ground at Novaya Zemlya, estimated by the long-range nuclear analysts at 200 megatons, easily the biggest ever staged. Within three days there were four more explosions, which proved to be "dirty" as regards fallout, making a total yield of more than 800 megatons, and it was obvious that there were more to come.

World reaction to this brutal disregard of the diplomatic niceties was intense. Lord Questing and his followers demonstrated outside the Soviet embassy in Kensington Palace Gardens, but made much more noise and disturbance outside the American embassy in Grosvenor Square. Scientists of dubious political affiliation issued grave warnings of the medical consequences and urged the U.S. not to make the situation worse by restarting tests in retaliation. President Artois, who was planning to test a small French H-bomb in the near future, said nothing.

The Pope publicly reiterated the theme *Pacem in Terris* of the famous Encyclical of Pope John XXIII, beseeching men who have the responsibility for public affairs to ensure that relations between states are regulated by the rule of truth, justice, and cooperation in the name of Jesus Christ, Saviour of the World and Author of Peace—to which Turganov, who claimed those titles for himself, privately reiterated the equally well-known dictum of the rehabilitated Stalin, "How many divisions has the Pope?"

Over Peking radio, Marshal Ho Cheng warned that China's 850 millions would not sit idly by while the handful of guilty men who represented only 200 million Russians polluted the peace-loving people's air. To which Turganov asked himself, "How many long-range missiles has Marshal Cheng?" and answered himself with a reassuring "None."

In a television broadcast relayed around the earth by satellites President Brandenberg addressed the free peoples and those few behind the Iron Curtain with the temerity to tune into him. Speaking in a flat, unemotional voice, he said, "As you all know, the United States and her allies have never relaxed their efforts in the quest for peaceful coexistence with the Soviet Union. We have worked unceasingly for peace, because total war makes no sense in an age when an exchange of nuclear missiles could bring only devastation to both sides and release poisons that might make even neutral countries uninhabitable. But, unfortunately, over the past years and in particular during the last few months, the Soviet leaders have gone out of their way to promote such a virulent campaign of hatred against us that they have debased international politics to the continuation of war by other means. They have cut off all cultural and trade relations. By strengthening the monstrous barbed wire curtain, they have deliberately widened the chasm between East and West and set back the hopes of all people of goodwill for an open world and open skies.

"Now, without provocation, the Soviets have broken the agreement to ban nuclear explosions in the atmosphere. My efforts to prevent this at ambassadorial level and by direct negotiation on the telephone with Premier Turganov have been negative. The hot line from the White House to the Kremlin, which we installed in the hope of preventing such offhand developments, proved of no value. Premier Turganov never made himself available for discussion on the four occasions on which I attempted to consult him during the last two days. In their first explosion of this new series the Soviets released more radioactivity into the atmosphere than was produced by all previous nuclear tests.

"In the face of such a truculent attitude, I would be negligent in my duty as Commander-in-Chief of the U.S. forces if I failed to take the necessary precautions to preserve our liberty and way of life. So, with the unanimous approval of the Chiefs of Staff, and after consulting with our NATO allies, I have ordered a resumption of nuclear tests at the Pacific proving ground. A big task force is already being assembled for this purpose. I am advised that the new weapons devised by our scientists will be comparatively clean and that the contribution they will make to global fallout will be negligible.

"We remain dedicated to the task of securing a world governed by reason and not by force. With God's help, we shall go on trying to resolve our differences by peaceful negotiation, but at the same time we must reaffirm our determination never to be subdued by threat of violence."

The first American 100-megaton bomb was rocketed into the atmosphere above Johnston Island within three weeks, giving *Pravda* "proof" that the imperialists had been all set to resume tests anyway and an excuse for praising Premier Turganov for beating them into the lead. Within three months a combined total of 2,000 megatons had been exploded.

The monstrous fireballs mushroomed high into the stratosphere, carrying with them tons of radioactive debris. There, the minute particles of strontium 90, radioiodine, and other malignant materials were caught up in the stream of great dry winds and distributed around the earth. Slowly, under the inexorable influence of gravity, they leaked down into the cloudy atmosphere so that when it rained the floating fallout was steadily washed to earth.

The months which followed the tests were remarkable for excessive rainfall throughout the Northern Hemisphere. Winter storms flattened the furrows of the farmland and flooded the fen dikes and ditches. Warm spring and early summer downpours had greened up the clover and the deer-sedge, giving an early bite to the dairy cattle and moorland sheep. They plumped the potatoes, crisped the lettuce, swelled the grain of the prairies and the cobs of the corn belt. In China, Japan, and Southeast Asia rain like torrents of tepid tea engulfed the paddy fields.

As usual the H-bombs were blamed for the weather, and this time, because of the known effects of high explosions on the electrical layers surrounding the earth, no scientist of repute would deny that they might not be responsible. Hourly, day and night, the strontium 90 and other fission products built up in the soil, where they were absorbed by the thirsty roots of growing grass, grain, and vegetables. In time, this radioactivity found its way into the bodies of millions of people who ate the affected plants or consumed the milk and dairy products from the cattle which had grazed them. The daily intake was negligible, but once in the body, the atoms of strontium 90 tended to remain forever, locked inside the bones and every few seconds one of them exploded like an ultramicroscopical bomb, causing tissue damage which was minute but, in accumulation, could be as destructive as the tiny surges of pressure inside a root forcing its way through concrete.

The Agricultural Research Council issued reassuring figures, and the Medical Research Council was not unduly worried. Previous fallout scares had proved unjustified, and the Government was determined not to cause unnecessary concern again and bring about a slump in the consumption of milk, which had been boosted to record levels by a long and highly expensive advertising campaign. The levels of radioactive intake regarded as safe had been raised again by the Medical Research Council, on the grounds that, previously, they had been unnecessarily cautious when less was known about the effects of radiation. So, in spite of the massive yield of the new weapons being tested, it was expected that the level of global fallout would be held well below the new tolerance limit. This optimistic view was strongly challenged by Lord Questing and other scientists, who suspected that the diminished value placed on human life had unconsciously conditioned the authorities to accept safety levels which their predecessors would have rejected. But their arguments had little impact on the public, who simply asked themselves, "If there was any real danger, would the Russians have started the tests when they will get just as much of the fallout as we will?"

But though the general public might not be perturbed, Sir Robert Harvey, Dr. Thomas Holmes, and a few more people with special information were greatly alarmed. Three more cases of severe irradiation effects brought on by normally safe dosages of X-rays had been reported. A fifty-five-year-old scientist at Harwell, whose body had been accidentally exposed to a burst of radiation from which he should have recovered, died within forty-eight hours from a form of radiation sickness more acute than any previously on record.

On top of these developments, which had been hushed up until more fully investigated, Shirley's mice experiments were beginning to show a disquieting result. She had sent Robert a graph of her preliminary findings. It confirmed that Juvenex definitely increased sensitivity to X-rays, but with a high degree of individual variation. Roughly five percent of the mice lapsed into rapid senility when given a dose of X-rays only one-third of what they would have been able to tolerate had they not taken Juvenex. A further thirty percent lapsed when the dosage was raised to two-thirds of the normal safe level. The rest showed greater resistance but more and more of them went into decline as the dosage was raised.

During a restless night in the lonely bedroom in Salisbury, Shirley's graph intruded into Robert's dreams, heaving its humped shape to the size of one of the burial mounds abounding on the Wiltshire plain, with her neatly penciled crosses expanding into more ominous symbols.

chapter 26

Shirley was lying in the warm sun ruminatively crushing the friable leaf mold in her hand and running it through her fingers. Margaret had failed to start divorce proceedings and in spite of persistent prompting from Shirley, Robert did not feel that he could live with his conscience if he divorced her for her short lapse with Fayverdale. So he and Shirley were living together in London, which he visited two or three times a week, while waiting for the grounds of desertion to mature—a flexible situation which he found better suited to his busy life than the rigid bond of remarriage. He had visited St. Patrick's Hospital that morning to inspect the mice experiments, and they had taken off in his fast new car for their favorite spot at Mapledurham, for Robert had never been in greater need of an ambience of calm.

"Obviously the Health Ministry must warn the hospitals to stop using X-rays on people who've been taking Juvenex for longer than a year," Shirley said as they mulled over the results of her experiments. "Thank God that it's only rarely they have to be used now. The reduction in malignancies more than makes up for this side-effect."

"It's not the X-rays I'm worried about," said Robert lying on his back with his eyes shut and sucking at a blade of grass. "I attended a special emergency meeting called to advise the Cabinet yesterday. You see that clear blue sky? Well, the odds are that it's going to kill millions. And I shall be one of the first to go."

"For God's sake, what are you talking about?" Shirley asked, sitting up sharply.

"According to Sir Henry Taylor of the Atomic Energy Authority who chaired the meeting, that sky which looks so benign may hold more than twenty tons of strontium 90 and other fission products of which ten percent will fall to earth every year. You, me, and everyone else in the world are going to absorb a share of it into the bones. And if those of us who have been taking Juvenex are as supersensitive to radiation as the evidence suggests, then the strontium 90 may reach a lethal level for us all."

Shirley was too stunned by the prospect to comment.

Withdrawing Shirley's graph from his inside pocket and unfolding it on the ground between them, Robert said, "Fallout has a similar effect to X-rays. So, if the pattern of human sensitivity proves to be like that of the mouse, up to five percent of the free world's population, that's about three millions in Britain alone, might be doomed by the radioactive dust already on the ground or in the stratosphere. And the toll will rise steadily with each new bomb that's exploded."

208

"Oh, my God, I hadn't thought of that," said Shirley.

"We can't escape it because we've got to eat," Robert continued. "It's no good trying to hide underground or wear protective clothing. It'll snuff us out as quietly and effectively as this blanket of beech leaves blots out anything else that tries to grow here." He paused, wondering what was happening inside his bones at that moment.

"You know, we won't feel a thing. It'll be like conception, unfelt in the darkness of the tissues but fraught with tremendous consequence. Questing and his mob have been howling that some idiot would bring about the nuclear destruction of civilization by miscalculation, and now it looks as though that idiot is going to be me. What a turn of events! Who could have foreseen that the Doomsday Machine would come out of a hospital laboratory?"

"Well, why doesn't the Government warn the Americans and the Russians to stop the tests immediately?"

"The Americans have already stopped. Brandenberg and Morgan Owen are going to try to see Turganov this week to get him to stop too, but I'll bet he refuses."

"Why should he? Aren't they in the same boat?"

"No. You know very well that the Russians and the Chinese prohibited the use of Juvenex because of the economic fears, as I now see we should have done. So they're not going to be put at risk. The strontium 90 levels will be tolerable for them."

"Don't you see the implication?" Robert asked impatiently, when Shirley made no comment. "They've only to go on testing and they'll defeat the whole Western world without firing a shot, destroying a building, or sustaining a casualty! They can calculate the weight of fission products they need to release to bring the global fallout well above the tolerance limit for Juvenex-takers, while keeping it well below the safe limit for most of their own people who have aged normally."

"What about leukemia?" Shirley asked.

"Oh, they'll get a few thousand extra cases among the very sensitive members of the population, but that's a tiny penalty. It's a fantastic opportunity for Turganov. After spending billions of rubles on weapons which looked like having no purpose except to prevent defeat, he can suddenly use them to secure victory. If he knows about it, I don't see how he can resist it."

209

Shirley was horrified. "It's too cold-blooded. It's not possible," she said. "Turganov's a civilized human being, and I just can't bring myself to believe that he could be so fanatical as to sacrifice perhaps five hundred million people for a political idea."

"I can," Robert replied despondently. "There have been many men in the past who'd have done it in the name of religion. There are plenty still living who think we should have wiped out the Communists when we had a nuclear monopoly."

"It looks as though they were right."

"I'll bet that if you take all the wars that have ever been waged for ideals of religion or politics, the combined casualties must total fifty millions. All Turganov would have to do, if presented with the possibility, would be to convince himself that there's no moral difference between doing it over several centuries and doing it all in a few weeks."

"I suppose that if you can justify fifty million deaths, you can justify five hundred million."

"It would be easy for Turganov to do so. It's officially estimated that the global casualties in an H-bomb war could total five hundred millions in three days. The missiles capable of causing them have been at instant readiness for many years, and for all that time Turganov has been living in an atmosphere in which he constantly has to remind the world of his own instant readiness to use them."

"It's terrible to contemplate, Robert. But I suppose that when you've been forced to accept that each tomorrow might be the day when you cause five hundred million casualties, actually pressing the button isn't inconceivable, especially when, for the first time in history, all the casualties are going to be on the other side. But surely there's something the Government can do?"

"They're in a hell of a fix. They should warn the public, but that would cause a panic and give the game away to Turganov, if he hasn't already seen his opportunity. They're not going to tell him about the increased sensitivity if they can avoid it."

"What about antidotes?"

"The Americans are going to sponsor a crash program into medical protection against the effects of radiation. There are several drugs that show promise of being able to counter strontium 90 to some extent. We're going to do all we can here, but I think it's too late."

"You mean there may be enough stuff floating about up there already to take us all over the limit?"

"Yes, we just don't know how dirty those last Russian bombs were. And if the explosions continue at the present rate, the chances of finding some effective drug protection against it in the time are negligible, especially for me, when I've been taking Juvenex longer than anyone else."

"I haven't told you . . ." Shirley said.

"You haven't told me what?"

"Oh, nothing. It's not important. Are you going to advise your friends to stop taking it?"

"How can I? They've all been taking it longer than a year, and all the evidence shows that they'll age at about five times the normal rate if they stop now. And there's no certainty that stopping the drug will reduce their sensitivity to radiation. We lose both ways. What an appalling mess!"

Shirley put her arm around him to comfort him, but he was in no mood for affection.

"Now you must keep your mouth shut this time," he said almost savagely. "Don't say anything to Holt if you see him, or to anybody else. We don't want to start a panic. There's still an outside chance that the Russians might be induced to stop in time."

"Don't worry, I shan't be seeing Holt," lied Shirley, who had been meeting him with increasing frequency since she had moved back to London.

To President Brandenberg's great surprise, Turganov was available when he called him on the White House hot line and immediately agreed to see him and Owen in Moscow at their convenience, though he was given no indication of the extreme urgency of the situation. The visit was announced simply as a last-ditch effort to negotiate a reimposition of the test ban as a means of reducing international tension. Brandenberg and Owen had agreed that the particular plight of the West should not be revealed to Turganov, unless it proved absolutely necessary to do so.

Turganov was most affable when they met in his private office in the Kremlin, and his visitors soon learned why.

"Take as much as you like, gentlemen," he said in English, pointing to the ritual vodka and caviar served before the talking began. "The vodka has been bottled for three years, and there was no strontium 90 in the Volga when the sturgeon were caught." He raised the small glass to the toast position. "*Na zdorovye.* Good Health." The smile, which normally flickered around his full lips, disappeared. "Good Health—to all of us," he repeated.

"I know exactly what you are worried about, gentlemen," he said when the formal discussion began. "Our scientists have also discovered that the drug, which we call Omoloditel, makes the body more susceptible to atomic radiation. Let me tell you frankly, I'm very worried, too. I will confess to you that I have been taking Omoloditel for as long as you have. So I'm in the same danger. It's therefore in my personal interest to stop the tests as quickly as possible but, though you don't believe it, I'm in the hands of my Party. I will put your proposition to the Presidium, which will have to make the decision."

He paused to watch Brandenberg and Owen as they looked at each other, bereft of their briefings by this unexpected candor.

"We are prepared to put forward a new package deal," said Brandenberg, trying to regain the initiative. "It includes some disarmament proposals that would meet all your difficulties over inspection, recognizes the permanent partition of Germany, and provides for a nonaggression treaty between NATO and the Warsaw Pact. But it is contingent on the immediate suspension of nuclear tests."

"I urge you to examine the proposals, Premier," said Owen, eagerly. "They take us such a long way down the road of sanity."

Turganov smiled disarmingly. "Marshal Ho Cheng was as insistent as you in demanding that we stop the tests at first, but our military advisers assure us that they are absolutely essential if the deterrent is to continue to keep the peace, and the Marshal's presumably accepted that, because he's stopped complaining. Of course we are interested in your proposals, and if you let me have them in detail, I'll put them before the Presidium, but it will take time. We are a democracy here, you know, and the different aspects of these matters all have to be thrashed out in the people's interest. We are so little of a dictatorship that I assure you I am quite expendable."

There was little more to be said. Turganov had insisted on the usual bibulous reception for the visitors, followed by a display of virtuosity by the Bolshoi ballet, but Brandenberg, Owen, and the expert advisers who had accompanied them were too scared to enjoy it. They would have enjoyed it less had they known, as they soon did on their return to their embassies, that another 200-megaton bomb had been detonated at Novaya Zemlya just as they were halfway through "Swan Lake."

As he looked through the window of the Disonic jet across the runway of Sheremetyevo Airport, where the tall figure of Turganov could be seen waving them farewell, Sir Henry Taylor who was sitting next to Owen remarked, "Assuming that Turganov was telling the truth about taking the drug himself, do you think it's conceivable that he knew about the increased sensitivity to radiation before he restarted tests and deliberately organized them to produce this situation?"

"Well, it would be tantamount to suicide if you fellows are right, and he doesn't look tired of life to me," Owen answered glumly. "But who would know what goes on behind those sloping eyebrows?"

Power politics had ceased to be fun for orators like Owen since science had dominated statesmanship. After a hundred years in which the written word had been the supreme vehicle of influence, television had once more made the mouth mightier than the pen, but in the meantime the test tube had become mightier than either.

chapter 27

Spring had her vigorous foot firmly on winter's throat, and as the dairy cattle grazed on the flush of grass, the Harwell analysts reported a substantial increase in the burden of strontium 90 in the nation's milk. There were now so many cases of human reaction to

X-rays that the Health Ministry had sent out a confidential memorandum to all hospitals advising temporary cessation of X-ray therapy. This news had leaked to the press and caused disquieting speculation, particularly by John who, through odd remarks dropped by Shirley during their occasional evenings together, had strong suspicions that something more inscrutable was being concealed. More than a dozen questions on these developments were down for answer in Parliament, and the several ministries involved had been ringing Robert at his London office in the Medical Research Council headquarters for guidance in dealing with them. Now there was Dr. Holmes on the telephone, or rather, Sir Thomas, for in the midst of impending disaster the sideshow of honors still went on, and he had secured his knighthood for routine services to the Royal Household.

"If there is a last broadsheet on Doomsday, it will be the *London Gazette*," thought Robert as he said "Hullo."

"Can you come round to the London Clinic right away? It's Merton. It's fantastic."

Robert raced around. Without a word, Holmes, who looked haggard, took him up into Merton's private ward. There, propped up on pillows, was a large-size replica of the Greenway boy as Robert had first seen him. The lolling head with its drum-tight scalp, the pigeon face, and shrunken frame—all the symptoms were there.

Holmes pulled back the bedclothes.

"He went like that in a month," he said. "It's a misnomer for a man of his age but, apart from the nausea he's complained of, if that's not a case of progeria I've never seen one."

The radiation from the strontium 90 in Merton's bones had been strong enough to dehydrate his hypersensitive tissues, bringing his weight down to 70 pounds. He was still capable of being rational, but had reacted so emotionally to the mirror sight of his terrible relapse that Holmes had put him under heavy sedation.

Robert stared silently for a few moments, then said quietly, "You realize that you are looking at us, too?"

"What do you mean?"

"If my interpretation is correct, everyone of us who has taken Juvenex for more than a year will go exactly the same way. We have all become so supersensitive to radiation that it's only a matter of time before the build-up of strontium 90 in our bones will neutralize the effect that Juvenex has exerted on our cells and bring about this rapid degeneration. Merton and I were among the first to take it. If I go the same way, you'll know I'm right. It's probably only because of his age and all the milk he drinks that he's beaten me into being the first case."

Holmes was staggered by the prospect. "I was only called in last week when the symptoms began to look so like those of progeria. We've tried increased dosage of Juvenex, but either it had no effect or accelerated the aging."

"How long do you give him?" Robert asked, pointing to Merton's sleeping form.

"He might hang on for months, especially if we took some heroic measures to keep him in medicated survival. His mind's still clear and he still has the Mertonian sense of humor. He asked me what his expectation of death was. But he's requested euthanasia, and I'm going to see that he gets it. I may need it myself if what you say is true."

Robert avoided seeing Shirley that afternoon but decided to keep his date with her in the evening. On his way back to Shirley's pleasant flat in Eaton Place he noticed that the evening paper posters were announcing "Another Russian Blast." He decided to spare her the terrifying news about Merton and tried to behave as though things were no worse when they set off for an escapist evening at their old table in The Roaring Forties, but Shirley could see he was worried to the point of despair. At first he shrugged off her solicitous questions, as though his tension was due to no more than his general anxiety, exacerbated by pressure of work, but eventually he could no longer resist the need to tell someone the reason for his agitation.

"If you want to know why I'm worried, it's because I'm now convinced that I, Robert Harvey, may have been the means of destroying Western civilization."

"Why? What's happened?"

As the floor show worked up to its raucous finale, Robert told her about Merton and the possible implication of everyone else.

"But this may just be a fluke case," Shirley insisted. "He may have contracted some virus or something."

"What about the X-ray sensitivity? That's no fluke! God, I never thought I'd be so frightened at the prospect of death. I've always felt I'd such zest for life that even if my legs were shot off I'd somehow get to safety on the stumps, but here I am helpless, and the thought that millions might be involved after me is insupportable."

"It just can't be true, darling. It's too horrifying," Shirley said, squeezing his hand.

"I can't see any other explanation for Merton's condition. To think that I, who seemed to have hit the richest jackpot in medical history, should have to go out in a blaze of infamy. Those men," he said, pointing to a laughing, middle-aged group about to slide down the pole to the bar below, "the odds are that I'm going to kill them all, and a few millions more besides."

Shirley, who by then appreciated the full impact of his fears, tried to comfort him.

"But that bull-headed fool Owen is as much to blame as you, and the Russians even more so."

"I suppose Owen was the midwife to the monster, but it was I who fathered it," Robert said despondently as he toyed with the empty glass which had held his fifth whiskey. "And it was my vanity as much as his gluttony for power which pushed it prematurely into use."

On the way back to Shirley's flat in the taxi, Robert realized that he could no longer delay in making his increased fears known to the Government, and he secured an appointment with Owen next morning.

All that Owen knew about Merton was that he was mortally ill, a fact which had also become known to the newspapers. When Robert described what he had seen and gave his interpretation, Owen screwed up his eyes in silent empathy.

"You mean that you think it's started, then?"

"I'm afraid it has, Prime Minister."

"Well, we can't start a panic on just one case," Owen said as he began to pace the room. "I think you're being too pessimistic. The whole idea's fantastic. But if you're right, what can we do?"

"I suppose we could step up the efforts to find some therapeutic protection against radiation," Robert replied. "Another crash program," he added sardonically.

Owen was quick to respond to the allusion. "If people like you hadn't gone interfering in things you didn't understand, we shouldn't be in this mess now," he retorted testily.

"I warned you against pushing it too quickly, but you steamrollered all of us—Butcher as well."

"Butcher! There's another scientist who should have kept his nose out of politics!" Owen paused and shook his head. "I'm sorry, Harvey. This'll get us nowhere. Is there anything we can do that's constructive?"

Robert, who, as a doctor, had been taught that it was terrible to rob anyone of hope, thought for a moment and said, "The first thing we should do is to speed up the survey of cases which have shown sensitivity to X-rays. By checking how long they have taken Juvenex, we should be able to get a reliable forecast of future casualties. Then you might limit these by issuing any canned or powdered milk in the civil defense stockpiles to adults, so that they don't have to drink any more contaminated milk, which should still be safe for children who haven't taken Juvenex."

"That seems a sensible idea," Owen said, noting it down on his pad. "But how are we going to do it without causing panic when our fears are not absolutely firm?"

"There is a precedent, Prime Minister. When the fallout from the Russian superbombs was overestimated back in 1961, the Government warned the public that it might issue canned milk for babies as a routine precaution. You could issue it for babies now and include adults as an extra safeguard, that is, if you have enough to go around."

"I understand the stockpiles are small, but I'll check with the Food Ministry. Anything else?"

"I can't think of anything at the moment—except to hope that I turn out to be wrong."

Owen shook hands with him and stood for a few moments staring out of the window. He was to be telephoned by Brandenberg in an hour's time, and he was trying to make up his mind whether to tell him about Merton's condition or keep quiet about it.

Merton's death was explained in the newspapers as being the result of a heart attack. A weighted coffin was ceremoniously lowered into the family vault, but under the law which gave the health authorities compulsory powers to acquire any cadaver for research purposes, his mortal remains were divided between the nation's most eminent pathologists, mustered in the frantic search for any method of countering the effects of fallout.

Within a fortnight the newspapers announced the sudden illness and death by euthanasia of Lady Merton. They ran it as a broken heart story. "After sixty years of devotion to her famous husband, her life was too diminished by his death to retain sufficient purpose," was the theme of the obituary notices. In fact, as her bird-claw hand signed the certificate, and the fatal injection was prepared, she looked almost identical to her husband in his last hours, for the illness stripped the body down to its common framework, with all the outward ornament of vigorous flesh, which makes for muscular manliness and feminine charm, eliminated.

A few days later Holmes reported that Joseph Greenway had gone into a rapid decline with complete return of all his original symptoms.

Crippled with apprehension, Robert examined his face in the mirror almost hourly, looking for any decrease in the thickness of his upper lip or eyebrows and scanning his skin with tremulous fingers from forehead to throat in search of the first signs of taut, unhealthy shininess. Each morning he weighed himself and measured the girth of his calf muscles for signs of wastage. He detected no suspicious changes, but over the next few weeks there was an increasing number of cases of severe emaciating illness, which the newspapers were encouraged to report as "A mystery complaint probably caused by an unknown virus."

The first American cases occurred within two months of Merton's death, to be followed by sporadic cases in Europe. Soon the free world realized it was threatened by some new pestilence which, in the English-speaking countries, quickly became known as the Wasting Sickness. It was as virulent, as mysterious, and as chilling as the medieval plague. And the doctors of the time were equally as powerless to contain it.

chapter 28

The results of the survey showed that the human body, sensitized by Juvenex, was somewhat more resistant to X-rays than that of the mouse, but the curve of susceptibility was broadly the same as that worked out by Shirley. Linking them with the latest measurements of fallout, Sir Henry Taylor's team at the Atomic Energy Authority was able to make some predictions in a secret report to the Cabinet. The summary of the report stated:

It would appear probable that even if nuclear testing in the atmosphere ceases at once, there will be enough fallout to cause casualties among the more sensitive subjects, who possibly constitute about one percent of the community. Provision should therefore be made for some 600,000 casualties among the adult population within the next three months. If testing continues at the present rate of 100 megatons a week, the casualty figure could rise to two millions by the autumn and perhaps five millions by the New Year. There seems to be no practicable method for distinguishing the specially sensitive people in advance.

In a private letter to Owen, Taylor wrote, "If Turganov was telling the truth when he said he was taking SP47, our calculations suggest that his chance of being a supersensitive is about 100 to one against—not a bad gamble for such a huge prize, if he did deliberately plan it!"

After a telephone conversation with Brandenberg, who faced casualties four times greater, because of the bigger population, Owen flew to Washington with Taylor and a few other technical experts for discussions officially projected as "routine" at the White House.

"We're grateful to you gentlemen for your prompt response in coming here," said Brandenberg, who was showing no signs of the strain. "Our intelligence confirms that these Russian explosions are not military tests any longer. They are using up stocks of production weapons to create fallout in the hope of radiating us into surrender. Apparently, they estimate that the American people will accept occupation before they have sustained twelve million casualties. The British limit is put at three millions—presumably on the basis that such a figure would cause insupportable dislocation.

"Our medical advice is that we are already committed to pretty hefty casualties due to the sensitivity created by Juvenex, but before we consider any action, I would like you to see a presentation of the situation as we see it. The presentation will be given by the Chairman of the Joint Chiefs of Staff, General Jones."

Blinds were drawn, a silver screen was pulled down, lights were dimmed, and General K. C. ("Casey") Jones, impressive in his air force uniform with nine rows of ribbons, picked up a plastic pointer and asked for the first colored slide. Entitled "Project Skydirt," it showed a map of North America with the areas where fallout had been measured and its strengths. After a brief explanation, this was followed by slides showing forecasts of casualties.

"We've always operated on the principle that the Soviets might launch a thermonuclear attack on our cities any day, so we have an on-the-shelf capability to cope with thirty million casualties," the General said.

A series of slides then outlined the organization of the U.S. civil defenses.

"Of course, the situation we are now considering should be much simpler because there won't be any fire or physical damage to buildings. We're confident we can cope with the casualties threatened at the moment and still keep essential services in being.

"There is, however, one big disadvantage. We can't assemble key personnel in deep underground shelters, as we could for a thermonuclear attack, because we don't know who'll prove to be supersensitive and who won't. Meanwhile we're making a survey of all adults who haven't taken the drug, to see if we can form a nucleus of executives who can be guaranteed to survive.

"Now, as to possible countermeasures . . ." General Jones tapped with his pointer and a slide appeared showing the mailed fist and thunderbolt insignia of the Strategic Air Command, which he had once directed, with its motto "Peace is our Business." He tapped again and a chart showing the state of readiness of the Command replaced it.

"We've been at red alert for the past six weeks. All the Mars and Saturn missiles are at maximum readiness. So are the Cupid submarines."

Owen looked at Taylor and raised his eyebrows. Though the responsibilities of office had quickly dispersed the enthusiasm for nuclear disarmament which he had canvassed in opposition, he had never become attuned to the absurdity that while the cost of atomic war was down to sixpence a casualty, the cost of preserving atomic peace was prohibitive, and he still found the code names for the terror weapons harrowing. The choice of Cupid for the latest submarine-launched missile seemed particularly inept to a Welshman, whose romantic streak had not been entirely leached out by disillusion, but, as Taylor had reminded him, it was in tradition. The bomb which had razed Hiroshima was called The Little Boy, and the plane which dropped it, Enola Gay.

After a few frames of color film showing the missiles being fired in tests, the General continued: "As the next slide shows, in the present state of the art we can't launch a surprise attack for two reasons. First, signals from our reconnaissance satellites confirm that the enemy is fully alerted against a possible revenge assault by us. We face the certainty that they could take out most of our major cities. But more critically, even if we should succeed in bombing them into eventual surrender, as I believe we could, we should create so much fallout that it would quickly bring the radiation to a level that would kill us all."

"So," the General added, underlining with his pointer the words printed on the slide, "thermonuclear attack is not practicable.

"A non-nuclear attack is equally out of the question," he continued. "As this chart shows, we don't have the troops. We've alerted the NATO forces, but they are dependent on tactical nuclear weapons and they couldn't use them because they've almost all been taking Juvenex and couldn't tolerate the local fallout.

"Intelligence reports indicate a massive strengthening of conventional forces in East Germany, with a big concentration of air-lift capacity. It's the same story in the Vladivostok area. So it seems that these forces are being gathered for eventual occupation of Europe and North America. The Russians have even withdrawn troops from the border with China for this purpose. Presumably they consider this a safe move because the Chinese are not being affected by the fallout as they've never been allowed to take Juvenex.

"It is therefore the considered view of the Chiefs of Staff," he concluded, "that at this stage military intervention is not practicable."

"Thank you, Casey," the President said briskly, drowning Owen's aside to Taylor: "Fancy bringing us all this way to tell us that."

There was a short break for coffee during which the President was handed a report announcing a further 50-megaton explosion over Novaya Zemlya.

When the coffee cups had been cleared away, the President addressed the meeting.

"In view of the urgency of the situation, the Director of the Central Intelligence Agency was asked for an appraisal of the possibility of liquidating Premier Turganov, but he considers that such a move would not only be extremely difficult but unlikely to stop the tests already programmed. That leaves us with only the diplomatic channel. We must pin our faith in world opinion and do more than we've done so far to muster it against the Soviets."

"World opinion is a busted flush," Owen said bluntly. "It hasn't exerted the slightest influence on the Russians in more than fifty years."

"We've never had the opportunity to align it so solidly against them before," said Brandenberg. "And this is just where we think you can help us. We want to get the Chinese to throw their weight in. Marshal Ho Cheng represents eight hundred million people— two hundred millions of them of military age—and if we could induce him to get really tough about the fallout, Turganov might be obliged to listen."

Owen shook his head disbelievingly.

"The Central Intelligence Agency has devised a specific plan that might work," Brandenberg continued, taking up a small buff

222

folder. "But it involves a personal approach to Ho Cheng. We can't make it after refusing to recognize Red China and keeping her out of the United Nations so long, but you have diplomatic relations with him."

"What's the plan?" Owen asked.

"This folder contains a series of unpublished reports from Columbia University and the Department of Agriculture which show that rice seedlings are unduly sensitive to strontium 90. It describes experiments in which seedlings withered and died when transplanted to soil only slightly more contaminated by strontium 90 than the paddy fields of southern China are now. If these results could be brought to the personal attention of the Marshal, he might be convinced that his entire rice crop is being threatened by the Russian fallout. Famine is the one fear that would stir him to protest."

"Are the experiments genuine, Mr. President?" Taylor asked.

"Frankly, no. But if Ho Cheng can be convinced that they are, he's unlikely to waste time checking them. We've fixed the figure so that only four more fifty megaton bombs would take the rice crop over the limit. Correction! Three more. I've just had notice of a further explosion."

"I'd have thought that the Chinese knew more about rice than you, but at least it's a positive suggestion," Owen said.

"It might give the scientists more time to make a breakthrough with anti-radiation treatment," Brandenberg commented. "If it fails and we start getting insupportable casualties, I propose to tell the Russians that we'll take them with us unless they stop," he added grimly. "Strategic Air Command is with me to a man, aren't they, Casey?"

"They certainly are, Mr. President."

The sun was shining as Owen left the White House after agreeing to the text of a cover-up communiqué about "full and frank talks on issues of mutual interest," and he ordered his driver to make a detour to give himself thinking time on his way to the embassy. The cherry trees along the Potomac were heavy with blossom, and the roads were filled with gaily colored cars and taxis. In that artificial city, in which government was the dominating industry, the knots of lounging Negroes and occasional whites were the only signs of the unemployment and unrest affecting the rest of the country.

What an incredible situation, thought Owen. The richest nation the world had ever seen, driven to beg a lifesaving favor from the poorest—and unable to do it for herself.

Using the embassy facilities, Owen arranged for Sir Henry Taylor to fly secretly to Peking with the folder of research reports. After a week's face-losing delay, Taylor managed to explain them to the Chinese Foreign Minister, who seemed impressed, according to the interpreter.

Proof that the Marshal's attention had been drawn to them came within twenty-four hours in the form of a cable signed by Ho Cheng and addressed directly to President Brandenberg. It read, "Tell it to the United Nations."

John, who sensed that something more catastrophic than a mutated virus was responsible for the Wasting Sickness, the Washington talks, and the extreme official evasiveness to his inquiries, was sitting in his office dictating equally evasive answers to readers' letters when the news editor buzzed him on the intercom.

"There's a news agency bulletin announcing that Sir Robert Harvey is seriously ill in St. Patrick's Hospital. Will you find out what he's got and bring your obit up to date just in case?"

John raced around in a taxi to Shirley's laboratory at the hospital medical school to find that she was over at Robert's private ward. Hoisting himself onto the teak bench, surrounded by the microscopes, water baths, dissecting boards, and other accouterments of the researcher's craft, he settled down to wait for her. She was weeping when she returned. Robert's symptoms were closely following Merton's, and she had noticed a sharp deterioration since the previous day.

"Well, you see I was right," Robert had said in a cracked voice when the nurse had shown her in. "What's my HSR now?" he added, raising his withering arms. "I've decided what they ought to put on that statue in Madrid—'The Inventor of Instant Atrophy.'"

John put his arm around her as she wiped her eyes.

"He doesn't seem to want me," she sobbed. "He just wants Margaret and the children. She's with him at the hospital now.

He's convinced there's nothing to be done for him, and he wants Margaret to take him home to die in peace at Salisbury."

"Never mind, darling, I want you. In fact, I *need* you. I've needed you for a long time, and if what's ahead is anything like I suspect, maybe you're going to need me. There aren't that many of us who haven't taken Juvenex."

When Shirley started sobbing again, he assumed that she was still thinking of Robert, and after putting her jacket around her shoulders, he steered her toward the door.

"Come on, I'll take you home and you can pick up a few things. You can't live there now on your own. You can move in with me until you decide what to do—and I hope you'll decide to stay."

While Shirley was packing a suitcase in the bedroom she had shared with Robert, John noticed a familiar container among the perfume and makeup bottles on her dressing table. Snatching it, he saw that it was half-filled with pink capsules stamped with the initial J.

"These aren't yours, are they?" he asked apprehensively.

Shirley began to weep again and sat on the edge of the bed with her head in her hands.

"What's going to happen to me? I was taking them for two months before the scare began and I stopped then. Robert said I should be all right, but nobody can be sure."

John checked himself from saying, "I warned you . . ." and tried to reassure her.

"Oh, you didn't take them long enough to do you any permanent harm."

Secretly the admission frightened him, yet he was disturbed to find that in spite of his deep concern for this girl, whom he undoubtedly loved in his strange way, his dominant feeling at that moment was elation—elation at the knowledge that however much he might be involved in the horrific consequences of Juvenex to society, he individually would survive.

As the Russian explosions rumbled on through the spring and early summer, the Western governments made repeated efforts to induce Turganov to suspend them, but he acknowledged no notes and answered no hot lines. Thousands of balloons sent drifting over the Iron Curtain showered down leaflets explaining how the continued Soviet testing endangered the lives of people everywhere, but they produced no significant effect. The Kremlin-controlled radios dismissed them as a lying stunt to cover up tests by the imperialists which, so far as the Russian people knew, were still in progress. Propaganda broadcasts were effectively jammed. On Taylor's board the number of predicted casualties mounted beyond the million mark.

It was in June while the Color was being trooped on Horse Guards Parade and preparations were being made for Royal Ascot and the other social calendar occasions, which were not to be curtailed by anything short of shooting war or Court mourning, that Robert discharged the shell of what was left of himself from hospital.

There was no connection, not even in memory, between the wizened creature Shirley had visited for the last time, just before Margaret came to take him home, and the virile, self-assured man with whom she had once elected to spend her life. As for Robert, sunk in apathy and with his coercing demon exorcised by his debility, he was beyond deriving any advantage from Shirley's cheerfulness, had she been capable of providing it. The only feminine offering he could appreciate, apart from physical care and comfort, was the clemency of his wife's affectionate smile.

chapter 29

To the terrified children, it was as though the world was being invaded by grotesque creatures with bald, outsize heads set precariously on scrawny bodies that hobbled unsteadily in clothing far too big for them. The only way the females could be distinguished was by the gay summer dresses they had bought a few weeks previously, when they were fifty years younger, or by the veils they wore to hide their ugliness before they became too apathetic to care. Every day there were more of them in the offices, the factories, the shops, the streets, trying to go about their business as long as they could.

At first the *Daily Dispatch* had suppressed the terrible news that John had extracted from Shirley, but as more and more people lapsed into decrepitude throughout the free world, the truth about the Wasting Sickness and its real causes could be hidden no longer, and the millions who had taken Juvenex were soon convinced that nothing could be done to save them.

There had never been such creation of despair by such massive removal of hope. There had never been such leveling in life. All classes from the Royal Family to the dustmen who emptied the palace bins had their unfortunate representatives among the supersensitive one percent, accurately forecast by Taylor. Those affected were under no more immediate threat from death than any normal ninety-year-old, and in such a highly automated society the loss of physical strength was not incapacitating, but for thousands the transformation was too savage. The human mind had learned to accept the ugliness of normal senility—itself an astonishing accommodation, for there is no other creature in which the contrast between life's prime and its decadence is so sharp and the end result so shabby—but many of the sudden-old could neither stand the sight of themselves nor of their fellows. To men like Owen and Harvey, who had been hale and handsome one week and enfeebled and repulsive the next, the shock was shattering enough. To the women like Diana and Coral who had been young and beautiful, it was overwhelming. As Hastings Maclaren had predicted years before, it was disappointment on a cataclysmic scale, for which the mind was totally unequipped to cope by the evolutionary experience which makes it resilient to most insults.

Unhinged, and bewildered by their predicament, which presented three of the classic causes of self-destruction—the awareness of crumbling faculties, the decline in the value of life, and fear so extreme as to demand escape in its absolute form—thousands exerted their right to release by euthanasia, but as those who provided it became stricken, more freed themselves by their own hands.

These included many who wrongly feared they had detected the nausea, the patches of pallid shininess on the skin, or the shallowing of the voice, which were the first observable signs of the Wasting Sickness, and others who simply could not tolerate the dread of it. To exalt their violent gesture of protest, some contrived a spectacular exit, and as in the past, such suicides proved infectious. Leaps from the catwalks of the road bridges across the Firth of Forth and Severn became commonplace, and the nation was only momentarily shocked when its most popular screen star dived to her death from the radio tower off Tottenham Court Road. Determined to attract attention, men hurled themselves from skyscrapers, cathedrals, television masts, from the huge dish aerials at Jodrell Bank and elsewhere, using extravagant cunning to defeat the anti-suicide guards.

When height became hackneyed, people sought to lure publicity through the horror of their deaths, as Buddhist monks had once immolated themselves with burning gasoline. There were appalling incidents in steel plants and rolling mills. At Cape Kennedy a scientist hid in the flame bucket of a launching pad and achieved annihilation in the vaporizing jet of an interplanetary rocket. On the Yorkshire moors, two technicians with climbing gear broke into one of the radar domes at the Fylingdales missile warning station and cooked themselves in the concentrated beam of the transmitter.

In few cases did this abuse of ingenuity display itself more grotesquely than in the way Sir Henry Taylor hastened his embrace with what he believed was the inevitable. During a routine visit to the Harwell nuclear research station, in which he took inordinate interest in the detailed working of one of the experimental reactors, he fabricated a reason for staying the night with the director. Then, after bidding his host good night and in pretense of taking a breath of air, he returned to the hangar housing the reactor. Sidling in so as to be unobservable from the control room, he climbed to the top of the concrete shield, pulled out one of the lead plugs, and stood for twenty minutes in the beam of escaping rays until the general release of radioactivity triggered the alarm bells. He was gibbering about his guilt when he was taken to hospital, to die there in three days from frightful symptoms.

Masculine vanity reached its apogee in a wave of presuicide murders, fathers ensuring that their entire families would die with them, in the overweening belief that life could hold nothing for those left behind. This arrogance extended itself to holocausts in which deranged pilots drove their aircraft into mountainsides and engineers deliberately rammed their trains into the bumpers.

Such widespread misuse of machinery to effect sensational suicide disorganized society by forcing into awareness its unquestioning trust in the sanity of ordinary people. Those still healthy or with such tenacity to life that they held on in the hope that they would learn to live with their deformity were terrified to use public transportation or even ride in elevators in case those in command should suddenly decide to take their passengers with them to eternity.

The nation had endured casualties on such a scale in the First Great War, but those were psychologically acceptable as a masculine hazard in a hostile world. With the Wasting Sickness, they arose sporadically, without visible or audible cause, producing dislocation out of all proportion to their numbers, because such a high ratio of rejuvenated men who had held on to executive office were affected.

The young, who had been howling for opportunity, might have assumed control but proved incapable of organizing themselves. Without the older executives to instruct and direct them they were ineffective and deficient in powers of improvisation. They could not run the electric power stations, the gas plants, the waterworks, and trains. Still less could they operate the computers on which the country's transportation, communication, and supply systems had become dependent.

Flight has always been a human reaction to approaching danger, and many of those, including Paul Harvey, to whom vital tasks had been delegated, were among the first to make the futile retreat into the countryside. The experience of Ernest Hobson and his neighbors was typical of what happened there. Marauding bands of youths and girls, sleeping rough and living off the land, vented their bewilderment and fear in a fury of malicious damage and senseless slaughter. They burned down ricks and barns, slit open grain sacks, wrecked chicken coops, and set fire to heaths and woodland. In one of Hobson's pastures, a group of bedraggled Georgians cornered the sheep and knifed every one of them, leaving it like a battlefield. The outraged farmers banded themselves into vigilantes operating in Land-Rovers and armed with shotguns, and when they fired it was not always just to wound.

Though the compulsion to destroy was more infectious in the young, adults were far from immune to it, and their behavior under terror showed that even in the mature and cultured, self-control may be a light halter. As public services were progressively curtailed in the towns, there were vicious riots in which windows were smashed, cars overturned and set afire, and trains derailed.

The doctors and pharmacists who had supplied the lethal capsules and were impotent to treat their results were handy targets for frenzied vengeance. Throughout the land doctors' offices and pharmacies were stoned, doctors were vilified and commonly assaulted. Harley Street was a prime objective, and in one sacking by a crowd, which surged in suddenly from Oxford Street for no reason its members could have given, Sir Thomas Holmes was beaten to death.

"Killing me will solve my problems, but it won't solve yours," the emaciated royal doctor calmly told the menacing rabble as it burst into his consulting room. But the intruders were in no mood for reason.

No building associated with the art of medicine was safe from violence. A lunchtime crowd being harangued in the traditional Speakers' Corner in Lincoln's Inn Fields swarmed into the Royal College of Surgeons and went wild in the anatomical museum there, hurling down specimen jars and cases from the balconies until the floor below was heaped with broken glass and grisly human remains.

The wilder members of the Committee for Natural Aging burned Sir Robert Harvey in effigy in Trafalgar Square, cheered on by the bystanders, who have always enjoyed seeing their heroes fall. The Institute of Gerontology was sacked. When a mob stoned the windows of Robert's home in Salisbury, the man who had yearned so earnestly for recognition had to be smuggled out of the garden entrance into the street, where he was able to mingle with the watching crowd, unrecognizable among so many who looked like him.

The vandalism spread to the public monuments and churches. In Westminster Abbey, at Canterbury, Salisbury, and at Ely, tombs and effigies were mutilated. At Winchester the bones of Canute, Egbert, and other Saxon kings were spilled from their wooden coffers above the choir and wielded to break windows and sacred ornaments as they had been used by Roundhead troops three centuries before. In Coventry Cathedral the huge Sutherland tapestry of Christ in Glory was lacerated with bicycle chains, ripped and defaced with sump oil. Public galleries had to be barricaded after an epidemic of picture slashing in which portraits of monarchs, doges, popes, prime ministers, and other emblems of authority were singled out for the quick flick of the knife or razor blade. Libraries were ransacked, and the ignorant declared their animosity to learning in a joyous burning of books.

In this cultural chaos old political scores were settled. Greeks from Soho pounded the Elgin Marbles with hammers. The Stone of Scone was once again stolen from Westminster Abbey by Scottish nationalists who broke up the Coronation Chair for good measure. Three Indian students were shot in an abortive attempt to steal the Koh-i-Noor diamond from the underground jewel house in the Tower of London, on the pretext that it had been looted from the Punjab more than one hundred and thirty years before.

Pillage of the property of those too frail to protect themselves was rife, and in the cities lampposts were hung with bodies bearing the roughly scrawled warning, "Shot for looting!" Some of the culprits were ex-convicts who were among the healthy because they had been denied Juvenex while in prison, but most of them were decent people driven to release their fear in irrational extremes, as a badly frightened dog may savage its master.

Resolving to extract the maximum from life in defiance of death, millions abandoned themselves to dissolute excess, and the Gin Lane debauchery of Hogarth's England, with its gutter drunks, thieves' kitchens, whorehouses, sadistic assaults, and barbarous child neglect was relived with exaggeration.

Others reacted as in times of plague, and the churches were crammed with chanting crowds appealing for protection from the Virgin and those saints believed to wield special influence on disease.

On a stifling June afternoon, so still that the steamy plume from the chimney of the Bankside power station was curved on more than a saber, St. Paul's Cathedral was so packed that the vergers locked the doors, anxious for the safety of the great throng which

231

had spilled down into the crypt and up the stairs on to the Whispering Gallery. The few scores being refused admittance in the forecourt hammered and kicked on the doors, and when this brought no response they tore down one of the filigreed lampposts to use as a battering ram. The rhythmic thuds on the oak-paneled doors touched off a rush of human muscle-power as a pistol shot may send a herd of nervous cattle into mad stampede. From the overlooking offices of St. Paul's Churchyard, from Carter Lane, from Cheapside, and from Ludgate Hill men and women, knowing they were about to be involved in violence but not understanding why, came running to swell the heaving phalanx forcing its way through the splintered doors. Even reporters rushed up from Fleet Street to investigate the tumult could not resist augmenting it.

As the vergers had feared, the Whispering Gallery gave way as more were forced onto it, showering stones, balustrade, and bodies onto the seething, screaming crowd below.

When the energy of the mob was spent and it streamed out again into the sunlight, more than one hundred and fifty trampled corpses lay on the marble floor of the nave.

Police and troops armed with the latest anti-riot gases, which quickly incapacitated without causing permanent injury, managed to quell most of the disturbances in the streets. A 10 P.M. curfew was imposed, first for teenagers, then for all without special passes. But before the casualties from fallout and the fear it provoked reached even the quarter of a million mark, the Government was driven to proclaim a state of emergency and martial law.

By ill circumstance, a disproportionate number of the Cabinet proved to be supersensitive, and as in previous times of national threat, Parliament's reaction was to set up a coalition with a member of the Opposition as Prime Minister, as had happened more than fifty years earlier in the time of Ramsay Macdonald. Maclaren was chosen because he was the only member of either frontbench who could be reasonably sure of remaining fit for office, as he had not taken Juvenex.

With dreadful regularity the seismographs and micropressure meters were recording more Russian explosions, and with each bomb the arrows indicating the estimate of casualties and their expected dates were raised on the board in Taylor's old office.

News of the further explosions was withheld from the public, but in the absence of any official announcement that the tests had ceased, morale steadily declined. Everybody feared that they were "SS"—they whispered the initials rather than use the chilling "supersensitive"—and never knew when their call to disfigurement might come.

In such calamitous uncertainty the will to work was drained and the absenteeism alone was so widespread as to threaten industry with paralysis. To Maclaren it was clear that some panic on an even more destructive scale was inevitable. This could have taken the form of a revenge attack on Russia, initiated by some conspiracy of demented bomber pilots or missile men, but though it was attempted in the U.S. and France, the triggering drill had been locked up with so many fail-safe systems that it could not be launched.

As the disruption of the national life mounted toward disintegration, Maclaren decided to put into operation the emergency system of Government, which had long been prepared for the event of nuclear war. As a former Minister of Health in the Cabinet, he had been intimately concerned with the plans for resuscitating the nation after a devastating nuclear attack by means of a skeleton administration operating from deep underground bunkers.

Many of the trained staff earmarked to run these seats of government were still available, and with the rapid recruitment of a few hundred responsible people like John and Shirley, who claimed they had never taken Juvenex, Maclaren manned the Citadel, the central seat in a system of tunnels near Bath, and the main regional seats scattered through the country. Locked behind steel and concrete doors, the staffs were managing to keep their independent power plants going and were sustaining the secret channels of radio and telephone communication with the armed forces. Units of the Navy, Army, and RAF were detailed to keep order outside, supervise the distribution of food, protect the main radio transmitters, and keep as many services going as possible. They were centered in easily defensible barracks, castles, aircraft carriers, and other ships anchored in harbor or offshore, and they operated by means of armed patrols.

The seats of government kept in touch with them mainly by

telephone but also sent out liaison patrols which left and returned by secret back gates—tunnels that could be quickly sealed in emergency by flooding. There were stocks of canned food and water sufficient for many weeks of siege, and it was already clear that they would be needed. Some of the outsiders had tried to storm the centers, partly to gain access to the sanctuary of the filtered air but mainly to destroy the privilege of those within, and after they had succeeded in ransacking one of them by introducing skin divers through a flooded back entrance, Maclaren had ordered the guards to machine-gun any further attackers; they carried out his command in their own self-interest.

Had the nation been faced with the crisis of coming to grips with a ferocious enemy, as it was back in 1940, it would have remained steady to defend itself, but Maclaren understood enough of human nature to realize that courage would evaporate against an unseeable and unassailable foe that ravaged by stealth.

"It's like the devil," he explained to the rump of his Cabinet, when justifying his decision to take to the underground fortresses. "It's because people can't see the devil that they don't fight him. And the terror will be all the greater because so few have any genuine faith to lean on. The nation is going to pay for its godlessness now!"

Maclaren did all he could to drive godlessness from the Citadel. There was a Church of England padre on its staff, and Maclaren ordered nondenominational religious worship night and morning, partly as a uniting influence on morale within the fortress, but mainly because he was a devout believer in the power of prayer. The staff needed no whipping to attend. Even John, who at first was derisive about the rush to kneel under the pressure of fear— "We'd scoff at Buddhists whirling prayer wheels in front of a bursting dam"—found some relief in the communal intoning.

After the first week, Shirley noticed that his eyes were shut and his lips moving, though inaudibly, while the congregation joined in the Lord's Prayer. John denied that he was doing any more than resting his eyes from the incessant artificial light when she asked him if he, too, was resorting to prayer.

"Just because I appreciate the practical value of this State myth at this moment, it doesn't follow that I believe it," he told her.

But after inquiry, Shirley was convinced that he was too embarrassed to admit the truth. She had noticed that his lips parted in what seemed to be "Amen" immediately after the particularly meaningful plea for deliverance from evil, and she remembered he had told her in the Milan Cathedral that Roman Catholics do not recognize the conceding phrase about the power and the glory, which was never used by Jesus Christ.

As a further measure of internal security, Maclaren imposed the strictest moral code within the Citadel. The dormitories of unmarried men and women were mutually out of bounds at all times, and John and Shirley, who found that their fear was more than halved when they shared it, were allowed to resume their life together only after they had submitted to a proper ceremony. The padre conducted it, and the hands-and-heart bracelet bought by John as a peace offering stood in for a wedding ring.

It was after the first night of the "honeymoon," when Shirley was making their bed, that she discovered the object which John had been so careful to hide. Under the bolster was a rosary made from dried peas pilfered from the food store and fitted with a cross cut from the lid of a salmon tin.

Shirley did not mention her find, but when John realized that she must have seen it, he abandoned all pretense.

"I'm bitterly ashamed of myself for giving in like this. It's such a personal defeat," he said as they lay together that night in the darkness. "I'd convinced myself I'd never let fear alone drive me back to belief in God—not even on my deathbed. I had all sorts of caustic remarks stored up in case anyone ever started giving me the last rites. But now I'm so frightened that when I see you and Maclaren and all these others so obviously getting comfort and strength from faith, I desperately want to believe."

"I know, darling, I've noticed it for quite a while," Shirley said, cradling his head in her arm.

"I've gone through all the motions of trying to get my faith back: even to the nonsense of making that rosary."

"I didn't think that was nonsense, John. I was very touched by it."

"I suppose I'd even try going to confession if there was a priest here. But it wouldn't work. It would be just like it was last time. I don't believe there's anyone listening when I pray. And I'm just as frightened as ever. I've never disclosed my fears to anyone before, Shirley. Somehow I always suspected that if I admitted my weaknesses, people would use them against me."

"You can be sure I won't," Shirley said, giving him a reassuring hug.

"Well, I've been frightened for as long as I can remember," John admitted. "When I was a kid I was afraid of the dark, afraid of the priest, and afraid of my father. Since my life filled out and living from day to day seemed satisfying enough, I've constantly been haunted by vague feelings of impending disaster, even when things have been going well. Now at forty I'm more frightened than ever. I suppose I'm just a terrible coward, really."

"Darling, we're all frightened. You wouldn't be human if you weren't. And you're very human when you take off that armorplate you hide in."

"Maclaren isn't frightened."

"Maclaren is, in spite of his belief. I know he is. He told me yesterday that he couldn't stand being shut up in this rathole much longer."

"Neither can I. If I didn't have you, I think I'd ask to be put outside. I'm so dependent on you to keep my spirits up. You're the strong one really, you know. You've more to frighten you than I have, yet you have to listen while I do all the whining."

"That's one of the things that wives are for, John," Shirley whispered as she kissed him good night.

He slept sooner and sounder than he had done for a long time. In a way, in a considerable way, he had been to confession.

John and Shirley, who were on Maclaren's personal staff, were astonished by the ruthlessness of his determination to keep order in the Citadel and to restore it above ground. The Prime Minister found that the frontier between kindness and stupidity, which had always been less vague in his mind than in most, was sharply defined by emergency. So those who had falsely stated that they had never taken Juvenex to get on the Citadel staff were ejected at the first sign of decline, as were those who became mentally unbalanced by the claustrophobia. No exception was made of those members of the Coalition Cabinet known to have taken Juvenex, whom Maclaren had been unable to keep out of the Citadel. The first of these to degenerate was Albert Hodges, the old Conservative Minister of Labor who was forced out, struggling and shouting, into the violence.

"We can't afford to house any useless mouths," was Maclaren's curt reply to Shirley's plea for compassion, as it had been when the aged but still active Lord Questing offered his services, as one of the minority of adults exempt from the evil of Juvenex.

"How can a man like you, who genuinely cared so much about the sanctity of human life, be so cruel?" Shirley asked him.

"I'm no different from all those decent people who are destroying everything outside," he replied with a shrug. "We all have the lion and the lamb inside us. It depends on circumstances which one of them shows."

chapter 30

Maclaren made radio appeals for order and restraint almost daily, but he was no more capable of forging mass fealty with words than he had been of swaying the House of Commons. Even before his administration had taken to its subterranean life, he had made his rule unpopular by destroying all accessible stocks of liquor to subdue the debauchery and in the belief that the pillaging of public houses and liquor stores would aggravate the looting. But criminal ingenuity had quickly neutralized this measure. The dismantled distilleries were replaced by hundreds of illicit stills producing liquor loaded with wood spirit and blinding fusel oil.

With his troops he had managed to defeat several attempts to seize power by the Communists, to quell some ugly riots, and to crush a full-scale rebellion raised by Scottish nationalists in Edinburgh, but there was nothing he could do about the final and unforeseeable panic.

On a sunny August morning Robert and Margaret, supporting each other in their frailty, eased thenselves into their car, which had just sufficient gasoline for the journey that both knew they had to make. Debilitated beyond centenarian weakness, Robert had to drive slowly, but he had no alternative, for his route to Bournemouth was choked with others who had all experienced the same compulsive urge.

On beaches ranging from Cornwall to Cape Kennedy, through Alaska's shore to Waikiki, Bondi, Durban, and the Costa Brava, thousands of shriveled, shuffling figures were collecting to stare at the sea until the running tides approached. Such automaton reaction to miserable existence had not been seen since the contagious dancing mania of fourteenth- and fifteenth-century Europe, when men and women were seized with the frenzy to whirl themselves into collapse or drown in the rivers with ecstatic indifference. But this time it was quiet and purposeful.

Robert and Margaret clambered out of their car, abandoned with a thousand others, and hobbled across the rippled sand to stand among the great crush at the water's edge, shivering slightly in the on-shore breeze. Whatever might have momentarily intruded into their distorted minds about their children, their possessions, their achievements, or their past responsibilities was overwhelmed by the obsession to free themselves from their squalid disfigurement. In these circumstances the sense of solidarity with the community, which normally inhibits suicide, promoted it, and as though in silent communication, like a flock of birds wheeling in unison, all those at the water's edge made no retreat as the hissing foam began to wash over them. Then, with no lament that was audible above the breaking waves and the mewing gulls, they began to move out, wading deeper, until with feeble strokes they embraced drowning water.

On another Channel beach farther east, at Littlehampton, the gnome who had once been Frank Butcher awaited his turn as a bedraggled crowd, infected with death-wish, surged forward to hide themselves in the sea in front of the pillaged vacation camp. As the flapping tarpaulins of the deserted fun fair cracked like distant gunshots, the memory of a day when he watched another horde of frightened creatures moving to certain destruction

238

erupted into consciousness. He could see the carcasses piled like cordwood, but in the confusion of his mind they were not of hares but of people.

To the knots of still-young watching this slow stampede from the promenades, the clifftops, and the dunes, it did not seem like deliberate dispatch. It was more as though these people were seeking to get somewhere yet failing for lack of strength, like the lemmings of Sweden's mountains, which swim out to sea in droves to a quick and bloodless end when they have increased beyond a number that can survive. One moment there was an advancing mass of bobbing, hairless heads. Then they disappeared, dragged down by the burden of their sodden clothes, making no attempt to save themselves or each other as more came on behind.

From a distance they seemed as disciplined as the soldiers at Dunkirk wading out to the little ships, but the only vessels standing off the coasts that day were the ubiquitous Russian trawlers which patroled on espionage duties and had received unexpected radio orders to advance within the three-mile limit. Their astonished captains were not there to pick up survivors but to dictate messages to Moscow as they scanned the hideous scene through their binoculars.

On the shore some of the young watchers screamed out hysterically, pressing their clenched fists to their faces, as they had done so often under happier circumstances when sent into ecstasy by jazz singers; some prayed, silently on their knees or aloud in small groups; a few took photographs through habit. Others, standing with the banners of the CNA, shouted and jeered to relieve their terror. Most just stood with their arms around one another, whimpering, sobbing, and wondering what was in store for them.

As night fell, the crush was still building up at the tide's edge and continued far into the following morning, with the ebbing currents washing away the multitude of corpses to return them later to the sand and mudflats as a banquet for the beachcombing carrion birds.

The magnitude of the catastrophe convinced the survivors that Maclaren's iron fist held no answer to the terrifying threat menacing them all. Spontaneous calls for immediate surrender to the Russians from every town and village were whipped up by the

Communists and others, who urged that it was better to be Red than bleached by radiation. But Maclaren had no stomach for surrender.

"We must stand firm," he declared over the radio. "All the resources of the free world's scientists are being concentrated on the discovery of protective drugs. Miracles have saved Britain before. Remember 1940—our finest hour—when it seemed certain that Hitler would invade. God can't be on the side of the atheists."

So he called for national prayer and ordered the rabble-rousers to be hunted down.

Hope that his prayers were being answered was raised when no explosions were recorded for five consecutive days, though the rush to the sea continued. Then the seismographs shuddered as three bombs were exploded in twenty-four hours, bringing the casualty forecast to the three million mark.

On those unprecedented dying days life behind the Iron and Bamboo curtains had gone on much as usual. Apart from an increase in the incidence of leukemia, which caused no national concern because the cases were scattered and lost in regional statistics, there was nothing attributable to fallout in the homes of ordinary Soviet and Chinese citizens. The scientists who had pursued their study of the long-term effects of Omoloditel on a few selected patients had reported a sudden incidence of progeria cases among them, noting, with satisfaction, in their official summaries, that the caution concerning its general use seemed to have been fully justified. The fatal degeneration of the former Soviet Ambassador to London went unmentioned in the public prints, as did that of Anthony Fayverdale, the former English lord, who had been released from the boredom of his friendless fate as a renegade in Moscow.

Even Moscow radio gave no immediate news of the wreck of the West, for its propaganda purpose was to promote a sense of national grief at the untimely death of Russia's beloved leader and father of his country, Maxim Turganov. No reason for his death was given, and it was assumed by Soviet listeners that it was from natural causes.

There was to be a state funeral, with millions of Muscovites given a holiday so that they could line the streets, but the customary lying in state, with the coffin lid removed, was to be omitted and the body was to be buried in the Kremlin grounds alongside Stalin's, not placed on permanent view in the Red Square Mausoleum. This was no disrespect to Turganov. It was simply that it was beyond the embalmer's art to make his body presentable.

The messages from the trawlers standing off the coasts of Britain, Europe, and America, and from other intelligence sources, piled up on the desk of Anatoli Belitsky who, like the rest of his colleagues, had been barred from taking Omoloditel and had managed to slide into the vacant seat of power, at least temporarily. They fulfilled all the predictions of the previous weeks, though even Turganov had not expected that the end would be so sudden and self-inflicted. As the impassive men of the Presidium met to discuss their next moves, after shouldering the coffin containing their leader to its resting place, they realized that the world would be theirs for the taking. All their major problems would be solved —the ideological conquest of capitalism, elimination of fear of attack and of sponsored counterrevolution; and the Chinese threat to spill over into Soviet territory could be liquidated by giving them Australia, New Zealand, and possibly parts of South America.

Speaking from the chair which was already actively coveted by at least three of the men about him, Belitsky announced, "Justice has delivered the capitalist criminals into our hands. France, Italy, Greece, Japan, and a dozen other countries are already negotiating for surrender terms, and the rest will soon follow. The takeover will pose tremendous logistic problems, but in the first place they will be sanitary rather than military.

"We will bury them, as the late Nikita Khrushchev predicted with such uncanny foresight," he added with a frosty smile. "And we must act soon to prevent epidemics that might become uncontrollable."

At this the retired Red Army marshal who was in charge of civil defense interrupted to say, "Already I've taken the precaution of assembling the disaster teams trained to cope with thermonuclear and bacterial attacks from the West, from which threat, thanks to our late beloved leader and consummate planner, Comrade Turganov, we have been freed forever."

"Excellent, excellent!" Belitsky interposed dryly. "We must not delay so long that the Chinese might infiltrate across the Pacific first, but neither must we hasten too precipitately. Academician Vladimirsky, who has guided us so competently on the number of bombs to explode, advises us that we can detonate five more before we reach the level of fallout regarded as the limit of safety for our own health. Therefore we can leave the capitalists to stew a little longer, so that in history they will not only be seen to have destroyed themselves through their fanatical belief in unplanned freedom, but will have been forced to beg the help of Communism to survive at all. I propose that we give the American and British rabble one month to entreat our help in delivering them from their chaos or at least to welcome our troops when they arrive."

Christianity is not the only faith to derive satisfaction from the fulfillment of sacred prophecy. So with no dissent, the Presidium agreed. Just as the Russians had delayed at the gates of burning Warsaw in the Second World War, while the retreating Germans eliminated the Polish resistance fighters who might one day have resisted their Red liberators, so they would delay again while history wrote itself for them.

chapter 31

In the air-conditioned atmosphere of the Citadel Maclaren and his staff were spared the nauseating smell of decay and the plague of flies blown inland from the beaches, but with nearly two million actual casualties, at least a further million unavoidable, and the explosions still going on, they were finally forced to admit that ordered servitude could not be worse than the predatory chaos that was increasing daily in the surface world outside. Maclaren could not hope to maintain the loyalty of the armed forces much longer, as more and more senior officers joined in the rush to hide their ugliness in the sea.

It was doubly bitter for a man who feared God and loved freedom to have to request the Communists to take over, but with each report from his patrols it became more obvious that he was wielding only a parody of power, and since it was clear from Moscow radio and intelligence reports that life was normal there, he guessed that the Russians would soon be invading anyway. He had contacted Brandenberg frequently on the direct line to Washington, and though the human wreckage and subsequent lawlessness there had been on a greater scale, especially since many of the senior officials had disappeared off the beach at Atlantic City, the President seemed unduly optimistic.

"Hold on, we're not beaten yet," Brandenberg had urged, shaking a defiant fist at the picture-phone. "We'd have taken far bigger casualties in an attack with nuclear weapons. The Soviets can't go on much longer or they'll be over the top themselves on radiation, Juvenex or not."

But when the President had offered no more specific reason for believing that the explosions would come to an end, Maclaren's reservoir of hope was so drained that he decided to seek surrender terms if the Russians staged one further blast, and the communications officer had just delivered confirmation of yet another heavy detonation.

"Well, that's it," he said to John with a heavy sigh as he wrote the surrender message. "Isn't it extraordinary? After all the struggle to avoid sending that message, the thing I fear most now is that the Russians will ignore it. Heaven knows what'll happen to us if they come, but they're our best chance of getting out of this place alive."

After the message had been passed to the transmission room, John and Shirley stayed with Maclaren in his stark, subterranean office, its quietness disturbed only by the soft hiss of the air conditioner. There was nothing left to do but wait and wonder what the waiting would bring.

When they broke the silence it was inevitably to return once more to the questions they had considered so many times, particularly since they had heard the news of Turganov's death on Moscow radio; questions which, in that cavern remote from the visual experience of the horror outside, they found they could discuss with strange detachment, as people had once joked and played cards in the shelters while the bombs rained down on burning London.

Had Turganov deliberately restarted nuclear testing in order to destroy his enemies, knowing it would destroy himself? Or had the tests been resumed for straightforward military reasons, before the supersensitivity of the Juvenex-takers had been anticipated by the Soviet scientists? And if the latter were true, had Turganov been prevented by Belitsky and the others from stopping them when the danger became known? In short, was Maxim Turganov the most callous mass murderer in history, prepared to eliminate millions, including himself, to secure the accession of his creed? Or was he as much an unwilling victim of the surfeit of science as those who died with him?

"Well, I suppose we'll soon get the truth firsthand," said Shirley with a shudder.

The communications officer was smiling excitedly when he reentered Maclaren's room holding a cable, which they assumed to be confirmation that the surrender message had been received.

"This came in from Moscow just as I was preparing to send your message, sir," he said to Maclaren. "So I held your message back. It's fantastic. They're asking for *our* help!"

Maclaren grabbed the cable and read it aloud in astonishment: "Chinese troops invading the USSR in strength along a four-thousand-mile front. Most earnestly beg your assistance in securing military aid from President Brandenberg and NATO. It is in our mutual interest to prevent westward penetration by Chinese imperialists. All nuclear testing terminated. Belitsky."

"Can we be sure it's genuine?" John said as he picked it up to read for himself. Before Maclaren could answer, Brandenberg was on the picture-phone from the White House.

"We made it! We made it! The rice plan came off! They've ended the tests!" the President shouted, thumping his desk. "Thank God you hung on! The National Security Council wouldn't let me tell you under the security restrictions, but soon after Taylor passed the phony research results to Ho Cheng, our intruder planes made a high-level biological attack on the rice crop in the Yangtze Valley. We knew it would take a couple of months for the bugs to take hold, but we figured that when they did, Ho Cheng would blame the fallout and issue an ultimatum demanding an end to the tests. He did better than that! He's invaded!"

"I know. Belitsky's just cabled me," Maclaren said. "But are we really out of the woods? The Russians will surely stop the Chinese with nuclear weapons. And won't that shower us all with more fallout than ever?"

"They can't, they can't," Brandenberg said jubilantly. "I've just had Belitsky on the hot line begging for military assistance. They've got themselves so near the threshold limit of fallout that their own troops and civilians couldn't tolerate the extra burden released by a nuclear attack. In any case nuclear weapons wouldn't be very effective against an assault mounted on such a broad front. Belitsky knows he's in for a long conventional war and he's terrified. The last thing he wanted was an invasion when his position's so insecure."

"He's asked me to intercede with you for help," Maclaren said. "He's warning us that if we don't help him the Chinese might get right through to Europe."

"I know, he tried to sell that to me. What he's after first is a guarantee that we won't attack in Europe if he moves his troops eastward. He's scared of having to fight on two fronts, though I think he realizes he's going to be saddled with that anyway. He'll be lucky if there aren't revolutions in the satellite countries as soon as he pulls his troops out."

"What did you tell him?"

"Oh, I just stalled. Let them sort each other out for a while. It'll take all our resources to clean up the mess here, and there's a lot of new casualties from the backlog of fallout to be faced yet."

"We're certainly going to have our hands full here over the next few months," Maclaren said, shaking his head. "We're in no position to attack anybody. As for military assistance, we shall need all the troops we've got to restore order, but with God's help we'll succeed. Incidentally, will you convey the gratitude of the British people to whoever it was who thought up the rice plan?"

"Sure will," said Brandenberg buoyantly.

Maclaren put down the telephone and turned to John. "Alert all staff over the loudspeakers to stand by for an important announcement in five minutes' time. We'll break the news to them and then we've got to think about how to get it over to the people outside."

American intelligence sources quickly confirmed that the Chinese had penetrated Soviet territory to depths of more than a hundred and fifty miles and were still advancing, but their interpretation of the reason for Marshal Ho Cheng's attack had been far from accurate.

chapter 32

The Chinese scientists serving Ho Cheng's regime were much more efficient than either Turganov or Brandenberg had judged, and what information they did not discover by their technical resources had been provided by intelligence agents in Moscow and Washington, where Mongolian faces were not out of place. They knew that rice is such an outstandingly poor absorber of strontium 90 that, when shown the reports submitted by Taylor, they had quickly declared them to be fakes. Their fallout measurements were also as accurate as any in the West, and their interpretation of them, submitted weekly to the Marshal's office in Peking, as perceptive as any of the appreciations circulating in Whitehall or the Pentagon.

Ho Cheng, therefore, had been informed almost as quickly as Owen and Brandenberg that the Russians were seizing advantage of the Western sensitivity to fallout. He was advised that the unprecedented magnitude of the test program required such a calculated risk, that it would take the Russians so near the normal medical limit for fallout, that they would be unable to wage nuclear war until much of the radioactivity had died away, which would take several years. And Ho Cheng's mind was as opportunist and as sharp as any in the Kremlin.

With Southeast Asia and Japan as overcrowded as his own country, and Australia so far away, he had long been persuaded that his colossal problem of living space could be solved only by expansion into the great empty areas of eastern Russia.

Believing that there could be no global movement for Communism without supreme power vested in one acknowledged master, he was convinced that only force would finally resolve his conflicts with either Russia or the West. There was also the monstrous perfidy of 1959, which had been indoctrinated into the minds of loyal Chinese Communists, when the arch-capitulationist Khrushchev had made the fraudulent concept of coexistence with the West an excuse for breaking his agreement to help China build a nuclear force of her own. That was a breach of solemn contract for which two decades of shaming inferiority had compounded the interest in revenge, for the national spirit fostered by the Chinese leaders had increased the oriental sensitivity to loss of face.

Yet all these prospects, so urgent for fulfillment, were being frustrated by the long-range nuclear missiles, which were making war impossible. So, though at first Ho Cheng has reacted violently to the air-polluting tests as a criminal act by an even greater enemy of the people than Khrushchev, he had quickly stifled his objections in the hope that the Russians would continue them and so provide his opportunity to unfreeze the map of Asia and then of the world.

In pursuit of his belief in the futility of peace, he had promoted Mao's injunction, "Every man a soldier," and had overwhelming superiority in infantrymen, especially since the strength of the Red Army had been halved through reliance on nuclear missiles. As a result of the national sacrifice that his austerity had imposed, he was also able to support them with tanks, guns, and tactical aircraft. All he would need, as his devious mind assessed the military requirements, would be a final rallying cause to convince his troops and his people of the justice of their attack. And suddenly, precisely at the right moment, Brandenberg's rice operation had provided it. What could be more incensing to a nation of farmers with such experience of famine than the threatened destruction of the crop on which most of them depended?

The American airplanes had not passed undetected as they flew over the Yangtze Valley, high on a moonless night: neither had the clouds of hen-feathers, loaded with a virulent strain of the fungal spores causing rice-blast, which had been dropped in self-destroying canisters. The Chinese defense authorities knew that just such an

247

attack had been planned by the U.S. to ruin the Japanese rice fields in the Second World War, and ever since the days when Chiang Kai-Shek had threatened invasion from Formosa, they suspected that it might be turned against them. They were therefore ready with countermeasures, but Ho Cheng reckoned that he could afford to permit the infection of the rice in the relatively small area to provide visible proof of Russia's ruthless wickedness for the whole nation.

Then, to dispel any last-minute doubt, came the news of Turganov's sudden death. With the Kremlin power struggle in unstable flux, he could never have dreamed of an array of circumstances so conducive to his aims.

"Justice has delivered the deviationist criminals into our hands," he announced in the final address to his generals before the khaki avalanche.

Though historians do not record it, there was a further cardinal reason for the Great Fratricidal War, in which the Chinese and Russian comrades fought, unaided, with such ferocity that their mutual defeat ruined the power and appeal of Communism as completely as the Second World War had wrecked Fascism. The incorruptible Ho Cheng had been taking Juvenex, smuggled in through Hong Kong, and unlike Maxim Turganov, he had been unwilling to sit, passively, and risk joining his ancestors for the sake of his ideals.